PENGUIN BOOKS

THE TRANSLATOR'S ART

Betty Radice read classics at Oxford and was an honorary fellow of St Hilda's College, Oxford, and a vice-president of the Classical Association. In 1964 she became joint editor of the Penguin Classics, contributing six translations of her own. She also wrote the reference book *Who's Who in the Ancient World.*

William Radice read English at Magdalen College, Oxford, and has a diploma in Bengali from London and a doctorate in Bengali from Oxford. He has published three books of poetry and two translations from Bengali. In 1986 he was given a Bengali literary award, the *Ananda Puraskār*.

Barbara Reynolds was, until her retirement, a lecturer in Italian language and literature at the universities of London, Cambridge and Nottingham. She is the General Editor of the *Cambridge Italian Dictionary*, and her translation of Ariosto's *Orlando Furioso* for the Penguin Classics won the Monselice International Award for Translation.

Betty Radice photographed in 1973 by John Gay

THE TRANSLATOR'S ART

ESSAYS

IN HONOUR OF

BETTY RADICE

EDITED BY

WILLIAM RADICE

AND BARBARA REYNOLDS

AND PUBLISHED BY

PENGUIN BOOKS

Penguin Books Ltd, Harmondsworth, Middlesex, England
Viking Penguin Inc., 40 West 23rd Street, New York, New York 10010, U.S.A.
Penguin Books Australia Ltd, Ringwood, Victoria, Australia
Penguin Books Canada Limited, 2801 John Street, Markham, Ontario, Canada L3R 1B4
Penguin Books (N.Z.) Ltd, 182–190 Wairau Road, Auckland 10, New Zealand

First published 1987

Made and printed in Great Britain by
Richard Clay Ltd, Bungay, Suffolk
Typeset in Lasercomp Bembo

CONTENTS

In Mandelstam's eyes 'philology' was a profound concept of moral importance – the word, after all, is Logos, the embodiment of all meaning . . . His whole life was devoted to the defence of 'philology' in his sense – it was connected in his mind with inner freedom . . .

Nadezhda Mandelstam, *Hope Abandoned,*
translated by Max Hayward (1974)

PREFACE

The aim of this book is not only to honour the achievements of Betty Radice, editor of the Penguin Classics from 1964 until her death in 1985, but to stimulate debate and reflection on the translator's difficult art. Seventeen distinguished translators have written essays on their personal experience of translating, and their ideas are as varied as the languages and authors they discuss. As editor, Betty Radice was responsible for the ancient and oriental languages in the Penguin Classics list, and nearly all of them are represented here. The contributors to the book are connected by their respect and affection for her as well as by their association with the Penguin Classics; their warmth of feeling shows on every page and has made the book possible.

In keeping with the spirit of the Penguin Classics, we have tried to marry specialized scholarship with general appeal. We encouraged contributors to write essays in the classic mould, with minimal notes and references; but it was more important that they should speak naturally and personally. Peter Green's exhilaratingly learned essay on translating Ovid, or Peter Whigham's 'Notes on Translating Catullus' (his thoughts, after twenty years, on a translation which has itself become a classic), confirm as vividly as the shorter essays the inescapable conclusion that, however self-effacing the translator's art may be, the translator's personality is never wholly suppressed; nor should it be.

We have included two examples of the art itself. Michael Alexander was unable, because of the illness and death of his wife Eileen, to write on translating from Old English; his translation of 'The Wanderer' is reproduced here instead. We also offer Betty Radice's own translation of the Sayings of the Seven Sages of Greece, originally published by the Officina Bodoni of Verona, and an unpublished article that she wrote on the Sages. Our special thanks are due to Martino Mardersteig for allowing us to reprint the translation, and to Professor Trevor J. Saunders for preparing the text and article for inclusion here.

Individual acknowledgements by contributors can be found in the Notes and References at the end of the book. It remains for us to thank the close friends who assisted Margaret Wynn in the writing of her heartfelt Memoir and the many readers all over the world whose esteem for Betty Radice and the Penguin Classics has made us feel that this book will not fall on stony ground.

The *Envoi* on p. 254 was found among Betty Radice's papers. We do not know for what purpose it was written; but it has surely met its rightful destiny in what we hope will be enjoyed as a celebration of translation, learning and paperback publishing.

William Radice
Barbara Reynolds
Oxford and Cambridge, 1986

INTRODUCTION

William Radice

❦ On 22 January 1964, Sir Allen Lane and the Directors of Penguin Books gave a party at the Arts Council in St James's Square in London, to honour E. V. Rieu on his retirement from the editorship of the Penguin Classics. The invitation card aptly quoted a line from 'Peter and Percival or The Penguins' Revolt', one of Dr Rieu's comic poems. The poem tells of the sad failure of prose-writing Peter and verse-writing Percival to win the hand of 'the Queen of the Penguins in Enderby Land', and their banishment to the South Pole. But they find compensation in their own amity, and joyfully resolve to found a new Republican Democracy:

> 'I observe you are ready,' said Perce, 'to rebel,'
> When a hiccough from Peter had broken the spell.
> 'And if you are ready, then why should we wait?
> Let us found a Reformed and Republican State!
>
> 'With freedom to live as we jolly well please,
> Freedom to hiccough, and freedom to sneeze,
> Freedom for Poetry, freedom for Prose –
> Let us dance the Democracy in with our toes!'
>
> So they tripped in their glee through the star-spangled night,
> Penguins in harmony, utterly right;
> While the silent Aurora went flickering forth
> And shivered the sky from the South to the North . . .

Anyone with the slightest acquaintance with the stormy history of Penguin Books Ltd will know that 'Penguins in harmony, utterly right' has been the exception rather than the rule (accounting, no doubt, for the explosive dynamism of the firm); but E. V. Rieu's retirement party was clearly one of those happy exceptions. It was a family occasion, not only for his immediate family, but for Allen Lane's Penguin family of editors and directors, and for the unique 'extended family' of translators that Rieu had built up. Nevill

Coghill, J. M. Cohen, Rosemary Edmonds, W. F. Jackson Knight, R. Lancelyn Green, Sir Desmond Lee, David Magarshack, Juan Mascaró, Sir Roger Mynors, Lewis Thorpe, Hugh Tredennick, Arthur Waley, E. F. Watling – nearly fifty of them were there, and among them at least six of the contributors to the present book. Leonard Tancock, translator of Zola, had been enlisted as Translator-in-Chief by Betty Radice, Rieu's assistant since 1959, to whom Tancock innocently wrote:

> Of course I should be delighted as well as honoured to be associated with a presentation to E.V.R. He has been a wonderful friend to me since about 1946 (I think) when he started me off on my first Penguin (now out of print!). I would have thought that even poor translators might be glad to go beyond 10/- as a maximum. In these 'affluent' days would £1 be excessive?
>
> If it is not indiscreet – of course nothing may yet have been decided – could one know who might take on the editorship of the P.C.? With one now in proof stage and another being tackled in the horrible early stages I am naturally curious.

The answer to his question was given by Rieu himself at the end of his speech at the party. He predicted 'a long and prosperous life for a series which, with its sister series, has already achieved a worldwide reputation. And it is because I have worked with my two successors, Mrs Betty Radice and Dr Baldick, that I speak with such confidence.' He also spoke with the self-deprecating charm and wit that all who worked for him had come to expect:

> The Penguin Classics, though I designed them to give pleasure even more than instruction, have been hailed as the greatest educative force of the twentieth century. And far be it from me to quarrel with that encomium, for there is no one whom they have educated more thoroughly than myself. For instance I remember admitting at one of our conferences that I was uncertain whether Goncharov had written *Oblomov* or vice versa. Now, of course, I know that *Oblomov* was the author. Or am I wrong? What does it matter between friends?
>
> I turn now to Dr Tancock and my other kind colleagues in the task of creating the Penguin Classics. By a grave failure in security (I name no names) I heard that this handsome presentation was being plotted and that Mr Watling had undertaken the task of gently bludgeoning all of you into contributing. And as this very amiable cat is now completely out of the bag, I may as well admit that I was privileged to see one or two of the many letters he received in answer. Here is one of them: it is from my son Christopher and I read it without his permission:

Dear Mr Watling,
Delighted to contribute to my father's retiring present. It's rather like robbing Paul to pay Peter. Or else you can regard me as a pelican in reverse . . . depriving itself of its life blood to feed its parent. Anyway, here's a pound for my aged Pa – Aeneas did more for his.
Yours sincerely,
C. H. Rieu.

I was deeply moved by his piety, and (I hasten to add) by your generous acknowledgment of the friendly way in which we have worked together for so long – so long in fact that quite a few have fallen out on the way: I think for instance of Dorothy Sayers, Una Ellis Fermor and poor Aubrey de Sélincourt whose pen dropped from his hand as he was translating a sentence nineteen pages from the end of Livy's *War with Hannibal*. From them, from those of you here and from those who live too far to come, I part with sorrow.

Retirement parties can be poignant occasions, but E. V. Rieu was fortunate to be able to retire with a magnificent achievement behind him, acknowledged by the leading publishers and newspaper editors who also attended the party, marked by the public honours* which so amply made up for his failure, because of a breakdown, to complete his Classical Greats degree at Oxford, and proved by the phenomenal sales of his own translations of Homer and of many other Penguin Classics. He had even won over the dons and heavyweight scholars who had initially looked down on the Penguin Classics as 'cribs' and had doubted Rieu's academic competence; indeed the learned journal *Greece and Rome* printed fifty four Latin 'Lines on the Retirement of Dr E. V. Rieu, Founder and Editor of the Penguin Classics' (with apologies to the poet of the *Heroides*), by the Revd Maxwell Staniforth (lately Rural Dean of Blandford in Dorset, and translator of Marcus Aurelius and the Apostolic Fathers):

quis fuit, o rudis atque indocta Britannia, caeci
qui tibi Maeonidae grande reclusit opus?
quis tibi, dic, varios cursus patefecit Ulixei?
(*Di, quantum Sosiis aes meret iste liber!*)

Fortunately for a nation now even more 'indocta', an English translation by the author has also survived:

* Hon Litt D (Leeds) in 1949; CBE in 1953; the presidency of the Virgil Society in 1951; a vice-presidency of the Royal Society of Literature in 1958; and the Benson Medal in 1968.

WILLIAM RADICE

Declare, O rude unletter'd Britain, who
Revealed imperial Homer's art to you?
Show'd you Odysseus roaming o'er the main
(And earn'd a fortune for Sir A—n L—e)?

Betty Radice did not inherit the whole of Rieu's empire: her sway was always limited to the classical and oriental languages (though there was not a single Penguin Classic translated from French or Russian or any other modern language that she did not read). But she was editor for even longer than he was – twenty-one years to his eighteen: more than enough to deserve a similarly affectionate retirement tribute with comparable public honours. After the early deaths of Robert Baldick in 1972 and his successor C. A. Jones in 1974, she remained the sole surviving scholar-editor working on the series, publicly regarded – whatever changes took place in Penguin editorial policy and the status of outside editors – as *the* Editor of the Penguin Classics, her name in most of the books. Fate, however, denied her the valediction permitted to Rieu, or elegiacs in *Greece and Rome*; for she died suddenly of a heart-attack on 19 February 1985. For the last two years of her life she had maintained that she was semi-retired or 'gradually retiring' from her editorship, and indeed it had been agreed with Penguins that she should cease commissioning new books herself. But there were over twenty contracted books on the stocks that she would have seen through to publication had she lived – hardly retirement.

The present book stems from widespread shock at her unexpected death felt among those who knew her personally or professionally, or both. Many people had come to rely on her; the gap that is left by a death is a measure of the significance of a person's life. It is even wider if the person has, in a way, been taken for granted. Betty Radice inspired great affection and loyalty in her translators, and won a large and admiring readership for the Penguin Classics. But influential though she was, she was self-effacing; famous though she became, she was never a public figure. She became a vital but almost invisible part of our contemporary literary world, a hidden linchpin enabling the wheels of classical literacy and broad humanist culture to continue turning. How would they go on turning without her? This was the question in the minds of many who attended her Memorial Service in June 1985. One wondered too whether she had been given the public recognition she deserved. Philip Howard wrote an appreciative profile of her in *The Times* in 1981, and soon afterwards her old college, St Hilda's, made her an Honorary Fellow, a tribute that gave her enormous pleasure and which persuaded her, for only the second time in her life, to speak in front of an audience – at a College dinner in 1984 (the other occasion was in 1982, at Hollygirt School in Nottingham, when she gave away prizes). She would have laughed at the notion of any public recognition beyond that; but implicit in the genesis of this book was the feeling that her memory, at least, should be honoured.

The Penguin Classics sprang from the kind of inspired guess that was Allen Lane's trademark, from his ability to recognize and back a winner despite cautious advice from collaborators. His biographer J. P. Morpurgo counts the Penguin Classics among those of Allen Lane's ventures that 'would be classed as lunatic had they not proved so successful'. E. V. Rieu had, up to 1946, followed an orthodox career in publishing, first as manager of the Oxford University Press in India and then as educational manager and managing director of Methuen & Co. He started re-reading Homer in about 1931, and found such pleasure in it that he translated it aloud to his wife in the evenings. She encouraged him to write it down, and he offered it to Allen Lane at the end of the war. Morpurgo records the doubts expressed by other Penguin editors, about the viability of yet another translation of the *Odyssey*, about Rieu's competence as a scholar, and about whether there was scope for a rival to established series of classics such as the Everyman Library and the World's Classics. Whether consciously or not, Allen Lane must have felt that Rieu's *Odyssey* had a fresh, modern, readable, 'friendly' quality about it that conformed to the Penguin ethos. If it could be done for Homer, it could be done for other classics: Rieu was appointed editor, with a free hand in the commissioning and supervision of further translations. The series was announced in *Penguins Progress* for July 1946:

> The first volume of our new Classics series, the editor's translation of *The Odyssey*, appeared in January. The series is to be composed of original translations from Greek, Latin and later European classics, and it is the editor's intention to commission translators who could emulate his own example and present the general reader with readable and attractive versions of the great writers' books in good modern English, shorn of the unnecessary difficulties and erudition, the archaic flavour and the foreign idiom that renders so many existing translations repellent to modern taste. Each volume will be issued at Penguin prices and the

series will include, besides *The Odyssey*: Homer's *Iliad*, Xenophon's *The Persian Expedition* (translated by Rex Warner), three plays by Ibsen, three by Chekov, Ovid's greatest poem, *The Metamorphoses*, Voltaire's *Candide*, Turgeniev's *On the Eve*, Gorki's *Childhood*, and a selection of de Maupassant's short stories. Dorothy Sayers's version of Dante's *Inferno*, and E. F. Watling's translation of Sophocles's *Theban Plays* are already being printed.

The Penguin Classics strove for a typically Penguin combination of popularity and quality; but unlike the Pelicans or the Penguin Specials there does not seem to have been any great missionary or educational impulse behind them. The war was over: relaxation, pleasure, expansion, reconstruction – these were the orders of the day that Rieu and Lane exploited with such success; and despite the sobriety of the Penguin Classics, and the austere typographical covers that were still at the time one of Allen Lane's sacred cows, there was something sunny about them. With the passage of time, this can sometimes now seem coy or quaint, the tone being set by Rieu's own rather cosy introductions and a 'house style' of translation that D. S. Raven wickedly parodied in *Poetastery & Pastiche* (1966). Horace *Odes* I. vii. 15ff. ('Albus ut obscuro . . .') is rendered three times: 'Literally translated by an Oxonian', 'Done into English prose by the Rev. Urijah Rufflebotham, M.A.' and in 'A new translation for the Pumpkin Paperbacks':

> It has been remarked that the South wind often has a cleansing effect, and acts as a detergent on clouds as they deface the sky, so that this wind's reputation as an unvarying bringer of tornados is in fact illusory. My advice to you, Plancus, is to follow this allegory, and to show the good sense to set a reasonable limit to the more unprepossessing and laborious aspects of your existence. You will find mellow wine astonishingly helpful in fulfilling this principle; and its assistance will not be dependent on changes of *locale*: you may avail yourself of it among the comparative restrictions of military life with its 'bull' and its accoutrements, and no less in the homely atmosphere and surprisingly luxuriant greenery of the Tiber. Let me tell you a story illustrative of my point . . .

At its best, however, Rieu's lead could work magic, the magic of pure, new, unfusty language, of the rediscovery of classical literature too long buried in school-books, that was almost Miranda-like in its innocence and delight. In his introduction to the *Bhagavad Gita*, Juan Mascaró quotes the Nausicaa episode in Book VI of the

Odyssey, in Rieu's translation, to illustrate 'the conception of Karma', of joy in work:

> In due course they reached the noble river with its never-failing pools, in which there was enough clear water always bubbling up and swirling by to clean the dirtiest clothes. Here they turned the mules loose from under the yoke and drove them along the eddying stream to graze on the sweet grass. Then they lifted the clothes by armfuls from the cart, dropped them into the dark water and trod them briskly in the troughs, competing with each other in the work. When they had rinsed them till no dirt was left, they spread them out in a row along the sea shore, just where the waves washed the shingle clean when they came tumbling up the beach. Next, after bathing and rubbing themselves with olive-oil, they took their meal at the riverside, waiting for the sunshine to dry the clothes. And presently, when mistress and maids had all enjoyed their food, they threw off their headgear and began playing with a ball, while Nausicaa of the white arms led them in their song.

There was for Rieu and for all who shared in his great venture something of the same joy in doing their work beautifully.

It was, then, into an atmosphere still on the whole as happy and purposeful as this that Betty Radice stepped when E. V. Rieu made her his assistant editor in 1959. 'Stepped' is the right word, for there is a recurrent image in his letters to her from 1959 to 1965 of Rieu seeing her from his study window as she stepped up the crunchy gravel drive of his modern house in Hurst Avenue, Highgate:

> Dear Betty,
> Don't you dare to stay up in Yorkshire and leave me holding all the babies that drop in. I count on seeing your cheerful face coming up the drive on Tuesday next with you behind it . . .
>
> (11 September 1963)

The image is with him still when he writes during the post-retirement tour that he and Mrs Rieu made of Australia, shocked to learn of the extent of a childhood ankle injury that Betty had at last got round to showing to an orthopaedic surgeon:

> We were shocked by your news. How could you keep it all to yourself? I think you are a very brave girl, and far from having anything to forgive you, I feel a bit of a brute myself when I think of you trotting up our drive with a huge load (and a smile on your face) and later *almost* running off with something even heavier still – and all with an ankle tied on with string. Well, dear Betty, you write with your customary courage and optimism, but nevertheless I feel you are having a pretty

tough time; so do be careful and get thoroughly well – long before we get home . . .

(12 February 1964)

And it is there again at the end of the last letter that has been preserved:

> I look forward to seeing you come up the drive one day under your own power – though perhaps with *one* stick?
> Goodbye, my dear Betty, from
> Yours ever
> Victor (17 April 1965)

Perhaps he noticed her coming up the drive on the day he first invited her round to his house to discuss the translation of Pliny's Letters that she had sent him. She would have come on foot, because she also lived in Highgate. Indeed her entire association with Rieu and the Penguin Classics can partly be attributed to this fact: that they were close neighbours, so that she could visit him frequently without having to disrupt her duties as *mater familias*. She told the story herself in her article on Rieu for *The Times Higher Educational Supplement* (19 October 1984):

> I am accordingly an outstanding example of one whose good fortune depended on being in the right place at the right time. We were near neighbours in Highgate and twice a week I walked round to spend a busy morning and take away material; these mornings included coffee, and sometimes lunch with his wife Nelly, whose quick wits and ready tongue were always a delight.
>
> At first this was on a purely personal basis, but before long he asked Allen Lane to pay me a modest salary as his recognized assistant. By this time Tony Godwin had brought all his energy and acumen into the firm to effect its necessary expansion and can't have been pleased to find me added to the Penguin staff without having been appointed by him; though we always got on well together when we met, and it was certainly his doing that I was made one of the two joint editors who took over the classics when E. V. R. retired.
>
> Meanwhile my concern was to try to keep the peace between the Edwardian old fogey and the half-educated young upstart, as they termed each other. E. V. R. had enjoyed the freedom gained from his long friendship with Allen Lane, and had had complete editorial independence, issuing contracts and apparently fixing royalties as he thought fit.
>
> It had been more fun in the early days, when there was a party at Canterbury to celebrate the publication of Nevill Coghill's *Canterbury Tales*, and Dorothy Sayers had arrived in Highgate for lunch with her

script of Dante, stayed to tea and then to dinner, still talking, and 'just when we were about to offer her bed and breakfast said she must go'.

The honeymoon phase of the Penguin Classics had faded by the time that Betty Radice joined Rieu; but the impression given by his letters to her is of an extremely warm and happy collaboration, of great pleasure in their mutual interests and confidence in the continuing improvement and vitality of the series. Indeed she probably gave him a new lease of life, cheering him out of the moodiness and 'beastly headaches' to which he was subject, helping him to come to terms with Godwin's changes such as Germano Facetti's splendid new picture covers – or at least to accept them with wry resignation:

> I have just opened a parcel containing two copies of V[ellacott]'s *Euripides* Vol. III – Medea, Hecabe, Electra, Heracles: new cover with a nice reproduction of a vase showing – Medea? Oh no, what an idea! *She* will no doubt be kept in reserve – to go on the Bacchae volume. This one shows a *maenad* – the one holding up a spotted dog – and they say so on the back cover!
>
> Oh my poor series, of which I used to be so proud!
>
> (9 April 1963)

It was a buoyant collaboration, and there is buoyancy too in Betty Radice's own early letters to translators, in her detailed and keenly interested comments on minutiae of style, accuracy and presentation. Here she was, forty-seven when she joined Rieu, suddenly finding her métier at last, flexing the scholarly muscles that had been carefully kept in training during her years of child-rearing but which she had had no chance to use or display, author herself of translations (Pliny and Terence) that broke even newer ground than Rieu's, and working with someone whom she found completely *simpatico*. It was a wonderful job for her: one cannot imagine any other suiting her better.

She was well aware of E. V. Rieu's foibles and limitations, and could joke affectionately about his devotion to the Athenaeum, or his 'prep-school' sense of humour, or his liking for garden gnomes. Some of his attitudes, such as his prejudice against German literature, or his acceptance (after translating *The Four Gospels*) of basic Christian belief, were alien to her. The changes that she was to introduce when she became editor reflected differences in their principles of translation and standards of scholarship. But she had the highest possible regard for him, and in their common modesty, domesticity and liking for plants, children and animals (he was better on birds, she on dogs, but they both loved cats), as well as their professional interests, they were soul-mates. She admired the seriousness of his hobbies – carpentry and petrology – and always spoke up for his light verse, which even now has perhaps not been fully appreciated. She wrote in her article on him:

> His collected poetry (*The Flattered Flying Fish and Other Poems*, 1962) much of it written long before I knew him, showed another side of him. It was light verse in the best English tradition of Cowper and Hood, Carroll, Belloc, Herbert and Milne.
>
> He took pride in his meticulous craftsmanship and the pleasure he could give his readers by his imaginative ingenuity, and I am sure he meant it when he sometimes said that he felt that he had achieved more in his verse than in his translations – *The Odyssey* and *The Four Gospels* not excepted. It was the right medium for his whimsical humour and irony and it also reveals that beneath his delight and relish for a schoolboyish pun or joke (a 'Dr Rieu joke' was a recognized category in my family) there was keenly felt sympathy for the young, the foolish, the innocent and helpless in an unkind world.

Her dedication of *The Letters of the Younger Pliny* to E. V. Rieu, with the tag *magistro discipula*, was truly meant: their relationship was indeed that of revered master with favourite pupil – one of the purest forms of love that there can be.

In what aspects of her own style of editing was she a follower of E. V. Rieu? Like him, she was always meticulously courteous to all her translators and correspondents, never failing to answer letters promptly, at surprising length and often in long hand. She learnt from him the difficult art of rejecting unsuitable work with politeness and tact, and a principle that she frequently enunciated was that of always replying even to the 'batty' letters an editor is bound to receive. Early on in her work for Rieu, she was brought up short when she suggested that a letter that had come was too mad to answer: for his part, he said, he did not wish to give the writer the last push round the bend by failing to reply. Young correspondents were always treated with special care. Copies of her handwritten replies are not preserved in her files, but one can be sure that this letter, for example, received a royal reply, with some free Penguin Classics enclosed:

> Dear Ms Radice and Mr Baldick,
> I am a student in the United States and spend much of my time reading.

As it happens, I am also a lover of books, both in physical appearance and in the quality between the covers. I wanted to let you know that Penguin Classics are outstanding in both areas.

Penguin Books last a long time. The pages don't fall out and the covers close after two readings. When I write passages in the margins, my ink does not leak through. The pages are all the same size so none of them become frayed and later ripped. The covers are (almost always) elegant; they have class. The blurbs on the back are informative and intelligently written. And I appreciate the subject headings, also on the back, since I have a filing system.

Inside, quality is always excellent. I never comprehended quality in translation until I read some butchered accounts for a class. You and your people are aware that most of us do not study the history and language of Greek and Latin . . .

On matters of translation and presentation, those who did books for her could be certain that their scripts would be thoroughly read and that they would be given guidance that was always scholarly, practical and level-headed. She had a fine sense of prose style, and many translators must have felt that they would not have attained the requisite balance between accuracy and readability, modernity and permanence without her help. She had an excellent ear for verse, too. Here she is, writing to a translator who had been having difficulty with his blank verse:

All I ask is that you should not hurry this. I would rather wait until next summer if necessary for you to take your time, especially over the problems of blank verse, which I am sure are greater than is generally believed. I do think one must always try to write it and think of it in larger units than the single line. It is because Milton and Shakespeare can sweep us on in the flow of a whole paragraph that they can break all the rules. The five-beat can conflict, up to a point, with the natural stress when one reads, but only if it is supported by the lines around it, if you see what I mean. If I were reading the lines you quote from *Winter's Tale* I should feel that the spoken stress doesn't fall on 'but' but slides over on to 'Looks'. We have one quite regular line here and two irregular –

> The sélfsame sún that shínes upón his cóurt
> Hídes nót his vísage fróm our cóttage, but
> Lóoks ón alíke.

But even at the risk of monotony, we lesser mortals do better to stick to the rules, don't you think?

If I were you I should soak myself in Milton.

Translators from Greek and Latin received detailed comments on meaning and nuance, and she was particularly alive to the dangers of letting the style and syntax of the original over-influence the English sentence structure. Above all, she was, like Rieu, always imaginative and open-minded, forever on the look-out for the new, the fresh, the surprising and original. And this must stand as one of the foremost achievements of the Penguin Classics, that the series has never seemed staid, predictable or 'old hat'. Sometimes, because she was responsible for trail-blazing books such as Peter Whigham's Catullus, she has been praised for being more daring than Rieu. But this was probably only because she belonged to a younger generation, and was more attuned to contemporary literary developments than he would have been. The list of Penguin Classics published up to 1958 – a year before she joined Rieu – is actually full of daring and surprising choices: *The Autobiography of Benvenuto Cellini*, Camoens, *The Lusiads*, *The Four Gospels*, *The Koran*, Rabelais, *Gargantua and Pantagruel*, Zola, *Germinal* and so on. Like Rieu, she was prepared, sometimes, to stick her neck out for translations or introductions that might be idiosyncratic or open to attack from scholars, but which nevertheless seemed to her to carry conviction, internal coherence, integrity. This was particularly so with translations from oriental languages. She would seek the opinion of scholars in the field before accepting any translation from a language she did not know; but sometimes she would publish even in the face of strongly negative readers' reports – trusting her own taste and judgement, just as Rieu trusted his.

Thus in many ways Betty Radice was an editor in the manner of Rieu. Her letters became famous for the way in which she interwove comments on the work in hand with personal and family news, anecdotes, accounts of holidays; his letters were like that too. Her translators became friends just as his did. But there were differences between their periods of editorship as well as broad continuity. Some of these differences came about through changes in the way the Penguin Classics were being used and read; some of them were a result of problems and upheavals in the management of Penguin Books; some of them derived from her personal life and the conditions under which she had to work – which were not the same as Rieu's.

Three years after she became editor, a translation of Ovid's *Ars Amatoria* and *Remedia Amoris* arrived that had been commissioned by E. V. Rieu but which turned out to be unsatisfactory. She sought the opinion of an independent scholarly reader, who agreed with her that the translation, introduction and notes all fell below the standards of the Penguin Classics – and the Penguin house-editor, Giles Gordon, agreed too. The translator was angry and mortified, but there was nothing he could do: he even forfeited the advance due on delivery, as his script had arrived three years late. It was an unpleasant and embarrassing episode, but not unique; such things are bound to happen from time to time in the running of a series. In her letter to the translator, Betty Radice admitted that she was surprised that E. V. Rieu had given the original contract on the basis of some very 'unpolished specimens'; but the translator had done two other Penguin Classics that were good, and Rieu no doubt had confidence that his eventual translation would be better than the specimens. She did not say that she thought that Dr Rieu would have agreed with her opinion, but there is little doubt that he would have done, because the translation was apparently sensational and smutty in a way which would certainly have offended his sense of propriety. Nevertheless, the reasons for the rejection of this translation are a clear indication of the way in which the series had moved on since Rieu. Firstly, the introduction and notes were 'unscholarly'; secondly the colloquial and contemporary prose adopted by the translator failed to convey the elegance and witty sophistication of Ovid's verse. Betty Radice was careful to say in her letter that the choice of prose rather than verse in the translation was not the issue, as 'the original agreement had been for prose' and 'polished stylish prose could, I think, very well convey the wit of the original'. But her independent reader favoured verse, and the appearance, fifteen years later, of Peter Green's verse translation is proof that this was her preference too.

Here, then, were two very important points of departure from Rieu's editorial principles. His own introductions and those that he encouraged were deliberately unspecialized: to reach the general reader, the Penguin Classics must be free of the dead weight of scholarly apparatus.* Betty Radice, in her introduction to Pliny's *Letters*,

* This is not to imply that Rieu's approach was slipshod or that he undervalued scholarship. His son, C. H. Rieu, who translated *The Acts of the Apostles* for the Penguin Classics (1957), has commented: 'Pa told me that he usually began in the early stages ... by inviting dons to submit work. But he found that very few of them could write decent English, and most were enslaved by the idiom of the original language ... As a consequence Pa began turning to writers, professional wielders of the pen, like Rex Warner. Some of these were

showed that it was possible to present solid and authoritative scholarship in an appealing way – and this is what she strove for in the books that she edited, which included major revisions of many of the early Penguin Classics, with new introductions and notes by acknowledged experts. In the matter of verse translation, she also parted from her mentor. Rieu did not believe that poetry – especially lyric poetry – was translatable: a prose version, which could be a means towards appreciating the original but not a substitute for it, was best – hence his own prose translation of Virgil's *Eclogues*, printed with a facing Latin text. Betty Radice had far greater faith in verse translation, and under her editorship it became the norm, culminating in her own triumphant collaboration with W. G. Shepherd in his translations of Horace and Propertius. These two fundamental changes were not just a consequence of her personal preferences; they arose from the way that Penguin Classics were being increasingly used in school and university teaching – especially in the USA – and the way in which readers with sophisticated literary sensitivity were expecting to find in English translations the poetic and aesthetic qualities of the original.

These were demanding aims: to produce books that were authoritative works of scholarship and of high literary merit, as well as readable and appealing in the manner of the early Penguin Classics. They made Betty Radice's task far more strenuous than Rieu's, and far more open to attack, from scholars and academics on the one hand, from poets and aesthetes on the other. The sheer strenuousness of her task, and the difficulty of pleasing such diverse and specialized groups (not the 'general reader' of the Rieu years), was the first reason why the sunshine of her years of collaboration with Rieu faded, making the experience of editing far cloudier and stormier than he had known. ('I can't please everyone, and sometimes wonder if I may end by pleasing nobody but myself,' she wrote wryly at the end of her article in *The Times Higher Educational Supplement*.) In 1968 the American journal *Arion* published a special feature which was symptomatic of the new strains the Penguin Classics were enduring by their very success and ubiquity. 'Penguin Classics – a report on two decades' (*Arion*, Vol. 7, No. 3, Autumn 1968, p. 393f.) is referred

---

immensely scholarly, like Dorothy Sayers, Nevill Coghill . . . I myself was certainly unscholarly in the sense at least of not spending a lifetime studying the original language, but I think my English was OK and I did my best to use other men's scholarship in the introduction and notes.

to later in this book, by Michael Grant in his essay on translating Latin prose; but it is worth looking at in some detail here as well, and at Betty Radice's reply in the Spring 1969 issue, for the debate between her and her Texan critics brings us to the heart of what a series of Classics in translation can do or should be expected to do.

The main thrust of the Report – if we disregard what she rightly described in her reply as 'the opportunities missed, the uneven quality of the individual reviews, the errors and omissions, even the occasional cheap taunt' – was against the inadequacy of many of the Classics 'for classroom adoption on the American campus', and against the 'mediocrity' of many of the translations as literature. In his introductory remarks, D. S. Carne-Ross wrote:

> As Miss Radice [sic] and Mr Baldick survey the work done by Penguin Classics in this field over the last two decades, they must be aware that a good deal of it is at best mediocre, some very bad indeed. Assuming this critical awareness, do they – the interesting question is – propose to do anything about it? Do they mean to recall certain translations and look for new, better ones?

He then proceeded to propose grandly an entirely new policy for the series:

> The proper course for a series of this sort would be to set up two flexible but well-defined categories. In the first category come the masterpieces, that is creative translations by writers of strong original gift. In the second come the service translations, competent versions by men with some scholarship and a decent prose style. With these categories in mind, the editor could draw a rough balance-sheet, the available talent on one side, the work to be done on the other.

Clearly the purpose of this new dual policy was to satisfy the two new categories of readers defined above: college students on the one hand, 'creative' or poetically inclined readers on the other. In her reply, Betty Radice wrote that she was fully prepared to meet educational needs, and that 'we are currently engaged in a major overhaul of the prose translations, starting with the historians. Many of these on reprinting will have new critical introductions by experts, bibliographies, and more adequate notes . . . but how far we ought to offer some guidance to the original text is the real crux.' It was easier to do so with prose than with poetry, though it was her conviction that in translating poetry, the text should be provided (she had wanted a facing text in Whigham's Catullus and Watts's

Propertius, but 'both texts were axed in an economy drive'). As regards 'creativity' in translation, however, she gave a spirited defence of her views. Her own translations of Pliny and Terence had been criticized by Douglas Parker and Gareth Morgan for being unimaginative, but would it have been true to the original to make them more so?

> It comes as no surprise to me that as a translator I don't come high in the *Arion* rating, and I hope Mr Douglas Parker will soon provide us with *his* version of Terence. My prose is 'relentlessly nice' because I see this as a flaw in the poet – the Latin is beautiful but lacks variety, the characters are too lightly sketched, and that is why the Romans themselves found him lacking in *vis comica* and a 'half-sized Menander'. I confess I was often tempted to improve on my original, from the dramatic point of view, and should have been more 'creative' had I done so. We also need a Pliny from Mr Gareth Morgan, to bring out the latent poetry in one who has hitherto been judged as a master of conscious *prose* style; and while he's at it he should include the *Panegyricus*, which might well prove more acceptable in canto-style verse than in its present form.

She went on to criticize many of the translations published in *Arion* for 'their lack of responsible relationship to the original'. Comparing a translation of a piece of Seneca by Ted Hughes with E. F. Watling's Penguin version, she wrote:

> Dense and overloaded as it [Watling's] is, it represents more faithfully what Seneca wrote – the density is his, not the translator's, and it is what the Elizabethans admired and we do not . . . perhaps the Penguin Classics aim at the impossible, in our struggles to be scholarly without being pedantic, to write good contemporary prose which is not ephemeral, to find poets who can present classical poets to non-classical readers and at the same time stimulate rather than infuriate those who know the original.

Betty Radice was undoubtedly stung by the attack in *Arion*. Her Pliny was the result of years of work, refined during odd hours snatched from housework and bringing up her children. In a letter to Lewis Thorpe she wrote:

> Pliny is a conscious stylist of immense versatility and every letter is beautifully written in what must have been the best prose of his day. I care very much about his prose style and it was a great challenge; some of those short notes which say little but say it elegantly I did again and again, reading them aloud when I had the house to myself . . .
>
> (10 November 1964)

There was little that she did not know about Pliny's style. But D. S. Carne-Ross's grand blueprint for a new-style Penguin Classics series must have seemed more comical than anything else. He admitted that his proposals were 'Utopian' – but only because no publisher would take them on. What he did not seem to appreciate was how utterly impractical they were from an editorial point of view. No series such as the Penguin Classics can be methodically planned by drawing up a list of books in advance and then finding translators for them. Right from its beginnings under Rieu it had grown far more haphazardly than that, for the simple reason that no editor can guarantee that translators for particular books will be available at a particular time, or can be relied upon to finish translations on time. And as for finding 'real poets' to translate poetry:

> I think it is true to say that for all the remaining major poets we are always on the lookout for the right translator and indeed, some years ago we were happy to commission a poet to translate a poet. Four years later he saw no prospect of finishing and we had sorrowfully to cancel his agreement and we are back where we started. The Muse cannot be held to a contract; *Arion* should know the problems. How many creative poets are there who will submit to the drudgery of translating the stretches of a classical poet which don't particularly inspire him? And is it his job, *qua* poet, to do so?

In her work as editor, Betty Radice was always dealing with people – highly sensitive, wayward or touchy people; and to this often exasperating part of her job the critics in *Arion* seemed quite blind. Moreover, by making the Classics more scholarly, bringing in academic experts to write new introductions, she was often up against varieties of donnish affectation or arrogance that E. V. Rieu was on the whole spared.

If *Arion* attacked the series for being uncreative, the series of reports on all the Penguin Classics that were commissioned by James Cochrane and Dieter Pevsner from Professor M. I. Finley in 1968 represented the kind of fire that could come from more orthodox academic quarters. This episode resulted from a phase in Penguin editorial policy when the highest priority was given to tapping the educational and university market. The Penguin English Library was begun around the same time, and the idea behind the Finley reports was to arrive at the same reliable academic package in the Penguin Classics as was being achieved in the new series. For Betty Radice, it was a thoroughly dispiriting experience. Not only were Professor Finley's reports almost invariably negative, she did not in any case need him to tell her where many of the older Classics were deficient. Furthermore, the Penguin chief editors decided at this time to inaugurate a new Classics series, the Pelican Classics, to be edited by Professor Finley. The idea behind this was to cover classics of philosophy, politics, economics or even history. To publish Darwin's *Origin of Species* or Hobbes's *Leviathan* was fine, but when it came to the inclusion of translations, how could overlap with the Penguin Classics be avoided? Were there not many Penguin Classics that could arguably be transferred to the Pelican Classics? Betty Radice had to fight tooth and nail to preserve her territory at this time: she was especially resistant to the notion that books that had been commissioned by the Penguin Classics could be transferred – over the head of the translator – to the Pelican Classics, and she felt especially sore about St Augustine's *City of God*, an immense feat of translation by Canon Henry Bettenson, which was press-ganged into Professor Finley's new series with an introduction by David Knowles that fell far below her own editorial standards.

The Pelican Classics were not a success, and her resistance to them was vindicated by the eventual reprinting of the *City of God* as a Penguin Classic in 1984, with a new introduction by John O'Meara, though Canon Bettenson did not live to see it. But the uneasy collaboration into which she was dragged with Moses Finley (whose prowess as a Roman historian she respected highly) was the nadir of her experiences as editor of the Penguin Classics. Some of her letters from this period are a bitter contrast with the cheerfulness and confidence of her years with Rieu or immediately afterwards. Moreover the aggravations of the *Arion* attack, the Pelican Classics episode and gruelling complications of the policy of revising the early Penguin Classics all came on top of the shattering death of her daughter Catherine from disseminated lupus erythematosus in March 1968.

This terrible blow is described more fully in the Memoir that follows this Introduction, but we cannot omit it from an account of the harsh aspects of Betty Radice's editorship. Catherine first became ill in the winter of 1966–7, so that editorial work had to be combined with nursing her at home for many months, as well as facing up to the incurability of her condition and the eventual torment of bereavement. Her death hangs over the following letter to Moses Finley like a brooding cloud, and it is worth quoting the letter extensively because it shows at what great cost the revision of some of the major

Penguin Classics – perhaps Betty Radice's finest legacy as editor – was achieved:

Dear Moses,
How *nasty* your letters can be to receive; I often dread the sight of the Cambridge postmark, though I know better than to take them personally. And I do appreciate how it is a great saver of your time not to have to choose your words, and how the building up of what the TLS calls your famous bite is a very useful ploy in the gamesmanship of the academic rat-race. It must be an agreeable feeling to use it.

In any case I have called for the full treatment this time by being careless. I had been thinking that the page-heads included the chapter references to the Greek text, which of course only I or you can do. Now I have the marked text and see that you have already put the chapter numbers in margins, so of course these can be copied by the copy-editors. I know we agreed on having them, but I had forgotten the state of play. I do apologize. The fact is that I am very tired and I have you and Cawkwell and Burn all at the same stage of these revisions. It will be a relief when this batch at least is settled. Cawkwell's donnish facetiousness I find rather tiresome, and still more so his affectations – refusing to entrust his MS even to a registered post, and always wanting to know if I shall be 'perchance' in Oxford. Burn is as disenchanted as yourself, but largely because he has gone beyond what he was asked and started rewriting great chunks of the translation between the lines, interspersed with fierce comments on the late de Sélincourt, all in ink; so the marked copy can't be used and one of us will have to mark up another one.

There is no disagreement between us about the policy of asking people to read the work of distinguished contributors. I have always felt very strongly that once one has chosen the best person, he should be left to handle his subject in his own way. It is an impertinence to ask a possibly lesser man to comment, and an embarrassment to the man asked. So you may be surprised when I tell you that in February '69 I was seen by Dieter and told that you had advised him that all these new introductions must be read by an academic expert, but you would refuse to do this yourself. It seemed to me at the time natural enough that you should doubt my competence, and very proper that having suggested the introducers you would not want to sit in judgement on them. I was a bit dismayed, I admit, and I pointed out that no one person could possibly give expert advice in all these fields. But I haven't much pride to be damaged, so I said I would try to do what you/he wanted. The important thing is to get these books improved . . .

But it was very clever of him to say that he was acting on advice from you, saving us both from embarrassment, and ensuring that I should not put up resistance, because he knows that I can't hope to win in an argument with you. People of your character can always brush aside people of mine.

But damn it, if I'd known this was Dieter's own idea I'd have argued all right, and refused to be a party to such nonsense. I just shan't do anything now about Burn's introduction, which is brilliant and idiosyncratic, unsatisfactory in parts, but the sort of thing you can't touch. Cawkwell's I still don't really like, but we must publish it, yours and Ogilvie's are very good, and Seager is all right too.

Sorry to bother you with all this, but I value your opinion, and I'm feeling thoroughly dispirited with Penguin work generally. I wonder if I ought to retire and let them find someone younger, and yet I do enjoy particularly all I learn from working on the oriental side. In fact I was born like you in 1912, but a lot of my resilience died with Catherine. Perhaps I'll feel better after a holiday.

(10 September 1970)

The 1970s brought continuous difficulties, many of them resulting from troubles in the management of Penguin Books. Not that Penguins had ever been entirely free of such troubles; but Allen Lane's conflict with Tony Godwin, to take a famous example, did not take place against a background of falling profits – on the contrary, in commercial terms Godwin's chief editorship was highly successful. The troubles of the late sixties and early seventies were financial and much more serious, not solved by the merger with Pearson Longman in 1968 or the period of severe retrenchment under Jim Rose and Peter Calvocoressi. Betty Radice had to fight for every title and every reprint during those difficult years (her own translation of Terence was out of print between 1970 and 1976). When the turn-around began under Peter Mayer, with the move of all the Penguin editorial staff to the new building in the King's Road, she was up against two further problems: a policy of 'easing out' outside editors (by then she was officially called 'Advisory Editor' rather than 'Editor'), so that some books such as *The Travels of Sir John Mandeville* (1983) and a translation of *The Exeter Riddle Book* by Kevin Crossley-Holland, were published over her head; and the appalling load that was piled on to house-editors (their numbers kept to a minimum to save expense), so that in her latter years as editor she was putting much of her energy into making up for the inability of house-editors to keep up with the flood of correspondence and new books. (Yet she always stood up for them, explaining to translators how overworked they were, defending them against complaints.) She was ageing physically according to the family pattern (her mother and sister both died in their early seventies), and her growing number of grandchildren brought new tasks which were delightful, but often also exhausting. As always, translating and editing had to be fitted in round domestic responsibilities:

> I have covered 19 elegies, and with 6 more to go should finish well before you go on holiday. I'll take everything to the cottage tonight, but next week I'm going to Leixlip (outside Dublin) for the inside of a week to stay with friends from college days . . . It will be a nice break from domestic organizing – a spate of grandchildren's birthdays and all three families off on holiday so that borrowings and transferrings must be done before they go. May William have our sleeping bags for camping in France? May John have my second drop-side cot at the cottage for his 4th as Sarah will still need the one permanently there – so it must be collected from Wm & Elizabeth who have had it on loan . . .Is Helen's 4th birthday to be celebrated in France or after their return? I enjoy it of course, but it involves a lot of *remembering*.
>
> (letter to W. G. Shepherd, 22 July 1983)

But as we look at her twenty-one years as editor of the Penguin Classics, shall we say that the aggravation, the obstacles, the complications, and the sheer unmitigated hard work dominate the story? That the pleasures of the job were Rieu's, or belonged to the years of their collaboration? That her experience of it was an increasingly bitter and exhausting one? In some ways she would have been prepared to accept this as inevitable right from the beginning, for struggle, loneliness and bereavement had long been familiar to her. Rieu's Homer sprang from the leisure of evenings spent comfortably at home with his wife; Betty Radice's Pliny was done amidst domestic chores and squabbling children (at the family cottage at Berrick Salome, she would retire to the garage, in wet and chilly April weather, to seize some peace to get on with it).*

* For her, the translator's art was always arduous. She wrote to me in October 1974: 'I don't want you to be under any delusions about translating being more creative than critical writing – in the sense that nothing in my experience involves so much drudgery, minute application, exasperation at being tied to another's thought processes. Great self-discipline is needed if one is to be a faithful interpreter and not fall into the temptation of "improving" one's original. For me there is satisfaction in a job well done and a reasonably well-phrased sentence, but every time I start on a new translation I have to push myself to get down to it and wonder why I thought I could . . . You can only learn if you can translate by working on something fairly substantial. Be prepared to find that like some poet-translators I know, you find the process too limiting and demanding.'

But the dominant impression – against the odds – is not a bitter one: indeed many would be surprised to hear that there were difficult aspects at all. The sweet spirit of E. V. Rieu – the delight in learning and literature that she shared with him – survived, in a way that was often heroic. Betty Radice is remembered as a life-enhancing person, who wrote and edited life-enhancing books. Pliny, or Abelard and Heloise appealed to her sombre feelings, but Terence and Erasmus brought out her sense of fun. Her translation of *Praise of Folly* sparkles. She loved Gibbon for his wit (she was half-way through an edition of *Decline and Fall* for the Folio Society when she died). *Who's Who in the Ancient World* was written in the wake of Catherine's death, but it is not a sad book – on the contrary it is a tonic: one finds oneself reading it straight through, captivated by its graceful leaps from classical topics and themes to the use to which they have been put through the ages. It is subtitled 'A Handbook to the Survivors of the Greek and Roman Classics', and her introduction ends on a note of optimism that the Classics *will* survive: her book has added, she hopes, to our awareness of the past, 'yet I should like to continue in the hope that the future will fill out its pages'. Betty Radice herself was a survivor, and she ensured that her Penguin Classics series was a survivor through times more difficult and uncertain than E. V. Rieu knew. Will it go on surviving without an editor like her at the helm? There has been a fundamental change: the Penguin Classics and the Penguin English Library have been amalgamated, with a new format. Classical specialists may wonder if the Latin and Greek bedrock of the series will not now be submerged under waves of English language classics, as well as the translations from modern languages. But Betty Radice would have wished the new series well, would have been proud to see W. G. Shepherd's Propertius, with her introduction, appearing among the first batch of new 'consolidated Classics'. E. V. Rieu would have wished it well too, would have admitted it, no doubt, to the cheerful democratic state that Peter and Percival founded at the South Pole. Our present world climate may at times seem no less inhospitable to the survival of classical learning and humane literacy; but Homer and Pliny and Virgil and Horace and Euripides and Cicero and all the many others are still with us, still surviving, and will continue to do so, thanks to what two great but humble editors achieved.

BETTY RADICE: A MEMOIR

Margaret Wynn

❦ It is a great good fortune to be brought up in a world never forgotten and to which the memory returns throughout life. In an article for the Women of the North Luncheon brochure, written a few months before she died, Betty wrote:

> I think every northerner born has some sense of nostalgia; mine will always be for the great estuary of the Humber, the winter sunsets and windswept skies, the rhythm of the waves and honking of the migrating geese, the birds on the mud-flats and the white pebbles idly tossed into the waters during hours spent looking across to the Lincolnshire cornfields changing with the seasons.

Betty was brought up in a 'country Yorkshire family dedicated to self-improvement', among aunts, uncles and cousins. The rambling old house and garden at Hessle looked south over the Humber. It was a corner of East Yorkshire that still had, when she was a child, relics of smuggling and of early industry: 'I can just remember the chalk being pulled up from the quarry by great shire horses to be loaded on brown-sailed barges, the Humber keels.'

The idyll of childhood was broken when her father died of post-war influenza, leaving her mother with a small income and three young children. All her life Betty recalled her father's death, not only as a sadness, but as a loss of the world he would have provided. William Dawson was founder and head of a firm of solicitors in Hull, a member of the City Council and chairman of the Education Committee and a member of many national bodies. At the last meeting he attended he was spoken of as a future Member of Parliament; he was a Liberal candidate with a good chance of success. He was a gifted musician and a man of wide learning. His room in the family home was lined from floor to ceiling with books and was kept as he left it. It became a place of retreat for the three children, and especially for Betty. Much of his library rested finally at the Radice cottage in Oxfordshire.

Betty and her sister Nancy went to Newland High School in Hull. She broke with school tradition in specializing in Latin and insisting on reading Greek in the sixth form in order to apply to Oxford, again a break with traditions. She spoke of coming home to tea 'with my new worlds of Greece and Rome in my satchel'. She was made a scholar at St Hilda's, the only classicist of her year.

The first impression of Betty as an undergraduate was her dazzling fairness of skin and her whiter than flaxen hair which she wore all her life braided round her head. Some years later a London consultant took one look at her and identified her as coming from East Yorkshire where 'this throwback to Viking ancestors occasionally appears'. Both her parents were of East Yorkshire stock. To her delight the white hair reappeared in a granddaughter.

Oxford was a great opening up of life. She was one of a group of northern girls of the early thirties all of whom were first from their schools to reach Oxford. She had a hard and lonely road to achieve her scholarship and never lost the sense that the pleasures of learning are a hard-won delight and also something of a surprise. She said to a northern friend, 'I believe our children miss something. To us it was all magic. To them, given some hard work, it is all a matter of course. We knew our good fortune in being there. They do not.' She was the most brilliant student of her year and planned to become a don, and a first in Mods made this seem possible. One day returning from a tutorial she slipped in Addison's Walk, badly spraining an ankle. A passing undergraduate helped her to hobble back to college. They talked and found both were classical scholars. They fell in love, and so began a deep attachment which lasted until her death within months of their golden wedding.

Betty and Italo de Lisle Radice married as soon as Betty left Oxford. De Lisle began his career in the civil service; Betty taught English and classics at Westminster Tutors. The world, new to her, of London was a shared joy which they never lost and which never slackened. London theatres, music, art galleries were explored together and Betty became an ardent Londoner. Like all their generation youth was lived under the increasing shadow of a coming war which gave a poignancy and sense of ephemeral joys to their first five years of marriage.

Betty belonged to that generation whose youth exactly fitted between two wars. She was just over two when the first war started in 1914 and her first child Thomas was born in the first year of the second. The aftermath of war deprived her of her father. She grew up among adults to whom the war remained a topic of talk and memory. The second war deprived her for five years of her husband. She returned to Hessle for the birth of Thomas and although she had the companionship of a much loved and admired mother she was very lonely. In a short story written during the war she sees herself as Penelope waiting, and knowing her Odysseus may not come:

> I can wonder whether the pain of temporary separation has any qualities in common with what is a complete end, by death. Possibly in all forms of unhappiness the first thing one knows about is living at two levels of consciousness . . . at the best times it is curious how the intelligence can be wholly and genuinely engaged in external matters, or even the heart warmed by spontaneous gaiety, and still one can perceive the pain below.

Her Penelope came to the self-knowledge that she needed her own life and not to endure only as a waiting wife:

> One must think, analyse, coordinate and be occupied with profitable intellectual activity . . . she was aware that she had emerged with a mind matured and toughened, that the new interests were real and enduring.

She felt herself trapped by the inescapable but too small duties of caring for a little boy. In their weekly letters she and her husband discussed all events of the day, the Beveridge Report, the latest *Horizon* or *New Statesman*, and each tried to show the other how thoughts and feelings developed in their separation. In the only one of her wartime letters which she kept Betty wrote of her fear that a love of solitude might be incompatible with family life:

> I think, you see, that some people, of whom I am one, have difficulty in reconciling the inner and outer self . . . Do you remember the famous passage in the *Republic* about the cave? The bulk of mankind, you remember, lives in the cave and has only *opinions* based on the shadow of real things. Those that get out and once see the 'real' meet to tell those who remain. These views are not welcomed and they can never return, and according to Plato would never wish to . . . There are activities which seem to me to be undeniably out of the cave and those which are undeniably in. But in the middle are several things about which there can be no certainty and they are the material for great literature.

A family of young children is not a recipe for the solitary life. There is a paradox in her love of solitude and her happiness in having young children about her, for she was never happier than in her nursery – the traditional sunniest room in the house, prettily decorated and smelling sweetly of powder and babies. Betty's evenings became her solitary life, her time for outside the cave, her space for herself. When her third child was born she was found by her obstetrician reading the *Odyssey*. He glanced at the Greek and suggested that, for a newly delivered mother, perhaps something lighter . . .? She replied, 'I put it down as soon as the baby whimpers.' At this time too she took out her undergraduate translation of Pliny and began her long revision.

When the war ended she returned to the house in Highgate which they had lived in briefly before the war. De Lisle had two months of leave and then had to complete his military service. He joined the military government in Germany and was away for seven months. When he was demobbed, Betty found herself like so many women of her generation with a husband taking up an interrupted career, the prospect of a small income, the hope of children to come but also the certainty of an absence of any domestic help, and the desire for a 'profitable intellectual activity' which would make her contribution to the new post-war world. It would be a juggling act needing a lot of skill, a lot of self-discipline, hard work and good humour.

This too was a period when she shared all the political enthusiasms of the day; the post-war decade of Beveridge reforms and founding of the National Health Service caught her imagination. The lights went on again, children could go out and learn to name the stars. Four families stood in a dripping November garden and heard their children gasp and shout when the first Roman Candles and Chrysanthemum Fountains they had ever seen sprang into the air. There was the first Christmas of the peace and its hymns of thankfulness and hope, and there would be another, and another. Betty had her knowledge of generations of European history. The barbarians were driven from the gate but civilization must make haste to go forward before they returned, as they always had returned.

In remembering Betty the years of family happiness should first come to mind because they were the preparation for the work this book commemorates and by which she will be remembered. From 1945 until the end of 1966, when Catherine, her second child, became ill, were the halcyon years of family life, the purchase of the cottage at Berrick Salome near Oxford, family holidays, and her own holidays abroad with de Lisle. By the time Catherine died at the age of twenty, Betty had had some years of teaching at Channing School, her translation of Pliny's *Letters* was published and she had been editor of Penguin Classics for four years. How did she 'fit it all in'? First there was the day-to-day management of a household of growing children on a limited income, then her own intellectual interests and the life shared with her husband. There was no domestic staff behind her. 'It is all very easy to be a liberated woman if you have a cook and a good nanny,' she said of an exponent of women's liberation who had a pyramid of domestic help beneath her. There was a succession of au pair girls, often as much responsibility as help but whose loyalty she won. She seemed always to give smooth running of domestic life priority but this smooth running created the gaps and pauses when she could concentrate on her own work. She could write a paragraph, edit a text, or translate a few lines while dinner cooked. She seemed always available to children or friends but she was also available to herself. She never spoke of her rights to time, she simply made the time and used it.

Sadness came to these happy years when Teresa, born in 1949, died of a heart condition at six months. Like all such grief it was intense. Later she said, 'This is the first year when we have not remembered Teresa's death as a date in the family calendar. One must not have milestones to grief.' Two further sons followed, William born in 1951 and John in 1953.

It was in these happy years that Betty and de Lisle began their tradition of holidays which were famed among friends. There were journeys of discovery, each with a purpose and theme prepared for by reading. Each visit to the renaissance in Italy, to the baroque art of a German city, or the medieval towns of France, was to visualize the past, to form connections in time and space. They were in effect a preparation for the work at Penguin Classics and helped her later to expand the series into other than classical times, into Early and Middle English and Celtic languages. In the introduction to her *Who's Who in the Ancient World* she wrote:

> But I am not as pessimistic as some about losing the classics altogether. I think it is more likely that we are beginning to be afraid of doing so, and to revalue and appreciate our heritage . . . More people travel, and many of them more intelligently, thanks to an awakened interest in the past which has been helped by television and even the colour supplements . . . If we travel in Greece we really need to know why Apollo was important at Delphi and Delos, or why we keep coming across Lapiths battling with centaurs.

She could convey to schoolgirls the sense of the ancient world being in close continuity with our own. The boarders of the sixth at Channing School, young women but still in school uniform, found themselves in a pretty drawing-room with jasmine creeping at the window, to be greeted by a motherly lady with her 'banana smile'. There was a baby in its cradle at her feet, a tea-tray set, and on the table their work and her own. She read a passage of her translation of Pliny's letters and asked their opinion. Had she met the ideal of the translator's art – the principle of equivalence, creating the same impression in the mind of a common reader today, as the author had done for his contemporaries? Was her version a pleasure to read? Then turning to their schoolgirl work she asked the same questions.

How did Betty contrive to bring up a family of scholars, not to follow in her own profession but to be people with a scholarly attitude to chosen professions and lovers of scholarship? She could say with William Cobbett:

> My family are a family of scholars and . . . I could safely take my oath, that I never *ordered* a child of mine to *look into* a book in my life . . . the everlasting mixture of amusement with book learning made me, almost to my surprise, find that I had a parcel of scholars growing up about me.'
>
> (*Advice to Young Men*, 5, 'To a Father', 1825)

She never read to her children once past baby days but they saw both their parents with their heads in a book for their own pleasure. Reading was a part of family life. On evenings or on wet days at the cottage, reading was the pursuit of adults. They were welcome to join, or they could go off on their own games and pursuits. Her children lived with their mother's enthusiasm for European culture. They saw that worlds existed into which they might if they chose eventually enter. They witnessed as teenagers how Betty would carefully record her future reading from the TLS and other reviews, how she was an indefatigable user of the local public library and how she read systematically and daily. When Betty asked: Do you read Thackeray? she meant not: Did you have to read *Vanity Fair* at school?, or: Have you ever read him?, but: Do you return to read him and enter into the world he lived in? Catherine's diaries, unread by anyone until after Betty's own death, contained lists of her reading, ranked and commented on, and comments on what her parents read and thought.

Catherine gave her parents twenty happy years. Betty was proud of her lively, rebellious and imaginative daughter, the family cat-fish keeping them all on the hop with new ideas, plans and projects. She was the centre of family fun, initiator of Christmas games with neighbours and new things to do on holiday.

Betty's work with Penguins was now flourishing and years of family pleasures and professional successes seemed to lie ahead. When Catherine returned on vacation during her first year at York University, where she was supremely happy, mother and daughter found themselves on the new ground of an adult friendship. There had been conflicts while Catherine was at school. Which of them was to organize the men of the family? Catherine was rather proud of the family's old battered car, the hand-on clothes and willingness to be slightly eccentric, but Betty had the juggling act to perform on domestic economies and the reconciling of conflicting demands. When Catherine became ill of a rare and incurable condition Betty at once accepted the foreboding of doctors and finally their prognosis. For eighteen months she had to carry this acceptance while de Lisle, Thomas and the younger boys found it difficult to face the fact that Catherine, the mainstay of the family, was dying. This was a time of great loneliness. Catherine was buried in the churchyard at Berrick Salome. Afterwards Betty looked round the room full of Catherine's school friends, contemporaries from York, young cousins, themselves undergraduates at Oxford, and said: 'They are all quite bewildered. I feel for them very much. They never think, and should not have to think, of death and now they must.' She understood, as her Penelope had understood more than twenty-five years ago, that in grief, one lives 'at two levels', that grief comes and goes and divides. 'I make a remark to de Lisle,' she said to a friend, 'about one of the boys or something coming up in the garden and it seems to him a deadly triviality because just then he is in the trough of grief, and when he talks to me perhaps I am only wanting to be alone and weep.' Her Penelope had said, 'the most permanent feature of prolonged sadness seemed to be a sense of isolation'.

Many years before she had written to a friend on the death of a baby, 'Don't let your private grief overshadow the growing up of the others.' So now she set herself to act on that resolve. 'Evidently,' said her Penelope, 'if the heart had once been fully alive it would struggle to live again almost of its own accord,' perhaps recalling the letter of sympathy from Servius Sulpicius to Cicero on the death of a beloved daughter: 'Are you then so distressed for the life of one poor woman? . . . There is no sorrow that the passage of time does not diminish and soften. It is unworthy of you to wait for this to happen, and not use your wisdom to anticipate it.' Betty had a strong sense that in ancient times life was accepted as short, that beauty was fragile and 'the brave efforts of man in his short-lived season' were always at risk. The worlds she had studied did not have our modern expectation that life is long, untroubled and happy. Presenting a copy of *Who's Who in the Ancient World*, she waited until the delighted friend turned to the dedication to Catherine and gently translated:

Sunt apud infernos tot milia formosarum – 'there are already so many beautiful young girls in Hades'. Propertius goes on: 'Surely one could be spared?' The sad double spondees at the end of the verse convey beauty vanishing, beauty passing, and the ancient world expected young women to die in the prime and joy of youth. Today we don't accept it and it seems outside the course of nature as we imagine it. Catherine is harder to let go than she would have been in the ancient world.

In his Betty Radice memorial service address William Radice said:

I don't believe she would have been able to attain such heights as a translator had she not felt so deeply in her own life. She shows us that translation is not just a matter of handling words and meanings; it requires deep imaginative insight into the person whose works one is translating . . . The sympathy she could feel for these figures from the past was a truly feminine sort of sympathy and it was of course the same sympathy that she extended to friends and colleagues.

She set herself to 'let the heart recover again almost of its own accord'. Her first grandchild was born five years after Catherine's death, and eight others followed. Her sons' families treasure the dressed dolls, the toys and inimitable cards which she sent them. Each was considered as a unique person. 'Fairy godmothers are essential,' she said, 'bringing the scarcely hoped-for wish, achieving the impossible and producing rapture.' Her own children and grandchildren knew this magic wand. At the end of the war, learning that a friend's little daughter had a passionate longing for a doll with a real, that is a china, face, she traced a doll of her own childhood to an attic in Ireland, arranged an escort to Highgate, dressed it and knocked on the door with the doll in her arms. Years afterwards it was returned for her own grandchildren, preserved as a fairy godmother's gift merits.

When her brother died, as her father had done, in his forties, she became a very essential aunt and, later, great-aunt. She was renowned for her memory of family events, recalling in detail her own childhood, tales of their father and grandfather and bringing forth little possessions, toys of long ago which told a million stories. Her power to fascinate children rested on this sense of family wholeness and presenting time to children in objects of delight. Her own grandchildren would run in and seek out the old dolls' house and its treasures of long ago or play respectfully with the marvellous doll which had a china face and sat on its own chair. When her sister-in-law died, she visited her niece and her children and at once began a tale of her long-lived tortoises and their wicked habits of eating her lettuce or refusing to be found when hibernation time came around. At the end of the visit the eldest great-niece asked 'Will you be our Granny now?' Her 'Yes, of course' meant that they were included in the yearly calendar of birthday cards and presents and visits for tea and games. She treated children's own interests with respect. Her niece recalls her 'in her seventies, striding up the hill from the station, map, *circa* 1950, in hand, full of new history about the town we lived in, stories of my own childhood, and fitting in to our family as though the intervening years were of no consequence'.

Betty felt herself more liberated than many of her friends and contemporaries. She did not perhaps appreciate that a job at home or just up the road is a very different problem from working nine to five in Whitehall or teaching full-time when children are young. As assistant to E. V. Rieu and later as Penguin editor she could 'chug on in my own time'. Her daughters-in-law faced very different problems. Her rather austere conviction that any woman with a good degree – preferably from Oxford or Cambridge – could 'make a contribution', have a career, and bring up a parcel of scholars began to seem inadequate. As the ever-helpful Gran she saw the difficulties of domestic help, coping with childhood illness and all the inevitable emergencies: she came perhaps nearest to sympathy for feminism or the women's movement in watching her daughters-in-law.

Her translation of Pliny's letters was her most heartfelt book. He was, in fact, a household familiar, living under the bed in a box. 'If you are going to be quarrelsome,' she would say on a wet afternoon, 'I shall go upstairs and find my Pliny more entertaining.' She felt that Pliny had been neglected and that he waited for her to bring him into the mainstream of European classical works: 'I want to put him in the repertoire of the classics, only it is taking me a long time.' Her introduction to his letters is not only to the common reader of our times but reads as though she speaks to his contemporaries and says: I am taking up the cudgel for him, never fear that he will be neglected again. Family and friends knew her as Pliny's advocate long before Penguins knew her as his translator.

Betty came of a generation of women to whom women friends were one of the most important things in life, kept by long hours of letter writing and long journeys. She was a woman's woman and her closest friends were women. She had a sense of the physical problems of being a woman, the indignities of childbearing and menstrual tension, long before these became fashionable subjects. Sorrow enlarged her understanding of others and her sympathies. During the long wartime separation she wrote of other women: 'Unhappiness was a widespread phenomenon . . . but there are too many of us, too many Penelopes waiting at home, and no one has cared to tell us what we have in common.' A friend from her first days at Oxford wrote, 'I valued her scholarship and felt proud of her but it was her humanity and interest in everyday things that made her the glorious, caring, domesticated person that she was.' During her happiest years she seemed the first confidant to many, but during her periods of sorrow she judged whom to visit and whom to spare. Her friends found her a very private person. Something of her self went into each relationship but in each there were reservations. A slight deafness, in spite of two operations, was so well concealed that some lifelong friends had hardly heard of it.

Betty once described herself as 'tone-deaf to religion', but she had a convinced and express faith founded on her classical studies. Her work for the translation of classics was seen by her as a contribution to keeping alive the important part of our inheritance handed down generation after generation from the classical world and from the literature of Europe to this day. She saw her own work as helping to defend the Roman qualities: *gravitas*, a sense of responsibility, *iustitia*, a sense of justice, and *pietas*, a man's duty to his dependants. She wrote of the war against Hannibal: '*Hannibal ad portas* became part of the tradition of Rome . . . Those of us who remember the years 1939–45 can surely recognize the moment when a Hannibal stood at our gates and there seemed nothing to hold him but the obstinacy of the people's refusal to accept defeat.' It was as a woman with this experience of her generation that she came to the deeply held conviction that the traditions of European culture are not safe in the hands only of scholars. Not only shall we be the poorer 'if poets and painters never draw from Greece and Rome again and they cease to provide a common language and a range of living symbols' but the common reader must be involved. There was something of the general about her when she spoke of making recruits for the defence of the best tradition by recruiting enthusiasts from her readers. What man comes to love he will defend. There was nothing patronizing about her attitude to her non-classical reader. He must be served by the highest standards of scholarship; respect for him as well as for the scholar made her provide each translation with its 'line references, notes, indexes, bibliographies and fuller introductions'. 'I myself begin as a common reader,' she said of a possible addition to the series from the Far East. So as the scope of the Penguin Classics grew, her sense of what was to be defended also grew: 'I know much is offered by the literature of China and Japan, India and the Middle East', she wrote in a tribute to E. V. Rieu, but added a practicality: 'Translations of this kind are not easy to sell.'

Betty would refer to herself as a humanist in words which recall her description of Gibbon's 'humanist belief in the rational thinking by which a man can rise above bigotry and superstition and try to make sense of his experience'. In her own life this was transfigured by the depth of family affections, by her sympathy for friends, and a gusto for life. Erasmus had sympathy for his fools and Betty comments:

> This warms the heart, for somewhere amongst them it is more than likely that we can see ourselves. And surely it is a simple truth that we do all 'look for a bit of gaiety and fun in life'. The spontaneity and warmth of our personal relationships, our endeavours, hopes and joys may be foolish and illusory *sub specie aeternitatis*, but what would life be without them?

In reading Betty's introduction to the letters of Abelard and Heloise one is reminded that she was taught at school and college by a generation of women, many of whom had lost young husbands and lovers in the First World War. Heloise lost Abelard as a lover at the age of nineteen, after only eighteen months of passionate happiness. She, too, had to put an unrecoverable past behind her and build her future. We are left with a vision of Heloise as one of the Church's great abbesses guiding her nuns, novices and students, and administering farms, fishponds, vineyards, mills and tithes. We may hope 'that her fine intelligence and administrative abilities found full scope in what we should now call a rewarding career, and that with passage of time she achieved "calm of mind, all passion spent"'.

We cannot know whether she found a vocation but surely she 'came to feel that her service to the Paraclete was a true form of devotion to God'.

Friends who themselves have a religious belief felt that Betty had such belief, but defined in other terms than their own. Her knowledge of Jewish traditions and the role of the Christian Church in history made her place Christian values among her list of things to be defended. A Quaker friend wrote of her: 'Betty had a great faith which she was unaware of and which carried her forward when her mother died, baby Teresa died, and Catherine died.' In later years she became very close to one of her translators who is herself a nun. This friend wrote:

> I was struck by her quality of – I can only call it – truth. I think her recognition of quality and her instinctive suspicion of sentiment struck me very much; and also her humility in asking always for other opinions, without in the least causing respect for her ability to drop . . . She seemed to receive every moment, and all things, fresh from the hand of God who made them. Cant and hypocrisy and affectation were quite alien to her mind. Perhaps her approach to scholarship was close to the ascetic approach to prayer, a clearing of the mind from its own absorption in order to receive reality in truth.

Betty had only a short last illness. On her last afternoon she spoke cheerfully of the holiday in southern Spain which she and de Lisle had already planned. She died in the small hours, on 19 February 1985, and is buried beside Catherine in the churchyard of Berrick Salome.

'THE WANDERER'

from The Earliest English Poems, 1966
translated by

Michael Alexander

Who liveth alone longeth for mercy,
Maker's mercy. Though he must traverse
tracts of sea, sick at heart,
– trouble with oars ice-cold waters,
the ways of exile – Weird is set fast.

Thus spoke such a 'grasshopper', old griefs in his mind,
cold slaughters, the death of dear kinsmen:

'Alone am I driven each day before daybreak
to give my cares utterance.
None are there now among the living
to whom I dare declare me throughly,
tell my heart's thought. Too truly I know
it is in a man no mean virtue
that he keep close his heart's chest,
hold his thought-hoard, think as he may.

No weary mind may stand against Weird
nor may a wrecked will work new hope;
wherefore, most often, those eager for fame
bind the dark mood fast in their breasts.

So must I also curb my mind,
cut off from country, from kind far distant,
by cares overworn, bind it in fetters;
this since, long ago, the ground's shroud
enwrapped my gold-friend. Wretched I went thence,
winter-wearied, over the waves' bound;
dreary I sought hall of a gold-giver,
where far or near I might find
him who in meadhall might take heed of me,

furnish comfort to a man friendless,
win me with cheer.
He knows who makes trial
how harsh and bitter is care for companion
to him who hath few friends to shield him.
Track ever taketh him, never the torqued gold,
not earthly glory, but cold heart's cave.
He minds him of hall-men, of treasure-giving,
how in his youth his gold-friend
gave him to feast. Fallen all this joy.

He knows this who is forced to forgo his lord's,
his friend's counsels, to lack them for long;
oft sorrow and sleep, banded together,
come to bind the lone outcast;
he thinks in his heart then that he his lord
claspeth and kisseth, and on knee layeth
hand and head, as he had at otherwhiles
in days now gone, when he enjoyed the gift-stool.

Awakeneth after this friendless man,
seeth before him fallow waves,
seabirds bathing, broading out feathers,
snow and hail swirl, hoar-frost falling.
Then all the heavier his heart's wounds,
sore for his loved lord. Sorrow freshens.

Remembered kinsmen press through his mind;
he singeth out gladly, scanneth eagerly
men from the same hearth. They swim away.
Sailors' ghosts bring not many
known songs there. Care grows fresh
in him who shall send forth too often
over locked waves his weary spirit.

Therefore I may not think, throughout this world,
why cloud cometh not on my mind
when I think over all the life of earls,
how at a stroke they have given up hall,
mood-proud thanes. So this middle earth
each of all days ageth and falleth.'

Wherefore no man grows wise without he have
his share of winters. A wise man holds out;

he is not too hot-hearted, nor too hasty in speech,
nor too weak a warrior, not wanting in fore-thought,
nor too greedy of goods, nor too glad, nor too mild,
nor ever too eager to boast, ere he knows all.

A man should forbear boastmaking
until his fierce mind fully knows
which way his spleen shall expend itself.

A wise man may grasp how ghastly it shall be
when all this world's wealth standeth waste,
even as now, in many places, over the earth
walls stand, wind-beaten,
hung with hoar-frost; ruined habitations.
The wine-halls crumble; their wielders lie
bereft of bliss, the band all fallen
proud by the wall. War took off some,
carried them on their course hence; one a bird bore
over the high sea; one the hoar wolf
dealt to death; one his drear-cheeked
earl stretched in an earthen trench.

The Maker of men hath so marred this dwelling
that human laughter is not heard about it
and idle stand these old giant-works.

A man who on these walls wisely looked,
who sounded deeply this dark life,
would think back to the blood spilt here,
weigh it in his wit. His word would be this:
'Where is that horse now? Where are those men? Where is the
hoard-sharer?
Where is the house of the feast? Where is the hall's uproar?

Alas, bright cup! Alas, burnished fighter!
Alas, proud prince! How that time has passed,
dark under night's helm, as though it never had been!

There stands in the stead of staunch thanes
a towering wall wrought with worm-shapes;
the earls are off-taken by the ash-spear's point,
– that thirsty weapon. Their Weird is glorious.

Storms break on the stone hillside,
the ground bound by driving sleet,
winter's wrath. Then wanness cometh,
night's shade spreadeth, sendeth from north
the rough hail to harry mankind.

In the earth-realm all is crossed;
Weird's will changeth the world.
Wealth is lent us, friends are lent us,
man is lent, kin is lent;
all this earth's frame shall stand empty.'

So spoke the sage in his heart; he sat apart in thought.
Good is he who keeps faith: nor should care too fast
be out of a man's breast before he first know the cure:
a warrior fights on bravely. Well is it for him who seeks forgiveness,
the Heavenly Father's solace, in whom all our fastness stands.

(1961–2)

THE OLDEST CHINESE POETRY

Arthur Cooper

In July 1968 I had just retired from a career under the Foreign and Commonwealth Office when I received a letter from Mrs Betty Radice, whom I did not know personally but who said she wrote at the suggestion of Michael Alexander, a common friend. It was a most interesting and sympathetic letter, though it flattered me by consulting me about subjects on which I could not possibly be regarded as an authority; and was to be the start of correspondence and conversations over the years thereafter: always generous, patient, stimulating and encouraging, and concealing by her manner how busy her life must have been. One knew only by starting to count all her quiet achievements in any year.

Among subjects on which she sought my opinion in that first letter was a proposal to have translations from the oldest Chinese anthology, the *Book of Odes*, in the Penguin Classics: could I suggest anyone to undertake this?

I answered that it would be difficult to find such a person either among scholars of Chinese willing to put up work to stand against Arthur Waley's *Book of Songs* (1937) and Bernhard Karlgren's *Book of Odes* (1950), the former a work of literary distinction and generally quoted when examples were given and the latter based on new philological examinations and interpretations of the ancient texts; or among poets against Ezra Pound's *Classic Anthology Defined by Confucius* (1955) which, though idiosyncratic and not a scholarly work, was often entertaining and much acclaimed by literary critics.

Any new translation would have to be fundamentally different from any of these in order to justify publication: to explore anew the original meanings of texts which have become encrusted with, one might say, layers of scholastic attempts at elucidation made during the 2½–3 millennia of their esteem as a sacred classic among the Chinese, who for centuries had to learn them by heart as an essential part of their education, but have had to depend on currently favoured glosses and commentaries for an interpretation of the content and intention of each.

The Chinese have not in fact read the originals without reliance on such for the past two thousand years. In recent centuries the interpretations of the twelfth-century neo-Confucian scholar and philosopher Zhu Xi (Chu Hsi) have reigned as orthodox, so that there would be a case even for two translations: one, based on these, to show how the Chinese have long understood the Odes, quoting from them like Latin tags; the other, likely to be of more general interest to modern Western readers, endeavouring to recover the ancient poets' original intentions in so remote a time, which may be put at about the eleventh to the sixth centuries BC. It is, of course, with the latter that scholars and translators are now most concerned.

That distant time in China may be said to be roughly contemporary with the Psalms of David and the Homeric poems on our side of the world; but the linguistic problem posed is entirely different and much greater, thanks to the nature of the ancient Chinese language and, especially, its script. The main problem in the language itself is its lack of formal distinction of different parts of speech and of most of what we are accustomed to regard as 'grammar', by which one can 'parse' and find the structure of a sentence before studying the meanings of the individual words (in a language one cannot know well) and so seek its intention. There are no grammatical concords to catch hold of like a handrail; no necessary distinctions of such things as number, gender, person, tense. All this, not expressed by the apparatus of the language, had to be provided by the reader's perception of the context. As Mencius (372–289 BC) said of understanding the Odes, already difficult in his own time, the reader 'must not let the use of a word in it spoil his comprehension of a phrase, neither must he let the phrase spoil his comprehension of the intention; but he must let his thought go to meet the intention as he would a guest'. In other words, he must start with some conception of the intention, confirming his hypothesis by all that is contained in the language used to express it, rather than by analysing the language first in order to discover the intention. For a similar process one may compare reading newspaper headlines lacking normal grammar for the sake of brevity and 'punch' – qualities the Chinese language makes possible to a singular degree by its nature. (I have used forty-four words of English above to render fully the meaning of what Mencius was able to express in fourteen monosyllables of his language, each written with one character of its script.)

But just as newspaper headlines may be baffling if one cannot guess the subject they refer to, so can a simple Chinese lyric, like many in the first section of the *Book of Odes*, often require guessing a context in order to recognize what it is about. That is indeed hardly unusual with poetry in any language, which must demand an active, creative contribution from its audience's uninstructed imagination to make it work; but with a language such as Chinese it widened the scope for later glossators and commentators to force on these revered and ancient poems supposed historical and didactic interpretations which in their eyes could alone explain their commendation by the Sage Confucius himself, so near to the time when they were composed. As Arthur Waley remarked, 'this type of reinterpretation is not confined to China. Parts of our own Bible have been explained on similar lines, particularly the Song of Solomon and certain of the Psalms'. Although such reinterpretations of the Odes have been altogether discarded by modern scholars, their didactic spirit sometimes dies hard in the work of translators; even in Arthur Waley's own, as will be seen in an example below.

The Book of Odes consists of several sections and different classifications; with both short and long poems, from simple lyrics of private emotions to grand odes for great occasions. All were 'odes', songs for performance with accompanying music and probably dance. Twelve tunes for twelve songs survive out of some three hundred, and one of these tunes is for a song of which a performance was praised highly by Confucius. To him the music will have been quite as important as the words.

The first section of the anthology is called the *Guofeng*: 'Winds (airs or fashions) from the States' (forming the religio-feudal empire of the time, perhaps roughly comparable politically with the Holy Roman Empire), and is arranged under the names of these States, as if it were a collection of regional folksongs. Although the language, style and content are similar for the different States, there are differences statistically in the types of verse structure favoured by each, and so presumably also in their musical fashions; however, there is no reason to suppose that these were truly folksongs rather than courtly compositions like others in this Book of Odes, but as they include the simplest poems I shall choose examples from them.

As a first example let us take a little song, *You Hu*, 'There's a Fox'

有狐綏綏在彼淇梁心之憂矣之子無裳
有狐綏綏在彼淇厲心之憂矣之子無帶
有狐綏綏在彼淇側心之憂矣之子無服

蝃蝀在東莫之敢指女子有行遠父母兄弟
朝隮于西崇朝其雨女子有行遠兄弟父母
乃如之人也懷昏姻也大無信也不知命也

Book of Odes, No. 51, 'A Rainbow' (left) and No. 63, 'There's a Fox'. (Read columns downwards from the right.) *Calligraphy by Shui Chien-T'ung*

(No. 63 in the usual Mao edition)* of three short stanzas of the playful type where each stanza repeats the preceding one but for the change of only a couple of words carrying the rhyme. I give the nearest I can as a word-for-word translation in English monosyllables, with glosses in italic and a little punctuation to help the sense (rhythm: 2 + 2 = 4 syllables to each of the four lines in a stanza):

There's	fox	creeps	creeps	1 *Ch'i*, river name
on	yon	Qi[1]	dam[2]:	2 or *weir*
heart —[3]	the	grief	oh!	3 *heart's*
The[4]	child(e)[5]	lacks	robe[6].	4 *This*
				5 of gentle birth here, as 'Childe' Harold
				6 (rhymes with *dam*) *lower or long garment*
There's	fox	creeps	creeps	
on	yon	Qi	ford[7]	7 *stepping stones*
heart	the	grief	oh!	
The	child(e)	lacks	belt[8]	8 (rhymes with *ford*)
There's	fox	creeps	creeps	
on	yon	Qi	side[9]:	9 *other side, having crossed?*
heart	the	grief	oh!	
The	child(e)	lacks	costume[10].	10 (rhymes with *side*)

My crude rendering of this song in English monosyllables (never, of course, exactly equivalent to the Chinese) could not be sustained for the last word for which I have put 'costume', instead of 'clothes' as it is commonly translated. The Chinese word here did not originally mean 'clothes' but what was *customary*, so proper to wear; and in this resembles our own word, which is derived from Italian *costume* = 'custom', with the earliest use as a 'set of garments' occurring in English as late as the last century according to the *Oxford English Dictionary*. The similar sense-development occurred in China many centuries earlier, but from a verb meaning 'to make submit' and so 'to submit to custom, *mores*'. The creeping fox can be recognized as a rival suitor by the use of the same image in another of the Odes where a 'male fox creeps creeps' and plays that part. Here I think he is seen approaching and crossing the river, on the other side of which (as often in the Odes) dwells the lady; while the unfortunate 'childe' lacks the proper costume, including the long robe and ceremonial girdle, to go courting her himself.

* Named after Mao Chang who commented on the Odes and compiled an edition in the second century BC. It has long been the standard edition, though with additional comments.

One has, of course, to contribute from one's own imagination a scenario for such a little poem, but from the words contained in it and observing the rule of Occam's Razor: not contributing more than is necessary. Here I have only had to suppose that 'side' in the last stanza was intended to mean the other side of the river. The Confucian interpreters, however, could not see such a simple little song as worthy of a place in the Odes admired by Confucius and so had to contribute much more to the scenario in order to provide it with an historical background and a didactic purpose. Thus in the 'Little Prefaces', compiled early in our own era and many centuries after the date of the song itself, it is regarded as an attack on the government at the time in the state of Wei, to which it is assigned in the *Guofeng*; because couples lost chances to marry according to the strict rites that had to be observed, which it claimed in times of trouble in antiquity had been relaxed so that the population might be increased. The twelfth-century neo-Confucian Zhu Xi, mentioned above, objected that this interpretation was not founded on the words of the ancient song, as he maintained interpretations always should be. We now should agree with that, but we then find his own interpretation to be quite as remote from them: in times of national disorder, he says, when people became dispersed, opportunities were lost for the proper pairing of couples: a widow saw a widower whom she desired to marry and this was intended to excuse her. I am unable to explain how Zhu Xi arrived at such a conclusion but it will be evident to the modern reader that the 'Little Preface', though rejected by Zhu Xi, had contributed greatly to his own interpretation and that his own scenario appears to have as little to support it in the words of 'There's a Fox'.

To Confucians, who believed that the purpose of the song must be didactic, it seems that the last phrase, 'without (the proper) costume' – or 'custom' – had the effect of dominating their approach to the whole; because they saw the proper observance of ritual as of vital importance both in the transactions of individuals and for good order in the state. Any suggestion of its absence should thus be severely condemned or else convincingly excused by exceptional circumstances. How they supported their interpretations in the rest of the little poem it is impossible to say; for they gave 'the right answer', as it were, without showing their 'workings'. Mencius' advice about reading the Odes, as quoted above, had been carried to lengths that he never intended: as if 'going to meet the intention' should be almost regardless of 'words' and 'phrases'! It is useless therefore to seek for guidance as to the ancient poets' original intentions from the commentaries made after Confucianism had become the state religion.

Nevertheless these were faithfully included in the first European works on *The Book of Odes*, as in the translation of James Legge (1871), who even mingled them together and sometimes thereby seems to have added to his own puzzlement. Later translators, even when rejecting them, seem often unable to escape their influence; as may be seen in translations by various hands of another little song from the *Guofeng* section, *Di Dong*, 'A Rainbow' (No. 51 in the *Mao* order).

I give first the translation by the French sinologue Marcel Granet (1884–1940), who introduced modern social anthropology to the study of the ancient Chinese anthology, from his *Fêtes et chansons anciennes de la Chine* (1919):

L'ARC-EN-CIEL

L'arc-en-ciel est à l'orient!
Personne ne l'ose montrer!
La fille, pour se marier,
Laisse au loin frères et parents!

Vapeur matinale au couchant!
C'est la pluie pour la matinée!
La fille, pour se marier,
Laisse au loin frères et parents!

Or la fille que vous voyez
Rêve d'aller se marier,
Sans plus garder la chasteté
Et avant qu'on l'ait ordonné!

The translation by the great Swedish phonologist and sinologue, Bernhard Karlgren, in the prose version of the whole anthology he made from his own textual and phonological studies incorporated in his *Glosses on the Odes* (the first, *Guofeng*, volume of this was published in 1942), differs little from Granet's:

1. The rainbow is in the east (a), nobody dares point to it; when a girl makes her journey (b), she goes far away from father and mother and brothers.

2. At dawn there are rising vapours in the west (c), it will rain all through the morning; when a girl makes her journey, she goes far away from brothers and father and mother.

3. That she was such a person! She was eagerly thinking of marriage; she was very unreliable, she did not understand the will of Heaven.

The words, but not the general purport, of the last stanza differ from Granet's translation. Karlgren provided notes: (a) A bad omen. (b) Going to her new home . . . The marriage should not be precipitated, against the warning of evil omens; it is a serious business, since the girl can no longer fall back on her own family. (c) [He argues that, because the verb 'to rise' used here is elsewhere said to be used of 'rising vapours', that must be the intention here also.]

Arthur Waley's version in *The Book of Songs* differs more, especially in the last stanza and in his notes provided to the whole:

There is a girdle in the east;
No one dares point at it.
A girl has run away,
Far from father and mother, far from brothers young and old.

There is dawnlight mounting in the west;
The rain will last till noon.
A girl has run away,
Far from brothers young and old, far from mother and from father.

Such a one as he
Is bent on high connections;
Never will he do what he promised,
Never will he accept his lot.

Waley noted that the girdle is the rainbow and that

its appearance announces that someone who ought not to is about to have a baby; for the arc of the rainbow typifies the swelling girdle of a pregnant woman. No one dares point at it, because pointing is disrespectful, and one must respect a warning sent by Heaven. The second verse opens with a weather proverb. The 'mounting' . . . typifies the swelling girdle; the rain means, I think, the tears she will shed, when she finds out that she has been deceived. For the lover is bent on forming powerful connections that will improve his lot in life, and whatever promises he may make now, he certainly will not fulfil them.

It will be observed that, alone of these three translators, Waley's scenario introduces a male, 'he'. Waley also makes the naughty girl, who is pregnant as a result of her foolish trust, *run away* from home; but none of this is implied, that I can see, in the original. Waley, in fact, seems here to have imposed his own scenario with as little justification as the Confucian commentators often did on the Odes; but, out of justice to the memory of a great English translator, who did more than any other to introduce Far Eastern literature to the public of the English speaking world, I have to say that, if Homer sometimes nodded, Waley nodded here: it would be very unfair to treat this as a sample of his work. (In an 'Additional Note' at the back of his book, he makes clear how much anthropological reading had influenced him at the time.)

Where all these versions agree is in their moral condemnation, which accords with the Confucian view of the poem. In the 'Little Prefaces' it is said to concern the good influence of the Duke Wen of a particular state, who made people ashamed of sexual immorality;* but Zhu Xi says no more than that it was written to attack such. Not only these, but all translations of the poem that I can find, accept, in one way or another, this kind of view of it, however various the scenarios the nature of the language may seem to permit.

The question that has to be asked is if any of these scenarios would have been chosen, were it not for the tradition of Confucian moralizing interpretations. When a rainbow is seen in the east, it is of course evening, with the sun on the opposite side of the sky in the west. There have always been these weather proverbs in Chinese: 'East rainbow – sunshine; west rainbow – rain' and 'A rainbow seen at dawn in the west means that it will go on raining, in the evening seen in the east means that the rain will cease.' (There is no need to repeat 'rainbow' in that proverb and no need either to repeat it in the second stanza of our ode: it is of course a rainbow that arises now in the west at morning time, not 'vapours' and still less 'dawn-light'!) The girl who is to leave her own family to marry into a strange one looks for omens for her future. In the first stanza she sees a good one, but it would be unlucky ever to draw attention to a good omen. Then in the morning when a rainbow arises in the west, she knows that it is going to go on raining all morning. The omens she seeks about her future are conflicting. I interpret the third stanza: *'So this is how she is, as she nurses in her bosom thoughts about her wedding and marriage: she greatly lacks confidence and does not know*

* The sexual theme was introduced because the rainbow was seen as an irregular fusion of rain, which belonged to the Yin, female principle, with sunshine, which was Yang, male; but this idea need not have been in the mind of the songwriter. It came to dominate the minds of commentators, as lack of 'costume' ('custom') did in 'There's a Fox'.

her fate.' ('Fate' is all that the last word expresses; it might of course be used for 'the will of Heaven', especially if 'of Heaven' were in the text; but it is not and there is no need to supply it unless one is determined to make this into a pious and moralizing poem!)

Other translators, such as Legge, the earliest in English, see the rainbow as the subject also of the second stanza; yet they all fail to see the connection with the third, which they too force into condemnation of the girl instead of an expression of sympathy for her. Sympathy, compassion for all kinds of suffering, sometimes with anger against its causes, are themes everywhere in this Chinese anthology and, I think, give it its greatest distinction among ancient poetry. There are indeed odes celebrating victory in battle, but many more songs that tell of the suffering of soldiers on campaign and of their anxious families at home. Even heroes in this anthology are allowed to tremble with fear. Those who sought exhortation in it for the modelling of individual behaviour according to their own ideals, and condemnation of whatever they saw as antisocial, had often to force senses on the words against anything unprepared minds would take as their probable intention.

Chinese may lack 'grammar' as we think of it from our experience of our own and other languages, but it does not lack rules; first among which is its necessary rule of economy. Seeking economy in expression, it demands it in interpretation. The various scenarios that can be imagined for the interpretation of the words of this song cannot be accepted as probable unless they obey that rule. If any other but the interpretation I have suggested above had been intended, the rule of economy in expression would have demanded making sure that it was understood by expressing it in another way which would rule out the one I have given. I have compared the way we understand newspaper headlines; let me give a rather absurd example of one I saw years ago before capital punishment in this country was abolished: LABOUR CALL FOR DEATH PENALTY SUSPENSION. One might argue that LABOUR CALL *might* in headlinese mean 'call for labour'; FOR commonly means 'on behalf of'; and SUSPENSION certainly means 'hanging'; qualified by DEATH PENALTY to show the kind of hanging meant? Nobody, however, would expect to find a story about a recruiting drive for hangmen under that headline! Yet, if one really *wanted* to impose that meaning on it, I suppose one could; provided one did not stop to think how that would more probably have been expressed, and was unaware of or prepared to disregard common usage in the language concerned. The language of the Odes was often sufficiently unfamiliar to people centuries later for the Confucian commentators to impose on them the didactic meanings they so earnestly wanted them to bear.

Not only are modern scholars still sometimes too much influenced by the Confucian idea of the nature of the Odes, but they may also allow false analogies drawn by themselves to obscure their view, as in Granet's and Karlgren's 'rising vapours', where the verb means only 'to rise', because in another of the Odes it has been taken by Chinese glossators as referring particularly to 'morning vapours' in the mountains – an approach by these two scholars quite contrary to Mencius' advice.

These examples will perhaps be enough to justify the opinion I offered to Betty Radice in 1968: that there was a need now to discard many of the notions that have grown around the Odes and for a fresh examination of them before attempting any new translations. One requirement that I have come to see as of paramount importance is a deeper look at the script in which they are recorded; which, having started from pictograms and ideograms, as did other scripts of the Ancient World, is generally supposed to have evolved as they did into a system aimed rather at giving the sounds of words than their meanings, at first through the medium of the *rebus* – a pictogram or ideogram used only for the sound of the word it represented and not for its meaning. As in other scripts in which a whole word may be represented by one symbol, the symbol was often divided into two elements to help the reader: one for the approximate sound of a word; and one to assist him in recognizing the word intended, by depicting a class of meaning for it. For instance in English, in addition to the word's sound, a hand might be depicted if the verb 'bear' were intended in the meaning of 'carry', but a symbol for an animal if for the noun. Such a system well suited Chinese as a language of monosyllables not subject to grammatical changes; but in Chinese, I no longer believe that the element apparently chosen for its sound was only for that: no more than a rebus and irrelevant for its meaning. It was, I believe, originally etymologically *related* to the words for the writing of which it was employed, and the early Chinese who chose it were conscious of this. Etymology had not yet become an interest only for academics, but *made* language.

To elaborate my reasons for coming to this view, in the years since Betty's first letter, would be far outside the scope of this essay;

but let us look at an example. The Chinese word and character used in the title of this ancient anthology, and translated by Legge and Karlgren as 'Odes' and by Waley as 'Songs', is now pronounced *shï* and written

詩

The character divides vertically with 'words' for the class of meaning on the left; and the supposed rebus, as an approximation to the ancient sound, on the right. But when one looks at this supposed rebus in its earliest written forms it can be seen to have represented a 'hand' and a 'foot' and, as a character itself, to have such meanings as 'to attend, wait on', an 'attendant', and a great 'hall' or 'court' as a place of 'attendance'. In our own language a 'minister' and to 'minister to' are from the Latin for an attendant or servant, and 'minstrel' is also derived from this. Does that not suggest a similar derivation for the Chinese word written with this character? That these Odes or Songs were originally composed for the entertainment of the great ones of the land in their halls and courts? Many kinds of song might have suited their taste on these occasions, from the light and witty to the noble and solemn, for these may have been like the operas, concerts and even masses of our own time; but such audiences would be unlikely to want moral homilies sung to them, as imagined for the Odes by the Confucians when, centuries later, theirs had become the state religion.

There are very many characters with a pronunciation like *shï* (roughly as if 'shr') in Standard Modern Chinese (I count over seventy in a middle-sized dictionary!) as a result of phonetic decay, but the script still distinguishes them in writing. The apparent ability of the Chinese language to put so much meaning into one simple syllable relates less to the spoken language now than to the script, which still shows the history of the words; although to the Chinese now it is mostly just the way to spell a syllable in a given context, like our own spelling, and as they have learned from their teachers who would be unable to give any reasons but precedent.

In all languages etymologies are forgotten as words extend their uses away from the shared observations and experiences that gave them birth. But as one goes back in time, so these become more and more relevant to the way a word may be used; and this is of course especially so with the oldest poetry. In 'A Rainbow' I have rendered a single Chinese syllable by 'nurses thoughts in her bosom' because that is the image its character reveals: 'to enclose' in the 'breast', where it opens, of a 'jacket', in which one may secrete things; with 'heart or mind' to show the kind of secreting the word refers to. The etymon can mean 'to nurse' and so 'to comfort' and 'to cherish', or physically 'to carry in the bosom or on the lap', or mentally 'to harbour thoughts or feelings'; and can according to context be translated in any of these ways or others. But in the ancient poems it is as well to refer to that image, from which the three translators quoted seem to depart more and more: Granet's *'rêve'*, but little; Karlgren's 'is eagerly thinking of', more; and Waley's 'is bent on', most. The sense of 'desire' that all of them take to be meant is of course perfectly possible, but only if other things point that way. The language had not yet reached the stage where the original observation or experience in the living world had been detached from the word created by it: where the word could instead be tied to an abstract generality such as 'desire' from which it could move on to 'eagerness' and being 'bent on', away from the image. The script like the language was, in fact, a creation of what Vico called 'the Poetic Age'; as were all languages in their origins. The Chinese language seems to be unique for the extent to which it has kept a record of its own *poesis*.

Modern sinologues prefer the rebus explanation, on account of parallels with other ancient scripts, to what I suggest as having been the *poesis* of the Chinese script. For instance Bernhard Karlgren, one of the greatest and still most influential, discusses a phrase *yao diao* occurring repeatedly in the first of the *Guofeng* Odes in the Mao edition. Mao's gloss on this phrase is translated by Karlgren as 'dark and secluded' but rejected by him because he cannot find any textual parallel for such meanings before later dates when Mao's work was already well known and influential for the interpretation of the Odes as part of everyone's education. Instead, Karlgren argues that each syllable of the phrase simply meant 'beautiful' as a description of the bride in this Ode, the famous Prothalamium known from its first line as *Guan Ju*; treating *yao* and *diao* as if rebus spellings of synonymous words for this, but without apparently considering at all the images in the characters with which they are written. Each of these characters had a 'cave' over it, to guide the reader towards the sense in which it was intended, while the etymological (so-called 'phonetic') element in *yao* meant 'young, tender' and in *diao* something like 'mysterious'; why the words were so written is not evident, but the fact that each had an image of a 'cave' over it must be seen as significant and the meanings more than just 'beautiful' therefore.

Arthur Waley solved the problem ingeniously and well in his translation of this song by alternating 'lovely' with 'shy' as the phrase *yao diao* recurs in different stanzas and, in attempting a version following the original Chinese four-syllable metre, I have borrowed 'shy' from him. The whole line in which it comes is *yao diao shu nü*, where *yao diao* and *shu* are both adjectives qualifying *nü* 'girl'. Karlgren, translating this as 'The beautiful and good girl', as if *shu* just meant 'good', took no notice of the image in its character, for the guidance of the reader, of 'water or a stream' which implies 'purity'. To translate these words just as 'beautiful' and 'good' is not, however, attempting to translate the poet's intention. For the equisyllabic version, which has to be very free because of what David Hawkes has described as the 'different specific gravity' of the Chinese and English languages (using up syllables on such words as 'he' and 'the', not needed in Chinese), I have made *shu nü* into a 'nymph' but not altogether inappropriately, for she is also here associated with the purity of streams and with grottoes. 'Lord' or 'Prince' I've made 'Shepherd': the character consisted of a 'mouth' for calling and a 'staff'; adding 'sheep', it meant a flock of sheep.

Two slightly different versions of this translation were published in the Introduction of two editions of *Li Po and Tu Fu*, commissioned by Betty Radice for Penguin Classics; in the following I have tried to make a somewhat closer translation:

'*Guan, guan!*' Ospreys
On the island,
Shy the Nymph our
Shepherd's chosen!

Water Gentians
Strew around her,
Shy the Nymph he
Waking, sleeping,
Never reaches,
Waking, sleeping,
Longing, longing,
Turning, tossing!

Water Gentians
Harvest for her,
Shy the Nymph we
Greet with zither,
Water Gentians

To array her,
For the shy Nymph
Bell, drum make glee!

'*Guan, guan!*' is for the call of the ospreys, but the Chinese suggests 'Guard, guard!' The birds are traditionally taken as ospreys, which mate for life; but the characters really only imply a pair, a cock bird and a hen bird. The flowers, which I had translated before as 'water-lilies', were in fact 'water gentians' (*Nymphoides peltata*), little yellow water flowers and more suitable than waterlilies (*Nymphaea*), which are generally thought of as white (the colour to the Chinese not of weddings but of mourning). The verbs I have now translated as 'strew' and 'harvest' had those meanings, but the one which I've translated as 'array' has been associated by scholars with 'to cook' a wedding feast because of a passage in the ancient *Record of Rites* where it has been taken as 'cooking' a fish with certain water plants for this; whereas in fact it meant 'covering, garnishing' it with them. Here it was the bride herself who was covered or 'garnished', arrayed with the flowers. The last word in the song, 'glee', resembles the English word by being capable of meaning both 'music' and 'joy' in Chinese.

This, my only attempt at rendering such a song from *The Book of Odes* equisyllabically, inevitably omitting some detail but so that it can be sung to its own tune, was inspired by the music for it, recovered by the work of Dr Laurence Picken from its old Chinese notation as recorded in the twelfth century by Zhu Xi, and by Dr Picken's generosity included in my book. He is of the opinion that this music, although not itself of the time when the song was originally composed, is likely to be very closely related to the music which so delighted Confucius, 'filling his ears' (*Analects* VIII, XV) when he heard it performed by a new Master of Music at court. In the words as written above, I have followed the editor Mao Chang in giving the song only three stanzas, not four as in my book, with the second and third stanzas each having eight lines; and Dr Picken wishes also to alter the double bar-line after the sixteenth bar of the music there (p. 47) to a single one. He thinks that the last eight bars (lines of the poem) constituted the coda (*luàn*) which particularly pleased Confucius (551–479 BC) at that performance.

Confucius also (*Analects* III, XX) praised the words of this song for their 'joyousness without licentiousness and feeling without excess'; but later pious followers made the bridegroom into a faultless, sage-like ancestor of the reigning dynasty in order to improve the poem by adding an important historical dimension. They then thought that such a person could never be represented as tossing and turning on his bed with longing for a mere girl; so interpreted the poem as if it was the bride who worried anxiously about selecting handmaidens (the water gentians) to be her ladies-in-waiting and, according to custom, his concubines. Confucian piety, but not Confucius himself, did much to destroy the oldest Chinese poetry.

TRANSLATING THE *MABINOGION* AND EARLY IRISH TALES

Jeffrey Gantz

My first view of Betty Radice was a reassuring one. It was November of 1973. An American just out of graduate school and with no publications other than a few bad poems in my college literary magazine, I was in London to translate the *Mabinogion* – the famous Welsh repository of myth and fable – for Penguin Classics. Of her appearance, I remember only that she wore her white hair in a braid coiled about her head, but I know that in every respect she met my expectation of what *the* Penguin editor should look like. And act like: we met in the cafeteria of the British Museum, but she was so easy and unaffected, we might have been sitting in the kitchen of her Highgate home.

The idea of translating the *Mabinogion* had been given to me by my twin brother, Timothy, in the fall of 1972, when I had my Harvard degree in hand but no job in sight. Six years earlier, Timothy had proposed that I pursue a doctoral degree in Celtic languages and literatures. Despite my German name, I have ancestors from Scotland, Ireland, and Wales, so perhaps my affinity for the soft soughing of Gaelic and Welsh is hereditary. I was attracted to the paradoxes of the Celtic sensibility, what in the *Mabinogion* I describe as the tension between the 'rich and concrete beauty of the mortal world' and 'the flickering shadowy uncertainty of the otherworld'. I was attracted by the beauty, the colour, the mystery and the myth. So, happily, was Betty Radice.

The choice of a prospective publisher for the *Mabinogion* was the easiest part. I had grown up believing that Penguins were the ultimate in classic literature; I had always wanted to produce one of my own. My aim – to provide an idiomatic but faithful translation, and to furnish the kind of background material these stories require – seemed right for Penguin. And when Betty Radice read my version of the first story, 'Pwyll Lord of Dyved', she was able to see through the corruptions and the lacunae and the longueurs of oral transmission (not to mention my occasionally lame English) to the genius of Celtic art beneath. I had planned on doing just the first four stories – the Four Branches of the Mabinogi, as they are called – but she encouraged me to go on and do all eleven tales in the collection. She also saw to it that I got the necessary space for the index (thirteen pages right there), bibliography, pronunciation guide, map, and individual introductions – 'extras' that were, to me, just as essential as the translation.

I had no lack of enthusiasm. Already I knew how the general introduction would open: with the burning-tree image from 'Peredur Son of Evrawg' ('On the bank of the river he saw a tall tree: from roots to crown one half was aflame and the other green with leaves'), a sort of Welsh precursor to the last lines of 'Little Gidding'. Besides, many of the decisions a translator ordinarily has to make had in effect been made for me. The content of the book was set: the eleven stories that have been handed down to us as the *Mabinogion* are virtually the only ones of their kind, so there was no choosing to be done. The text too was a given. Our one complete manuscript is found in the Red Book of Hergest (*c.* 1400). A slightly earlier version, with some missing sections, appears in the White Book of Rhydderch (*c.* 1325), but the differences between the two manuscripts are immaterial to a literary translation – I never had to decide between 'sullied' and 'solid', for example. Medieval Welsh is closer to modern Welsh than medieval English is to modern English; it is surprising how many medieval words turn up in the modern dictionaries.

Even the philosophy behind my intended approach seemed pretty simple. William Arrowsmith has said that the act of translation presupposes a prior act of criticism. My presupposition was that my material did not need improving, modernizing, Anglicizing, or Americanizing – in short, I was ready to line up with Walter Benjamin: 'A real translation is transparent; it does not cover the original, does not block its light, but allows the pure language, as though reinforced by its own medium, to shine upon the original all the more fully.' I had faith in my originals, and in the artistry that underlay them; I figured that any tale which could offer white hounds with red ears in the second paragraph ('Pwyll') did not need much help from me. My goal was not to repaint the *Mabinogion* but simply to restore it.

None the less, I soon discovered that the task of turning my manuscript into flowing English which retained its Celtic colouring would be far from straightforward. I was right in thinking that Welsh words are sharply defined and single-minded; one does not face the epistemological and philosophical problems that arise in more sophisticated (or at least Platonist) European languages like German and Italian (where, for instance, in rendering *carità*, the translator is stranded between 'love' and 'charity'). But reproducing the Welsh idiom turned out to be a formidable assignment. The stories of the *Mabinogion* took shape over a number of centuries, via oral transmission, before being written down. The material they present may be even older. So it is hard to find the right tone. I worked toward an English that would be weighty but not leaden and formal but not stiff – not modern, but not a burden to read, either. To that end I rejected contractions like 'he's' and 'hasn't', and since the Celtic languages have no equivalent of English yes and no, I excluded those words as well. On the other hand, I decided against archaisms like 'a-hunting', on the ground that medieval Welsh does not sound anything like that archaic to a modern Welshman; in the same way I avoided the use of the pronoun 'thou' and its attendant verb forms.

These were relatively easy decisions; it was much harder to capture the distinctively passive, noun-centred quality of the text. The *Mabinogion* begins thus:

> *Pwyll Pendeuic Dyuet a oed yn arglwyd ar seith cantref Dyuet. A threigylgweith yd oed yn Arberth, prif lys idaw, a dyuot yn y uryt ac yn y uedwl uynet y hela. Sef kyueir o'y gyuoeth a uynnei y hela, Glynn Cuch. Ac ef a gychwynnwys y nos honno o Arberth, ac a doeth hyt ym Penn Llwyn Diarwya; ac yno y bu y nos honno.*

An absolutely literal rendering would read something like this:

> Pwyll Ruler Dyved that was in lord over seven hundred Dyved. And once upon a time that was in Arberth, chief court to him, and coming into his mind and his thought going to hunt. This is direction from his realm that desired to hunt, Glynn Cuch. And he that set out the night that from Arberth, and that went as far as Penn Llwyn Diarwya; and there that was the night that.

You can see that Welsh idiom is quite different from English: articles and personal pronouns are often omitted, relative pronouns are everywhere (and often require interpretation), verbs are turned into nouns – in fact, just about everything is turned into a noun.

A less literal though still faithful version might read thus:

> It is Pwyll Ruler of Dyved who was lord over the seven hundreds of Dyved. And once upon a time when he was in Arberth, his chief court, it came into his mind and his thought to go hunting. It is this part of his realm that he desired to hunt, Glynn Cuch. And it is he who set out that night from Arberth and who went as far as Penn Llwyn Diarwya; and it is there that he was that night.

Even at this short distance from the original, speculations and sacrifices have been necessary. Is Pwyll lord over seven of the hundreds of Dyved or over *the* seven hundreds of Dyved? Is Arberth *a* chief court of his or *the* chief court? As for the characteristically Celtic copula/relative-clause construction ('It is X that Y . . .'), it is beguiling in one paragraph, but would it prove tiresome over three hundred pages? I decided it would. A storyteller with a dramatic and varied delivery might make it listenable, but I could not do so in print.

So a further step was necessary. This is what I finally settled on:

> Pwyll Lord of Dyved ruled over the seven cantrevs of that land. One day, when he was in his chief court at Arberth, his thoughts and desires turned to hunting. Glynn Cuch was the part of his realm he wanted to hunt, so he set out that evening from Arberth and went as far as Penn Llwyn on Bwya, where he spent the night.

Here some real verbs ('ruled', 'spent') have been provided, the third and fourth sentences have been run together, some repetition ('Dyved' in the first sentence) has been avoided, the connecting conjunctions have been omitted, and in general the construction has been made more fluid, more varied – and more English. Looking back at this paragraph now, I wonder whether I did not do too much, whether I might not have hewed a little closer to the Welsh without rendering the result unreadable. If that is the case, I erred on the side of caution. I wanted a translation that people could enjoy, and the one thing I am told about the *Mabinogion* is that it is readable.

The dialogue was another area where I took the liberty of smoothing things out a bit. In the second paragraph of 'Pwyll', our hero encounters the mysterious Havgan, who tells him, '*Hynny ansyberwyt oed, a chyn nyt ymdialwyf a thi, y rof i a Duw, mi a wnaf o anglot itt guerth can carw.*' This I might have rendered as 'That discourtesy was, and though I do not avenge myself on you, between me and God, I will do you dishonour the worth of a hundred stags', but instead I bowed to the easier 'That was your discourtesy, and though I will take no vengeance, between me and God, I will dishonour you to the value of a hundred stags', avoiding any possibility of ambiguity in the first clause. Later, when I came to translate my second volume for Penguin, *Early Irish Myths and Sagas*, I took a more conservative line with the dialogue where I thought it would not put too great a strain on the English – or the reader. Thus, in 'The Wasting Sickness of Cú Chulaind', when Cú Chulaind tells his wife, Eithne Ingubai, '*Is olc do menma*', I rendered it as 'Angry you are' rather than the more natural (for English) 'You are angry'; and later, when Lí Ban answers the question of where Labraid Lúathlám ar Cladeb has gone with '*Ni handsa*', I settled on 'Not difficult that' instead of 'That's not hard to say.' As odd as these expressions may sound to English or American ears, they're quite natural to the Irish, and in an effort to produce a richer translation I gambled that Penguin readers would get the hang of them without too much trouble.

Where the text was puzzling or doubtful, I had to choose between rendering it literally and trying to make sense out of it. Guessing is not translating, but when that was the only way to produce coherent English, I did it. At one point in 'The Wooing of Étaín', the text reads, 'If the host had not been spied upon, there would have been no better road in the entire world. Flaws were left in it afterward.' Nowhere does the Gaelic say that the holes were left because the workers were spied on, but that seems the only sensible conclusion. So I rendered it as 'If the host had not been spied upon, there would have been no better road in the entire world; but, for that reason, the causeway was not made perfect.'

Sometimes, however, I had no choice. A little farther on in 'The Wooing of Étaín' the following appears:

Cuirthe i lland tochre i lland airderg damrudh trom an coibden cluinitar fir ferdi buidne balcthruim crandchuir forderg saire fedhar sechuib slimprib snithib sciathu lama indrochad cloena fó bith oenma duib in digail duib an tromdam tairthim flatho fer ban fomnis in fer mbraine cerpai fomnis diadh dergae fer arfeidh solaid fri ais eslind fer bron fort ier techta in delmnad o luachair for di Teithbi dichlochad Midi indracht coich les coich aimles.

This is a type of dense, alliterative Irish poetry called a rosc. Such passages tend to be older than the rest of the text, and also more corrupt. Confidence in this particular section is not improved by the appearance, a few paragraphs earlier in the story, of a sentence that begins similarly: '*Coire a laim, tochre i laim, urdhairc damrudh.*' The general sense of the rosc is that of the earlier sentence: it is the song of those who are building the road, there is reference to the excellent oxen, to the clearing of trees, to the goal of winning Étaín for Mider. But to provide a line-by-line translation would have entailed wholesale speculation. Since the gist of the rosc was to be found elsewhere in the prose, I retired gracefully and omitted it from my translation.

Arriving at an acceptable English idiom for Welsh and Gaelic proved to be one of the two major hurdles I had to surmount in translating the *Mabinogion* and *Early Irish Myths and Sagas.* The second obstacle was even more of a surprise to me: establishing the spelling of proper names. There are some four hundred of these just in 'Culhwch and Olwen', so it is no small matter. Both medieval Welsh and medieval Gaelic are reasonably phonetic – meaning that if you know how a name is spelled, you can figure out how to pronounce it; but the spelling rules can be a little complicated. In the first paragraph of 'Pwyll', you may have noticed that 'Dyuet' in the original becomes 'Dyved' in my translation. In fact, the letter 'u' in Welsh manuscripts stands for both the vowel 'u' and the consonant 'v'. And the letter 't', when not initial, usually designates the sound of 'd'; in the same way, 'c' is often used for 'g'. Previous translators had modernized these spellings, so that 'Dyuet' became 'Dyfed' (in modern Welsh the letter 'f' stands for the sound of 'v') and 'Kicua' (Pwyll's daughter-in-law) 'Cigfa'. I decided to naturalize the spelling rather than modernize it, to create in effect a phonetic version of the medieval spelling. So 'Dyuet' became 'Dyved' and 'Kicua' 'Kigva', and they are pronounced about the way you would expect.

That was a simple, satisfactory solution, and when it came time to establish spellings for *Early Irish Myths and Sagas*, I expected to do the same. I was quickly disillusioned. Many of the Irish names are well established in English, so it is not easy to change them. Worse, many Gaelic sounds have no easily indicated English equivalent. Take the name 'Mider' in 'The Wooing of Étaín': the 'd' has been softened to the sound of 'th' in 'father'. How to write this? 'Mither' would be misleading, since in medieval Gaelic 'th' stands for the sound in 'thin'. Modernization? In modern Gaelic 'Mider' is spelled 'Midhir' – but 'dh' in modern Gaelic is no longer pronounced as a soft 'th', so some kind of note would still be necessary. Reluctantly I adopted the original spellings, made them as consistent as I could, and explained them as carefully as possible in the pronunciation guide. The decision to enforce absolute consistency led to some unfamiliar results

– Derdriu instead of Deirdre, for example, and Cú Chulaind (by analogy with Fand) rather than Cú Chulainn or Cuchullin; but I was loath to except some names and not others.

Establishing the original spelling was not always easy either. In 'Branwen Daughter of Llŷr', the name of the Irish king is spelt 'Matholwch' in the White Book of Rhydderch and the Red Book of Hergest but 'Mallolwch' in the 'Branwen' fragment of Peniarth 6 (*c.* 1235). Which is right? Both versions look like a Welsh attempt to transliterate the name of a real Irish king – in which case the Irish royal name Máel Sechlainn presents itself as the likely original. Since the Welsh 'll' (rather like 'h' + 'l') seems the better approximation of what in Gaelic would be pronounced 'lsh', I opted for 'Mallolwch'.

The name 'Branwen' presented a similar difficulty. Here the variant spelling – 'Bronwen' – appears in just one instance in the White Book, and yet the Celtic scholar Proinsias Mac Cana has argued that this form, which means 'White Breast', is the original, and that 'Branwen' ('White Raven') developed only later, by analogy with her brother's name, Brân. I found this argument persuasive – White Breast looks a better name than White Raven; but I was unwilling to change the title character's name, and a well-established one at that, on the strength of a single manuscript reading (at least in Peniarth 6 'Mallolwch' appears six times and 'Matholwch' not at all), so I left 'Branwen' as it was, with regrets. In the case of 'Bendigeidvran', however, I did not hesitate, even though I had no manuscript support at all. The name means 'Brân the Blessed', and the 'Blessed' is clearly a Christian accretion, so after its first appearance I reduced it to its original form, Brân.

Sometimes it is not clear what is a proper name and what is not. In 'Pwyll', we are told that 'Pendaran Dyuet' is the name of the foster-father of Pwyll's son, Pryderi. Now 'pendaran' means 'chief', and so 'Pendaran Dyuet' looks more like an epithet than a name, just as 'Pendeuic Dyuet' is an epithet that means 'lord of Dyved'. But then why does he have no name? I translated it as the 'Chieftain of Dyved', with some doubts.

These are, certainly, small points. You might well think that, in the wider context of mythic meaning, they do not amount to much – and you would be right. And yet sometimes they *do* affect the wider context. In 'Branwen', during the fighting between the Irish and the British, one 'Morddwyd Tyllyon' rises up and says, 'Beware of Morddwyd Tyllyon!' This could be the name of one of the British heroes, but he does not appear anywhere else in Welsh literature, and it seems more than a coincidence that the name means 'Pierced Thighs'. Like Akhilleus, Brân is wounded in the heel while on a quest to bring a woman back from a foreign land. And in some of the Grail stories, Bran or Bron is the name of the Fisher King who is wounded in the thighs. Is that the meaning of Brân's wound? Is 'Morddwyd Tyllyon' Brân himself? If indeed he is, then 'Branwen', with its magic cauldron, becomes a link between Greek tales of a heroic raid upon the treasures of the otherworld (Demeter and Persephone; Peirithoös and Persephone; Orpheus and Eurydike; Menelaos and Helen) and the quest for the Holy Grail.

Sometimes these ideas arise outside the translation proper. One of the more confusing episodes in 'Pwyll' is the episode in which Pwyll's son gets his name. The storyteller would have us believe that the boy is named after the relief his mother feels when he is returned to her; but in that case his name should be 'Escor' ('relief') and not 'Pryderi' ('anxiety'). There is nothing the translation can do to resolve this enigma; the notes, however, can suggest (as mine did) that since the storyteller considers 'Pryderi' important enough to warrant this nonsensical explanation, we might wonder whether the Welsh scholar W. J. Gruffydd was not right when, years ago, he proposed the idea that Pryderi was originally the central character and hero of the Four Branches of the Mabinogi. Like Peredur, Pryderi is a young, naïve hero who takes part in a quest for an otherworld cauldron. Could Pryderi be a form of Peredur, the Welsh equivalent of Perceval and Parzival? It is a question the act of translation raises.

Throughout this act of translation, and the raising of such questions, the text got bigger, richer, more complex. That in itself justified the task I had undertaken. But there was more: I could now share these stories with a large audience of readers – though the tales were different, they had not stopped being themselves. The following, from 'The Exile of the Sons of Uisliu', may not be in Gaelic, but it is Irish none the less:

> One day, in winter, Derdriu's foster-father was outside in the snow, flaying a weaned calf for her. Derdriu saw a raven drinking the blood on the snow, and she said to Lebarcham, 'I could love a man with those three colours: hair like a raven, cheeks like blood and body like snow.' 'Then luck and good fortune are with you,' answered Lebarcham, 'for such a man is not far off. In fact, he is quite near: Noísiu son of Uisliu.' Derdriu replied, 'I will be ill, then, until I see him.'

Certainly it is a thrill to see the text of a great work translated into your words. There is an even greater thrill, however, in seeing it translated into its own.

ON TRANSLATING GOD'S NAME

David Goldstein

The English word 'cabal' indicates intrigue, secretiveness, and is especially applied to a political group that uses devious means to achieve rebellion or revolution. It derives from the Hebrew *kabbalah* which at root signifies 'tradition', in the strict Latin sense of 'that which is received, or passed on'. (In modern Hebrew it means among other things a commercial 'receipt'.) Originally, *kabbalah* indicated any religious tradition. But the word came to be used especially of mystical tradition, a secret set of beliefs and practices handed down within groups of initiates or devotees.

Kabbalah in this sense has a long Hebrew literary pedigree going back to the Bible itself. Jewish mystics traced the origins of their communion with the divine back to Ezekiel's vision of the heavenly chariot, Isaiah's experience of God in the Temple, even indeed back to Moses at the Burning Bush, and his encounter with the Lord at Sinai, a meeting which was accompanied by fire, thunder and smoke, and the sound of trumpets.

Biblical accounts of ecstatic visions have parallels in later Talmudic literature, where we read, for example, of four scholars who gained access to *Pardes*: Ben Azzai died, Ben Zoma went mad, Elisha ben Abuyah became a heretic. Only Rabbi Akiva emerged in peace.

Contemporary with the Talmud are mystical paeans of praise glorifying the Creator, and describing the ascent of the soul towards the celestial Throne of Glory.

None of these texts, however, not even the Bible, occupies as important a place in Jewish kabbalistic tradition as the *Zohar*. To attempt a translation of the *Zohar* into English is to involve oneself in intellectual convolutions which at one moment lead to the brink of absurdity and at the next to the most glorious insight into religious truth.

According to the Jewish mystics themselves, the *Zohar* contains divine revelations granted to the second-century rabbi Simeon ben Yohai and his son Eleazar, while for thirteen years they hid from the Romans in a cave. These revelations were accurately preserved and transmitted within small groups of enlightened mystics, both by word of mouth and in writing, until they were disseminated more widely by a rabbi named Moses de Leon who lived in the second half of the thirteenth century in Spain, principally in Ávila. These revelations when circulated were given the name *Zohar* (brightness, splendour).

Modern critical scholarship questions the authenticity of this view of the *Zohar*'s origin, and holds instead that the *Zohar* was indeed written about the year 1280 by Moses de Leon, and based to some extent on earlier source material, but that in the main it was the unaided work of Moses de Leon himself.

It is written in the most typical form of all rabbinic works – a commentary. For the Jew nothing can be more important and more challenging than to interpret the Bible, especially the Pentateuch, which is considered to be the *ipsissima verba* of God, revealed to Moses at Mount Sinai. Since Scripture is the single and unique written communication that God saw fit to share with mankind it must necessarily embody not only its superficial meaning but also countless layers of hidden connotations which the human mind armed with ingenuity and inspiration can unravel. Through their commentaries the rabbis of every generation have been able to express their own individual views of God and man, and the major commentaries have themselves attracted super-commentaries. Only a few Jewish religious thinkers wrote independent philosophical or ethical monographs. Most of them were content to append their ideas to the thoughts of others, and eventually to the written divine word.

The *Zohar* is such a work, concentrating its mystical interpretation on the Pentateuch, the Book of Esther and the Song of Songs. This is the first hurdle to confront a prospective translator. Moses de Leon could assume with complete justification that his readers would be as familiar with the text of the Bible as we are with the National Anthem. The patriarchs and their wives, Moses and Joshua, Saul, David and Solomon, and all the events connected with them were part almost of the Jews' own biographies.

But this is not all. Jews who recited many of the Psalms daily in their prayers, who heard the words of Scripture proclaimed regularly in their synagogues, and who studied rabbinical interpretations in their schools, saw every Biblical verse through Jewish eyes. Every phrase went hand in hand with exegesis. A reference to a phrase conjured up at least one interpretation. Let me give two examples.

1. Cain, on hearing of God's curse, exclaims, 'My punishment is too great to bear' (Genesis 4:13). The Hebrew word here for 'punishment' usually means 'sin'. With a different intonation and without any change in the text the verse can be read 'Is my sin too great to bear?' Cain asks whether God's compassion is so limited that He cannot bear (that is, forgive) Cain's sin.
2. Noah is described as being 'righteous in his generation' (Genesis 6:9). An old rabbinic comment states that had Noah lived in any other generation he would not have been described as righteous. In other words, Noah was righteous only when compared with his depraved contemporaries.

It has taken several lines to explain these two interpretations, but a reader of the *Zohar* would know them instinctively, because the Bible was not taught independently of the interpretation. When therefore the *Zohar* proposes its own explanation of these verses, that explanation becomes an additional layer, gaining significance from the interpretation that preceded it.

Moses de Leon's work refers consciously and unconsciously to a myriad of such insights: to deep moral deductions from the Scriptural text, or to verbal conjuring tricks, to the substitution of numbers for letters (since the Hebrew alphabet also acts as a numerical sequence), to legends connected with Biblical heroes and heroines, to the celestial world itself and the nature of God, whose traits are delineated in the Hebrew Bible if only one knew how to read it 'correctly'.

We are therefore dealing with a language which although in this case emanating from Spain is as esoteric as the Tibetan *Kanjur*. And this is true of all Hebrew texts that depend on Biblical quotation and imagery, including secular poetry whose authors made use of this medium in order to achieve spectacular metaphorical and allusive effects.

The *Zohar*, however, requires us to go one stage further, into a world even more remote from our everyday experience. It uses the Bible, together with all its rabbinic trappings, to explore a mystical universe, whose terminology is not only strange but also at times paradoxical.

Moses de Leon deals in essence with the eternal theological problem of how an infinite God can create a finite world. He solves the difficulty by suggesting that the creation of material things was the final phase in a long chain of emanatory processes which began in the unknowable depths of the Godhead. The links in this chain are designated as *sefirot*, often depicted in kabbalistic diagrams as spheres, the last of which is the *Shekhinah* (the divine presence). The *Shekhinah* is the aspect of God which is closest to man, and for all but the most adept and knowledgeable of mystics the only area of the divine that can be apprehended.

This chain of processes that links the unknowable God to the *Shekhinah*, and thence to the terrestrial world, has a continuous dynamism. It is not a long-drawn-out series of events that happened over a period of time in the past and then ceased, but an ongoing activity. Divine beneficent influence flows down from one *sefirah* to another, and the flow can be encouraged or stopped by the quality of man's deeds. There is a continual cross-influence between the celestial and the physical worlds. When a Jew sins he has an adverse effect upon the world above, interrupting the divine flow, and this in turns bodes ill for the lower world. Conversely when a Jew fulfils a *mitzvah* (commandment) well, especially if he does so with the correct intention and concentration, he has a good effect on the celestial world, increasing the flow of influence there, and hence benefiting the physical world too.

In order to convey this constant interplay of forces the *Zohar* uses a number of simple images. Indeed, one of the paradoxes of the book is that a complex array of supernal forces is expressed by a severely limited vocabulary, heightened only by a number of obscure neologisms which were probably deliberately added in order to convey an impression of antiquity.

The images used are those common in most mystical literary systems. The continuous flow of influence is a stream of water, channelled from one *sefirah* to another. The water has its origin in an ever-flowing source, or in a well which never runs dry. Or the imagery used is that of light. Each *sefirah* illumines the one below it in the chain. Rays of light emanate from the source of all light. Each aspect of the Godhead is distinguished by a specific colour. The lowest *sefirah*, the *Shekhinah*, has no light of its own, but is nothing more than a mirror that reflects the light shed upon it from above. In this respect, the *Shekhinah* is also seen as the moon, entirely and utterly dark except when it conveys the light that it receives from the sun, who is the central *sefirah*, *Tiferet*, also called 'the Holy One, blessed be He', around whom all the others revolve.

One can see how by using images such as these the *Zohar* can pour new meanings into old Biblical vessels. 'I am black but comely'

(Song of Songs, 1:5) is the appeal made by the *Shekhinah*, who is female, to the male *Tiferet*, expressing her forlorn state when she is deprived of light. 'The sun shall not harm you by day, nor the moon by night' (Psalm 121:6) becomes a direct assurance that the individual *sefirot* symbolized in the verse will be beneficent toward Israel.

Another range of images concerns food and drink, nourishment and sustenance, and these are frequently associated with the view of the *sefirot* as members of a family. So we read of how a mother nurses her children, and this must be understood as a higher *sefirah* transmitting influence to the lower *sefirot*.

The complete structure of the ten *sefirot* in the celestial world is portrayed as a tree, an upside-down tree, with its roots in the higher realms, and its topmost branches closest to the world below. Or the structure is described in terms of the human form, *Adam Kadmon* (primordial man), each *sefirah* representing part of the body. *Tiferet*, which is the trunk of the tree in the previous image, is now the torso which transmits influence to the *Shekhinah* by means of an intermediary *sefirah*, called *Yesod*, the penis of *Adam Kadmon*.

Through these terms, which are basically simple and elemental, the *Zohar* tries to express concepts which are actually beyond mortal comprehension, because we are face to face with the inner workings of the divine. This apparent paradox comes to the fore in the way in which the *Zohar* moves rapidly from one image to another, as if to say that no language can express the ineffable, and that all terms are on the same level when confronted by the Supernal One.

The translator faithful to his text must therefore write that the branches of the tree shed light, that water flows from the boughs, that the mother illumines her children, that the sun has intercourse with the moon, and that the stars are nourished. He must ask his reader to suspend disbelief and to surrender all expectation of normal logic; so that when he comes across a phrase such as 'the highest depth' he does not throw up his arms in despair and close the book, but realizes that *Keter* (lit. 'crown') is the highest apprehensible point in the Godhead, and that it is also the depth from which all influence flows throughout the sefirotic world, and that therefore to call it 'the highest depth' is natural, logical and simple.

Nevertheless, because as we have seen the *Zohar* takes the form of a commentary to the Scriptures, the reader (and the translator before him) has to work hard. For Moses de Leon every Hebrew word in the Bible offers a potentiality for mystical insight, or to put it in terms used by the kabbalists themselves 'the whole *Torah* [i.e. the Bible, or more strictly the Pentateuch] is the name of the Holy One, blessed be He'. Even the word *zot* ('this', feminine) can refer to the *Shekhinah*, in whatever context it happens to occur. The opportunities therefore for mystical exegesis are unlimited.

Take, for example, the use of the word *olah*, which means a sacrificial burnt-offering. It occurs many times in the Bible, particularly in Leviticus, where sacrificial legislation is concentrated. *Olah* is derived from a verbal root meaning 'to ascend', since the sacrifice is meant to ascend to God. But since it is in the feminine gender it can also be translated as 'she that ascends'. The *Zohar* uses the word both in its original Scriptural sense and as descriptive of the *Shekhinah*. The *Shekhinah* in the sefirotic realms ascends towards her 'husband', *Tiferet*, when she is stimulated by acts of worship, such as sacrifice, in the terrestrial world.

This perpetual play on words abounds in the *Zohar*, and the translator has no choice but to annotate his translation in order to clarify the meaning. How far is such annotation a confession of failure? To some extent it is; but perhaps not so much a failure on the translator's part as an inevitable limitation in the language of translation. Even English, with its enormously rich and varied vocabulary, cannot be expected to match the verbal gymnastics of an alien tongue. The translator can draw some comfort from the fact that even in English, Elizabethan puns need explanation in the twentieth century.

Frustration at the inability to convey these nuances in a direct manner is balanced however by confidence that the text of the original is at times both simple and weighty enough to cross the barrier of language. Here is a description of the *Shekhinah* nourishing her children, before the redemption:

> What is 'the hind of the dawn' (Psalm 22 : 1)? It is a particular animal, a merciful one, than whom there is none more merciful among the animals of the world; for when time presses, and she needs food both for herself and for all the animals, she goes far away on a distant journey, and comes back bringing food. And she has no desire to eat until she has returned to her place. Why? So that the other animals may assemble near her and she can distribute the food. When she returns all the other animals assemble near her, and she stands in the middle, and distributes food to each one of them. A sign for this is 'She rises while it is yet night, and gives food to her household' (Proverbs 1:15). And she is satisfied by the food that she distributes, as if she had eaten more than

anyone else. And, when the morning comes, called 'the dawn', it brings to her the pains of exile, and she is therefore called 'the hind of the dawn', because of the blackness of the morning, when she experiences pain like a woman in childbirth. This is the meaning of the verse 'As a woman with child, that draws near to the time of her delivery, is in pain, and cries out in her pains, so have we been at your presence, O Lord' (Isaiah 26:17).

The darkness before the dawn, the final pains of exile before redemption, are here cryptically conveyed, but not so enigmatically as to prevent our perceiving the slow, repetitive build-up to an eschatological conclusion.

The kabbalist, however, is not solely concerned with future hope, or with a theoretical view of the divine powers and their relationship with affairs on earth. He believes with absolute conviction that in the religious life he can have an effect, for good or ill, on the Godhead, and that this effect will reverberate in practical terms on himself, on the Jews, and on the universe as a whole.

His principal enemy in this endeavour is *sitra ahra* ('the other side'), the power of evil. Although in theory 'the other side' is subservient to God, and cannot act without God's permission, it is portrayed so vividly in the *Zohar* that it assumes an independent life of its own, and this indeed has led to the accusation that the *Zohar* preaches a kind of dualism, which is absolute anathema to traditional Jewish monotheism.

The charge of dualism is fuelled by the fact that the *Zohar* sees 'the other side' as parallel in many respects to the sefirotic world of the Godhead. It is structured in a similar way. The *Shekhinah* and *Tiferet*, the female and male elements in the celestial sphere, are matched by Lilith and Samael, the demons of the lower regions, who, like their heavenly counterparts, have myriad forces at their command.

As one would expect from similar portrayals in the work of Milton and Blake, 'the other side' is depicted in a far more striking manner than the forces of good. Samael's world is described as the domain of the husks, of chaff, of refuse, of dregs, of all that is discarded after processes of purification. He and his minions live in 'the crevice of the great deep'. They emerge at night to launch their assaults on humankind. Lilith is particularly vicious. Having been provoked by Samael's infatuation with Eve in the Garden of Eden she wreaks her vengeance by taking away the lives of babies and little children. (Hence the widespread use by Jewish women, particularly in North Africa and the Middle East, of talismans and amulets to protect them against Lilith when they are about to give birth.) She appears to men in their dreams and excites them sexually. She becomes pregnant by their nocturnal emissions and produces evil spirits.

> She dresses herself in finery like an abominable harlot and stands at the corners of streets and highways . . . her hair is long, red like a lily; her face is white and pink; six pendants hang at her ears; her bed is made of Egyptian flax; all the ornaments of the East encircle her neck; her mouth is shaped like a tiny door, beautified with cosmetic; her tongue is sharp like a sword; her words smooth as oil; her lips beautiful, red as a lily, sweetened with all the sweetnesses in the world . . . The fool turns aside after her, and drinks from the cup of wine, and commits harlotry with her, completely enamoured of her . . . The fool wakes up, thinking to sport with her as before. But she takes off her finery, and turns into a fierce warrior, facing him in a garment of flaming fire, a vision of dread, terrifying both body and soul, full of horrific eyes . . .

For the kabbalist, however, this is not the most serious assault from 'the other side'. Samael is more powerful than Lilith, and his designs are not directed against flesh and blood alone. The object of his desire is none other than the *Shekhinah* herself. As we have already seen, she is that aspect of the Godhead which is closest to the physical world, and therefore also the most vulnerable to Samael's attacks. Were he to seize and master her, divine beneficent influence on mankind would immediately cease, and 'the other side' would be immeasurably strengthened by that very same influence, which would be channelled into 'the great deep'. Chaos and anarchy would ensue on earth.

The responsibility of the Jewish people, and hence of every individual Jew, is to safeguard the *Shekhinah*, and this can be done only through the Jews' fidelity to the commandments. The kabbalists fulfil these commandments with the precise intention of influencing these supernatural worlds.

Once again the whole panoply of Biblical images is brought into play by the *Zohar* in order to describe 'the other side' and the efforts that must be made to overcome it. The antagonists of Israel, particularly the Amalekites and Egypt, are frequently used in this context. The Exodus is seen as a victory over Samael, which was vitiated, however, by the fact that the Jews took out with them 'a mixed multitude', who persistently thenceforward had a baneful effect upon them. Abraham's descent into Egypt, when there was famine in Canaan, is seen as an incursion into the enemy territory of 'the other side', from which he emerged victorious.

Such images can be multiplied. The translator has the daunting task of trying to persuade the reader at the outset, and preferably all the way through, that for the *Zohar* the Bible is not the book that we have been accustomed to. Even if the reader has some knowledge of the Biblical text (and he will be a rarity) he will be surprised to find some verses translated in quite a different way – and in many cases not unjustifiably so. The same Hebrew words can be made to say very different things.

In the end the translator must ask the reader, temporarily at least, to take the leap of faith into the kabbalistic world, into a world that is at times opaque, and at others translucent, often confusing but sometimes suddenly revealing, a world which is at the very root of all subsequent Jewish mystical movements.

The kabbalist sees the world made up of many layers. He must try to peel them off one by one like the layers of an onion, until he reaches the supernal truth at its heart. The key to this truth is the name of God, the *Torah*, but the *Torah* also has layers.

The *Torah* has a body. The commandments of the *Torah* are the bodies of the *Torah*. This body is clothed in garments, which are the narratives of this world. The fools in the world look only upon the clothes, which are the narratives of the Torah; they know no more, and do not see what is beneath the clothes. Those who know more do not look upon the clothes but upon the body beneath the clothes. The wise, the servants of the supreme King, those who stood at Mount Sinai, look only upon the soul, which is the foundation of all, the real *Torah*. And in the time to come they are destined to look upon the soul of the soul of the *Torah*.

TRANSLATING LATIN PROSE

Michael Grant

❦ A translator of French poetry, Wilfrid Thorley, wrote that although translations of prose involve complications 'the matter is obviously ten times more intricate when we come to poetry'; and Paul Selver agreed that this distinction is axiomatic.[1] Without wishing to minimize the excruciating difficulties of translating poetry, I would submit that statements such as theirs have tended to distract attention unduly from the peculiar hazards attendant upon the translation of prose.

The same bias was apparent in the questionnaire on 'The State of Translation' which the now regrettably extinct periodical *Delos* (National Translation Center, Austin, Texas) circulated to translators and published in 1968. It was encouraging that the thirteen questions included one asking 'Is there a difference between translating poetry and prose?' But the replies on the whole showed that little thought had been given to the problem. Twenty of the thirty translators who were interrogated did not answer the question at all. Four said, yes, there is a difference, Mary Renault adding that good prose should always be translatable. Three more pointed out the particular difficulties of poetry. Few said anything worth saying about prose translations. One of these was Robert Lowell, who saw that they could, on occasion, raise quite special problems: 'For some reason, a faithful, lucid prose translation seems to come nearer to being satisfactory than the same thing in verse. Not always; I would imagine *The Waste Land* might be easier to do than Cicero or Rimbaud's *Saison*, or the end of Moby Dick.'[2]

This is in line with the summing up of B. Q. Morgan:[3]

> On the whole, criticism of translations of prose centres on accuracy, which is, in theory, attainable. Yet even here there are pitfalls, particularly when the great writers of Greece and Rome are to be interpreted, or when differences in folkways offer verbal or spiritual difficulties.[4]

Selver quoted an example offered by Félix Boillot which illustrates the point very adequately. You must not, he said, render '*les terrassiers sont en train de déjeuner*' as 'the navvies are having their breakfast', because the appearance, attire, food and drink of 'navvies' (he was using the word in 1930) are completely different.[5]

D. S. Carne-Ross, formerly the editor of *Delos* and *Arion*, brought the translating of prose fairly prominently to the fore, with certain reservations:

In a sense (in *one* sense, not perhaps the most interesting sense) prose translation matters more than verse translation. Although it is in poetry that language is and means more intensely, we read poetry infrequently and then in a special Sunday way that limits its effects on us. This is an age of prose, and it is on prose that our feeling for language is formed – not so much the *Kunstprosa* of the higher fiction, which we must study as though it were poetry, but the everyday stuff on the labels of soup cans and the pages of the dailies and the weeklies and the quarterlies and the paperbacks. And on the translated prose that we read every day.[6]

However, Michael Hamburger's reply to the *Delos* questionnaire made a notable contribution on a more literary level:

The few prose works that I have translated have been as difficult to render – if not more so – than verse, because their style is highly idiomatic. (I am thinking of Baudelaire's prose poems, of Büchner's story *Lenz*, and of Hofmannsthal's play *The Tower*.)[7]

With regard to this more literary type of prose, Terence Kilmartin, translator of Proust for Penguin, has recently made a very valid point, in criticizing 'the defect of a virtue' which he found in his predecessor C. K. Scott-Moncrieff:

Contrary to a widely held view, he stuck very closely to the original . . . and in his efforts to reproduce the structure of those elaborate sentences with their spiralling subordinate clauses, not only does he sometimes lose the thread but wrenches his syntax into oddly un-English shapes: a whiff of Gallicism clings to some of the longer periods, obscuring the sense and falsifying the tone. The literal renderings of these French idioms and turns of phrase makes them sound weirder, more outlandish, than they would to a French reader.[8]

This is relevant to those of us who try to translate Latin prose. And, furthermore, the word-order of Latin prose is markedly different from that of Latin verse. Of course, the same is true of ancient Greek as well. But Latin prose presents a strange difficulty which Greek prose lacks: namely, its *apparent* resemblance to a sort of English prose – the wrong sort for today. As I have said:

It is worth considering, for example, how Cicero's rhetoric slides with catastrophic ease into an outdated English which, being unreadable, cannot be called a suitable rendering.[9]

That is to say, as Robert Lowell no doubt appreciated, that the translator is easily lulled into an entirely misplaced confidence by the superficial resemblance of Cicero's language to a certain unnatural kind of English:

> O come that easy Ciceronian style,
> So Latin, yet so English all the while.

When Alexander Pope wrote those words,[10] and even a good deal later, Cicero's abundant and rhythmical prose was by no means alien to contemporary fashion. Now the situation has changed. The translator is still insidiously tempted to utilize these analogies with an English that used to exist, and thus to produce Ciceronian English. But that is not the sort of English which is, or should be, written today. On the contrary, if contemporary readable English is to be written, these blandishments must be resisted, and sentences must be cast in an entirely different mould: to take a single example, a row of rhetorical questions is nowadays scarcely acceptable. In view of the strong temptation which constantly invites the translator of Cicero to ignore the steady widening of such divergences during the past century and a half, I observed in my translation of his *Selected Works* (Penguin Classics) that it is, in certain respects, harder to attempt a version of his writings than to translate from some language so alien that no such misleading analogies suggest themselves, such as Turkish.

And there are not only dated or outdated English renderings of Cicero, there are also dateless renderings: not in the grand sense of timeless, but in the deplorable sense of translatorese, 'that queer language-of-the-study,' as B. Q. Morgan rightly remarked, 'that counts words but misses their living force'. Ciceronian Latin lends itself with appalling facility to translatorese.

However, it is Pliny the younger, not Cicero, about whom I want to write now. For his *Letters* or *Epistles* were translated for Penguin Classics (1963) by the editor of that series, Betty Radice, whom I, like so many others, most sadly miss, and would like to honour by this all too inadequate tribute. Her work, like herself, was always admirable. Of course Pliny differs from Cicero very substantially in style – having lived in a later and entirely different epoch – but resembles him closely in one respect. That is to say, his

Silver Latin is just as difficult as Cicero's Golden Age prose to turn into English. Betty Radice gave us some idea of the problem that confronted her:

> Pliny can be elegantly formal, colloquial and conversational, analytically critical or tersely descriptive. He draws on legal language for his jokes with professional friends, quotes the poets in Greek as well as in Latin, and sets himself to describe a scene or a scientific problem in precise terms. No translator can hope to convey such versatility successfully, but a fresh approach can perhaps give a better idea of Pliny's gifts of accurate observation and clear description which put him high among the prose writers of any period.[11]

Pliny, remarked Gareth Morgan,

> is more of a poet than we have been prepared to realize – that he is also an antiquarian, a scientist and an administrator alternately optimistic and querulous (I suspect an ulcer) makes him a fiendish problem for a translator.[12]

So the task set herself by Betty Radice was a challenging one. But she handled it excellently.[13] Obviously, something had been lost. We all know the numerous epigrams indicating that some loss or other is inevitable in all translations. Total translations, as George Steiner declared, are impossible, because each writing represents its own complex, historically and collectively determined aggregate of values, proceedings of social conduct, conjectures on life. So translators have to decide what they are going to try to retain, out of all this, and what they are going to be willing to lose.

One thing that Betty Radice did not feel willing to lose was readable English.

Now, the editors of *Arion* dismissed the notion of 'readability' as 'simple-minded'.[14] On the contrary, however, it remains a real issue, though one could and should refine it by asking, readable *to whom*, an investigation which, in regard to translations, has still hardly begun. Anyway, readable today. (Incidentally, one wonders if criteria of readability have not already changed a little since those discussions of the 1960s.)

One interesting question is whether contemporary works on the one hand, and ancient classics on the other, ought not, on principle, to be translated into *different* sorts of language – whether, for example, Latin should not be made to sound 'harder and more bronze-like' and more antique than the resources of our own language normally permit. Certainly, as far as atmosphere goes, we must respect the spirit of the ancient work, and the effect it exercised on people living at the time (though this is very often a fairly wide open question) – but *not* if it means torturing the English until it is English no longer.

For nearly three hundred years translators have been anxiously asking themselves the question: 'If Pliny (etc.) had been living today, how would he have expressed himself?' This sort of inquiry has the authority of Dryden, though for imitation rather than translation:

> I take imitation of an author . . . to be an endeavour of a later poet to write like one which has written before him on the same subject, that is, not to translate his words, or to be confined to his sense, but only to set as a pattern, and to write, as he supposes that author would have done, had he lived in our age, and in our country.[15]

Since then, the same yardstick has been employed, in so far as it can be, for translation as well as for imitation. Possibly this 'if so-and-so were living today' business may sometimes become a little fatuous, since it partakes of the unreality of other historical might-have-beens. Nevertheless, venturing to translate Tacitus for the Penguin Classics, I still persisted in concluding that

> any translator – since he wants people to read what he writes – has to ask himself this question [i.e. how would he have written if he had been living today?], and even attempt, in his own way, to answer it.[16]

Robin Campbell, translating some of the prose works of another difficult post-Ciceronian writer, Seneca the younger, correctly (in my view) decided that some of the rhetorical fireworks of his style should be modified in translation, since the English reader would find them unnatural, contrived and unendurable.[17] In other words, as Benjamin Jowett (d. 1893) pronounced, an English translation has to be in English.

This is very much the attitude that I tried to defend in introducing my version of Tacitus:

> In translating in this series the fantastic Apuleius (1950), Robert Graves remarked: 'paradoxically, the effect of oddness is best achieved in convulsed times like the present by writing in as easy and sedate an English as possible'.[18] 'Sedate' is surely not an ambitious enough epithet for a good rendering of Apuleius or Tacitus – or for Graves's own excellent style; but his reminder that twentieth-century English has to be plain is still relevant. No amount of colourful or fanciful language will make the strange personality of Tacitus understandable to contemporary readers, who find rhetoric and grand style unnatural and

unreadable. Today the only faint hope of rendering his complexity lies in as trenchant and astringent a simplicity as the translator can achieve.[19]

Certainly, by aiming at 'natural' English something is lost. But it still seems to me that any alternative philosophy of Latin prose translation is likely to involve even larger losses. However, perhaps someone will give a practical demonstration to the contrary, and show I am wrong. At least I very much hope they will try.

Betty Radice would proably not have felt that the epithet 'astringent', which I applied to Tacitus, would have been exactly the right word to sum up the peculiar complications of Pliny. However, leaving that aside, I believe she was in a fair measure of agreement with the sort of ideas I had been expressing.

A word may perhaps be said here about her version of Pliny's *Panegyricus*, which she did not include in the Penguin edition but added to an amended reprint of the *Letters* for the Loeb series.[20] This literary oration sets any translator a special problem. It has been variously described as nauseously flattering, ludicrously artificial, obscure, over-long, a stupefying plethora of eulogistic verbiage tediously straining after antithesis, etc. Ought the translator to bring out these faults, or, on the contrary, try to make his or her version sound as appealing as possible? (Especially since the original, in its impact on the audience to which it was addressed, was no doubt a success.) One major difficulty is the fact that the whole conception of a panegyric is totally alien today. It is true that I have heard wildly eulogistic speeches in parts of the Middle East. But can you imagine anyone addressing any western statesman (or stateswoman) in the lush terms of this eulogy of Trajan?

For my part, I believe I have formed this impression of the Father of Us All as much from the manner of his delivery as from the words he has said. Only consider the seriousness of his sentiments, the unaffected candour of his words, the assurance in his voice and decision in his countenance, and the complete sincerity of his gaze, pose and gestures, in fact of his entire person![21]

This is pretty fulsome stuff; and, throughout this weird work, Betty Radice decided, in accordance with the principles enunciated above, not to be as epigrammatic and incantatory as Pliny allowed himself to be, in order to avoid making the work more indigestible still.

Gareth Morgan, contributing to 'Penguin Classics: a Report on Two Decades', had something to say about her version of Pliny's *Letters*, showing that he was not entirely happy about this policy of ironing out or mitigating Latin peculiarities that could not be exactly rendered into what is now considered to be English. The last chapters of the late Mr de Sélincourt's *War with Hannibal*,[22] he pointed out,

> were completed by Mrs Radice with enough skill and sympathy to make it difficult to recognize the break; so there is no doubt of her competence as a translator. The question raised by her *Letters of the Younger Pliny* is of a different order. A sentence from a famous letter may illuminate the difficulty: *Ab altero latere nubes atra et horrenda, ignei spiritus tortis vibratisque discursibus rupta, in longas flammarum figuras dehiscebat.* At first level, the translation can hardly be faulted. ['On the landward side a fearful black cloud was rent by forked and quivering bursts of flame, and parted to reveal great tongues of fire.'] What it does not suggest is that the Latin, though perfectly equipped with the grammar of prose, is more readily intelligible with the visual grammar of poetry. A series of impressions, each haloing its neighbours, has the conventional imposed upon it by an act of syntax. Pliny is more of a poet than we have been prepared to realize. (The light–dark, black–gold patterns of these letters repay analysis.)[23]

I referred earlier to this emphasis by Morgan on Pliny's poetical character, and general many-sidedness. But 'this fiendish problem,' he concludes, 'cannot be solved by the current Penguin "evenness", "equability", "sedateness", or what-you-will'. I cannot be expected to agree entirely with his assessment, since – unsurprisingly in view of its emphasis on readability – my *Tacitus* is one of the books he accused of displaying an excess of the same qualities. Certainly, if we are going to be *too* equable, etc. (let us get away from the word 'sedate'), this method is not perfect. Like every other method, it sacrifices something. But let us just imagine that Betty Radice had produced a more pepped-up, melodramatic version of Pliny's admittedly poetic phrase about Vesuvius. In English, though not in Pliny's sort of Latin, there would have been a danger of this standing out too jaggedly and rebarbatively from the whole, so that the reader would be stopped short rather than stimulated. (Incidentally, such purple passages are not all that common in Pliny, and to call attention to this point and say nothing else about Betty Radice's version of this author did not do her justice.)

It may be interesting, however, just to glance at her rendering of this particular sentence against two earlier translations. The eighteenth-century version by William Melmoth (1746) published in a previous Loeb edition with compressions by W. M. C. Hutchinson (1915) (a disastrous form of collaboration) read as follows:

On the other side, a black and dreadful cloud bursting out in gusts of igneous serpentine vapour now and again yawned to reveal long and fantastic flames, resembling flashes of lightning but much larger.

And this is the translation of J. P. Hieronimus (1952):

On the other side a black and frightful cloud, rent by quivering and twisting paths of fire, gaped open in huge patterns of flames.[24]

Both these versions are about as poetical as Betty Radice's. The point is, however, that Gareth Morgan seems to be asking for something new: for a *more* poetical way of tackling the problem than any of these translators has attempted. Once again, the most constructive way of considering the merits or demerits of this more poetical method, which he recommends, would be for someone to try it. That would not be at all easy. Certainly, although Pliny was writing in prose, you can sacrifice the greater part of this prose element if you really want to. Something, it must be repeated yet again, always has to go, and what Morgan was saying, if I understand him rightly, was that this is one of the best things to throw away. But, as far as I am aware, no one has tried this with Pliny. Perhaps it might be an impossible task; the whole thing could become *too* uneven for our toleration. That is why I have certain reservations about the procedure suggested by D. S. Carne-Ross:

I wonder if we are not putting verse and prose too much in different categories, demanding inspiration from the one and accepting mere competence – 'accuracy' – in the other. The verse translator is allowed to take certain liberties in order to get his text off the ground, but the prose translator is still stuck with this 'word-for-word thing' . . .

We have somehow come to assume that if a translator renders the 'sense', a novel will look after itself. In this field the criterion is still what schoolmasters call accuracy, and if a new Florio turned up, the chances are that his manuscript would be sent to a professor of French and rejected. 'Mr Florio's rendition is idiosyncratic; he seems to be writing a new work based on Montaigne.'[25]

This was all very welcome in that, as indicated above, Carne-Ross was taking prose translation seriously, but I am not sure that it led exactly in the direction in which we ought to go. Do we really, at this stage, want more loosely translating Florios and Amyots and Norths? Certainly we want them very much indeed, in one respect. That is to say we need translators who will make a real substantial impact on the general culture of our time – indeed that is one of our prime requirements, and it is one that has been somewhat lacking in modern times until fairly recently, apart from certain notable exceptions. But in order to achieve this, in our day and age with its heightened standards of translation, I doubt whether it is necessary for prose translators to take all the liberties which Florio, Amyot, etc., took. On the other hand, they must take *some* liberties. Absolutely literal translation will not do. John Dryden felt the same; when he was formulating his canonical distinctions between metaphrase (word-for-word) and paraphrase (translation with latitude) and imitation, he declared:

> 'Tis almost impossible to translate verbally, and well, at the same time . . . The verbal copier is encumbered with so many difficulties at once that he can never disentangle himself from all.

Unless we are prepared to take a terribly humble view of the function of translation, we must accept this standpoint and reject Vladimir Nabokov's assertion that 'the clumsiest literal translation is a thousand times more useful than the prettiest paraphrase' – and reject, also, the doctrine of Edwin and Willa Muir that even to change word order, however unavoidable this may seem, is to 'commit an irremediable injury'.

So much for the one untenable extreme. At the other end of the spectrum comes imitation, which is outside the scope of this discussion (Florio, etc., sometimes went near it). We are left with paraphrase. As Novalis said, successful translations simply cannot help being *verändernde*, metamorphic. Sir John Denham (1615–69) praised Sir Richard Fanshawe, translator of Camoens and Virgil and Horace, for accepting this:

> That servile path thou nobly dost decline,
> Of tracing word for word, and line for line.

The question that remains, then, is *how far* from the servile path one ought to be allowed to stray – how close or how loose the paraphrase can legitimately be.

About Scott-Moncrieff's version of Proust, Carne-Ross wrote:

> People complain of him that he hasn't got this word right or the exact sense of that phrase. Only the worst kind of pedant approaches verse translation in this way now.[26]

True; and so the same should also apply to prose.

But the crux of the matter is that the translator, especially if he is going to try to improve on his original, must first know exactly *what it means.* You can only take liberties if you are quite sure what liberties you are taking. I agree that a paraphrase might legitimately, on occasion, be looser than anything that prose translators have lately been allowed. But on one condition: that they *know* what the meaning is, and that they are building on a correct interpretation of what the original words signify, and not on a meaning that they have understood imperfectly or wrongly.

Among the contributors who gave *Arion* (1962–76) and *Delos* (1968–71) their vitality, Thomas Gould was somewhat exceptional in stressing this very point. Emphasizing that reliable translations of Plato and Aristotle are an absolute cultural necessity, he also had every intention of trying to discover exactly what they really said and meant.[27] In being able to do so he was a fortunate man; fewer and fewer people are in a position to conduct rigorous inquiries of this kind. To make such a complaint, I know, conveys a mellow whiff of hankering after bygone times, while sitting round the port. It was rather depressing, all the same, to be reminded by *Delos* of the procedure which translators of Chinese, for example, are forced to adopt. What they do, apparently, is work in couples, of whom one partner is good at understanding Chinese and the other good at writing English. Robert Lowell was hopeful about collaboration of that kind; he did not believe that one could tell the difference between versions refurbished from cribs ('trots') and translations done from originals. W. H. Auden, too, was receptive to this type of collaboration.

Others are less so. Thus Dudley Fitts, although hoping for the occasional happy accident, concluded:

> A puritan streak in my make-up persuades me, against my more generous impulses, that a man ought to know something of the language he's translating from.

Pierre Emanuel, too, was convinced that this was essential:

> I do not think that a translator who does not know the original can really translate. He mimics in his own rhythm, and sometimes with his own twists of language, something which remains alien to him.[28]

Still, this sort of collaboration could be tried out more than it has, for Latin and Greek. Indeed it will probably need to be, since the odds against the *same person* knowing the dead languages really well and writing good English are going to become small. Meanwhile, a translator of the calibre and linguistic knowledge of Betty Radice has played a staunch part in postponing the emergency. Her version of Pliny, for example, will hold the field for a long time, like her other translations. And for this and many, many other reasons we shall cherish her memory.

METRE, FIDELITY, SEX: THE PROBLEMS CONFRONTING A TRANSLATOR OF OVID'S LOVE POETRY

Peter Green

❦ It is still hard for me to accept the fact of Betty Radice's death, to realize that in my work, now, on Ovid I can no longer draw on her immense experience of translation and translators; that never again will I be encouraged, argued with, gently bullied, briskly cajóled, or tactfully steered away from the shoals of procrastination, *Angst*, and unseasonable polemic by her diplomatic ministrations; that henceforth there will be no still small voice of civilized common sense (too long taken for granted) to which I can appeal in moments of need. Like Ovid himself in his exile, I have lost a vital contact with reality as well as a much-loved friend, and the *Tristia* and the *Ex Ponto*, as I work on them, are that degree more glacial for her absence. What follows here itself owes an incalculable debt to discussions and correspondence between us over many years, while I was struggling to isolate the Ovidian voice in the *Amores* and the *Ars Amatoria*. Without that on-going dialogue, an essential dimension would have been lacking in my translation; and I am very happy to offer this essay in her memory, remembering how many of the ideas in it she either suggested or patiently midwifed into viable form.

I

Any would-be translator of Ovid begins with an awkward historical legacy. From Marlowe's day onward there has been a persistent vogue for translating Ovid into the rhymed iambic couplets so popular with Dryden, Pope, and other eighteenth-century poets. The habit is far from dead even today: Ovid still seems to be regarded, even if only at subconscious level, as a kind of honorary English Augustan. In 1954 A. E. Watt performed this metamorphosis on the whole of the *Metamorphoses*, a transformation so monstrous that the

Picasso line-drawings illustrating his text seemed tame by comparison. L. P. Wilkinson chose the same medium for the numerous illustrative extracts he cites in *Ovid Recalled*. So good a scholar as D. A. Little praised these versions fulsomely;[1] yet, immensely ingenious though they are, they do not sound anything like Ovid.

Quite apart from the matter of rhyme and assonance – a device that Ovid uses cleverly and sparingly, not with the predictable regularity of a metronome – there remain the awkward facts that a hexameter is not only dactylic as opposed to iambic, but is one foot longer than the pentameter; on top of that, it has what in English verse would be called a feminine, i.e. disyllabic, ending, whereas the pentameter is cut off abruptly with what used to be known as a half-foot: it is catalectic. Now Ovid was acutely conscious of this distinction. Uneasy about not writing epic, which would have meant using nothing but the hexameter, he made continual little jokes about Elegy's one lame foot when referring to the pentameter.[2] 'Let my verse rise with six stresses,' he says, 'drop to five on the downbeat'[3]; the traditional translator, presumably unable to count, with cheerful impartiality gives him five on both, and a chiming rhyme into the bargain. Even in the *Metamorphoses* the use of rhymed couplets to express hexameters sets up associations wholly alien to the original movement of the verse, not least in the matter of overrun: Matthew Arnold's characterization of the hexameter[4] as possessing, above all, rapidity and directness should be borne in mind here.

What is of prime interest, it seems to me, is to understand why such an odd convention should have persisted for so long. The answer takes us into a brief consideration of what might be termed the 'Homeric Problem' of verse translation.[5] To put it, I hope, succinctly: there are two fundamental and contrasting theories governing the translation of classical poetry, one arguing that the translator should, in the words of F. W. Newman, attempt 'to retain every peculiarity of the original so far as he is able, with the greater care, the more foreign it may happen to be',[6] while the other follows Dryden's precept, which excused anglicization of the original on the grounds that, as between Dryden and his original, 'my own is of a piece with his, and that *if he were living, and an Englishman*, they are such as he would probably have written'[7] [my emphasis]. In other words, Dryden's principle is a licence to render elegiacs, hexameters, sapphics, alcaics or, if it comes to that, choriambic dimeters in whatever local prosody is popular at the time of writing. Leaf through that perverse anthology of pastiche and potpourri, *The Oxford Book of Greek Verse in Translation*, and you will find epigrams in the Housman manner, Greek choruses a long way after Swinburne, and such oddities as Ibycus done up in the idiosyncratic manner of Marvell's ode on the *Return of Cromwell from Ireland:*

> Them might the subtle muses tell,
> The Heliconian sisters, well:
> No mortal man may trace
> Each vessel in its place,
>
> How Menelaus set his sail
> From Grecian Aulis to prevail
> In Dardan pasture-land
> With his bronze-shielded band . . .[8]

Translators, indeed, almost invariably reflect far more of their own age than that of their original; Dryden was simply elevating this unfortunate (and seemingly perennial) human frailty into a positive merit.

The result was that Pope (for instance) could take the end of Book VIII of the *Iliad* (lines 562–5) and produce this:

> A thousand piles the dusky horrors gild,
> And shoot a shady lustre o'er the field.
> Full fifty guards each flaming pile attend
> Whose umbered arms, by fits, thick flashes send;
> Loud neigh the coursers o'er their heaps of corn,
> And ardent warriors wait the rising morn.

We are given six lines for four, a clutch of gratuitous rhyme, and much additional decoration not in the original, including those 'dusky horrors', 'umbered arms', and 'ardent warriors', the last-named having usurped the horses. As Bentley said, with good reason, 'A very pretty poem, Mr Pope, but you must not call it Homer.' Those who so regularly applied the principle to Ovid presumably did so for two main reasons: first, because they knew Ovid was witty and neat, and felt that neatness and wittiness could *only* be produced in English by means of the stopped rhymed couplet; and second, because they were convinced that it was absolutely impossible to reproduce any Latin or Greek metrical pattern adequately in English. The opposing group, on the other hand, would argue with equal passion that the difficulty of the task was no reason for not attempting it, and that what Dryden's followers regarded as the 'equivalent' or 'corresponding' form in English merely set up false associations and took the unwary reader *away* from the original rather than bringing him nearer to it.

2

The problem of the English hexameter[9] is one that goes back as far as the Elizabethan Age. In 1586 William Webbe, who was associated in his ideas with the better-known Gabriel Harvey, wrote a *Discourse of English Poetrie*, advocating the use of Greek and Latin metres in English. Webbe's own version of Virgil's First Eclogue begins:

> Tityrus happilie thou lyste tumbling under a beech tree
> All on a fine oate pipe these sweet songs lustillie chaunting:
> We, poor soules, go to wracke, and from these coastes be remoued,
> And from our pastures sweete: thou Tityr, at ease in a shade plott,
> Makst thick grouves to resound with songes of braue Amarillis.

Now the first thing we see about this hexameter is that, inevitably, it is not metrical. As Omond said of Southey's efforts in this field, it 'is simply a triple-time six-cadence line, with falling accent, and without rhyme'.[10] This hints at the reason why almost all English hexameters or elegiacs, however brilliant, and even when sauced up continually with sprung rhythm, inverted stresses, or overrun, have a flat, limp quality that their classical models, however mundane, do not. If I pick an example from Longfellow,[11] that is not only because he did the job better than most, but also because he is here concerned, in verse, with the problem of the elegiac couplet:

> Peradventure of old some bard in Ionian islands,
>   Walking alone by the sea, hearing the wash of the waves,
> Learned the secret from them of the beautiful verse elegiac,
>   Breathing into his song motion and sound of the sea.
> For as the wave of the sea, upheaving in long undulations,
>   Plunges loud on the sands, pauses and turns and retreats,
> So the hexameter, rising and singing, with cadence sonorous,
>   Falls, and in refluent rhythm back the Pentameter flows.

Most critics, I think, would agree that this is pretty awful stuff; but *why* is it awful? The awkward inversions, the unnaturally stressed syllables or words, are symptoms of something deeper. Tennyson, who was a consummate craftsman and a fair classical scholar, knew the answer by instinct, though he never spelled it out. His lampoon on English elegiacs gets right to the critical heart of the matter:

> These lame hexameters, the strong-winged music of Homer!
> No, but a most burlesque barbarous experiment.
> When was a harsher sound ever heard, ye Muses, in England?
> When did a frog coarser croak upon our Helicon?
> Hexameters no worse than daring Germany gave us,
> Barbarous experiment, barbarous hexameters.[12]

The point he makes so succinctly by demonstration is this. Since all vowels in Latin and Greek have fixed quantities, either naturally or by position, the metrical pattern is independent of – indeed, contrapuntal to – accentual stress and ictus. The two schemes play against each other, producing a strong and springy resonance. In English, on the other hand, we have *only* accentual stress/ictus, and no fixed vowel quantities. Thus the trouble with an English stress equivalent to classical metre is that, having no firm metrical base, it lacks all counterpoint and tension. The usual solution is to create a stress-pattern that coincides at all points with the metrical schema: the line will then sound flat. To realize the truth of this one need only glance at a line or two of Cotterill's *Odyssey*:[13]

> Now when at last they arrived at the beautiful stream of the river,
> Here the perennial basins they found where water abundant
> Welled up brightly enough for the cleansing of dirtiest raiment.
> So their mules they unloosened from under the yoke of the wagon,
> Letting them wander at will on the bank of the eddying river . . .
> (*Od.* 6.85–9)

But, as Tennyson knew, the essence of a classical hexameter or elegiac is that its metrical schema should *not* coincide with the natural stresses of the words forming it: he therefore demonstrated the impossibility of reproducing classical metres in English by carefully creating elegiacs in which, wherever possible, natural stress and metrical schema should be at complete odds with each other. In Latin and Greek this would work excellently; in English it merely sounds awkward and grotesque. In addition, English is largely deficient in inflections, and so cannot achieve that dense flexibility which marks the *genre* in Latin. As Walter Shewring recently remarked, 'Early and late attempts in this direction have all in the end come to grief through confusion of quantity with accent, pitch accent with stress accent, and English spelling with English pronunciation.'[14]

The proof, for elegiacs, is contained in such versions of Ovid as Saklatvala's *Art of Love* or Lind's *Tristia*,[15] from which brief extracts should suffice by way of demonstration:

And now my sport's at an end. From my swans to descend it is timely,
  Who have borne on their lovely necks this yoke and harness of mine.
As once the young men, so now let my pupils, the lovely lasses,
  Write in their trophy and spoils: '*Ovid my master was!*'
(*AA* 3.809–12)

I'm criticized though I am blameless; it's a slender field that I'm ploughing;
  The praise of your deeds would require a plough-land far richer than mine.
If some little craft is contented to venture upon a small lagoon,
  It ought not therefore in its rashness trust itself to the broad sea.
(*Tr.* 2.327–30)

I seriously doubt whether someone not already familiar with the elegiac metrical pattern would be able to scan these translations – the second in particular – as they were intended. Note, apart from the flatness, the variable number of extra non-stressed syllables in anacrusis at the beginning of each line, the occasional violation of syllabic count (even on the caesura: 'rash*ness*'), the need to stress, in Tennysonian fashion, improbable words, or, worse, syllables ('lagoon'), the arch inversions ('my master was' – one syllable short there, too): all the result of trying to fight a metrical pattern with the weapons of a stress language.

Worse still, any attempt at variation, unless handled with the skill (and diacritical signs) of a Gerard Manley Hopkins, is liable to baffle a reader used to sensing the natural stress of a line. What kind of pentameter, for instance, is Lind's 'You will find in its entire contents not a single line that is sweet' (*Tr.* 5.1.4) or, more baffling still, 'Take care that my funeral rites are not ignored, without even a sound' (ibid. 14)? The first requires the discounting of 'you will', 'entire contents' pronounced with a heavy stress on the *first* syllable of each word, the swallowing of 'not', a stress on 'a'; the second calls for the dropping of 'take' and the complete omission of 'are not ig-', though I suppose a slurred 'aren't' would just carry one through. Clearly here we are in a metrical wasteland. On the other hand, there has to be some attempt to produce the *effect* of the original, since otherwise we would still be stuck with the pernicious tradition of 'local equivalence' – rhyming couplets or quatrains, blank verse, or even less appropriate English growths (see below). All translation must be, in some sense, a compromise. How, I asked myself when I first set about translating Ovid, could I save even a semblance of the Latin elegiac couplet, in a way that would keep Ovid crisp and witty, yet sounding like himself rather than a flaccid pastiche of Pope?

3

There was one interesting and in ways attractive model before me, that of Guy Lee's *Amores*.[16] This was the work of a sensitive and well-read literary scholar who knew very well Ovid's penchant for making puns and sly effects that can only be brought off successfully in a heavily inflected language where the juxtaposition of words is solely for emphasis and not essential to the meaning. Lee's answer, however, almost invariably, is to omit what he cannot get across. He also, as he himself admits, very often finds Ovid flat and long-winded (his epithets), and therefore boils down his decorative effects to nothing, remarking[17] that this is the converse of what students of classical verse composition are required to do when turning English poems into Latin, thus offering us two fallacies for the price of one. He reminds us that H. A. J. Munro turned Thomas Carew's lines 'He that loves a rosy cheek/Or a coral lip admires' into the following Latin elegiac couplet:

cui facies cordi roseos imitata colores
labrave curalii tincta rubore placent

which has to be his excuse for translating:

accipe per longos tibi qui deseruiat annos,
accipe qui pura norit amare fide
(*Am.* 1.3.5–6)

as 'I'll be your slave for life,/your ever-faithful lover', or indeed the delectable-sounding:

illa magas artes Aeaeaque carmina nouit
inque caput liquidas arte recuruat aquas
(*Am.* 1.8.5–6)

as 'She's the local witch – /Can reverse the flow of water', which apart from anything else completely loses the *pattern* of the two lines on which Ovid hangs so much, along with the verbal beauty. The staccato, variable free verse that Lee defends on the grounds of avoiding monotony (p. 201) makes hay of the whole elegiac concept, even (to take one obvious and gross example) in very often presenting a couplet – and the couplets are spaced out from each other in this version – with its second line both longer and stronger than its first. Lee's *Amores* jettisons a whole mass of fustian, and is sharply alive to jokes and nuances; but in reaction against its predecessors it boils all the formal richness out of the poems. What it offers us is Ovid dehydrated, almost in capsule form.

The solution that most appealed to me was one that had been developed over several decades, primarily by Cecil Day Lewis and Richmond Lattimore, who saw that the way to produce some real stress equivalent to the hexameter was to go for the beat, the ictus, since this was native to English, and let the metre, within limits, take care of itself. They worked out a loose, flexible line (but varied on occasion with one stress less or more) and a variable, predominantly feminine ending, that could take easy overrun, moved swiftly, and to a great degree countered the determination of the English language to climb uphill, where possible in iambic patterns, if given half a chance. Saintsbury had foreseen some of the dangers: 'Good dactylic movements in English,' he observed, 'tip themselves up and become anapaestic . . . the so-called 'Accentual' hexameter . . . is, when it is good verse, not a classical hexameter at all, but a five-anapaest line with anacrusis and hypercatalexis.'[18] That is true, on occasion, of both Lattimore and Day Lewis. But does it matter? This line at least catches the precipitate striding movement of the hexameter, while preserving its basic structure, including the caesura. What is sacrificed is the linguistically unattainable ideal of true metrical equivalence.

The relaxation sometimes tempted Day Lewis especially into slang, at inappropriate moments: '*Quo fugis, Aenea? thalamos ne desere pactos*'[19] emerged in his version as 'Aeneas, where are you off to? Don't welsh on your marriage contract!' But the overall sense of epic speed and flow were captured as never before. Let me quote two parallel passages: Hermes' flight to Ogygia from the *Odyssey*, and Mercury's similar mission to Aeneas in the *Aeneid:*[20]

PETER GREEN

I He stood on Pieria and launched himself from the bright air
across the sea and sped the wave tops, like a shearwater
who along the deadly deep ways of the barren salt sea
goes hunting fish and sprays quick-beating wings in the salt brine.
In such a likeness Hermes rode over much tossing water.

II Here first did Mercury pause, hovering on beautifully-balanced
Wings: then stooped, dived bodily down to the sea below,
Like a bird which along the shore and around the promontories
Goes fishing, flying low, wave-hopping over the water.
Even so did Mercury skim between earth and sky
Towards the Libyan coast, cutting his path through the winds.

My own apprenticeship to this line was served by translating Homer for the BBC Third Programme (as it then was) back in the fifties, and, a decade later, Juvenal for Penguin Classics. In Homer's case it offered speed, variety, formulaic strength, and chances for surging rhetoric, as in the arming of Agamemnon:

Then, last, he grasped
His two tough sharpened spears, each pointed with keen bronze:
And the light gleamed back to heaven from arms and armour,
And Athena and Hera sent the thunder pealing
In salute to the king of great and golden Mycenae.
(*Il.* 11.41–5)

But it was Juvenal who showed me how the almost infinite adaptability of the line could be utilized for pointing up wit and satire – as here in the middle of his anti-Greek diatribe:

Quick wit, unlimited nerve, a gift
Of the gab that outsmarts a professional public speaker –
These are their characteristics. What do you reckon
That fellow's profession to be? He has brought a whole bundle
Of personalities with him – schoolmaster, rhetorician,
Surveyor, artist, masseur, diviner, tightrope-walker,
Magician or quack, your versatile hungry Greekling
Is all by turns. Tell him to fly – he's airborne.
(*Sat.* 3.78–85)

The elegiac couplet poses somewhat different problems from those of the epic hexameter. In particular, it is hard to avoid the feeling, in English, of rhythmic monotony, if only because the opportunity for unlimited runovers is going to be severely reduced, since, *inter alia*, so many couplets, in Latin, form self-contained sentences. To make a sharp contrast between hexameter and pentameter is easy enough. Curtail the pentameter by at least a foot, and give it a masculine ending by setting a sharp stress on the final syllable. At the same time *always* give the hexameter a feminine ending. This solution was arrived at independently by G. S. Fraser, in some Ovid translations he did for a radio feature I wrote about twenty-five years ago,[21] and by Gilbert Highet in his book *Poets in a Landscape*.[22]

Let us see how the device works. Here, first, is Fraser: the opening of Penelope's letter to Ulysses:

> Your Penelope writes to you, long-delaying Ulysses –
>   yet send no letter home, come home yourself!
> Tall Troy is down now, loathed of Danaan daughters:
>   was Troy, was Priam worth the cost to me?
> Long since that adulterer's ship sought Lacedaemonia:
>   would the mad waters had then whelmed him down!
>
> (*Her.* 1.1–6)

Now compare Highet's version of Ovid's complaint to Cypassis, Corinna's lady's-maid:

> Expert in ornamenting hair in a thousand fashions,
>   but pretty enough to set a goddess' curls,
> Cypassis, my sophisticated fellow-sinner,
>   deft at serving *her*, defter for me –
> who could have betrayed the mingling of our bodies?
>   how did Corinna sense your love-affair?
> Surely I did not blush? or stumble over a word
>   that gave some evidence of our stolen love?
> Of course I said the man who loved a servant-girl
>   must be a hopeless idiot – of course!
> But the Thessalian hero loved the slave Briseis,
>   captive Cassandra fired Mycenae's king.
> Achilles and Agamemnon fell. I am no stronger:
>   so, *honi soit qui mal y pense*, say I.
>
> (*Am.* 2.8.1–14)

It is clear at once that Highet has gone further than Fraser in exploring the flexibilities of the form (so far, in fact, that at lines 7 and 9 he seems to lose the feminine ending to his hexameter altogether). Fraser is in serious danger of falling into the rocking-horse mode that remains the prime hazard for elegiacs: that is, unvarying stopped – if not rhyming – couplets, each rhythmically identical to the last. Highet's rhythms are subtler, and he has a sharp eye, like Guy Lee, for Ovidian sophistication, but he is still very much in thrall to the tyranny of the couplet. Over the short haul this may not obtrude on the reader's ear; but when, as in the *Art of Love*, he has to plough through hundreds of lines without a break, the old absence of metrical counterpoint, Latin's saving grace, produces a sense of relentless, repetitive undulation.

4

Bearing these dangers in mind, I decided to employ overrun whenever possible, and also to exploit the rhythmic contrast between the two lines of the couplet to the uttermost, sometimes reducing the pentameter to as few as three or even on occasions two stresses, and extending the hexameter with an extra stress in override, as it were, while on occasion cutting it back to a five-beat line. These devices are not so apparent in my version of the Cypassis poem as elsewhere, since it is comparatively short. However, you can observe both the overruns and (on the matter of tone) a more – I hope – relaxed, teasing, colloquial approach than Highet's: here closer to Lee (who starts off 'Cypassis, incomparable coiffeuse/who should start a salon on Olympus' – nice mood, but too far from the Latin), but linguistically trying to preserve Ovid's patterns:

O expert in creating a thousand hairstyles, worthy
  to have none but goddesses for your clientele,
Cypassis! – and (as I know from our stolen pleasures)
  no country beginner: just right
for your mistress, but righter for me – what malicious gossip
  put the finger on us? How did Corinna know
about our sleeping together? I didn't blush, did I,
  or blurt out some telltale phrase?
I'm sorry I told her no man in his proper senses
  could go overboard for a maid –
Achilles fell madly in love with *his* maid Briseis,
  Agamemnon was besotted by the slave-
priestess Cassandra. I can't pretend to be socially up on
  those two – then why should I despise
what's endorsed by royalty? Anyway, when Corinna
  shot *you* a dirty look, you blushed right up.

Now the immediate criticism of this format is going to be that it evokes no recognizable patterns in the mind of an English reader;

and that, in turn, raises the perennial question, yet again, of what a translation, a verse translation in particular, is *for*. What we may term, for short, the Dryden theory (see above, pp. 93–4) seems to assume tacit familiarity with the original, to invite applause for clever and appreciable pastiche. In the English Augustan Age this was, of course, the main motive for translation: anyone interested enough to read a new English version of Ovid or Virgil could almost certainly read them in Latin as well. The object was to produce a skilled assimilation to the literary mode of the moment, however alien that might be from the poet's own intentions. How, as Dryden asked, would he have handled the matter had he been writing in the translator's time and country? This produced, *inter alia*, Gilbert Murray's vastly popular versions of Greek tragedy, with the iambic *epeisodia* done over in rhyming couplets, and the chorus revamped as Swinburne-and-water; or (my favourite oddity) J. W. Mackail's *Odyssey* in the Fitzgerald *Rubaiyat* stanza:[23]

> Now at the hour when brightest shone on high
> The star that comes to herald up the sky
> The Dawning of the Morning, even then
> The ship sea-travelling to the isle drew nigh.
>
> The fields of Ithaca a haven hold
> Called after Phorcys' name, the Sea-God old.
> Two jutting headlands breaking sheer in cliff
> Stretch seaward, and the harbour-mouth enfold . . .

It has also produced, more recently, such metaphrastic curiosities, brilliant in their own right, yet arguably not translations in the basic sense of conveying a text to those who lack its language, as Pound's *Homage to Sextus Propertius*, Ted Hughes's version of Seneca's *Oedipus*, or Christopher Logue's marvellous variations on Homer (I am thinking in particular of Achilles' fight with the Scamander) that were originally broadcast on the BBC Third Programme. It would, I suppose, be surprising if an age of *Rezeptionsgeschichte*, determined to enthrone the critic as an integral element of the creative process, did not offer similar privileges to the translator.

This trend militates strongly against another, equally strong, movement in modern translations: the sense of responsibility to one's original and, in a different sense, to the reader, who today, nine times out of ten, knows nothing whatsoever of the original language, and is far more interested in getting an accurate impression of the poet's own texture and rhythms than in applauding the irrelevant ingenuity of a translator with a gift for clever pastiche. Let me give an example. One critic of my Ovid translation (from the safe anonymity of a reader's report) accused it of 'egregious dullness', and picked on the opening of Book II of the *Ars Amatoria*:

> Cry hurrah, and hurrah again, for a splendid triumph –
> the quarry I sought has fallen into my toils.
> Each happy lover now rates my verses higher
> than Homer's or Hesiod's, awards them the palm
> of victory. He's as cheerful as Paris was, sailing away from
> warlike Sparta, the guest who stole a bride,
> or Pelops, the stranger, the winner of Hippodameia
> after that chariot-race.
> Why hurry, young man? Your ship's still in mid-passage,
> and the harbour I seek is far away.
> Through my verses, it's true, you may have *acquired* a mistress,
> but that's not enough. If my art
> Caught her, my art must keep her. To guard a conquest's
> as tricky as making it. There was luck in the chase,
> but *this* task will call for skill. If ever I needed support from
> Venus and Son, and Erato – the Muse
> erotic by name – it's now, for my too-ambitious project
> to relate some techniques that might restrain
> that fickle young globetrotter, love. He's winged and flighty,
> hard to pin down . . .
>
> (*AA* 2.1–20)

Why my critic thought this version dull may be deduced from the rendering he offered, with evident approval, in its place (the fruit of what sounds like a fairly swinging Comp. Lit. seminar):

> O, shout hurray! and then whoopee!
> The long-sought prize is fallen to me!
> Beneath the old men's startled eyes
> I take the Nobel Loving Prize.
> So Paris felt, with Priam's bride,
> escaping o'er the shining tide.
>
> So Pelops on his foreign wheels
> showed Hippo's car some cleanish heels.
> But what's your hurry, callow youth?
> You're far from court, and that's the truth.
> I won your dolly by my art:
> Her body's yours, but where's her heart?
> You can't rely on Lady Luck
> for more than just an easy fuck.

Erato, Muse of loving name,
O Venus, Cupid, play my game!
My plan's ambitious: O what joy,
to pen that wayward, wandering boy!
His frown's a smile, his smile's a frown:
the problem is to pin him down.

As Bentley might have said, 'A very pretty poem, Mr X, but you must not call it Ovid.' Quite apart from incidental matters of accuracy, interpretation and taste (never mind the anachronisms and rhymes: Ovid never used a four-letter word in his whole career), what we have here is a fundamental divergence over method. What my critic wanted, in effect, was Dryden's licence: the old rhyming couplet, shorn of one foot and sauced up with contemporary allusions – a neat, recognizable package to which (as the current catch-phrase goes, dangling its transitive verb with insouciant abandon) modern readers can relate. It is, I think, no accident, as I suggested above, that pastiche translation is gaining ground again in an era of criticism when authors' intentions come a very poor second to critics' interpretative and structural – or deconstructional – fancies. The old joke about translations being like women – if they're faithful they're not beautiful, and *vice versa* – is getting a new lease of life.

I, on the other hand, start from the proposition that all translations are, in effect, crutches, second best substitutes for those who cannot read the original, rather than material designed to provide pasticheurs and infertile poets with a creative shot in the arm. Though it remains, admittedly, impossible to capture fully one's original text in translation, that does not relieve a translator of the permanent obligation to get as close to that unattainable ideal as he can. I would like, now, to examine some of the specific problems that this intention raises in producing an English version of Ovid's erotic poems.

5

Of the three elements in my title, the sex, I found, was by far the easiest to deal with. Social *mores* had moved on a long way since I was first commissioned, in 1957, to translate Juvenal, and Dr E. V. Rieu, the series' founder and guardian, asked me in a discreetly lowered voice, after a good lunch at the Athenaeum: 'Now, my boy, *what are we going to do about the smut*?' ('Translate it', I answered, and, since my progress was slow enough to catch the revolution of the Sixties, I not only did that, but got it published without trouble.) Despite the traditional air of *nequitia* – *frou-frou* might be a better word for it – that hangs around the *Amores* and the *Art of Love*,[24] Ovid almost never goes in for explicit sexual details. The penultimate line of *Amores* 1.5 is far more characteristic. Having catalogued Corinna's physical charms, and folded her into his siesta-time embrace, Ovid then writes: *Cetera quis nescit? lassi requieuimus ambo* – 'Fill in the rest for yourselves! tired at last, we lay sleeping.'[25] To borrow his own favourite image, what he offers, particularly in the *Art of Love*, is a guide to sexual siege-warfare and night-exercises. Pursuit forms the essence and major attraction of the game. Ovid spends nearly three books telling men and women how to manoeuvre during the chase, and no more than a few perfunctory lines[26] instructing them how to act when their quarry is safely bedded. This is very mild stuff indeed. Choose sexual positions, he tells the ladies, that conceal your physical defects (e.g., if you have striations from childbirth, have intercourse *a tergo*). Try to achieve simultaneous mutual orgasm – but if you can't come, fake it. No problems for a modern translator here: we are in familiar territory.

Significantly, Ovid tends to be far more violent – sometimes, indeed, downright embarrassing – when describing what he finds *repellent* about women. This is a side of his erotic persona that for some reason has attracted little attention. His evocation of ladies' dressing-tables[27] has a Swiftian quality about it; it reminds me of Jimmy Porter's remarks in *Look Back in Anger*: 'When you see a woman in front of her bedroom mirror, you realize what a refined sort of butcher she is. Did you ever see some dirty old Arab, sticking his fingers into some mess of lamb fat and gristle? Well, she's like that.'[28] For Ovid, women in their natural, unmasked state are not merely uncivilized, lacking in *cultus*, but actively disgusting.[29] In the *Remedia* there occurs the following passage:

Quo tua non possunt offendi pectora facto,
forsitan hoc alio iudice crimen erit.
Ille quod obscenas in aperto corpore partes
viderat, in cursu qui fuit, haesit amor:
Ille quod a Veneris rebus surgente puella
uidit in inmundo signa pudenda toro.

(*RA* 427–32)

Here we have two problems: how to translate *obscenas partes* in a way that conveys the curled lip of disgust without overloading the English, and how to convey the delicious double allusion of *pudenda*, as adjective and noun, implying that the man not only saw stains on a dirty bed, but associated them with his partner's vaginal secretions. I tried 'obscene parts', on the principle of adhering to the Latin whenever possible, but that sounded too heavy. In the end I came up with the following:

What could not give the least offence to your own feelings,
  in another man's judgement might well
Be a cause for reproach. One lover was stopped in mid-performance
  by a glimpse of the girl's slit as she spread
her legs, another by pudendal stains on the bedsheets
  when she got up after the act.

'Slit' conveys distaste but is not over-emphatic; 'pudendal' (surprisingly, not a coined neologism, but well-attested, and instantly comprehensible) conveys both senses of Ovid's ambiguity. At least what we achieve here is an approximation.

This kind of *double entendre* is, in fact, a regular Ovidian device,[30] and its punning allusions can cause the translator severe headaches. Sometimes the sexual teasing can be matched up with an identical English metaphor: the mistress's 'threshold' and 'grotto' (*R A* 786–9) clearly refer to her anatomy as well as to her house, and can so be read in any language. But there is also, in the same passage (783–6), a mythic allusion skewed to point a *risqué* allusion. Of Agamemnon Ovid writes: *Nam sibi quod numquam tactam Briseida iurat/per sceptrum, sceptrum non putat esse deos.*' Commentators[31] have not been slow to point out that in Homer it is Achilles rather than Agamemnon who swears by the sceptre:[32] but they all seem to have missed the point of Ovid's switch. What he clearly had in mind was the kind of situation envisaged in one of the *Priapea*[33] (whether actually Ovid's own early work or not remains a moot point), where Priapus parodies Homer's speech in reference to his own huge phallus-as-sceptrum: clearly the joke was both well-known and popular. Ovid, then, is making a salty joke, for which the sceptre is essential.

His Latin, as so often, is ambiguous; *numquam tactam Briseida iurat/ per sceptrum* can mean not only that Agamemnon swore by his 'sceptre', i.e. phallus, but also (taking *per* instrumentally) that Briseis had never been 'touched' by it, i.e., was *intacta virgo*. How to suggest this in translation? 'He swore that Briseis was still a virgin, by his sceptre,/But a sceptre (he figured) is no god.' I did wonder whether 'sceptre' might not, in English, be too free of any phallic associations, and thought of substituting 'staff of office,' but decided it was preferable to keep the Latin word and image.

A great deal of Ovid's wit is of this sexually allusive sort. *Nocuerunt carmina semper* (*Am.* 3.12.13) can mean both 'my poems have brought nothing but trouble' and 'spells have always been dangerous': the *praeceptor amoris* suddenly takes on the nervous persona of a Sorcerer's Apprentice dabbling in aphrodisiacs. (Ovid repeatedly plays with the word *carmen* in its double sense, promoting poetry as the true magic.)[34] In his address to Bagoas (*Am.* 2.2.63–4), Ovid insists that he and his beloved '*non ad miscenda coimus/toxica*'; *miscenda* and *coimus* both suggest sexual intercourse as well as an assignation. How to catch this in English? Perhaps 'we don't come together for the decoction/of poisonous doses'? In *Am.* 2.15 Ovid plays with the notion of achieving close proximity to his beloved as a ring, *anulus*, but cannot resist punning on *anulus* as anus too – *felix, a domina tractaberis, anule, nostra*: luckily 'ring' in English carries the same double connotation. Consider *Am.* 3.15.4, *nec me deliciae dedecuere meae*. The meaning most scholars attach to these words is, roughly, 'My poems may be erotic, but I'm respectable.' That is certainly one possible meaning. But *deliciae* can mean, apart from light verse, both 'darling' and 'sensuality', while the verb *dedecet* can convey the notion of 'unbecomingness' as well as 'dishonour'. So the phrase can also imply 'my girl-friend was quite smart enough for me', 'my elegies lived up to my reputation', or even 'my sensuality never failed me'. What is the poor translator to do? The best I could manage was 'A man whose delights have never let him down.'

There is a whole series of words on which Ovid puns, regularly and ingeniously, to produce sexual double meanings: *membrum*, *testis*, *neruus*, *latus*, *coire*, *miscere*, *surgere*, *cadere*, *iacere*, and so on. At *AA* 1.412 the *naufraga membra ratis* suggests erotic no less than maritime failure: a 'dismembered vessel', perhaps? *AA* 1.632 contains a marvellous ambiguity, *pollicito testes quoslibet adde deos*, which can mean either 'Call any gods you please to witness your promises' or 'Promise any sexual performance you like, and throw the gods in too': my version is 'Invoke any gods you please/To endorse your performance.' The same joke turns up at *Am.* 3.3.19, where the gods whom Ovid's mistress has falsely invoked are described as '*sine pondere testes*', i.e., both worthless witnesses and half-cock performers.

Try 'puffball witnesses'. We find it yet again at *AA* 3.398: *fructus abest, facies cum bona teste caret* can mean either 'A pretty face, unseen, gets no results' or 'A pretty girl, if never balled, won't get pregnant.' My version: 'Fruitless, the pretty face that goes alone.' The *adultera clauis* of *AA* 3.643 is not only a duplicate key but a duplicitous cock, just as *ianua* in the following line has vaginal connotations: that one defeated me altogether. Ovid, like Horace, is well aware that *neruus* often means not 'nerve' or 'muscle' but the penis. See *Am.* 2.10.24: *pondere non neruis corpora nostra carent* – 'Though I'm a lightweight, I'm hard.'

Examples of this sort could be multiplied: how to convey them in English without losing the dry and elegant touch of the original is another matter. The constant danger is of sounding vulgar – something Ovid never is. Yet the pitfalls of sexual allusion are as nothing to the difficulty of reproducing the verbal effects that this technically dazzling poet achieves by neat juxtapositions in a heavily inflected language. *Spectatum ueniunt, ueniunt spectentur ut ipsae* (*AA.* 1.99), pins down, for ever, the behaviour of pretty women in an auditorium. But how catch that perfect chiasmus – all done in six words, too? Ten was the fewest I could manage: 'As spectators they come, come, too, to be inspected/themselves' – strained, and it loses the crispness, but perhaps better than nothing. Oddly, by comparison the famous couplet (*AA* 2.23–4).

> *Daedalus ut clausit conceptum crimine matris*
> *Semibouemque uirum semiuirumque bouem*

proved quite easy to manage by redistributing some of the weight between hexameter and pentameter:

> When Daedalus had built his labyrinth to imprison
> the bull-man, man-bull conceived through a queen's guilt . . .

That last example brings me to the problem of topicality, of glossing for an alien audience references they cannot be expected to know, names (famous in their own day) which will mean nothing to them. All Ovid says to indicate the imprisonment in the Labyrinth is *clausit* – 'he shut [him] up'. We need the word *labyrinth* itself to remind us that what Ovid is talking about is the Minotaur. I first dealt with this problem in detail when translating Juvenal, and there in my introduction[35] I referred to the 'unfamiliar names, the obscure topical or historical allusions that translators are forever having to break off in mid-passage and explain to the layman. Nothing is calculated to annoy a reader more . . . than a text where every other line requires, and gets, some detailed marginal gloss before it can be understood.' Here Ovid, like Juvenal, provides endless problems. He, too, 'is full of recondite references that he takes for granted his readers will understand: he is writing for educated Romans who knew their own myths and history' and were familiar with all prominent figures of the day, not to mention a great number from their immediate or remote past. Here Ovid too is helped by what I then termed the 'silent gloss' – that is, the tacit insertion of a word or brief phrase to point up the reference. Sometimes nominative substitution helps. Ovid is very fond of periphrastic allusion: when he talks about the 'Maeonian and Ascraean sages' I will translate these characters, *tout court*, as Homer and Hesiod. A stylistic trick, hard for modern taste to swallow, is lost; much clarity is gained. But mythic parallels and *exempla* are so much part and parcel of Ovid's method that the reader has to be credited with at least a basic working knowledge of the main myths and legends, and referred to running notes as a kind of life-raft if he feels in danger of sinking.

The same is true of, say, Roman topography and the associations it carries. Consider the following passage from the *Art of Love*:

Tu modo Pompeia lentus spatiare sub umbra,
cum sol Herculei terga leonis adit:
Aut ubi muneribus nati sua munera mater
Addidit, externo marmore diues opus.
Nec tibi uitetur quae, priscis sparsa tabellis,
Porticus auctoris Livia nomen habet:
Quaque parare necem miseris patruelibus ausae
Belides et stricto stat ferus ense pater.

(*AA* 1.67–74)

My translation invokes all the aids outlined above, but I still found myself writing over two pages of commentary on these lines:

Here's what to do. When the sun's on the back of Hercules'
Lion, stroll down some shady colonnade,
Pompey's, say, or Octavia's (for her dead son Marcellus:
Extravagant marble facings: R.I.P.),
Or Livia's, with its gallery of genuine Old Masters,
Or the Danaids' portico (note
The art-work: Danaus' daughters plotting mischief for their cousins,
Father attitudinizing with drawn sword).

The Ovidian will at once notice the silent glosses. I have inserted the names of Octavia and Marcellus, and clarified Ovid's obscure reminder that the library in the Portico of Octavia (itself dedicated by Augustus) was built in memory of her son. I have also glossed Belus' daughters (Belides) – or, more precisely, granddaughters – as the better-known Danaids. But there is still much for which the reader must turn to the notes for enlightenment: e.g., the puzzling reference to 'the back of Hercules' lion', impossible either to omit or to gloss.[36] Such solutions are not, cannot be, perfect; but then all translation, verse translation especially, is an unending series of compromises between conflicting and often incompatible demands. In Ovid's case, if I have succeeded in keeping some proportion of any of these qualities – the balanced formal structure of the elegiac couplet, the elegant sexual innuendo, the crispness of aphorism, the well-read mythical and literary allusiveness, with its simultaneous flattery of, and demands on, the reader's cultural heritage, the sparkle and wit and fun – without, at the same time, losing too many of the landmarks that an intelligent non-classicist requires for his enjoyment of foreign poetry, then I shall feel that my task has been well worth while.

CLASSICAL PROSE AT ITS EXTREMES

Walter Hamilton

❦ Translation can take such diverse forms and be practised at such different levels that it eludes generalization, at any rate by me. If I am to say anything of the smallest interest about it, I must limit my field, and, as can be seen from my title, this essay will be almost entirely concerned with translation from and into prose, and with the classical languages of Greek and Latin. Whether such translation can ever rise to a level which deserves the name of art I am inclined to doubt, for reasons which will become apparent, but, whether it can or not, I am sure that my own productions cannot be so called, even on the most charitable interpretation of that regrettably wide and much abused term.

The translation of prose into prose is, of course, the easiest form of translation. It is also, with rare exceptions, the only form in which it is possible to produce, at a greater or lesser remove, an effect at all similar to a Greek or Latin original. To translate ancient poetry into prose inevitably loses the element of metre, and to translate it into verse, whatever verse form is chosen, involves an act of fresh creation, which of itself erects a barrier between the reader and the original. This is not to deny that there are many verse translations which may be good and even great poems in their own right. Samuel Johnson, who maintained in conversation with Boswell that poetry cannot be translated, nevertheless declared in his life of Pope that his Homer 'is certainly the noblest version of poetry that the world has ever seen'. Few people are now likely to be found who would echo this sentiment, and none, I am sure, who would deny that Pope has transformed Homer out of all recognition. Let me take another example, on a smaller scale, Housman's well-known version (*More Poems* 5) of the seventh ode of Horace's fourth book (*Diffugere nives* – 'the snows are fled away'). Housman, an incomparably better scholar than Pope, has given us what seems to me a profoundly moving and beautiful poem – I was once lucky enough to hear it read aloud by him with electrifying effect on his audience at the end of an unbelievably arid lecture on the text of the ode – but it still seems to me to smack more of the Shropshire Lad than of Horace. In prose translation of prose, by contrast, the translator can and should entirely subordinate his own personality to that of his author, and the merit of his work will largely depend on the degree to which he succeeds in doing so.

Subordination of one's own personality is at best a negative virtue, not, I venture to say, a quality normally to be expected in a creative writer, but there is a positive acquirement no less essential to any translator. It goes without saying that he must have a thoroughly sound knowledge of the language from which he is translating, but it is equally important that he should possess at least a more than average mastery of his own language. This is a combination not always found in the same person. The point was well made by Dryden in the preface to his *Sylvae*:

> There are many, who understand Greek and Latin, and yet are ignorant of their mother tongue . . . It appears necessary that a man should be a nice critic in his own tongue before he attempts to translate a foreign language.

Housman in his *Introductory Lecture* expressed himself with less urbanity:

> You might perhaps expect that those whose chief occupation is the study of the greatest masters of style would insensibly acquire a good style of their own. It is not so; there are exceptions, but as a rule the literary faculty of classical scholars is poor, and sometimes worse.

Perhaps one might add that long familiarity with the language from which one is translating can even bring with it a positive danger to a translator. There is a risk that his mind may be so soaked in the idiom of his original that he unconsciously transfers it to his own version, and 'escapes his own notice', producing what is frequently called 'translationese'. I have used the phrase 'escapes his own notice' deliberately. It is not natural English, but a literal translation of a common Greek expression, and therefore a good example of the kind of pitfall that I have in mind.

These are sobering thoughts for any translator, and I hope that no reader will take my emphasis on them to imply that I suppose myself to be immune from the weaknesses that they reprobate. But I have one other general point to make before I attempt to give some account of my own experience. There is all the difference in the world between a translation and a crib. A crib is by no means to be despised; it can be a most helpful tool to the student of an ancient language who wishes to see exactly how an editor construes his text. Their usefulness in this respect constitutes one of the chief merits of many of the volumes in the Loeb series. But by its very nature a crib has to stick too closely to the structure and syntax of its original to be continuously readable. The aim of a translation, on the other hand, is to convey to a reader ignorant of the language of the original as accurate an impression as possible of its style as well as its meaning without lapsing into stilted or unnatural or pedantic English. It is this aspect of a translator's work that I personally have found the most satisfying. It is no false modesty on my part to say that I am almost entirely devoid of originality; so much will be apparent to any reader of this essay. But I would go so far as to claim that I am capable of presenting the thoughts of a classical author in tolerably correct prose, and that I have a reasonably good ear for the rhythm of an English sentence. These are by no means rare or shining qualities, but, such as they are, I enjoy their exercise.

My own activity as a translator has fallen into two sharply contrasted halves, first, the *Symposium*, *Gorgias*, and *Phaedrus* of Plato, acknowledged masterpieces of a supreme genius, and, second, many years later, the major part of the late Roman historian Ammianus Marcellinus, who is hardly more than a name even to many respectable classical scholars. No two writers could have less in common, separated as they are by language, subject, style, intellectual power, and a gulf in time of more than seven hundred years. The problems that they present to a translator are no less diverse. That is why I have called this essay 'Classical Prose at its Extremes'. I was tempted to call it 'Plato and Ammianus or Pleasure and Pain', but that would have been untrue as well as unkind.

There have been so many translations of Plato that it may well be asked how I could have the audacity to add to their number. I can only reply that, when some forty years ago I was asked by Dr Rieu to undertake the *Symposium* for what was then the relatively new Penguin series, I accepted because the task was particularly congenial to me. Greek philosophy had been my special field of study, and Plato that part of the field with which I was especially familiar. There was the further advantage that the *Symposium* in particular, and to a lesser extent the two other dialogues with which I followed it, though they show Plato at the height of his artistic power, are not among the most difficult in philosophical content. The problems to be encountered were not, for the most part, problems of interpretation but problems of style and tone, though I confess that, like many others, I found it difficult to determine with precision the main theme of the *Phaedrus*.

It would be absurd in a slight essay to attempt anything but the most cursory description of Plato's style. His language at its best is Attic Greek in its purest form, fresh, limpid, and flexible, and it is almost a miracle that he could have evolved so sophisticated an instrument at a time when continuous prose composition had been practised in Athens for less than a century. Even more remarkable is his extraordinary range, of which the *Symposium* furnishes the supreme example. The scene is a dinner-party, at which the guests are Socrates and a number of other historical persons, who agree to entertain one another with speeches on the subject of love. The whole is represented as being reported by an onlooker, and this device enables Plato to move with complete felicity from anecdotal narrative, which includes a certain amount of light-hearted banter, through a series of speeches in which the speakers are clearly differentiated by their style, to an exposition by Socrates in the grandest manner of the philosopher's ascent to the vision of absolute beauty. The dialogue ends with a superficially humorous but fundamentally serious character sketch of Socrates by Alcibiades. It is obvious that a translator who attempts to give Greekless readers even a faint impression of all this is faced with the almost hopeless task of varying his own style over the same range. He must not, for example, allow the cold and pedantic speech of the doctor Eryximachus to read like the Rabelaisian fantasy put into the mouth of the comic genius Aristophanes, or fail to mark by a corresponding change of tone the complete transformation which comes over the party on the arrival of the drunken Alcibiades. Nor do his difficulties end here. How can he present with any approach to plausibility an account of such a conversazione cast in a form which has no counterpart in the literature of our own day? Cicero is reported to have said that Jupiter himself, if he had employed human speech, would have spoken like Plato. That in itself is enough to quench any incipient spark of self-satisfaction in the bosom of a translator.

Nevertheless, the substance of Plato's thought is more important than his style, which does not always, or indeed often, reach the heights of the *Symposium*. That Plato enjoyed the exercise of his superb literary gifts we can hardly doubt; there was indeed a story current in later antiquity that after his death a tablet was discovered on which he had experimented in several different ways with the order of the opening words of the *Republic*. All the same, there is evidence in the dialogues themselves that Plato, with whom the written exposition of moral, political, and metaphysical philosophy may be said to have come full-blown into the world, undervalued writing as a vehicle for the communication of philosophical truth. In the *Phaedrus* he speaks of it as a 'pastime', in which the philosopher may employ his leisure moments. This should perhaps not be taken too seriously, but it is certainly true that in his later and most profound works he is less and less concerned with artistic expression, though he retained the dialogue form to the end. We may, I am sure, feel quite certain that the first demand that he would have made on a translator would have been that he should faithfully transmit his *meaning*. This is no easy task, but it is a requirement that a translator need not feel quite so hopeless of fulfilling.

I turn now to the other extreme mentioned in my title. Ammianus Marcellinus (or, to anglicize his name like others of the same type, Ammian) is, as I have said, very far indeed from being, like Plato, a household name. But the comprehensive history of the Roman Empire which he set himself to write at the end of the fourth century AD, beginning significantly where Tacitus left off in 96 AD and going down to his own times, was expressly designed to continue the tradition of the great Roman historians. The work was very unequal in scale; the last eighteen books (all that survive out of thirty-one) cover only the years 354 to 378 AD, but they are the most important and reliable source for a period of exceptional interest, at the centre of which stands the apostate emperor Julian; and Ammian, a staff-officer in the Roman army, had lived through the events that he narrates and personally participated in many of them. Gibbon, never lavish with praise, described him as 'an accurate and faithful guide, who has composed the history of his own times without indulging the prejudices and passions which usually affect the mind of a contemporary'. When in 1978 Betty Radice, in a tone clearly expecting the answer 'no', asked me whether I would spend on him some of my recently acquired leisure, I was surprised to discover that, apart from the Loeb edition, there was no English translation of Ammian currently available. As one whose preferred language was Greek and whose interests were philosophical rather than historical, my ignorance of Ammian was profound, and my initial reaction was to refuse. But the novelty of the project was exciting in itself, and when I found in my friend Andrew Wallace-Hadrill a Roman Imperial historian who was willing to collaborate with me by supplying an introduction and notes (to which I must refer those as ignorant of Ammian as I was seven years ago), I decided with considerable misgiving to see what I could do.

I soon discovered why Ammian is not better known and more highly valued. What stands between him and a proper estimate of his merits is his extraordinary style. It was, of course, not to be expected that he would stand comparison as a stylist with writers of the golden or even the silver age, and his prose contains many departures from the idiom and syntax of classical Latin which have sometimes been ascribed to the fact that he was a native of Antioch of Greek origin who was not writing in his mother tongue. This, however, in itself presents no great obstacle to a translator. It is not the defects of his grammar which make him what one German scholar has gone so far as to call 'a torture to his readers'; it is the extreme artificiality of his manner, which he himself quite clearly regarded as a positive virtue. Such features as his unnatural word-order, his perpetual striving after effect, his reluctance to say a simple thing simply, his love for the most bizarre metaphors and the wildest hyperboles represent a conscious effort on his part to write in the grand style, and it has to be admitted that we have good evidence that it found favour with his contemporaries. There survives a letter from his fellow-countryman Libanius addressed to one Marcellinus in Rome, who is almost certainly to be identified with Ammian, congratulating him on the success of a public reading of part of his work. In fact, one might almost describe his history as a monument to the bad taste of his age, inspired by what to us are entirely mistaken views of what constitutes fine writing. There is nothing careless or slipshod about it, and there can be no doubt at all that he devoted immense pains to the cultivation of his style. 'Those turgid metaphors, those false ornaments' for which Gibbon finds fault with him were no accident, but the product of Ammian's careful and deliberate choice, and in his last sentence he recommends a similar style to anybody who may follow him. It is ironical to reflect that, whereas Plato would probably feel little concern about his translator's style, Ammian would be likely to be outraged by the liberties that have to be taken with his elaborate conceits.

How was such a writer to be made acceptable to an English audience? At first I was simple-minded enough to think that I might be able to produce a plain rendering of his meaning without paying undue attention to his idiosyncrasies. But that would have been entirely to misrepresent him, a complete betrayal of the duty which a translator owes to his author. Ammian's matter and his manner are in fact inseparable – *'le style est l'homme même'*. But something had to be done to clear a viable track through the jungle of his prose. In the end I had to content myself with abandoning any attempt to follow his word-order, dividing many of his unwieldy sentences into shorter units, and softening as best I could some of his wilder figures of speech. I am far from confident that I succeeded in striking anything like the right balance, but I hope that it is not vanity to record one impression that remained in my mind when I read through the result. I realized, as the complexities of his style had prevented me from realizing before, not only that, for all his faults, Ammian, apart from the more arid of his digressions, is continuously interesting, but also that at his best he can be a vivid and exciting narrator, especially of events in which he was personally involved. He deserves his title of the last great Roman historian, and, if I have helped in any degree to rescue him from the obscurity which he has to a considerable extent brought upon himself, I do not in the least grudge the labour that he has cost me. But I cannot pretend that I enjoyed translating him as I enjoyed Plato, or that I regard the result with the same degree of satisfaction.

It is, of course, a matter of sheer chance that I have found myself dealing with two authors, who, standing as they do at the opposite ends, and in Ammian's case, almost beyond the end, of the classical tradition, are so totally different in every respect that any conclusion that one might draw from comparing them would be meaningless. But it is relevant to contrast the nature of the problems faced by their translator. It is a commonplace that the masterpieces of the past need to be translated afresh in every generation if they are to retain their appeal by keeping in tune with the never-ending development of English idiom. That is the only valid reason for my attempts to translate Plato. The content of his dialogues was well known already from other versions, and my task was to convey their atmosphere and tone to readers of my own generation without falling further than was inevitable below the standard of the original. With Ammian it was very different. He is not a great, or even, except occasionally, a good writer, but he is a good, and even a great, historian. It was his historical content that needed to be made accessible in as readable an English version as I could achieve. If in the process something of the peculiar flavour of his prose could be preserved, so much the better. But this was not the primary object of the exercise; no one ignorant of Latin, and not many Latinists, would want to read Ammian for his style.

It will, I think, now be apparent why I hesitate to speak of art in connection with prose translation. Readers of Plato's *Gorgias* may remember that in that dialogue Socrates is represented as refusing the title of art to the oratory of his own day, which he classes with cookery, popular lecturing, and beauty culture as merely 'knacks acquired by experience', because, like them, it is based on no clearly established principles. I have a strong suspicion that much prose translation, certainly my own, falls into the same category. It is a 'knack acquired by experience'. In my case, such happy turns of phrase as may occasionally be found in my renderings were generally not the product of conscious thought. They came into my head at odd moments, in bed, for instance, or in the bath, when I was carrying the original at the back of my mind but did not have the text in front of me. But more often, I fear, and especially in dealing with Ammian, I had simply to slog through the text in much the same spirit as Johnson with his dictionary, when he describes himself as 'beating the track of the alphabet with sluggish resolution'. Perhaps it is worth adding that the antiquarian Hearne, in speaking of the indefatigable Jacobean translator Philemon Holland, incidentally one of my only three predecessors in the attempt to put Ammian into English, says that 'Dr Holland had a most admirable *knack* in translating books.'

All this, I fear, is very egotistical stuff, and I must emphasize that what I have said is based merely on my own experience of translating one Greek and one Latin writer. But I hope that it will not be out of place if I try to reinforce my point of view by adding a few words about a quite different kind of translation, to which, as both learner and teacher, I have over the years devoted a good deal of time and pains, the production of Latin and Greek versions of English originals. Composition, at least in prose, was, until comparatively recently, a standard component of a classical education, and the ability to compose successfully in verse an accomplishment held in considerable esteem. I was at one time what one of my teachers, the late Andrew Gow, called 'not utterly bad' at verse composition, and could at my best produce versions which might almost have been mistaken for lines by classical authors in their less inspired moments. But I have never at any period of my life had the slightest ability or impulse to compose original English verse or even an English verse translation. In my case, and I speak only for myself, the ability to write Greek or Latin verse was simply 'a knack acquired by experience', in fact a trick almost on a level with the ability to solve a fairly difficult crossword puzzle. If that can be true of translation into Greek and Latin I see no reason why it should not often be true of translation into English.

Much that I have said tends to the conclusion that in our time, at any rate, prose translators of the classics are fairly humble practitioners of the writer's craft. But that must not be taken to imply any depreciation on my part of the value of their activity. It is impossible to overestimate the contribution made by translation as a civilizing influence on human society. It has gone far to annul the curse of Babel, and immensely widened men's mental and moral horizons. More particularly, at a time when the ability to read Greek and Latin in the original is becoming, if it has not already become, an accomplishment confined to a small minority even among the highly educated, those who have made so many ancient authors accessible to English readers deserve to be regarded as national benefactors. On this roll of honour no one is worthy of a higher place than Betty Radice.

ON TRANSLATING SANSKRIT MYTHS

Wendy Doniger O'Flaherty

'Do you know Languages?' [asked the Red Queen]. 'What's the French for fiddle-de-dee?'

'Fiddle-de-dee's not English,' Alice replied gravely.

'Who ever said it was?' said the Red Queen.

Alice thought she saw a way out of the difficulty, this time. 'If you'll tell me what language "fiddle-de-dee" is, I'll tell you the French for it!' she exclaimed triumphantly.

But the Red Queen drew herself up rather stiffly, and said, 'Queens never make bargains.'[1]

Every translator from an obscure language sooner or later encounters a form of Alice's quandary; one can only begin to search for the English way to express a foreign thought when one knows what language it was thought in – that is, when one knows what assumptions, linguistic and other, are built into the apparent nonsense that is to be translated. I would like in this essay to face three aspects of this quandary one by one, beginning with the problem of determining the language from which one is translating, then considering the problem of determining the language into which one is translating, and ending with the problem of the role of talent in translating from the first language to the second.

The first challenge is a crisis of faith, not of reason: one must somehow come to *believe* that the text one is working on was actually written in a language other than one's own. When faced with a particularly opaque passage, especially after hours of frustrated attempts, one is often tempted to curse the original author for having been so Machiavellian as to take what was doubtless originally a perfectly straightforward thought and translate it into such a perversely diabolic code, just to make trouble for the translator who has to decode it. It takes faith to remember that the thought really was originally – and *naturally* – thought in another language.

Sanskrit, the language that I have worked with most of all, is particularly challenging in this regard, since many great Sanskrit texts were composed at a time when, even in India, Sanskrit had ceased to be a natural language and had become an artificial language (which is what the word 'Sanskrit' actually means, in contrast with 'Prakrit', the Sanskrit term for a natural language).[2] In modern American parlance, too, Sanskrit has usurped the place of Greek as the language symbolic of donnish obscurity ('It's Greek to me'); Walt Kelly's cartoon opossum, Pogo, referred to any particularly dry and obscure statement as 'Sandscrimps' ('Sanscript' or 'Sand-script', vaguely redolent of tablets unearthed in deserts, are the forms such defamations usually assume).

But if one cares enough about a text to translate it, one must believe that the text was composed by a human being who used that language, however obscure or artificial, to express a human thought; that any thought thought by one human being is capable of being thought by another human being; and that the task of the English translator is first to find that thought and then to figure out how one would have thought it in English. This is rather a heavy ideological burden for a translator to carry about, full of assumptions about universals in human nature, if not in human language; it is reduced to its absurd extreme in the Red Queen's hidden assumption that fiddle-de-dee is [in] a human language. This faith in the meaning of other people's nonsense is also expressed, on another level, in the many brilliant attempts to translate Lewis Carroll's 'Jabberwocky' into Latin, French ('*Il brilgue; les tôves lubricilleux . . .*'), and German ('*Es brillig war. Die schlichte Toven/Wirrten und wimmelten in Waben . . .*').[3] But no translator who did not assume most of what I have spelt out so bluntly could undertake the work of translation at all. This faith – the faith that anything that was beautiful and good to read in any language could be good to read in English – found its canon in the Penguin Classics, and its priestess in Betty Radice.

Having decided, then, that fiddle-de-dee is in a language, and that it is worth translating and capable of being translated, the would-be translator must decide what language – more precisely, the language of what *audience* – he or she is going to translate it into. Who is it for? How much work can one expect them to do? How much can one expect them to know? Our assumption that anyone can think any thought must be heavily qualified in action: they can be *taught* to think any thought, and one must find the particular way to teach them. This is the translator's version of the Buddhist faith in *upaya*, 'skill in means', the Bodhisattva's commitment to express the great

Buddhist truths in as many different ways as were required for all the different people who needed to learn them. But if one is going to publish one version of a translation, who is the particular person for whom it is designed?

I have modified my expectations of my audience – or, rather, I have changed my target audience – over the years of translating. One of the first articles I published, in 1968, was 'A New Approach to Sanskrit Translation',[4] in which I called upon the reader to do a great deal of work indeed. The article grew out of a seminar I had taken at Harvard with Dudley Fitts, in which each student presented a text in the original language and a polished translation. Students working in European languages could easily share their texts with the rest of the seminar; we were all assumed to have a working knowledge of French, German, Latin, and so forth. But what was I to do? I could hardly expect them to know Sanskrit. And so, as a basis for my discussion of the problems that I had encountered, I produced, in addition to what the others produced (my own translation and a transliteration of the Sanskrit text) a very literal, word-for-word translation, retaining the long, multiple compounds, and bracketing pairs of words to represent the puns and *doubles entendres* with which Sanskrit abounds. To my surprise, Fitts was more interested in that literal translation than in my 'elegant' rendition. It struck me that others might be interested in it too, and so I published a canto of a great Sanskrit poem, with each verse rendered in the following manner:

> The moon, grasping with rays like fingers the hair-mass-
> darkness, kisses the [night / evening] [-face with / -mouth] [closed- / bud-made-]
> lotus-eyes.

And I supplied elaborate notes: 'The moon is the lover of the (feminine) night, whose darkness is a mass of black hair. The face or mouth of the night is also a term for the evening (*i.e.*, the "opening" of the night); as the lotuses close at nightfall, so the woman's eyes close when she is kissed. Women's eyes are often likened to lotuses.'

I took pains to justify this approach in my introduction, too. John Brough had recently remarked that English must not

> strain to imitate structural features of the original which English cannot accommodate. The artificial use in English of long compounds, for example, would usually destroy more important poetical qualities of the original.[5]

And Daniel H. H. Ingalls commented that the long compound typical of Sanskrit appears 'even to some extent in English, where it usually produces a humorous or barbarous effect'.[6] Yet both Brough and Ingalls resorted to these long compounds in their introductory explanations in order to show the reader the true nature of the raw material. Ingalls offered such a translation of one verse ('. . . these soft under-the-branches-fallen-flowers . . .'), though he regarded it as 'so literal that it is almost unintelligible.'

Now, granted that such literal rendition of compounds is a highly unorthodox form of English *verse*, I argued, the English *language* can certainly strain to accommodate it; and, indeed, such language is basically more straightforward and more easily intelligible than the widely accepted English verse of Ezra Pound, e. e. cummings, and others. The problems involved in unravelling the lines of causation within the compounds face the Sanskrit reader as they do the English reader; there is no reason to suppose that the English reader, once aware of the challenge, will be less able to solve the puzzle, which is half the fun of the Sanskrit verse, a pleasure which all other forms of translation automatically exclude.

Certain concessions must be made to enable even the most enthusiastic English reader to use some of the tools at the disposal of the Sanskritist. Grammatical clues of gender, number, and case must be supplied, though an unambiguous rearrangement of the word order may sometimes provide the necessary links. The omission of the articles, though more faithful to the compact cadence of the Sanskrit, results in verse disconcertingly close to pidgin English, and so the articles must be supplied.

This was the argument with which I justified my inelegant rendition. I had reasoned that the people who were likely to read translations of Sanskrit poetry were not the same people who read the sorts of novels that one bought in airports; they were people who were genuinely interested in a foreign culture and who were willing to make a major investment of their intellectual energy in this enterprise. In this assumption I was simultaneously snobbish and naïve – a bad combination. I failed to realize two things: that anyone who was interested in fighting through that sort of translation would be likely to go ahead and *learn* the original language; and that people in airports were quite capable of doing that, too.

In the introduction to my second Penguin (the *Rig Veda*), I somewhat modified both my previous hope that the readers of translations from the Sanskrit might be willing to break their heads a bit and my previous élitist attitude to my potential audience. As for the first, I began much in the vein of my earlier reasoning:

> This austerity in commentary may often puzzle the reader. Good. The hymns are meant to puzzle, to surprise, to trouble the mind; they are often just as puzzling in Sanskrit as they are in English. When the reader finds himself at a point where the sense is unclear (as long as the language is clear), let him use his head, as the Indian commentators used theirs.[7]

Here is another hidden assumption of universalism, the assumption that we enjoy puzzle-solving in a way commensurate with the ways in which Indians enjoy puzzle-solving. This assertion not only supports the general enterprise of translation, as the other universalist assumptions do, but supports the belief that a translation that is *difficult* to read can still be successful.

Nevertheless, this time I was more reasonable in my expectations of my English readers:

> This is a book for people, not for scholars. Real scholars will read the *Rig Veda* in Sanskrit; would-be scholars, or scholars from other fields, will fight their way through [other existing] translations; they will search the journals for articles on each verse, and on each word; they will pore over the dictionaries and the concordances. But there is so much in the *Rig Veda* to interest and excite non Vedists; it seems a shame to let it go on being the treasure of a tiny, exclusive group, hidden as it is behind the thorny wall of an ancient and cryptic language.[8]

The idea of challenging the reader was, in principle, the same; but what I actually regarded as a legitimate challenge was entirely different. My Penguin *Rig Veda* was written in normal English sentences; no more brackets and hyphens. The difference between these two approaches to the audience for a translation came in part from the wisdom of the fifteen years that intervened between the two works but also, in very large part indeed, from what I learned from Betty Radice. It was she who rescued me from the Groucho Marx paradox ('I don't want to be a member of any club that would have me for a member') as applied to translation: 'I don't want to write a translation for anyone stupid/lazy/uneducated enough to make use of a translation.' It was she who provided, *in her own person*, the ideal audience for a translation from the Sanskrit: an intelligent, educated, intellectually curious person who did not claim to know very much about Indian literature. And it was she who, in her optimism and modesty, assumed that there would be thousands of people like her to buy such translations. And she was right.

The editors and publishers of the Penguin Classics were neither snobbish nor naïve; they discovered that people in airports were quite happy to read, along with the soft porn and the lurid biographies of movie stars, the world's greatest literature. The universalist assumption was there – how else could one have the bravado to flood the bookstalls of Kuala Lumpur and Bombay with copies of the *Orkneyinga Saga*? – but it was modified in an uncompromising way; when presented with an exotic oriental flower, one did not substitute a rose for it but rather left it as a *mallika* creeper trailing a footnote. The only requirement was, apparently, that the book be priced far below all other *serious* books, that it have paperback covers of stunning beauty, and that it be *well translated.*

This brings us back, full circle, to the question with which we began: if one has decided that the text is worth translating, and one has found an ideal audience for whom to translate, how does one translate it?

For me, the task was greatly (if, perhaps, artificially and self-seekingly) simplified by distinguishing between poetry and myth, and by deciding that myth, not poetry, was my bailiwick. Claude Lévi-Strauss has remarked that, where poetry is what is lost in translation, 'the mythical value of myth remains preserved through the worst translation'.[9] The myth, the core of meaning, survives to some extent even without language; the myth can be recreated again and again, re-inflated like a collapsible balloon. The Trojan horse and the myth of Eden survive as myths, free-floating without words; poetry, by contrast, survives only in language, despite the sustaining nature of the ancient core of truth that it embodies.

As long as I believed this – and I believed it for a long time – it let me off the hook. I needed no particular way with words; I just had to decipher the Sanskrit and put it into English and the myth itself would provide all the beauty. This was enormously liberating and exciting for me, and I am glad that I believed it. But I am afraid that my ignorance is no longer bliss. I have come to realize that myth, too, is carried on language as perfume is carried on a wind. Myth, like poetry, cannot be translated without *some* loss; and it is the translator's challenge to minimize that loss. For even a myth needs *some* linguistic detail, some spark of originality, to ignite it for us; it must eventually be re-inflated, re-tumesced, and if the language that attempts to do so is inadequate and unexciting, the myth will not come to life again. Sometimes it is art, and art alone, that can recreate the myth; and to do this the words must be the right words, the words of poetry. Some myths do not survive some translations.

There is a wonderful, little-known story by Rudyard Kipling, one of the last that he wrote, about the role of art, indeed of genius, in translation. This is 'Proofs of Holy Writ',[10] in which Kipling depicts a mellow, drowsily alcoholic encounter between Ben Jonson and William Shakespeare on a warm summer afternoon. As the afternoon rolls on, a liveried messenger arrives with a packet of papers for Shakespeare. It transpires that he comes from the Bishops of Oxford and Cambridge, to whom King James has given the task of translating the Bible; they have secretly engaged Shakespeare to advise them and, in fact, to ghost-write a lot of the translation for them. At the moment, they are tackling *Isaiah*. To Jonson's combined envy and horror, Shakespeare fashions verse after brilliant verse out of some mysterious source within him, pacing and muttering in a semi-drunken state of high creative excitement. Sometimes he steals from extant translations that he approves of (he asks Jonson to read him all the available translations of each verse before he creates his own, as all but the most high-principled translators still do).

Occasionally Shakespeare asks Jonson to tell him exactly what the Latin means, but he interrupts impatiently when Jonson launches into a long erudite explanation, and he pigheadedly ignores Jonson's pedantic objections to his mis-rendering of the Latin. Indeed, the whole story may have been inspired by Jonson's well-known comment on Shakespeare, that he had 'small Latin and less Greek' and that 'he took the Latin from the meaning, not the meaning from the Latin' – for taking the Latin from the meaning – the *human* meaning – is precisely what Shakespeare does in this story.

When even the grudging Jonson concedes, 'There's something not at all amiss there', Shakespeare merely remarks, 'My Demon never betrayed me yet, while I trusted him.' Later, when he has made a particularly felicitous line by joining bits of two inadequate extant translations of the line together, nose to tail, as he puts it, 'He began to thump Ben on the shoulder. "We have it! I have it all, Boanerges! Blessed be my Demon! . . . If those other seven devils in London let it stand on this sort, it serves. But God knows what they can *not* turn upsee-dejee!"' It is a very funny story, but it also contains some highly detailed, inspired reconstructions of the chains of reason, accidental association, research, and inspiration that produce a truly great translation. At the heart of it all is Kipling's implied suggestion that a translation as beautiful as the King James Bible cannot possibly be the work of scholars, let alone churchmen, but must be the work of our greatest poet, profane and Latin-poor though he may have been.

If one *had* to be a great poet in order to translate, the Penguin Classics would be a slender set of volumes indeed. But Jonsons, not Shakespeares, have always been the workhorses in the stables of translation. Even so, Betty Radice believed that a scholar of Jonson's ilk, when translating, should give as free a rein as possible to the poet in him. She nosed out scholars in whom the poet was not altogether dead, and egged them off the heavily trotted paths of dull academic ponies. Her offbeat choices, not only of 'classics' – which she redefined in a bold new way – but of translators, and of ways of translating, ensured that the myths and the poetry reached their exotic and not so exotic audiences with all vital organs intact, despite the violence and loss inevitable in the dangerous journey from one language to another.

THE PLEASURE CRAFT

Barbara Reynolds

If my late husband, Lewis Thorpe, were alive he would be writing this article, for Betty Radice was 'his' editor. She worked with him on his translations of medieval Latin texts: Geoffrey of Monmouth's *History of the Kings of Britain*, the *Two Lives of Charlemagne* by Einhard and Notker the Stammerer, Gregory of Tours' *History of the Franks*, and (a posthumous publication) *The Journey Through Wales and The Description of Wales* by Giraldus Cambrensis. As in the case of all her translators, collaboration soon developed into friendship. Lewis's visits to Highgate over the years to confer about problems of interpretation were always an enjoyable respite from university routine, and the pursuit of perfection became a shared creative pleasure.

In a sense Betty Radice was my editor too. She had no direct responsibility for translations from Italian: Dr E. V. Rieu was my adviser when I completed Dorothy L. Sayers's translation of Dante's *Paradiso*. But it was Betty who suggested that I should be invited to translate Dante's *La Vita Nuova*. A few years afterwards, in a light-hearted, holiday mood, I tried my hand at turning the first canto of Ariosto's *Orlando Furioso* into English rhymed octaves. I read the result to my husband, who laughed and said, 'Not bad! Send it to Betty Radice.' So I did, more for fun than anything else. She replied:

> I came in tired this evening after an exasperating day, and found your canto. It so refreshed and cheered me that I am sending it to Robert Baldick, suggesting that he should invite you to continue.

Thus began what was to prove, for me, the most enjoyable task I had ever undertaken.

Enjoyment is an essential ingredient in the translation of a work of art, especially of a poem such as *Orlando Furioso*, which was written above all to give pleasure. The translator should feel an urge to convey as nearly as possible the enjoyment received from the original. It is not an exclusively altruistic desire. The impulse to recreate, in one's own language, something that has given delight in another, is a self-fulfilling one. It is an operation of love, similar to that described by Virgil to Dante in *Purgatorio*, XVIII, 28–33:

> *... come 'l foco movesi in altura*
> *per la sua forma ch'è nata a salire*
> *là dove più in sua matera dura,*
>
> *così l'animo preso entra in disire,*
> *ch'è moto spiritale, e mai non posa*
> *fin che la cosa amata il fa gioire.*

> ... as fire mounts, urged upward by the pure
> Impulsion of its form, which must aspire
> Toward its own matter, where 'twill best endure,
>
> So the enamoured soul falls to desire –
> A motion spiritual – nor rest can find
> Till its loved object it enjoy entire.[1]

There are two ways in which a reader's enamoured soul can find rest: interpretative criticism, and translation. In a sense they are one and the same. But the more analytical process of criticism is not always enough. The soul cannot fully rejoice in the loved object until it possesses it 'entire'; and the more personal the metabolism, the deeper the satisfaction.

Learning poetry by heart used to be an unwelcome task imposed on schoolchildren. Yet there are times when we memorize a poem willingly, lovingly, in an attempt to absorb it, physically, into the rhythms and senses of our being. T. S. Eliot, speaking of his earliest awareness of Dante, recalled that when he had grasped the meaning of a passage which especially delighted him, he committed it to memory, 'so that for years I was able to recite a large part of one canto or another to myself, lying in bed or on a railway journey'. Eliot absorbed Dante's poetry not only by memorizing it but by transmuting it into his own: 'Still, after forty years,' he said, 'I regard his poetry as the most persistent and deepest influence upon my own verse.'[2] This is translation of a very inward and subtle kind. It is not a question of borrowing only, or of imitation, but of bringing forth in one's own language what has been experienced in another.

One of the lessons which Eliot learned from Dante was that a poet should be a servant of his language. This applies also, particularly, to a translator. English is a rich and flexible tongue, yet not many translators have the courage to let it speak for itself, especially if they are experts in the language from which they are translating. Laurence Binyon, though himself a poet, used a subdued style in his translation of Dante. Ezra Pound tried to encourage him to step out of the shadow of Italian, but failed, as may be seen from Binyon's statement of intent in the introduction:

> In making this version, the aim has been to produce what could be read with pleasure as an English poem. At the same time I have kept as close to the original as I could, and I have tried to communicate not only the sense of the words, but something of Dante's tone, and of his rhythm, through which in great measure that tone is conveyed . . . In some degree the effects produced by Dante can be imitated in English, and are attempted here.

The result of such contradictory aims was, inevitably, a somewhat Italianate English, which some readers admire. It depends on one's view of translation, especially of poetry.

It is often said that English is a language poor in rhyme compared with Italian. Consequently it is held that any attempt to translate *terza rima* into triple rhyme or *ottava rima* into rhymed octaves must end in failure. But what English lacks is not rhyming words but pure vowel sounds. It is remarkably rich in diphthongs, which produce perfectly legitimate impure rhymes, of a far greater range and variety than Italian can command. Dorothy L. Sayers pointed this out in the introduction to her translation of *Inferno*, but so powerful is the voice of received wisdom which echoes down the centuries that the myth is perpetuated. I am guilty myself of having added to it, unthinkingly, in a foreword to my translation of *La Vita Nuova*, where I said, 'English is less rich in rhyme than Italian.' I was hiding behind a time-honoured excuse for not having done better. When I came to translate Ariosto I was obliged to eat my words and I ate them with relish.

In self-defence I must add that T. S. Eliot said much the same: 'English is less copiously provided with rhyming words than Italian . . .' But he goes on to add:

> . . . those rhymes we have are in a way more emphatic. The rhyming words call too much attention to themselves: Italian is the one language known to me in which exact rhyme can always achieve its effect – and what the effect of rhyme is, is for the neurologist rather than the poet to investigate – without the risk of obtruding itself.[3]

This is the nub of the matter. English rhymes are preponderantly masculine. Consequently they tend to be more noticeable than Italian rhymes, since Italian is a language in which feminine endings are the norm. In English, feminine rhymes are reserved for special purposes, for lingering effects, for instance, or for humour. This is in the nature of the translator's medium. Like a carpenter who has to consider the grain of the wood, a translator who chooses verse has to bear in mind the need to avoid obtrusive rhymes where they are not required. There are various ways of achieving this. The fact that difficulties exist does not mean that they cannot be overcome.

Eliot implied that when Dante desired the rhyme to float gently by, almost unnoticed, he could conjure Italian words to do this in a way that is not possible in English. This may be so, but I am inclined to think that in both languages it is not so much the rhyme-words which set the tone, as the meaning of the lines which modify the effect of the rhymes. When, for instance, in *Paradiso*, XXVII, 67–72, Dante wishes to produce the effect of the lights of the Church Triumphant floating softly upwards into Heaven, as snowflakes drift gently downwards to the earth in winter, the rhyme-words do no more than waft the meaning on from line to line:

Sì come di vapor gelati fiocca
in giuso l'aer nostro, quando il corno
della capra del ciel col sol si tocca,

in su vid'io così l'etera adorno
farsi e fioccar di vapor triunfanti
che fatto avean con noi quivi soggiorno.

As through our air the frozen vapours leak,
In flakes down-drifting, when the heavenly Goat
To butt his horns against the sun doth seek,

So upward there I saw those vapours float,
Their triumph spangling heaven with the light
Of saints who sojourned with us, as I wrote.[4]

And yet the rhyme-words which Dante has used in this passage are not in themselves remarkable for their lightness: *fiocca*, *corno*, *tocca*, *adorno*, *triunfanti*, *soggiorno*. Taken out of context they are not very different from the following: *vele*, *fiacca*, *crudele*, *lacca*, *ripa*, *insacca*. But the context in which these occur gives them a much more obtrusive effect, intentionally so:

Quali dal vento le gonfiate vele
caggiono avvolte, poi che l'alber fiacca,
tal cadde a terra la fiera crudele.

Così scendemmo nella quarta lacca,
pigliando più della dolente ripa
che 'l mal dell'universo tutto insacca.

Then, as the sails bellying in the wind's swell
Tumble a-tangle at crack of the snapping mast,
Even so to earth the savage monster fell;

And we to the fourth circle downward passed,
Skirting a new stretch of the grim abyss
Where all the ills of all the world are cast.[5]

This picture of the monster Plutus collapsing like the sails of a snapped mast imparts a vigour to the Italian rhymes which here exceeds the force of the English. In the same canto (*Inferno*, VII), where Dante describes the souls of misers and spendthrifts trundling heavy boulders and clashing with their opposites in ponderous conflict, he uses the following rhyme-words, chosen for the abrupt effect of their double consonants: *Cariddi, s'intoppa, riddi, troppa, urli, poppa.* The meaning of the lines reinforces the impression of effort and collision:

Come fa l'onda sovra Cariddi,
che si frange con quella in cui s'intoppa,
così convien che qui la gente riddi.

Qui vidi gente più ch'altrove troppa,
e d'una parte e d'altra, con grand'urli,
voltando pesi per forza di poppa.

As waves against the encountering waves advance
Above Charybdis, clashing with toppling crest,
So must the folk here dance and counter-dance.

More then elsewhere, I saw them thronged and pressed
This side and that, yelling with all their might,
And shoving each a great weight with his chest.[6]

Here, in the first three lines, the English is lighter in effect than the Italian, suggestive more of water than of boulders. In the next three lines a more substantial effect has been achieved, but not, it will be noticed, by means of the rhymes.

Thus it may be seen that English rhymes are not necessarily more obtrusive than Italian. Sometimes, as in the lines above, they are less so and compensation has to be made in the rest of the line. This can be done by the use of monosyllables, which have a powerful effect in English. In the following passage (which immediately precedes the lines quoted from *Paradiso*, XXVII), Dante so constructs his verse as to throw withering contempt into the harsh rhyme-words. St Peter is concluding his famous rebuke to his degenerate successors:

In vesta di pastor lupi rapaci
si veggion di qua su per tutti i paschi;
o difesa di Dio, perchè pur giaci?

Del sangue nostro Caorsini e Guaschi
s'apparecchian di bere: o buon principio,
a che vil fine convien che tu caschi!

The rhymes are feminine but forceful, nevertheless. English masculine rhymes and monosyllables can produce a comparable effect:

Rapacious wolves in shepherds' garb behold
In every pasture! Lord, why dost thou blink
Such slaughter of the lambs within Thy fold?

Gascons and Cahorsines prepare to drink
Our blood. Beginning that so fair didst show,
To what vile ending wast thou doomed to sink! [7]

'Take care of the sense,' said the Duchess to Alice, 'and the sounds will take care of themselves.' When I came to translate *Orlando Furioso* into rhymed octaves I found this was true, again and again. It is part of what I mean by trusting the English language. When friends knew what I had embarked on they nearly all asked, 'How do you find all those rhymes?' But it is not the rhymes that are the chief difficulty. More challenging are the problems of getting the main stress on the right word, of making a point in the same way as the original, of catching the tone, mood, colour and movement of the ever-varying stanzas. But even with these problems English is there to help, if only the translator will allow it to. I first noticed that this was so when I was translating canto II. In stanza 35 the treacherous Pinabello is described as reclining beside a stream in a meadow:

. . . un cavallier, ch'all'ombra d'un boschetto,
nel margin verde e bianco e rosso e giallo

sedea pensoso, tacito e soletto
sopra quel chiaro e liquido cristallo.

The lines present no special problem and I proceeded without striving for any special effect:

Alone and silent, with a pensive brow,
Reposing in a shady grove beside
A green and flowery bank, he watches how
The limpid, crystal waters slowly glide.

I had not consciously tried to make the fourth line move slowly. The sense, combined with the sound, had done it for me. The Duchess was perfectly right.

As I gained in experience, I learned that it was often a question of allowing the original to have a physical, emotional, or imaginative effect on me, quite apart from, or as well as, my intellectual understanding of the vocabulary and syntax. It was then a matter of trying to find English which would produce the same or a similar effect. When, for instance, Ariosto describes Bradamante's feelings as she longs for Ruggiero to return to her, it was not only knowledge of Italian which came to my aid when I translated the following stanza:

Di qua, di là va le noiose piume
tutte premendo, e mai non si riposa.
Spesso aprir la finestra ha per costume,
per veder s'anco di Titon la sposa
sparge dinanzi al matutino lume
il bianco giglio e la vermiglia rosa:
non meno ancor, poi che nasciuto è il giorno,
brama vedere il ciel di stelle adorno.

She turns and tosses on her bed all night,
The downy feathers granting no repose,
Or window-gazes, eager for the sight
Of fair Aurora, old Tithonus' spouse,
Who scatters in the path of morning light
Her tribute of the lily and the rose;
And when day rises she no less desires
To see the sky ablaze with starry fires.[8]

Behind all our prose, written or spoken, lies a long tradition of poetry, ballads, nursery rhymes, puns and jokes. It is ready, waiting to be uncovered. Words which are associated in meaning often rhyme and jingle together conveniently. It is natural that they should: that is partly how languages develop. I noticed this with surprise and amusement when I came to canto XXVII, stanza 130. Rodomonte has arrived at an inn where he decides to stay for the night. In English the most natural phrase is 'to put up at an inn'. I had by then trained myself to be bold and not avoid what seem difficult rhymes. So I began:

> The night was coming on, the air was dank,
> So Rodomonte thought he would put up
> For shelter at an inn along the bank . . .

The rhymed octave requires three rhymes twice in the sextet and a pair of rhymes in the concluding couplet. So I had to find two words to rhyme with 'up', which on the face of it looks unpromising. But, not surprisingly after all, there are two words which rhyme with it and which are exactly what the context requires: 'sup' and 'cup'. I had not thought of them when I put 'up' in the rhyme position. I trusted the English language to produce them. It did, and I was able to proceed:

> . . . Where a kind host invited him to sup.
> His horse being stabled, he then ate and drank,
> But not as Moslems should: for in his cup
> Were poured choice wines from Greece and Corsica,
> Which by Mahomet's law forbidden are.

It was not always as easy as that. Sometimes I had to spend several days on a stanza before I could get it right. But the solution was there all the time, in among the resources of English, which is so much vaster than any one individual's command of it. It is awe-inspiring to experience a sudden disclosure of its possibilities. My most exciting moment occurred in canto XIV, stanzas 83–4. Ariosto here introduces one of his few allegorical figures, Discord. In stanza 83 she is described as being a rag-bag of tatters and conflicting colours:

> *La conobbe al vestir di color cento,*
> *fatto a liste inequali ed infinite,*
> *ch'or la cuoprono or no; che i passi e 'l vento*
> *le giano aprendo, ch'erano sdrucite.*
> *I crini avea qual d'oro e qual d'argento,*
> *e neri e bigi, e aver pareano lite;*
> *altri in treccia, altri in nastro eran raccolti,*
> *molti alle spalle, alcuni al petto sciolti.*

He knew her by her multicoloured dress,
Made of unequal lengths, one up, one down,
Which sometimes covered her, now more, now less,
As the wind blew her tattered, unstitched gown.
Her hair, one tress of which was gold, one tress
Was silver, and another black, or brown,
Was looped in ribbons, or else tightly plaited,
Or hung about her shoulders, loose and matted.

After this startlingly prophetic picture of punk comes the idea of legal disputation. Discord is hung about with documents, like a personification of the Circumlocution Office or the Court of Chancery. A key word caught my eye in the original: *chiose* – glosses. Feeling bold, I put it in the rhyme position. What would rhyme with it that was relevant to the context? The documents were stuck all over with seals: very well – 'seals and bosses':

Her hands were full of legal documents,
Bundles of charters, hung with seals and bosses,
Counsels' opinions, summonses for rents,
Verbatim records, affidavits, glosses,
Powers of attorney, deeds and instruments,
? ? ?
Ready at hand, to illustrate the code,
A group of notaries about her strode.

The sixth line eluded me. The meaning to be provided was that poor men were the victims of all this. For hours I twisted the idea round and round, juggling the Italian words against the English. I thought I might have to give up the rhyme in -osses and begin again. Suddenly, without conscious effort on my part, a line dropped into place, like a string of beads into a groove:

Which lawyers' pockets line with poor men's losses.

I could hardly believe my luck. The meaning was right, the rhyme was relevant, the stresses were perfect, there was even a touch of alliteration and the whole line had a proverbial ring. If I hadn't persevered I should never have found it. The exhilaration was so great I was obliged to go out into the garden and run and leap about. I could do no more work for hours. I was rejoicing, not in my own cleverness, but in the English language.

There have been many warnings against the folly of trying to translate the *Orlando Furioso* into English verse. Among the moderns,

Guido Waldman, who translated it into prose, was particularly trenchant:

> How could any translator show fidelity to the original when he had to lay his version on the Procrustean bed of the 'Englished octave' and accept the tyrannous demands of its rhyme and metre, lopping off here, padding out there? . . . to compare the finished artefacts, the Italian and the English, is enough to make one weep.[9]

These are solemn strictures, but they can also be levelled at the intrinsic disadvantages of prose.

I did not find the resources of English rhyme and metre restrictive. On the contrary, I quite often found them liberating. Nor is English unsuited to the Italian of Ariosto. Our inheritance from Elizabethan English included a rich vein of Italian elements which have become naturalized. Moreover, modern English possesses a direct, unrhetorical vocabulary and style which correspond to the direct, unrhetorical elements which are to be found in the *Furioso*. It is the mixture of many styles, the modulations from the epic and the elaborate to the earthy, the homely and the humorous that make it such a varied and lively work. And the octave, in English as well as in Italian, as Byron demonstrated in *Beppo* and *Don Juan*, as well as in his translation of the first canto of Pulci's *Morgante*, is admirably suited to this variety. Unravel the octaves into prose and half the character of the work is lost: the pivotal turn between the sextet and the couplet, the airy, often witty dismissal of an image or a topic by means of the change of rhyme, the neat turn of phrase that marks an aphorism, the heightened meaning, force or pathos which words acquire from their position in a line of verse, the cumulative effect of thousands of octaves, varying in style and pace yet forming a pattern – all this is sacrificed in prose.

Not only is form sacrificed in prose, but the very content of the poem is distorted. That essential ingredient of epic, the catalogue of names, resonant with heroic or barbaric associations, falls as flat as a telephone directory without rhyme and metre. Then there is the question of speed. The pace of prose is too fast. Ariosto's octaves move slowly, more slowly than Dante's *terza rima*; he intends them to. Ariosto, who was much influenced by contemporary painting, offers the reader not only the entertainment of narrative but also visual delight.

A famous instance is Ruggiero's first sight of the naked Angelica, chained, like Andromeda, to a rock. Looking down at her from the sky where he is hovering on a winged horse, he thinks she is a statue, until he sees a tear trickling down her cheeks and over her breasts, and the breeze stirring her golden hair. Richard Hodgen rendered this in prose as follows:

> From high overhead, Ruggiero wondered if she were not a perfect statue of pale pink alabaster, with gold for hair, the sculptor's greatest masterpiece. But circling lower, he could see tears falling from her cheeks to her breasts, and he could see a gentle breeze stir her long, golden hair.

This is pleasant, though not quite accurate: in Ariosto's original, the alabaster is not pale pink and there is no mention of gold in that part of the stanza. Inaccuracy apart, the point is that prose cannot by its very nature render the shape of the octave, the relationship of its parts, its balance, all those elements of the art of Ariosto which are as much a part of what *happens* in the poem as the action itself. Verse is not in itself a guarantee. A bad verse rendering may incur more loss than prose, as in the notorious rendering of this passage by the Elizabethan translator, Sir John Harington:

> Roger at the first had surely thought
> She was some image made of alabaster,
> Or of white marble curiously wrought,
> To show the skilful hand of some great master,
> But viewing nearer he was quickly taught
> She had some parts that were not made of plaster,
> But that her eyes did shed such woefull tears,
> And that the wind did wave her golden heares.

Modern English verse can do better than that:

> He might have thought she was a statue, made
> By skilful and ingenious artistry
> Of alabaster or fine marble, laid
> Upon the rock, but that he chanced to see
> A tear steal down her countenance, amid
> The roses and white lilies, tenderly
> Bedewing the young fruit, so firm and fair,
> And breezes softly lift her golden hair.[10]

Among the elements which verse by its very nature can convey better than prose are exuberance, fun, lightness of touch, playfulness, wit, irony and, above all, a sweet sensuousness, which the shape of the stanza engenders, holds for a moment as in a caress, then gently disengages. An example of this occurs at the beginning of canto XXV. Astolfo has ascended to the moon, where he will find Orlando's wits and take them back to earth, eventually to restore them to him. Ariosto, who often compares himself half mockingly with Orlando in his sufferings for love, opens the canto with two stanzas which soar to the moon and return to the arms of his beloved with a sigh of bliss:

> Who will ascend for me into the skies
> And bring me back the wits which I have lost?
> The dart you aimed, my lady, with your eyes
> Transfixed my heart, to my increasing cost.
> Yet I will utter no complaining cries
> Unless more triumph over me you boast;
> But if my wits continue to diminish,
> I know that like Orlando I will finish.
>
> But to regain my sanity, I know
> I have no need to journey to the moon
> Or to the realms of Paradise to go,
> For not so high my scattered wits have flown.
> Your eyes, your brow, your breasts as white as snow,
> Your limbs detain them here, and I will soon
> Retrace them with my lips, where'er they went,
> And gather them once more, with your consent.

Translating a long and varied poem such as *Orlando Furioso* (and long it certainly is – 4842 stanzas long) was an exhilarating experience. It lasted six years. A love-affair, it shed a radiance on everything I did. My own life mingled with it, flowing through it, so that even now, when I read it, a backcloth appears, like a tapestry, reminding me of where I was and in whose company, when I translated certain passages. One of my best stanzas was written while I was sitting at the foot of the Campanile in St Mark's Square, Venice, with the crowd swirling round me. So little apparatus was required – a clipboard, paper, a pen and a page of stanzas – that I could work on it anywhere, at any time. All the interstices of time, normally wasted, were joyously filled: waiting to get through on the telephone, sitting under the hair-dryer at the hairdresser's, in a dentist's waiting-room, on trains, on aeroplanes (it was fun to translate stanzas about the hippogrif while actually flying) – and above all, queueing. 'Ask me some questions, love,' said the conductor one day as I boarded a bus. (He took me for a pollster.) The translation of poetry is a physical process, as well as an intellectual one. Movement, variety of scene and contact, everyday life as well as rare, inner moments, all nourish it.

Translation is also the slowest and most observant form of reading possible. Having taught the Italian Renaissance epics for many years, I thought I knew the *Furioso* fairly well. I was mistaken. To translate it into verse is to shine a torch into every nook and corner and to floodlight every pageant and every combat. I never realized, until I was faced with having to account for them in my own words, how perfectly choreographed Ariosto's battles are. I discovered that a precise map could be drawn of the siege of Paris in cantos XIV–XVIII. The poet knew the exact position of all the troops and kept track unerringly of his main characters. This is not apparent at a normal reading pace because Ariosto deliberately whirls the reader round, concealing precision in a dazzling kaleidoscope. I never knew, until I translated them, how magnificent are the stanzas in canto XXXIII where the host in Tristan's castle displays the murals which depict the history of Italy from the earliest invasions down to the sack of Rome. And there are all the minor works of art with which the poem is adorned: fountains, palaces, gardens, sculptures, embroidery. There are the exquisite descriptions of female beauty – verbal paintings and statues. It was a joyful privilege to be entrusted, however unworthily, with the responsibility of recreating so much splendour and beauty.

The personality of Ariosto also became familiar to me. Despite the horrors of war (especially of artillery, which he so deplored) and the troubled state of Italy, he never gives way to despair. He rejoices in courage, loyalty and love, and is always on the side of life. One of the loveliest moments of self-revelation comes at the beginning of the last canto. Imagining that he is returning from a long voyage, he pictures all his friends standing on the quay to welcome him home, and mentions them by name. Perhaps they feared he would never make port; he feared so himself sometimes. But now they all rejoice:

> Now, if the bearings of my chart speak true,
> Not far away the harbour will appear.
> On shore I'll make my votive offering to
> Whatever guardian Angel hovered near
> When risks of shipwreck threatened, not a few,
> Or of for ever being a wanderer.
> But now I think I see, yes, I am sure,
> I see the land, I see the welcoming shore.

A burst of joy which quivers on the air,
Rolling towards me, makes the waves resound.
I hear the peal of bells, the trumpets' blare,
Which the loud cheerings of a crowd confound;
And who these are I now become aware
Who the approaches to the port surround.
They all rejoice to see me home at last
After a voyage over seas so vast.

Betty Radice it was who set me off on a voyage over seas so vast. I am grateful to her. It was her gift of enjoyment, which showed in everything she did, which enabled her to respond so generously to my first faltering attempt. As General Editor of the Penguin Classics she responded to a wide range of authors of many different cultures and periods. This, in an age of specialization, was most unusual and inspiring. She was also a specialist, of course: a classicist by training, a scholar by inclination and a humanist by nature. I once told her that I considered her a modern Madame Dacier, who translated the ancient authors for the court of Louis XIV and, like Betty, happily combined professional work with family life. I sent her a book to prove my point: *Madame Dacier*; *Scholar and Humanist*, by Fern Farnham.[11] I am not sure whether she acknowledged the resemblance. Perhaps not, for she was very modest about her attainments. Strange to say, the name DACIER is an anagram of RADICE.

TRANSLATING THE TRANSLATORS: PECULIAR PROBLEMS IN TRANSLATING VERY EARLY TEXTS

N. K. Sandars

❦ There are times, particularly when we are young, when some large body of knowledge is indistinctly perceived though still unpossessed, when it is infinitely enticing. There is a moment, discovery hovering just out of reach, attempted and not yet achieved, which is more delightful than achievement itself. One day it will be known and possessed but then it may have lost its glamour. So too there is a moment when a poetic substance is sensed but not yet revealed: partially hidden or latent, it needs to be uncovered, and the process of uncovering is more delightful than possession of the whole meaning when it is understood. Something like this was my state of mind when I first met the Epic of Gilgamesh in praiseworthy translations from Akkadian, Old Babylonian, Hittite and Sumerian originals. The contours of a great poem were discernible, but overlaid and partly distorted by the barbarities of scholastic jargon; and yet, to anyone not possessed of all the ancient languages in which the texts were written, those barbarities were the only available way into a still unknown, almost unimaginable world.

To say this is in no way to disparage the painstaking, sometimes brilliant, always necessary, labour of dedicated scholars elucidating the meaning of extremely difficult and fragmentary texts; but *their* interest is not literary. They are engaged in a wrestling match with meaning and interpretation. They need to include *all* the meanings possible, or equally to exclude all but one, and which one? Then comes the search for equivalent ideas, since the meaning when arrived at is still an archaeological object which has to be articulated into life.

After the strange names – Gilgamesh, Enkidu, Ninurta, Anu – a phrase hits you between the eyes:

I looked over the wall and I saw the dead bodies floating on the river and that will be my lot also . . .

and this is no longer an unfamiliar world, a strange Sumerian *ensī* with a crinkly beard dressed in a stiff fleece. The speaker is a man, any man in the grip of the first realization of his mortality; although a king, he too must die like these.

The Epic of Gilgamesh appeared in Penguin Classics in 1960 and owed an immense debt to the advice and encouragement of Dr Rieu, the founding editor. The original material is magnificent but Gilgamesh is unique, and after its acceptance by the reading public the question naturally arose of what else might be recovered from the same store of lost literatures. In this search and in the presentation of the new matter, Betty Radice, first with Dr Rieu and later herself alone, gave enormous help and encouragement which I remember and acknowledge with gratitude, the help of a friend as well as an editor.

The Babylonian Creation known as *Enuma Elish* (from the first words of the opening) is the most imposing Akkadian text after Gilgamesh. Its six tablets and their relative completeness made it an obvious choice. A Creation and a Descent into Hell occur in almost all great literatures, so it seemed well worth while to discover what the early inhabitants of Mesopotamia, with whom we already had a frail line of communication, made of these universal themes.

A first encouraging look at *Enuma Elish*, as the subject of a translation for the non-specialist reader, was quickly offset by the much greater strangeness of it all. The weird scenario, the alien words and names were all daunting beyond measure; and though so much more was known about the setting of the poem, the times and occasions of its performance, its purpose and the part it played in the life of the people of Babylon as the climax of the annual celebration of the New Year Festival in the Temple of Marduk, none of this really made up for the fundamentally alien feel. Whereas the gods of the Greeks are household names, and even Thor, Odin and Wayland Smith stir childhood memories, if no more, what was to be made of a long poem a great part of which circled round outlandish ideas, and names like Apsu and Tiamat . . .?

> Lahmu and Lahamu
> were named; they were not yet old
> not yet grown tall
> when Anshar and Kishar overtook them both . . .

But a closer look again showed that all these names had specific meanings which revealed a great deal about the poem. Apsu and its

Sumerian form Abzu, the great deep, are in English 'abyss'. Tiamat, related to Hebrew *tehom*, is any great expanse of water into which silt is deposited (Lahmu and Lahamu). To equate Tiamat with the dragon, as is sometimes done, is misleading. Unlike the timeless and limitless waters, the silt is a tangible thing which has a property of limitation, giving an horizon to heaven (*An*shar) and earth (*Ki*shar). In this way the perpetual physical features of the Babylonian world – water, empty skies, banks of silt or sand, reed-beds – are conjured up, a vast empty theatre for wind, storm and hurricane which then duly take over the action of the poem. All this is present in the language; the proper names themselves paint the picture.

You only have to think of the landscape of Greek or Nordic myth to feel the power of locality. There is no Olympus; in *Enuma Elish* the only mountain is the one that Marduk piles on top of Tiamat to hold down the flood.

Seeing the Babylonian Creation as a poem of locality made sense, and familiarized the strange names up to a point, but to a point only, for to possess the meaning of a name is not the same as truly to understand it. Anki, which is made up of Sumerian *An* (heaven) and *Ki* (earth), represents everything, the totality, the whole cosmos; but this said, what *we* understand by the cosmos can bear little relationship to a second millennium BC inhabitant of Babylonia's understanding of the totality of his heaven and earth.

With the more active gods the problem is different. Enlil, literally Lord Wind, did at one time embody the power of the wind; he was wind itself tearing across the low horizons of the Gulf. This more primitive Enlil has been projected back from later writings into the pre-literate and proto-literate fourth and third millennium, the milieu of Inanna's Journey to Hell, in which, however, he is a background, almost paternal, figure. By the time that the Babylonian Creation was composed, he had become a god who *controls* the winds. He employs them as weapons, they are his cohorts obeying his commands, while he himself stands aside. Yet the earlier more absolute personality is embedded in the later person, as contemporaries would have been well aware, though to convey this today is beyond translation. These changes also have a political dimension with the change from the simple needs of village life to the factions and hierarchies of walled cities and great temple complexes. The earliest temples built before 5000 BC, like that at Eridu, once at the head of the Persian Gulf but now far inland, consisted of a simple room with reed walls like the reed hut through the walls of which Ziusudra, the Sumerian Noah, heard the voice of his god speaking to him. Then by the end of the third millennium temples were built as tall stepped towers reaching almost to heaven, ziggurats from the top of which priests communed with the gods. There were wide platforms, stairs and processional ways. This period of several millennia corresponds to two short chapters of Genesis from Noah to Babel.

The names of other gods are equally descriptive, though their characters and functions change as much as Enlil changed: Enki Lord Earth, Inanna Lady of Heaven, Ningal Great Lady, Ninhursag Lady of the Foothills, and so on. Society was already old in Uruk, in Ur, in Eridu, in the third millennium when the first written texts come to hand. We have to jump in in midstream, for the myths and the gods are in movement and everything is changing all the time. I think the translator is better without too much theoretical lumber about myths and mythology. One should, where possible, limit oneself to a particular meaning in a particular place at a particular time.

Enuma Elish has a great many themes which recur elsewhere: war in Heaven, order formed out of chaos, the emergence of a supreme god, the building of the city and the temple, the creation of man and his destiny and finally, and most bafflingly, the great Hymn of the Fifty Names of Marduk which did not begin to make sense until one realized that all the names were the attributes of the omniscient, omnipotent deity, a truly noble concept. The Babylonians never got nearer than this to monotheism, not as far as the Egyptians with the Akhnaten heresy, though the early emergence of a Personal God, a guardian who stood in the relationship of parent to child, was a tentative step in that direction. Marduk of the Fifty Names is something quite different, a being of awe and majesty of whom Thorkild Jacobsen, a pre-eminent scholar and translator, has said that through him 'order pervades both nature and society . . . in a universe that is moral and meaningful and the expression of a creative intelligence with a valid purpose: order, peace and prosperity'.[1] Even as an ideal it did not last very long. Political disasters overtook Babylon, Marduk was carried away captive, and the Creation that he had usurped from Ninurta was given in turn to another, more dubious, figure.

In amongst the rhetoric of the catalogue of names, it is possible to find strange suggestive ideas, condensed fragments of mythology. Under Nebiru, the planet Jupiter, Marduk conquers Tiamet whose waters are commanded to recede into the *future* and to 'stay away for ever', which can only belong to ideas of circular time and the Myth of the Eternal Return.

In date, in cultural and historical setting, the poems brought together as Inanna's Journey to Hell are quite unlike the Babylonian Creation, and although much older, they are also probably more accessible. The Underworld, the Netherworld, Hades, Tartarus, Hell, Sheol, the names evoke ideas related, and yet unlike, while the name that is truest and nearest the bone is given us by the Sumerians, the Land of No Return.

Half a century ago Maud Bodkin, writing about 'archetypal patterns in poetry', saw behind Coleridge's 'measureless caverns' and Dante's 'dolorous valley of the abyss', memories of dark galleries and tortuous passages that lead down to Paleolithic sanctuaries deep in the mountain, often reached after crossing underground streams, their walls painted and engraved with animal- and bird-like figures. Nor is this beyond the bounds of possibility. I have suggested elsewhere[2] that when climate changed and the ice retreated, new and dense forest cut the roaming hunters off from their usual camping places and their religious sanctuaries which they could no longer visit from season to season. The image of the cave may not have entirely died, but remained a memory confused and misunderstood. As well as the physical barrier, thick undergrowth, lost entrances, fallen rocks and subterranean waters, there was also a spiritual barrier so that the half-remembered journey into the caves becomes the journey to Hades, Styx, Acheron, the 'descent' of mystery religions, and the road taken by Inanna in the Sumerian poem to the Land of No Return.

Although this Land is a dreary, dusty place of drought and hunger inhabited by sinister and baleful beings, without any joy, it does not have the tortures and horrors found in the Egyptian Netherworld, and still more in Tartarus and the medieval hell as it can be traced in ever more horrific details from the fifth-century vision of St Paul onwards. Inanna dies, she really dies when she tries to outface the Queen of the Underworld, and her naked body is hung on a spike; but she suffers oblivion, not torment. The small 'devils', the *gallê* who follow her up from hell, and who fall upon Dumuzi and pursue him through the desert, have the power to inflict pains, but hovering over the earth as watchers and spies they are more allied to the Erinyes than to the tormentors of medieval 'visions' and paintings.

In many of these early writings one becomes aware of resonances sounding forward into quite different times and scenes, and probably sounding backwards as well if we had the key. The rescue of Inanna has a different outcome from that of Eurydice, though in both hell claims its victim. This is no Harrowing, but still the reader who is familiar with Langland's *Piers Ploughman* may hear some of those odd resonances. The two maidens who come walking towards hell, one from the west called Mercy, and one from the east called Truth, when they have met together, ask each other 'about the great wonder that had come to pass – the noise and darkness, and then the sudden dawn'. Out of that strange light that is hovering over hell they hear a voice, 'Princes of Hell, unbar and unlock your gates, for there comes here a crowned monarch, the King of Glory . . . Unbar the gates quickly, you lords of this dreary place . . .'[3]

> And Hell itself will pass away,
> And leave her dolorous mansions to the peering day.[4]

However, one must not allow these resonances to influence the actual process of translation. If they are there plainly recognized, well and good, but the choice of words must be a true translation of the thing intended and not one that draws consciously on other treasure. That would be to work in a back-to-front mode. What matters more is the depth given to the later poem from the antiquity of its themes.

At the beginning of Inanna's Journey there is a puzzle. Nowhere is it ever explained why the heavenly goddess should have undertaken this dangerous experiment. Classical journeys to Hades have more motivation: to fetch back a lost wife, to capture the fearsome guard-dog of Hell Gate, or even to carry off the Queen of the Underworld herself. One day a text may come to light which gives a reason for the journey, but at present Inanna's action is arbitrary: either curiosity, bravado, envy of her sister the Queen of the Land of No Return, or simply the whim of a spoilt woman. Or again there may be some liturgical or mythological purpose behind the action of which we are still ignorant. The existence of a puzzle does not spoil, it may even enhance a story: the unasked question in Wolfram's *Parzival*,[5] or why Heilyn son of Gwyn the Old opened the forbidden door 'towards Cornwall that brought the recollection of loss and sorrows' to the seven who carried the head of Bran to the White Mount in London.[6]

The scholars who have worked on these texts, translating and commenting in English, German, French and other European languages, have provided so great a choice of interpretations (and with such distances to cover we are often in the area of interpretation rather than translation) that many different criteria have to be applied. *They* are generally best when they are most technical, and least happy when they try to 'lighten' the tone with slang, or worse still coyness, as when a great and awful goddess is accused of 'fibbing'. The translator has always the terrible consciousness of what Robert Lowell called 'the sprawl of language, neither faithful nor distinguished, now on stilts, now low', though it should be less difficult to avoid the pitfalls of 'metrical taxidermy'. A true poet can afford occasionally to be 'reckless with literal meaning', but in translations such as these, literal meanings are the sheet-anchor.[7] But literalness has its dangers too, and then commonsense has to step in. When Enkidu the 'wild man' is led by the hand to eat with the shepherds, the word used is *gupu* which means table. In such circumstances a table is an anachronism. One translator has used 'board' in the sense of provisions, as less specific, but even this gives an awkward impression. Sometimes the meaning is quite impenetrable, and not infrequently scholars disagree. Dr Rieu used to say 'make up your mind as to what it means and say that as clearly as you can'. Good advice, but following it will mean that sometimes one goes widely astray.

The discovery of a common humanity, such as we find when Gilgamesh looks over the city wall at the dead bodies in the river, may lead to the perfectly legitimate aim of searching out a contemporary equivalent, so that the peculiar conditions of the third or second millennium BC in Mesopotamia are transposed into the modern world on the assumption that, because humanity has not much altered, *we* will react in a similar manner to the tyrants of today as the people of Uruk did to Gilgamesh. This has in fact been done by several adapters of Gilgamesh in the past. It is not the way of Penguin Classics, and I think rightly so, for though there are gains in the shock of a contemporary challenge, at the end we are left probably knowing less rather than more about human nature by peeling off the historical dimension and substituting a present-day event. It is better, I think, to avoid this species of temporal juggling and keep the scenario, as far as possible, that of the third millennium or whatever period seems to be represented in the different texts.

In translating Gilgamesh the purpose was to make a smooth consistent story, with intelligibility of first importance, so that the overall tone was fairly uniform even when rendering the very different style and idiom of Sumerian and Akkadian originals. The chronological hiccups were to a large extent smoothed away, in doing which something was lost. A good case has been made for using what is now known about the sources and the manner in which the Gilgamesh material was put together by different ancient compilers and redactors in order to throw light on the processes by which a great epic such as the *Iliad* could have reached its final form. If we take the seventh-century Assyrian text of Gilgamesh as a 'final' compilation, within this compilation the different poetic worlds of the story can be separated out, and also the political and theological changes that shaped it can be followed through. A case in point is the role of the sun-god Utu-Shamash, who changes from a god of the rising sun in the eastern Zagros, to whom prayers are addressed but who remains distant and aloof, to a prime mover and inspirer of the action, warring against evil, with the cedar forest now placed for political reasons in the western Lebanon. Or there is the change in the character of Enkidu from the servant of the Sumerian story to the beloved friend and companion of the later Akkadian version.

In Poems of Heaven and Hell the problem was different. The Creation is itself consistent in style, though some of the chief characters may have changed roles in the course of time, and some earlier material is embedded in the late-second-millennium poem. Of the Hymn of the Fifty Names of Marduk, I have already said something. But with Inanna's Journey the parts of the text differ so much that any attempt to unify them would have been misplaced. Whereas the first two sections comprising the greater part of the poem are fairly consistent in a rather grand and public manner, thereafter the texts are not only scattered, fragmentary and often overlapping, but also in a different style of writing. Some are quite simple and primitive laments, perhaps part of seasonal rituals; there are separate lyric pieces such as Dumuzi's Dream, and the songs and laments put into the mouths of his mother, his wife and his sister. These are in line with a series of courtship and marriage songs, the setting for which is closer to the village society of the fourth and early third millennium and which reminds one of the timeless life of folksong. Many have the beginning, 'As I walked out . . .' – almost as universal as the storyteller's 'Once upon a time . . .' A wife mourns her dead husband:

> He is dead and has left me . . .
> only the north wind sings your song my husband . . .

Though far separated in place and time, we may be reminded of another song:

> The trees that do grow high, and the leaves that do grow green
> The time is gone and past my love when you and I have seen . . .
> For now my love is dead and in his grave does lie
> The green grass was growing over him so very high.[8]

This also finds an echo in Dumuzi's 'I am not shoots of grass in a dead land.'

Many years ago Maurice Baring published a collection of his favourite quotations taken from many literatures of the world, which he called *Have You Anything to Declare?* He imagined himself arriving in the nether regions and faced by a custom-house official in place of Charon, who demanded that he should declare the literary baggage with which he had travelled during his life. He began with Homer and ended with St Augustine, having passed by many countries and many authors. I would be very well pleased if some future traveller, meeting at the same custom-house, should find some words of an old Babylonian or Sumerian poem in his baggage. I believe too that Betty Radice, who did so much to increase the range and riches of our literary belongings, would be glad of that declaration.

THE PENGUINIFICATION OF PLATO

Trevor J. Saunders

❦ 'Translations (like wives) are seldom faithful if they are in the least attractive.' In an age of translations (I say nothing of unfaithful wives), Roy Campbell's *mot*[1] is a salutary reminder that attractiveness in a version may conceal gross infidelity to the content and meaning of the original; and that even if by some miracle a translator should succeed in reconciling the demands of readability and accuracy, his work is necessarily 'at best an echo'[2] of the ancient text, or – to use Platonic language – a copy reproducing its model only imperfectly.

But before the translator grapples with that problem, he has many other jobs to do. Nowadays a Greek or Latin work is to most people a rather strange object, whose structure and conventions and world of ideas are very far from being readily intelligible. The translator must perforce go to some trouble to *present* and *interpret* his text to his modern readership. He must, to put it crudely, be something of a showman.

For purposes of showmanship, the *Laws* of Plato seems at first sight monumentally unsuitable. It is the last and longest of his works, and has little dramatic or conversational sparkle; written in ungainly Greek, it stumbles oddly from one topic to another, and to read it continuously would seem to require dedication on a heroic scale. Small wonder, we may say, that it is among the least known of Plato's dialogues. Yet its faults are very much on the surface; dig a little deeper, and you find that the *Laws* is one of the most fascinating of works about political philosophy. It contains no less than Plato's blueprint for a practical Utopia, to be founded in Crete in the middle of the fourth century BC. In his ripe old age Plato gives us his plans, in all their brilliant detail, for his second-best ideal state. Even when I was an undergraduate, it seemed strange to me that the *Laws* was so little discussed; and later, when I was a research student, I concluded that at least part of the reason was the lack of a good translation in the modern idiom. And so in February 1965 I set about translating this neglected work, in the hope of making it more accessible to modern readers.

My first problem was the sheer size of the *Laws*. The translation, which was to appear as a Penguin Classic, would amount to well over five hundred pages, which would have to be broken up into natural constituent sections and sub-sections, each of which would need to be attractively labelled and listed so as to give the prospective reader an idea of the contents, and short enough to encourage him to dip his finger into the pie – the *Laws* being far better taken in nibbles than as a continuous meal. Here is part of section 12, as listed in the contents table (which occupies no less than ten pages):

	(p.)
Bk VII §12. EDUCATION	270
Written and Unwritten Rules	270
Education in the Womb	271
The Importance of Movement: the Evidence of Corybantic Ritual	273
How far should a Child be Humoured?	275
Unwritten Rules: a Reminder	277
Early Education	278
Ambidexterity	279
Physical Training (I)	281
The Dangers of Innovation in Education	282

The titles are such as Plato himself might have used, if he had known the modern device of headings and sub-headings.

But appetite-whetters are not enough. The actual dialogue moves on three more or less distinct levels, which I thought it helpful to articulate typographically. First we have the private philosophical conversation of the three speakers: the Athenian Stranger (in effect Plato himself), Cleinias a Cretan, and Megillus a Spartan; then there are the public persuasive preambles to the various parts of the legal code, which are intended for the ears of the farmers and others who are to make up the new state; and finally there is the legal code itself. The dialogue often oscillates rapidly between these three levels; and in addition the legal code is in places very detailed and complex. Accordingly, the philosophical discussion is printed in the ordinary manner; the preambles and legal code are distinguished by indentation; and in addition the complexities of the code are articulated by the insertion of 1, 2, 3, *a*, *b*, *c*, etc., to introduce the various clauses in the manner of a modern statute, the clauses being also spaced out on the printed page on a generous scale. Few ancient texts demand such typographical elaboration; in this as in other ways the *Laws* is in a class of its own.

Several other aids to the reader proved essential. Elementary information about names and places, customs and institutions had to be peppered appropriately at the bottom of the pages in the form of footnotes; bibliographies were needed for readers who might wish to study the *Laws* further; and an index of names would obviously be useful. For ease of reference, the Stephanus numbers had to be placed in the margin (rather than at the tops of the pages).

But above all I felt I had to explain, especially to a reader new to the *Laws*, its importance as a document in the history of political philosophy and its relevance to various modern issues. Now to set an ancient work in its historical, literary, and philosophical setting, simply but not superficially, attractively but not *too* 'popularly', and in the modest space of twenty-five pages, is a fairly taxing business, as anyone will know who has tried. When the work is as huge, diffuse, and many-sided as the *Laws*, the task is quite ferociously difficult. Consider what you have to do: you have to 'catch' your casual Greekless general reader with the first word of your introduction and carry him through to its end, mixing *dulce* with *utile*, so that almost without realizing it he learns something about the work and is left with a desire to read the translation. The broad difference between an ancient and a modern reader is that the ancient already possesses a 'conceptual framework' in which he may read the work, whereas the modern does not. The aim of an introduction is to supply the lack, to give that frame to the modern reader, so that he can read the translation with something like the outlook and reactions of an ancient; and it should also give him some sort of indication as to how he might assess the work from a modern point of view. All this, I am aware, is an impossibly tall order; but it has to be attempted. Hence I thought it worth while to lavish a great deal of labour on the introduction; and in order to reinforce it at a more particular level, I also inserted at suitable points in the text a page or two of italicized commentary, in the manner pioneered by Cornford. The *Laws* is a devious work, and from time to time a reader needs to be told of the reasons for the twists and turns of the discussion.

It may be that I am labouring the obvious, and that the need to take a lot of trouble about presentation can be taken for granted. If so, it is a measure of how far we have come since the days when it was thought sufficient to give the reader little but the translation, on the assumption that all educated people had at least some classical background. That has been quite unrealistic for a very long time.

But however good its 'packaging', a version must stand on its own merits as translation. Now up to a point, as every classicist knows, to make a good translation is perfectly simple. By this I do not mean that it is enough if you merely turn the literal meaning of the Greek into bare English, without grace and art: obviously that would be intolerable, and you would deserve to gather dust on the shelves. I mean it is not at all difficult to express in decent English one's conception of the meaning, by forgetting the form, expression, and structure of the Greek and constantly asking oneself, 'How does one *say* that nowadays?' Given time and application, the right form of words will come, and one's sentences and paragraphs can be licked into shape; and one will get a sense of creative achievement by satisfying a crucial test: that in point of literary style your version should read as little as possible like a translation. The Greekness of the Greek should not poke through into the Englishness of the English, which should read like an original composition. I learned very early on, through painful experience, that literary mannerisms of the Greek should not be reproduced in the English if the cost is too great. I happened to translate book ix before the others, and after a short time the following confronted me: [Our laws may not be able to subdue obdurately wicked persons.] *Ὧν δὴ χάριν οὐκ ἐπίχαριν λέγοιμ' ἂν πρῶτον νόμον ἱερῶν περὶ συλήσεων, ἄν τις τοῦτο δρᾶν τολμᾷ.* Misguidedly, I spent a lot of time trying to render the jingle *χάριν ἐπίχαριν*, 'on their unpleasant account', and eventually came up with 'for their forsaken sake'. A friendly critic, reading my version of the whole passage, blinked. 'Why do you have that curious expression?' he asked. I had no answer; 'forsaken' became 'dismal'. The merits of a partial reproduction of the jingle are outweighed by the mystification felt by the reader: such frigid whimsy is alien to modern English. The example is perhaps a trivial one; but a large part of a translator's business is in fact to cope with a long series of such minor problems, to which perfect solutions are rarely attainable. A combination of instinct, inspiration, and judgement must be brought to bear on each; the only rule is that there are no rules.

Nor is it even difficult to vary one's style within the same work, to take account of the tone of particular passages. For instance, I found it was the least of my problems to write informal and colloquial English when the dialogue demanded it. Take for instance the following piece of genial conversation, in which Megillus tells the Athenian Stranger that he may talk for as long as he likes (642 b–d):

ἀκούων γὰρ τῶν παίδων εὐθύς, εἴ τι μέμφοιντο ἢ καὶ ἐπαινοῖεν Λακεδαιμόνιοι Ἀθηναίους, ὡς ‘Ἡ πόλις ὑμῶν, ὦ Μέγιλλε,’ ἔφασαν, ‘ἡμᾶς οὐ καλῶς ἢ καλῶς ἔρρεξε’ – ταῦτα δὴ ἀκούων, καὶ μαχόμενος πρὸς αὐτὰ ὑπὲρ ὑμῶν ἀεὶ πρὸς τοὺς τὴν πόλιν εἰς ψόγον ἄγοντας, πᾶσαν εὔνοιαν ἔσχον, καί μοι νῦν ἥ τε φωνὴ προσφιλὴς ὑμῶν, τό τε ὑπό πολλῶν λεγόμενον, ὡς ὅσοι Ἀθηναίων εἰσὶν ἀγαθοὶ διαφερόντως εἰσὶν τοιοῦτοι, δοκεῖ ἀληθέστατα λέγεσθαι· μόνοι γὰρ ἄνευ ἀνάγκης αὐτοφυῶς, θείᾳ μοίρᾳ, ἀληθῶς καὶ οὔτι πλαστῶς εἰσιν ἀγαθοί. θαρρῶν δὴ ἐμοῦ γε ἕνεκα λέγοις ἂν τοσαῦτα ὁπόσα σοι φίλον.

When the Spartans were criticizing or praising the Athenians, I used to hear the little children say, ‘Megillus, your state has done the dirty on us’, or, ‘it has done us proud’. By listening to all this and constantly resisting on your behalf the charges of Athens’ detractors, I acquired a wholehearted affection for her, so that to this day I very much enjoy the sound of your accent. It is commonly said that when an Athenian is good, he is very very good, and I’m sure that’s right. They are unique in that they are good not because of any compulsion, but spontaneously, by grace of heaven; it is all so genuine and unfeigned. So you’re welcome to speak as long as you like, so far as I’m concerned.

‘Done the dirty on us’, ‘done us proud’, ‘you’re welcome’, ‘very very good’ (a whimsical reminiscence of the girl with a curl in the middle of her forehead) – all this lightens the tone and makes it casual and everyday. By contrast, the Athenian sometimes preaches in a most earnest manner, and it seemed necessary to rise to a modest solemnity (727 d–728 a):

οὐδὲ μὴν πρὸ ἀρετῆς ὁπόταν αὖ προτιμᾷ τις κάλλος, τοῦτ’ ἔστιν οὐχ ἕτερον ἢ ἡ τῆς ψυχῆς ὄντως καὶ πάντως ἀτιμία. ψυχῆς γὰρ σῶμα ἐντιμότερον οὗτος ὁ λόγος φησὶν εἶναι, ψευδόμενος· οὐδὲν γὰρ γηγενὲς Ὀλυμπίων ἐντιμότερον, ἀλλ’ ὁ περὶ ψυχῆς ἄλλως δοξάζων ἀγνοεῖ ὡς θαυμαστοῦ τούτου κτήματος ἀμελεῖ. οὐδέ γε ὁπόταν χρήματά τις ἐρᾷ κτᾶσθαι μὴ καλῶς, ἢ μὴ δυσχερῶς φέρῃ κτώμενος, δώροις ἄρα τιμᾷ τότε τὴν αὐτοῦ ψυχήν – παντὸς μὲν οὖν λείπει – τὸ γὰρ αὐτῆς τίμιον ἅμα καὶ καλὸν ἀποδίδοται σμικροῦ χρυσίου. πᾶς γὰρ ὅ τ’ ἐπὶ γῆς καὶ ὑπὸ γῆς χρυσὸς ἀρετῆς οὐκ ἀντάξιος.

And when a man values beauty above virtue, the disrespect he shows his soul is total and fundamental, because he would argue that the body is more to be honoured than the soul – falsely, because nothing born of earth is to be honoured more than what comes from heaven; and anyone who holds a different view of the soul does not realize how wonderful this possession is which he scorns. Again, a man who is seized by lust to obtain money by improper means and feels no disgust in the acquisition, will find that in the event he does his soul no honour by such gifts – far from it: he sells all that gives the soul its beauty and value for a few paltry pieces of gold – but all the gold upon the earth and all the gold beneath it does not compensate for lack of virtue.

Dignified vocabulary, and a certain amplitude of expression, serve to elevate this piece above the common style.

But if you compare closely the Greek of these two passages with my English, you may well wish to remonstrate: 'Aren't you going too far? Your versions are louder than the originals. "Done the dirty" and "done us proud" are surely over-translations of *οὐ καλῶς ἢ καλῶς ἔρρεξε*, "treated us well or ill", and "a few paltry pieces of gold" says rather more than *σμικροῦ χρυσίου*, "a small piece of gold". The tone of the first piece is not as chatty as you make it, nor that of the second as solemn as your diluted-biblical style implies.' The rebuke is just. I confess the fault, and boast of it. A cardinal principle of translation is involved. The style of a version must, it is true, be determined partly by the nature and purpose of the original text; but it must be determined also by the current status of the text and the characteristics of the intended readership of the translation. What is the status of the *Laws*? It is Plato's bulkiest work, and probably his most neglected; it has few partisans, and the intended readership is indifferent or lukewarm. In that situation, the best service the translator can do for the *Laws* is to ensure that it shall be *read*. If, perish the thought, I ever had to translate the *Laws* again, in an age when it was as well known as the *Republic*, I should probably wish to proceed rather differently. One sometimes hears it bemoaned that translations are a product of their day and age. So they should be. There is no such thing as an 'ideal' or 'standard' translation. A calculated and deliberate – and modest – exaggeration of certain relatively unimportant features of the text is a perfectly legitimate method of enticing readers, if it helps to rescue a great and undeservedly neglected work from obscurity.

But over-translation is one thing; mistranslation is another. Should one ever dare to cultivate inaccuracy? Consider for example the first sentence of the whole dialogue:

θεὸς ἤ τις ἀνθρώπων ὑμῖν, ὦ ξένοι, εἴληφε τὴν αἰτίαν τῆς τῶν νόμων διαθέσεως;

Tell me, gentlemen, to whom do you give the credit for establishing your codes of law? Is it a man, or a god?

The literal translation of *xenoi*, 'strangers', would have jarred in modern English, so I took the liberty (and others have taken it before me) of using throughout 'sir' for the singular and 'gentlemen' for the plural, words which catch something of the three elderly speakers' staid formality. Here is another example of deliberate technical inaccuracy (721 d):

If a man ... reaches the age of 35 without having married, he must pay a yearly fine (of a sum to be specified; that ought to stop him thinking that life as a bachelor is all cakes and ale), and be deprived too of all the honours which the younger people in the state pay to their elders on appropriate occasions.

The words in the bracket translate *τόσῳ καὶ τόσῳ, ἵνα μὴ δοκῇ τὴν μοναυλίαν οἱ κέρδος καὶ ῥᾳστώνην φέρειν*. 'Cakes and ale' was, literally, 'profit and ease' – yet the Shakespearean expression seemed to me to catch the tone of the remark so well that I deliberately jettisoned accuracy for readability. For the reasons I have outlined, in certain small and inessential points, idiom and colour may be allowed to prevail.

To a very large extent, the quality of a version will increase with the skill and labour of the translator. But the most skilled and the most painstaking translator in the world will in the last analysis be frustrated by the sheer impossibility of producing a translation which is at once wholly accurate, utterly readable, and completely intelligible. Readability and accuracy are at odds, and *all* translation is mistranslation. Let me try to justify this doctrine of despair. Here is a sentence from the *Laws*, translated baldly and literally (904 c):

ὅπῃ γὰρ ἂν ἐπιθυμῇ καὶ ὁποῖός τις ὢν τὴν ψυχήν, ταύτῃ σχεδὸν ἑκάστοτε καὶ τοιοῦτος γίγνεται ἅπας ἡμῶν ὡς τὸ πολύ.

For in whatever way he desires, being of whatever kind as to his soul, in this way on nearly every occasion each of us becomes just like that, on the whole.

That is accurate but unreadable; indeed, it is nearly unintelligible. Here is what I printed, after much head-scratching:

You see, the way we react to particular circumstances is almost invariably determined by our desires and our psychological state.

That is readable and intelligible enough; but does it accurately represent Plato's intentions? I suppose him to be saying merely that soul determines desires and desires determine action. If that is right, I could have purchased even greater precision at the cost of even greater length and elaboration: '. . . by our desires, which are determined by our psychological state'. I am fairly sure this would convey Plato's meaning; but obviously to print it is to thrust before the unsuspecting reader a very particular interpretation fully defensible only in the light of an equally particular interpretation of the wider context (which I have in fact expounded in detail elsewhere).[3] And it must be confessed that 'react to particular circumstances' is a considerable inflation of 'on every occasion becomes just like that'. Just how much of his own opinions is the translator entitled to put into his version? However diffident he may be, he cannot do as students sometimes do in translation exercises, and simply leave a blank: he is obliged to print *something*, which must, and indeed should, be what *he* thinks the Greek means. To translate is to interpret, and one may interpret wrongly.

You may think I have chosen an extreme, because obscure and controversial, example. True; but take the word 'soul' in it, which would be impossible to translate even if the context were not difficult. To start with, the Greek word only partly overlaps in meaning with the modern – so to use the latter means foisting back on to the ancients our own conceptions. Secondly, few modern men would say that their soul affected their actions in the way this passage seems to: it simply is not a modern way of speaking. I have used an up-to-date and palatable expression: 'psychological state' – but at the probable cost of some falsification. Have I conned the modern reader into thinking he knows what Plato is talking about? R. D. Hicks, lamenting the decline of the practice of translating Aristotle into Latin, put the matter harshly but truly:

> The terse simplicity, not to say baldness, of literal Latin is now discarded for that rendering into a modern vernacular which, whatever its advantages, is always in danger of becoming, and too often is, a mere medley of specious paraphrase and allusive subterfuge.[4]

You can now begin to see why it is so dangerous to be beguiled by the school of thought which holds that the modern reader should be given a total illusion that he is reading modern English. Beware of the translator who tries to write what he thinks the ancient author would have written if he had been writing today. I am prepared to accept this as a proper aim, as I have explained, in small matters where there is a clear gain in readability and only a trivial loss of accuracy (e.g. 'sir' for *xenos*). But the sad truth is that any ancient author said many things which you simply cannot say today, and if he were alive now he would never think of saying them anyway. To take a minor example: *polis*, as every schoolboy used to know, means 'state' or 'city' or 'city-state' or 'country' – yet by common consent all these version are inadequate: a *polis* is a *polis* is a *polis*. A translation should not lift the reader out of the ancient world, but immerse him in it; and the reader must be prepared to think himself imaginatively into that world. Lazy people do not deserve to have the text translated for them, and good translation is a cooperative enterprise of translator and reader.

This is, of course, a counsel of perfection. In practice, 'city' or 'state' as an equivalent of *polis* is not too rough to be acceptable, and my version 'psychological state' is perhaps good enough for 'of whatever kind as to his soul'. When translation is unavoidably imprecise, one simply has to use one's judgement.

But translation is not always unavoidably imprecise, and certain kinds of detail it is vital to get right. The *Laws* covers an immense variety of topics, and appeals to lawyers, sociologists, historians, philosophers, theologians, and many others, who can only be misled if the translator misunderstands the technicalities in their fields, or fails to maintain a consistency of usage from one passage to another. There are some passages of the *Laws* which are crammed with technical terms not always fully intelligible even to the experts; and some of those that *are* intelligible are rendered wrongly even in standard reference books. Many times I had to suspend translation and go away to do homework on the Greek jargon. Doubtless this is very good for one's Greek and one's soul, but it is immensely time-consuming. At one point I found myself consulting, in a specialized library, a report issued in 1932 by the Department of Scientific and Industrial Research on the weathering of building stones – and very useful it was.[5] Try to translate out of reach of a good library, and you ask for trouble. And the translator should be quite honest with his readers: if a passage seems irredeemably opaque, let him admit his perfectly understandable ignorance in a footnote, and if possible refer to some useful discussions.

In technicalities, of course, consistency of usage is simple, for words do not change their meaning with the context; the translator has simply to decide on his English version and stick to it. But the matter is more difficult when he is faced with vaguer words like *epitēdeuma* ('practice', 'pursuit') or *aretē* ('virtue', 'excellence') or *psuchē* ('soul', 'life'). Readers notoriously tend to assume here too a one-for-one equivalence. But to render the same word by the same word all the time is to put the ancient author in a straitjacket: it denies him the freedom to use a word in different senses and with different nuances. On the other hand to vary the translation of a term too much can conceal part of the ancient framework of ideas: it is *revealing* to see the same Greek word being used in two instances where we would be inclined to use different ones. There is no way out of this dilemma except by using transliteration for key terms; but transliterations need explanation – which can often be conveyed by a well-chosen translation. If, as I have argued, to translate is to interpret, then translation is to some extent its own commentary. My policy was to maintain consistency of usage wherever I could, but to abandon it for good reason. However, I found it impossible to formulate any general notion of 'good reason', and it seemed best to treat each case separately on its merits.

To return to those cakes and ale: in using Shakespeare I have the support of Benjamin Jowett, who in his essay on translation wrote:

> Equivalents may occasionally be drawn from Shakespere, who is the common property of us all; but they must be used sparingly.[6]

This essay is still one of the best short accounts of the trials and tribulations of a translator, and much of its advice is very sound. A sentence in the opening paragraph expresses my own feelings exactly:

> Experience has made [me] feel that a translation, like a picture, is dependent for its effect on very minute touches; and that it is a work of infinite pains, to be returned to in many moods and viewed in different lights.

There cannot be many sentences in my first draft that survived wholly unaltered into the final version. This first draft took two and a half years, and was sent round to a team of readers who winkled out many infelicities; further revision took up another twelve months, and the last thing I did before the final version went to the printer was to try to put myself in the position of a user, and to read it through simply as English, without reference to the Greek. It was humiliating to find that even then a lot of unnatural English had to be recast (with due regard to the Greek) in a more idiomatic form. Even in the proofs many 'minute touches' were added. The whole process made me very sensitive to the way things are said in English: many a time I would hear in casual conversation, perhaps at a party, some word or expression and almost jump with excitement: '*That's* how one says it! Now I can catch that slippery nuance that eluded me last week.' And sometimes, for no apparent reason, days or weeks after tackling a passage, a good word or phrase would force itself to the surface of my mind, and I would scurry back to the manuscript to make yet another alteration.

For five years I lived the *Laws*; but it is the only way: the translator must be *pickled* in what he translates. Jowett put it more grandly than I can; let him have the last, and Platonic, word:

> [The translator] . . . must ever be casting his eyes upwards from the copy to the original, and down again from the original to the copy (*Rep*. vi. 501A) . . . [H]e . . . may be excused for thinking it a kind of glory to have lived so many years in the companionship of one of the greatest of human intelligences, and in some degree, more perhaps than others, to have had the privilege of understanding him.[7]

FOR HORACE AND PROPERTIUS

W. G. Shepherd

I remember clearly my first meeting, in 1980, with Betty Radice. She had before her a typescript containing my translations into English poetry of twenty-seven of Horace's odes, which I had submitted to Penguin Books with the suggestion that I should translate all the odes and they, of course, publish the resultant book. Betty expressed approval of my MS, then gave me a very direct look and said, 'One thing I do need to know – how good a Latinist are you?'

Conscience and an eye for consequences prevented me from answering, 'Oh, first class, first class.' Other considerations ruled out the truth – A-level Latin in 1952; complete disconnection from the language for twenty-two years; belated discovery of ancient Roman poetry in 1975; intermittent absorption in Horace's odes since then. I replied, 'Um, I think that must be apparent from the translations you've seen.' In about three civilized, painless moves, Betty acquired a clear view of the position, diagnosed that I needed the help of a classicist to prevent me from making a fool of myself (or Horace) on the academic side of the project, and proposed that she should be that person. I was extremely pleased – but it was only as we proceeded that I learned the true extent of my good fortune.

In addition to writing as the introduction to *The Complete Odes and Epodes* an admirable essay on Horace, Betty guided me expertly and conscientiously through the linguistic and textual bases of my work: repeatedly her scholarship cleaned my lenses so that I saw with enhanced clarity a line, a stanza or even a whole poem. Having prepared herself by collating texts and reading or re-reading critical works (some of which she then recommended to me), she went through my typescript of all the poems at two separate stages in its evolution: I have pages bearing as many as a dozen annotations, varying from '!' to learned, pithy comments. However, Betty insisted that hers was a critical, not a creative mind and pointedly refrained from contributing to the making of the English poems ('That's *your* job,' she would say) – except sometimes in a negative way, as when she took strong exception to my use (‘*three times*, Bill . . .’) of the word ‘overly’. (I changed it – three times.)

Our collaboration took the form of correspondence and of occasional meetings at Betty’s home in Highgate. The latter, which I came to think of as tutorials, were extraordinary and memorable events. The work would proceed intensively and at what was for me a headlong pace, but there were many digressions: Betty would talk, with obvious love, of her husband and the other members of her family; she gave me the benefit of her trenchant views on a hundred and one literary and miscellaneous topics; she brought in splendid anecdotes – as that of the eastern European diplomat who began an after-dinner speech with, ‘Ladies and gentlemen, I will not keep you long. I know your English saying: early to bed and – up with the cock!’ Having laughed heartily, Betty remarked, with her usual critical acumen, ‘It’s so *nearly* plausible, isn’t it?’

These divagations were not monologues: I was required to give an account of myself as well. While I did so, Betty was closely attentive, and her comments pointed: ‘I should think you’re a person to whom it’s important to be liked,’ she once put in. This bluntness stopped me in my tracks, but it sprang so plainly from kind interest, with no ulterior edge, that it enabled me, speaking for once with equal simplicity, to answer, ‘I am, yes.’

Although so much has been written and said about Horace’s lyric poetry, I have the impression that certain aspects have not yet been sufficiently explored. First, there is the occasional but very expressive use, in a strikingly *modern* way, of metaphor. Perhaps the most remarkable example is in *Odes* III.10, where the poet says to the girl who resists his love:

> Resign to Venus your graceless pride
> lest the rope fall back from the whirling wheel.

In the course of a covering letter to one of my typescripts, I wrote to Betty Radice that the second line is marvellous: no specific machine is indicated – yet the meaning (emotional and intellectual) is very specific indeed, and forcefully conveyed. We grasp the idea of a simple pulley without needing to visualize – this is *shorthand* metaphor. (I illustrated my observation with a diagram of a reeling man who clutched a broken rope falling back from a wheel and allowing a weight marked ‘love’ to plunge to earth: Betty replied that Horace’s line was indeed very clear, and that my picture reminded her ‘irresistibly of an “ongoing situation” in *Private Eye*’.)

The shorthand quality I have mentioned is in at least one instance so cryptic as to remain immanent – one could well overlook (were it not for Gordon Williams's perceptiveness) the cooking metaphors which my translation stresses in *Odes* I.13: speaking to Lydia of his jealousy of his rival Telephus, the poet says in the first stanza, 'my simmering liver swells with crotchety bile'; in the second he mentions his 'inward maceration above slow fires'; in the third, confronted with bruises and love-bites, he announces tersely, 'I am charred'.

But my favourite example of Horace's impacted metaphor occurs in *Odes* II.7: speaking frankly and humorously of his cowardice at the battle of Philippi in 42 BC, where he fought for Brutus against Octavian (later the emperor Augustus, and Horace's friend), the poet says to his 'friend and oldest comrade' Pompeius:

> Luckily Mercury
> bore me away, in my fright, in a cloud:
> but the undertow sucked you back
> to the weltering straits of war.

The wave of the last two lines has broken before we know of its existence. The images of 'the undertow' and 'the weltering straits' are so strongly expressive that this does not matter: events *had* gathered and crashed in one catastrophe (Philippi), more *would* gather and crash in the 'weltering' civil war.

The last quotation illustrates also another Horatian quality I have found inadequately investigated, namely the mercurial shift of mood and viewpoint. The fine sombre metaphor of the broken wave succeeds without intermission or modulation upon a humorous, even playful, line and a half in which Horace ranks himself ironically with epic heroes who are rescued in Homer from tight corners by the intervention of a deity.

Usually, however, these dexterous swerves or shifts move in the opposite direction – from seriousness, even high seriousness, into humour. *Odes* II.2 ends by declaiming that Virtue

> teaches the people
> to call things by their
>
> right names, granting power, a secure crown
> and especial laurels only to the man who can gaze
> on mountains of treasure without glancing
> over his shoulder.

The last five words interrupt, cut short, yet somehow round off the earnest preaching by zooming in like a camera lens so that Horace's unjudging eye can share with us not so much a man tempted as a man ascertaining whether it is safe to allow himself to be tempted – a bright touch of a kind of humour which is surely perennial.

A Horatian scholar might object that I am merely repeating a commonplace of criticism: that Horace's work contains many abrupt changes of mood, to such an extent that his character or *persona* is very elusive. But I have not seen it remarked how very far Horace develops this mannerism, so that the effect is positively startling. *Odes* III.14 consists of seven stanzas. In the first three, Horace tells us that he looks forward eagerly to Augustus' victorious return (in 32 BC) from his Spanish campaign, and to the public ceremony of welcome. There is absolutely no reason to doubt Horace's sincerity, that is to say his patriotism and his personal liking for Augustus – and in the last four stanzas he arranges his own private celebration of the event: he sends for perfume, wine and a girl –

> Bid witty Neaera make haste
> to put up her hair and scent it with myrrh.

A practical difficulty occurs to him and he adds:

> If that evil, grumbling janitor causes
> delay, ignore him.

The subject of the janitor rankles, and Horace spends a stanza upon his resentment of the man, concluding:

> I would not have borne this in my fiery youth, when
> Plancus was consul.

And here the poem ends – and I am baffled. I cannot believe either that Horace intended some parody of a 'laureate' poem (why should he?), or that he was unaware of or indifferent to the shotgun marriage of genres he had effected.

Even more remarkable is the case of *Odes* III.2. This is one of a group known as the 'Roman' (*i.e.* patriotic, moralizing, militaristic) odes, and includes the famous line:

> It is sweet and proper to die for one's country

(*dulce et decorum est pro patria mori*) – 'the old lie', Wilfrid Owen called it, but we have no grounds for impugning *Horace's* honesty.

Yet in the last two (of eight) stanzas Horace finds time to hope that no blasphemer shall

> lie beneath
> the same timbers or sail the same dinghy
>
> as me – slighted, the Ancient of Days is apt
> to confuse the innocent with the guilty . . .

My problem is not that these lines are intellectually incompatible with the sentiment that 'It is sweet and proper to die for one's country' (they are not): it is that in a hymn to manhood, indeed to Manhood, grim enough to satisfy Shakespeare's Volumnia and her son Coriolanus, Horace is indulging in a kind of mock-religious levity – or else displaying a degreee of simplicity it is more than hard to reconcile with his urbane intelligence. Who will explicate this riddle? Does it matter? Yes, it does, because it prejudices perceptibly not Horace's personal credibility, but the artistic integrity of his poem.

My final comment is simpler. We hear much of the urbanity, charm and gentleness of Horace (quite rightly), but very little of the harshness, which surfaces rarely but memorably. There is a moral and military absolutism in the 'Roman' odes at the beginning of Book III, but the qualities I am concerned with blossom fully only in Book IV, and even there only in a few passages.

At the military level we have *Odes* IV.14: in celebrating his victory over an Alpine tribe, Horace writes that Augustus' stepson Tiberius (later emperor) was

> a fine sight in martial combat
> for the chaos he made in havocking
> those resolved to die unconquered . . .

Is that not ungenerous? Crassly so? A corresponding coarseness invades Horace's convivial mode in IV.12: the familiar recommendation of wine acquires a vehement bitterness in the final stanza:

> Set aside delay and thought of gain
> and mindful of darkness burning mix
> brief sottishness with wisdom while you may:
> it is sweet to play the clown upon occasion.

What a sombre, desperate pleasure this denotes! And Horace the charming, insouciant lover writes in IV.13, addressed to an ex-mistress he calls Lycë, that Cinara, his dearest (imaginary?) love died young,

> but Lycë shall be long
>
> preserved, an agèd crow,
> that burning young men may study
> (not without much laughter)
> the torch collapsed in ashes.

Spiteful cruelty? Yes, and magnificent imagery. I can imagine nothing more expressive of erotic despair than the fact that, since they too are burning, the young men in this bleak tableau must themselves end as ashes, just like the old crow they mock. What intrigues me is that each time we are confronted by the brutal vein in late Horace we are offered, as I hope the foregoing quotations show, profoundly impressive poetry.

By the time I had brought my translations of all the odes and epodes to the stage where they required only minor adjustments as the result of *n*th thoughts, I was exhausted. This was owing to my method of working, which I felt compelled to take up and then stick to. As soon as Penguin Books offered me a contract, I became engrossed, obsessed with the task, and worked at it intensively day and night. My wife, children, friends and job (I mean that by which I make a living) were all neglected shamelessly. I was involved in an intoxicating alternation of Horatian frustrations and triumphs. I resented time spent sleeping. Then there was the problematical relationship with the whisky bottle: 'enough' (a quantity not to be measured, only subjectively felt) stimulated invention, but 'more' blunted judgement. For months I lived a kind of harrowing exaltation, feeling as a matter of plain fact, 'This is what I am *for* . . .'

It was lucky for my health, I think, that two years elapsed before Penguin Books commissioned me to translate all the extant poems of Propertius – and then it took me several resentful months to force myself into the mental overdrive which enabled me to work for Propertius as I had for Horace. I was inestimably heartened in this by the fact that Betty Radice had again undertaken to write the introduction and supply the learning I lack – a task all the more onerous because the textual difficulties in Propertius are less only than those in Catullus. We worked together exactly as we had done for Horace.

FOR HORACE AND PROPERTIUS

My pleasure at my first 'tutorial' in two years was great. It was a cold winter day and I arrived on the Radices' doorstep wearing one of those pseudo-fur teacosy hats of vaguely Russian provenance: Betty opened the door to me – and broke at once into laughter. Being entirely friendly and straight from the heart, this was very infectious. Having regained her breath, Betty observed that her husband had 'a hat like yours, but yours is much funnier!' It was not for me to embrace Mrs Radice, but I did so mentally, for transmitting still such lively warmth.

Before translating Propertius, it is necessary to overcome Sextus Pound's syndrome. I accept, of course, that *Homage to Sextus Propertius* is sophisticated art, and that Ezra Pound is a better poet than I am – more specifically, the *Homage* includes passages of English poetry which are quite beyond my scope. However, the fact remains that the work, a collage of short or shortish extracts, some of them fairly closely translated, others loosely paraphrased, represents only a few of the expository and stylistic aspects of Propertius. Moreover, Pound changes the tone, the human flavour, of some of the most striking passages he does tackle: for example, in his rendering of II.34(a) he heightens and dramatizes the irony, allowing his own creative exuberance to override Propertius' impeccable 'sincerity'. The poet who speaks in the *Homage* is not so much Propertius as one of Pound's personae, whom I have dubbed Sextus Pound. It is as though the *Homage* had been written by Hugh Selwyn Mauberley – or even as though Pound (Ezra) had invented Propertius (as Peter Russell has invented Quintilius). A literary editor wrote to me during my Propertian endeavours that I was undertaking an appalling task 'in the wake of Pound'. He was mistaken: the *Homage* offers us enjoyment (plus a few brilliant insights) and commands our admiration, but for the poet who sets out to empathize strenuously and to represent fairly every extant line that Propertius wrote, it is, frankly, irrelevant.

The salient theme in Propertius is erotic love – in particular of course his love for the woman he calls Cynthia. The opening lines of the first poem in Book I state clearly:

> CYNTHIA was the first
> To capture with her eyes my pitiable self . . .

Propertius sees himself in a passive role, a captive and worthy of pity. However, he relishes his subjection: he loves Cynthia even as he abuses her for unfaithfulness, dissipation or reckless spending. His masochistic glee (blended with masculine complacency) finds its most explicit statement in III.8:

> Be rash, come on, attack my hair,
> And mark my face with your shapely claws,
> And threaten to burn out my eyes with close-held fire,
> And rip my tunic and leave me bare-chested! –
> Indubitable signs of sincere affection:
> No female is so vexed, unless by onerous love.

(Incidentally, III.8 has tacked on to its end four lines addressed to an unnamed rival of Propertius which include the ultimately dire curse:

> May your home be never quit of your mother-in-law
> And your wife's father prove immortal . . .)

But Propertius' subjugation is not a condition he can always view with equanimity: at the end of the road stand the concluding lines spoken to him by the dead Cynthia's ghost in IV.7:

> 'For now, let others possess you: soon I alone
> Shall have you: you shall be with me,
> And I shall grind down bone entwined with bones.'

Surely this statement of intent (to grind his bones to dust in skeletal love-making) is more a gruesome threat of ultimate annihilation than an affectionate pledge of perpetual reunion.

Further indication that Propertius' love was no passion in a mainstream romantic vein is provided by his erotic poems *not* concerned directly or predominantly with Cynthia. To cite just one example, in II.23 Propertius speaks, as a libertine, with genuine warmth (it seems to me), of a prostitute in exotic sandals, preferring her favours to those of what he calls (later in the same poem) ' "virtuous" girls':

> By contrast, she's nice who goes at large, her wrap
> Thrown back, fenced off by no guardians' threat,
> Whose dirty moccasins wear out the Sacred Way,
> Who won't allow hindrance if anyone wants to go with her:
> She never prevaricates or garrulously wheedles
> For what your tight father deplores he gave you:
> Nor says 'I'm frightened, please hurry, get up at once,
> Bad luck, my husband gets back from the farm today . . .'

Contrariwise, one could, needless to say, compile a selection of exalted declarations of loyalty to Cynthia – such as this, in a 'high', myth-fraught style, from II.14:

> Not so did Agamemnon rejoice in his Trojan triumph,
> When the mighty power of Laomedon fell;
> Not so did Ulysses, his wandering drawn to a close,
> Delight when he touched his dear Dulichia's shore;
> Not so Electra, when she beheld Orestes safe,
> Whose supposed bones she had grasped, and sisterly wept;
> Not so did Ariadne perceive her Theseus unharmed,
> When he found his Daedalian path by the leading thread;
> As I have gathered joys this bygone night:
> If another such comes, I shall be exempt from death!

(Note that in two of his four *exempla* Propertius implies comparison of himself with the heroine rather than the hero of the relevant myth. I read this as reflecting his empathy with Cynthia, the heroine of the 'myth' he is living and writing.)

Propertius, like his elder contemporaries Virgil and Horace, was a protégé of Maecenas. As well as being a patron of the arts, Maecenas, though he never accepted any official position, was Augustus' right hand in civil matters. Inevitably, therefore, pressure was exerted on these poets to write patriotic verse celebrating Rome (legendary, past and present), its current regime and above all its first emperor, Augustus. Virgil and Horace complied, the former with his *Aeneid*, the latter with some of his odes (most notably the *Centennial Hymn*). With the dubious exception of one elegy (IV.6), Propertius refused to oblige, and did so quite explicitly in some of his poems, with irony, wit and even scorn. Since Propertius chose, bravely or foolishly, to publish these pieces, we must see him as, among other things, a political writer, a 'dissident' – it was no light matter publicly to tease and disobey Augustus. In his admirable book *Propertius*, J. P. Sullivan has drawn our attention to, and explored in some detail, the political aspect, the 'refusals', of Propertius. I propose to offer here two plausible *reasons* for refusal, and the effect on what I take to be Propertius' greatest poem.

In I.22 (the last poem of his first book) Propertius asks:

> Do you know our fatherland's Perusian graves,
> The Italian massacre in a callous time,
> When civil dissension hounded the Romans on?

This refers to the fact that during the civil wars following the assassination of Julius Caesar, Octavian (later the emperor Augustus) bloodily subdued the town of Perusia (the modern Perugia) in 41 BC in order to defeat Mark Antony's brother Lucius Antonius. Propertius continues:

> (Hence grief for me especially, Tuscan dust, for you
> Have allowed my kinsman's limbs to be flung out,
> You cover with no earth his pitiful bones.)

Who was this kinsman, whose unburied state would condemn his shade to wander in limbo, debarred from the underworld? Conceivably, he was Propertius' father, for in IV.1 the seer Horos says to Propertius:

> Though not of an age for such gathering, you gathered
> Your father's bones, and were compelled to a straitened home:
> For many bullocks had turned your fields, but the pitiless
> Measuring-rod took off your wealth of ploughland.

In the second couplet Horos refers (presumably) to the widespread confiscation of land for the resettlement of the soldiers of Octavian and Mark Antony after their defeat of Brutus and Cassius at Philippi in 42 BC. Thus, whether or not the 'kinsman' of I.22 was his father, it is clear that Propertius, with the impressionable sensitivity of a child some six years old (he was born about 48 BC), may well have formed a hearty and radical aversion to the man who was to become his emperor.

Then there was the nature of Propertius' love for Cynthia, and of Cynthia herself. The duty of a responsible Roman citizen (male) was to marry and beget more Roman citizens. If in parallel he resorted to prostitutes or slaves (male or female), this was no great scandal. But Propertius was a bachelor and Cynthia had the temerity, the effrontery, to ignore the code and be her own woman, not only sexually adept and beautiful, but intelligent, strong-willed and independent. It must have been sad for right-thinking citizens to see Propertius in the toils of such a termagant prodigy, wasting so much valuable time and energy on her – but what when he actually taunted the emperor with this 'love'? For in III.4 Propertius encourages Augustus to make glorious war against India and Parthia, and prays that he may live to see his emperor's triumphant return,

> And leant on the breast of my precious girl I'll undertake
> To read the names of captured towns . . .

Hardly the participation Augustus might reasonably hope for from a Roman patriot!

In his masterpiece, III.5, Propertius states his position with unflawed clarity – the opening couplet requires no gloss whatever:

> The god of peace is Love, we lovers venerate peace:
> Hard battles with my mistress suffice for me.

He continues:

> My heart is not consumed for hateful gold,

and this is a fair gibe: glorious conquest was indeed not unconnected with the desire for riches (i.e. loot). The falsity of the distinctions of status created by such conquest is pithily exploded:

> You shall carry no riches to Acheron's waters:
> Naked, fool, you'll be borne on hell's ferry.
> Victor and victim shades are mingled as equals . . .

Even

> When heavy age has interrupted Venus,
> And age's white has brindled my black hair,

Propertius will not attend to his civic or patriotic duties: he will instead 'study nature's ways'. His ensuing list of the questions that will occupy his mind, with its grave tone, lively curiosity and boundless scope, reminds me somewhat of Sir Thomas Browne. The list concludes:

> If underground are tortured Giants; gods' laws;
> If Tisiphone's head is maddened with black snakes;
> Alcmaeon's Furies, Phineus' hunger,
> The wheel, the rock, the thirst amid the waters;
> If Cerberus guards with triple jaws the pit
> Of hell; nine acres too strait for Tityus:
> Or fictions have come down to hapless folk,
> And no alarms can be beyond the pyre.

Now there only remains the electric jolt of the last couplet:

> Such going out is what is left to me. You
> Who welcome war, bring Crassus' standards home.

Propertius' obscurity, being mainly allusive, is only one level deep, and can be elucidated by brief notes. During Augustus' reign Parthia was the most hated and feared of all Rome's enemies. In 53 BC the army of Marcus Licinius Crassus had been totally defeated, and Crassus and his son killed, by the Parthians at Carrhae in Mesopotamia. Shamefully (from the patriotic viewpoint) the Roman survivors had settled among their captors. The disgrace rankled profoundly in the Roman military mind for many years. Hence the last line of III.5 must have read like treason to Propertius' orthodox contemporaries, including the emperor himself: its curt, dismissive force could hardly be surpassed.

Absolutely nothing is known about Propertius' life after the publication (about 16 BC) of his fourth book, which contains a substantial crop of further 'refusals'. I wonder – though this is baseless speculation – if some busybody, hoping to ingratiate himself with Augustus, had Propertius murdered?

Betty Radice and I read the final proofs of *Propertius: The Poems* in January 1985. A month later her son William told me of her death. The extent of my grief took me by surprise. My consolation is that we did our very best for Horace and Propertius. I say 'for' deliberately: our plan was from the first to represent the work of both writers as accurately as we possibly could by genuine poems in English. It occurs to me now that I and Betty Radice collaborated rather like an athlete and his trainer.

FALSE FRIENDS AND STRANGE METRES

Brian Stone

❦ A translator of poetry who was happily briefed by E. V. Rieu, and after him by Betty Radice, to translate medieval English poetry into modern English, using the original metres as far as possible, must contribute to a discussion of translation by focusing on two aspects rather than on translation alone. Both parts of the brief involve considerations peculiar to the task: on the language side, the 'translation' is into modern English from a source language which is already recognizably English – and that it is, however early or remotely regional the form of the language in the particular original; and the prosodical practice prescribed involves acceptable resurrection of a number of poetic forms which are largely dead to the uninstructed modern reader.

If the well-known accusation, '*traduttore traditore*' (the translator is a betrayer), is applied to both the linguistic and prosodical factors mentioned, it may take two specialized forms. On language, the argument that 'true' translation can never be achieved is augmented by the argument that it is unnecessary, especially if a student readership is envisaged, to translate medieval English into modern English. And with regard to prosody, it is argued that it is bad taste, necessarily involving the use of archaisms of language and poetic practice, to bring back dead poetic forms when the language that sustained them has changed.

Granted that it is always better to read an original poem rather than its translation, both the above arguments seem to me insufficiently to take into account the understanding that any reading of a poem is an act of interpretation in which the words and lines on the page make a particular impact peculiar to the mind which registers them. In such an act, the re-forming of the poem in time and place, with all that that implies of historical, linguistic, social and personal factors, is 'normal'. It is impossible to respond to *Sir Gawain and the Green Knight* as those in the circle of the original poet did; and even they no doubt responded differently from each other, just as critical interpreters of today respond, each in his or her own way, to a new poem.

George Steiner has written, 'No two human beings share an identical associative context',[1] though of course interpreters of the same period are likely to share more elements of approach to a poem, whether translated or not, than interpreters of different periods. And within the same period, readers drawn from the same group, such as a particular student year whose members have been taught the same ideas and techniques in responding to poetry, would share an even wider, though still not identical, associative context. A translator of medieval English poetry into modern English, therefore, must attract readers as a creative critic who aims to establish a personal interpretation by means of a complex act of imitation based upon knowledge of the original and using his own 'associative context'.

The pain of such a process lies in the effort to produce a verse text which may be seen and felt to stand as poetry in its own right, and is not perceived merely as versified translation. Above all, since the different kinds of medieval poetry are the product of diverse rhetorics, each owing much to history, each located at a particular stage of development, and all serving a still predominantly oral tradition, the translator's work must be *heard* as poetry. Openness of texture, not the impacted syntax and imagery, and the lack of flow, of much modern poetry, must be striven for. The lines must attract reciting skills, even the semi-chanting skills which seem to have been used in early times to perform epic and other kinds of narrative poetry.

To complete what is offered as a guarded apology for the kind of verse translation suggested, it is necessary to mention the overwhelming reason for its existence – the pragmatic cultural argument that translators serve society at large by bringing the poetry originally written in strange or unknown languages within the reach of non-specialist readers.

In written Middle English, during the whole of the thirteenth and fourteenth centuries there were marked regional differences. Uniformity of spelling did not exist anywhere. The process of shedding inflexions varied in speed; as late as the end of the period, Chaucer could freely decide whether to use them or not, according to the syllabic demands of his chosen metre. Then, the farther north and west the scribal origin of the text, the greater the number of words which are now obsolete. But in all forms of English there were many words, perhaps a majority, which still exist in our language:

many had the same meanings as they possess now, but others, the tricky ones for a translator, had different meanings from their modern ones. In grammar, the basic structures were largely the same as they are now, and the catches are the idiomatic and syntactical constructions which have since either changed or disappeared. One hardship for the modern translator is the impossibility, in modern English, of distinguishing between the familiar and the formal modes of address simply by using respectively the singular and plural second person pronouns; that is constant practice in establishing register in medieval poetry.

So two opposite predicaments of the translator are to find that the odd line of medieval poetry may stand without alteration, and that the entire structure of the original must be collapsed and the parts translated and re-assembled. Often these predicaments come in quick succession, so that the problem is to make harmonious wholeness of the resulting translation. Bearing on all these considerations is the fact that nearly all texts of medieval English poetry have been skilfully edited more than once, so that the translator has variant interpretations to ponder, as well as the original text or facsimile.

Of the characteristics mentioned so far, the one which requires that almost every word must be carefully thought about before being translated is what Steiner calls the 'false friend' – the word which still exists in modern English, but may have one or more other meanings in the medieval. Take for instance the common word 'free'. I have seen it asserted that Middle English *fre* does not mean modern 'free'; and though that may be correct in most cases, the word is sometimes used in medieval poetry in exactly the modern sense of 'at liberty' and 'unrestricted'. See, for example, *Pearl*, line 299, where the reading 'noble', which some recommend, seems to me absurd:

The thrydde, to passe thys water fre –

The modern meaning of 'free' is in fact the first given in *A Chaucer Glossary*.[2] But it is followed by a group of meanings which relate to a society formally stratified in a way in which our society is not: *fre* means 'of free (independent) condition', 'not a bondman'. Linked to the condition of freedom are meanings which can attach only to people of birth or rank: 'noble', 'gracious', 'magnanimous' and even 'generous'. *Fre* in this sense is sometimes used as a noun, to indicate a woman of rank, as in *Sir Gawain and the Green Knight*, line 1549:

Thus hym frayned that fre and fondet hym ofte.

Nevertheless, the OED indicates that the primary meaning of 'free', of which the modern sense is a development, is

> 'dear'; the Germanic and Celtic sense comes of its having been applied as the distinctive epithet of those members of the household who were connected by ties of kindred with the head, as opposed to the slaves.

Although many common words are not limited in meaning to their primary sense, it does so happen that all the medieval meanings of the word which then applied to people of rank are still current, sometimes with slight variation. The word 'free' is a nice example of the tendency of language to be based on binary structures, in this case the polarity between the noble, which carries the suggestion of particular virtues, and the base. But, as I have argued, it is sometimes possible to translate *fre* as 'free', and I can think of only one modern meaning of the word which has no equivalent in medieval English: 'gratis'. For that meaning Chaucer has 'free of dispense'. From all this, then, it seems that the translator must judge from the context of *fre* in the poem which meaning is appropriate.

A similar problem is presented in translating such an important word of multiple meaning as 'sense', which is given thirty applications in the OED, many of them deriving ultimately from medieval theology.[3] But one of its common modern meanings, that relating to the five senses, is not found in medieval English. There, those outward bodily functions are 'wits', as still occasionally in Shakespeare. So Tom o'Bedlam's compassionate 'Bless thy five wits!' to Lear in the second storm scene in Act III, if paraphrased, would run, 'God bless your five senses!'

Equivalents exact or rough can be found for most medieval words, but medieval technical language, such as that related to warfare, can rarely be matched satisfactorily by modern words. A dictum of Steiner's may be followed in such matters: 'The translator enriches his tongue by allowing the source language to penetrate and modify it.'[4] For instance, in the work I am engaged on at present, the alliterative *Morte Arthure*, which is full of terms describing items of weaponry, I am pondering introducing the word 'fewter' from the original into my translation, with an explanatory note. The fewter is the socket fixed to the saddle of a knight which is not simply a 'rest', but supports the spear-butt in the charge and takes the brunt of impact; 'socket' may be regarded as a technically correct translation. But the modern word 'socket' indicates the hollow space into which a butt or shaft fits without, it seems to me, allowing for the violent buffer function of the medieval item of knightly equipment; this is still how we think of 'socket' today:

> O sir, the good die first,
> And they whose hearts are dry as summer dust
> Burn to the socket.
> (Wordsworth: *The Excursion*, I, 500–502)

Such annotated importations into modern English ought to occur only when they exceed in accuracy and vividness of effect any modern translation that can be devised. One alternative to Steiner's enrichment of this kind is to incorporate the annotation or interpretation in the translation, if this can be done without straining the rhythm or the metre. It was on this principle that I described the Green Knight's *ax*, which is amplified to a *spetos sparthe* in the next line, as a 'hideous helmet-smasher'.[5] Modern English has just the one word 'battle-axe' to describe such a weapon – choppers are for woodmen, not knights or giants, and I thought that my amplification, which was suggested by a conjectured etymology for another kind of battle-axe, the halberd, was justified by its effect of intensification centred on precise function: in descriptions of medieval battles, helmets are always being smashed by battle-axes.

A more serious translation problem than that offered by technical terms is presented by the debasement of strong words over the centuries. The translator is as afflicted as any other writer by the difficulty of using with their earlier force such words as 'terrible', 'ghastly' and 'awful' in one field, and 'lovely' and 'gay' in another. Who can now say with Yeats, 'Hamlet and Lear are gay'? A friendly reader who advised me over *Medieval English Verse* opined that I simply could not use 'lovely' for *lufsum* or other medieval synonyms for 'beautiful'. In my use of words like 'terrible' and 'lovely', I have hoped that their so figuring within their earlier cultural context might help to restore some of their original force. It would be a pity if we were ever to lose the effect of

> A terrible childbed hast thou had, my dear.
> *Pericles*, III, i, 56

Where modern equivalents of old strong epithets are wanting, the translator may find that judicious use of vivid verbs, which seem not to have suffered the same kind of debasement, will help him through.

I turn to metrical questions. As a translator who habitually uses the original metres, I have developed pragmatically through years of practice what I take to be a heretical view. Broadly stated, this is that Romance poetic prosody, with its predominantly iambic and occasionally dactylic measures and its integumental rhyme schemes, is not as harmoniously attuned to the way the English language works as accentual metre, which in Old as well as Middle English is alliterative as well as accentual. I judge that my work on alliterative poetry has produced verse translations more accurate, of more natural word order, and more memorable as poetry (the latter being the acid test, I suppose) than any of my ventures into the translation of accentual-syllabic poetry, where success, though possibly attainable, has been rarer and more hardly won. When flowing iambic or dactylic lines figuring in a tight and demanding lyric stanza exactly mould the poetic idea, something is achieved which is generally denied to unlimited alliterative verse. Hence the Gawain-poet's brisk borrowing from Romance prosody to create the bob-and-wheel terminal shaping to his stanza-paragraph. And he was not alone among medieval alliterative poets in doing something of the kind.

When I aired my view about Romance prosody and English poetry among colleagues – probably in stronger and more conversational terms than I use here – one of them was quick to counter with, 'Nuns fret not at their convent's narrow room,' the first line of the sonnet in which Wordsworth expresses himself content

> . . . to be bound
> Within the Sonnet's scanty plot of ground.

There can be little disputing that; in all the arts, tight formal requirements of organic beauty have proved the best moulds for such qualities as intensity of expression, economy, and purity and power of focus. But the genius of medieval poetry in my view lies in narrative rather than lyric. I find the Harley Lyrics, for example, comparatively lacking in interest and subtlety, though they are strong in musical *afflatus*. The trouble with their poets is that in using Romance metres, they retained their English addiction to alliteration. The result is concentration on excessive decoration with formulaic alliterative phrases and necessarily restricted rhyme patterns, to the virtual exclusion of consecutive original sense.

Indirect support for my view exists in the liberties historically taken with strict Romance prosody by the English poets, beginning, of course, with Chaucer, our greatest Frenchifier in this respect, who apologized for varying the accent and number of syllables, and gave new flexibility to both the dominant iambic rhythm and the placing of the caesura in his four- and five-stressed lines. In his innovations he left behind English contemporaries such as the orthodox Gower and, as well as giving a permanent place in English to the rhymed pentameter couplet, created a new Romance stanza which we know as 'rhyme royal', the seven-line stanza of iambic pentameter rhyming ababbcc. To translate into that metre, as I found when working on *The Parliament of Fowls*, and as translators of *Troilus and Criseyde* must find, is demanding.

It is worth pausing to consider one consequence of working to the rhyme scheme of such a metre, even as the original poet, and a single instance will do. *Troilus and Criseyde* is set in Troy, a word which would therefore often occur in the narrative. It is the last word in thirty-one lines, and every time it is rhymed with 'joy', the only rhyming word for it which Chaucer could accept. So 'Troy' figures thirty-one times together with the presence or absence of joy – a considerable limitation of the possibilities of interesting meaning. Moreover, since there is only one word available to rhyme with 'Troy', 'Troy' can appear at the end of a line only when in the a or c position of a stanza which rhymes ababbcc; the b position would require three rhyming words. I believe that such an analysis of the use of any common rhyme sound would produce similar evidence; the effect of rhyme on meaning has not been sufficiently recognized.

As for the tyranny of the iambic rhythm over English poetry, there is a limit to the extent to which the interplay of weak and strong accent, inversion and variable caesura can palliate it. A nice example into which I stumbled when reading poetry on Arthurian subjects is from Tennyson. That musically-eared poet finds it hard in *Idylls of the King* to accommodate the Round Table. Iambic tyranny almost always forces the ugly inversion, 'Table Round'.

That is a startling example, the result of the iambic requirement alone, but attention must be drawn to the perennial consequences to word order of obedience to rules concerning both accentual-syllabic line structure and rhyme. Most English poets of the last five hundred years have recognized inversion as a blemish, except when it is resorted to for rhetorical effect, and have tried to avoid or limit its appearance in their poetry. In the passage from *Cleanness* with which this essay concludes, inversion is rare in the original and virtually absent from my translation.

It is germane to my argument to note the resistance, which developed from late pre-Romance times in English-speaking and indeed other Germanic lands, to what I have called the iambic tyranny. It begins with the heritage of Anglo-Saxon poetry, with its four-stress alliterative line, in which the number of unstressed syllables before, between and after stressed syllables may vary. This characteristic was enhanced by the even looser requirements followed by the medieval alliterative poets, such as allowing a line to have five stresses, three of them before the caesura, and the alliterative components to occur in different places in the line. The strong stresses of spoken English work well in such a metre, and many of our major poets, including Chaucer and Shakespeare, who have not, however, recorded their practice except by their unorthodox use of iambics, have worked over their whole careers towards the freedom in English afforded by accentual verse. Milton, Coleridge, Hopkins and Auden may be specifically instanced.

Milton's well-known note on 'The Verse' added to *Paradise Lost* in 1668 makes two points. He attacks rhyme, 'the jingling sound of like endings', which he stigmatizes as 'the Invention of a barbarous Age, to set off wretched matter and lame Meeter'. He also defends syllabic verse, 'true musical delight' in poetry consisting, according to him, 'only in apt Numbers, fit quantity of Syllables, and the sense variously drawn out from one Verse [i.e. line] into another'. Milton notes that rhyme had already been abandoned by English tragedians, and that unrhymed syllabic verse is especially suitable for long poems. But in his later work, like Shakespeare, who progressively reduced the number of end-stopped lines and rhymed passages (except for special purposes, such as choruses or masques), Milton developed great freedoms. In *Samson Agonistes*, though the iambic rhythm remains, the intensity of the hero's first lamentation about his lost sight breaks the decasyllabic mould towards the end (lines 80–109, beginning 'O dark, dark, dark, amid the blaze of noon'), and syllabic flexibility is combined with formal rhyme in the closing chorus:

> All is best, though we oft doubt,
> What th'unsearchable dispose
> Of highest wisdom brings about,
> And ever best found in the close.

> Oft he seems to hide his face,
> But unexpectedly returns
> And to his faithful Champion hath in place
> Bore witness gloriously; whence Gaza mourns
> And all that band them to resist
> His uncontroulable intent,
> His servants he with new acquist
> Of true experience from this great event
> With peace and consolation hath dismist,
> And calm of mind all passion spent.

Coleridge, who like his fellow Romantics knew his Milton, formally made the adjustment from iambic syllabic verse to accentual verse in *Christabel*. In his letter to Byron of 22 October 1815 he writes, 'I count by Beats or accents instead of syllables', and in his Preface to the poem of 1816, he notes that the syllables

> may vary from seven to twelve, yet in each line the accents will be found to be only four. Nevertheless, this occasional variation in number of syllables is not introduced wantonly, or for the mere ends of convenience, but in correspondence with some transition in the nature of the imagery or passion.

The loftiness of the latter claim may obscure the underlying truth that the accentual metre Coleridge thus developed made the stressed English language thoroughly at home:

> There is not wind enough to twirl
> The one red leaf, the last of its clan,
> That dances as often as dance it can,
> Hanging so light, and hanging so high,
> On the topmost twig that looks up at the sky.
> (ll. 48–52)

Hopkins's explanations of his 'sprung rhythm', in his letters to Bridges (22 August 1877) and to Dixon (5 October 1878), show him drawing, like Coleridge, on the natural features of English and on early popular forms of its poetry, such as the ballad. The opening of *The Windhover*, for all its original splendour and concentrated imagery, is positively Old English in style and feeling:

> I caught this morning morning's minion, king-
> -dom of daylight's dauphin, dapple-dawn-drawn Falcon, in his riding . . .

Both poets, as the above examples demonstrate, often incorporate alliteration in their accentual verse, thus moving ever nearer to the style of medieval alliterative verse. Hopkins's reasons for writing in 'sprung rhythm' are thus justified to Bridges:

> Because it is the nearest to the rhythm of prose, that is the native and natural rhythm of speech, the least forced, the most rhetorical and emphatic of all possible rhythms, combining, as it seems to me, opposite and, one wd. have thought, incompatible excellences, markedness of rhythm – that is rhythm's self – and naturalness of expression . . .[6]

Some of Hopkins's successors have used accentual metres in lines of from three to seven feet in length, in a manner often redolent of medieval alliterative verse, but the general preference has remained for the four-stress line. Thus the Second Tempter in Eliot's *Murder in the Cathedral*:

> Yes! Men must manoeuvre. Monarchs also,
> Waging war abroad, need fast friends at home.
> Private policy is public profit;
> Dignity still shall be dressed with decorum.

And in the subtle villanelle that Auden puts into the mouth of Miranda in *The Sea and the Mirror*, the two repeated key lines are regular medieval alliterative, thus standing out amid the other un-alliterated four-stress lines, to structure and eventually to seal the poem:

> So, to remember our changing garden, we
> Are linked as children in a circle dancing:
> My dear One is mine as mirrors are lonely,
> And the high green hill sits always by the sea.

I have written this much about accentual alliterative verse in order to indicate its strengths and specifically English domicile; to familiarize readers with it, and modestly to recommend it to poets. I am surprised at the strictures on it contained in P. M. Kean's comments on the changes in English poetry effected during Chaucer's times:

> The alliterative style continued in use until the early sixteenth century, in spite of Chaucer's preference for a less idiosyncratic, more universal kind of language.[7]

It is not clear to me how the kind of language employed in *Piers Plowman* can be lumped together with that employed in *Patience*, as characteristic of 'alliterative style'. While denying that there is anything idiosyncratic about the metre, or about the language of its practitioners (which is Miss Kean's exact point), I accept that the metre has one disadvantage which is comparable to either of the disadvantages of the Romance metres that I have mentioned. This is the obligation to alliterate, mostly by head-rhyme, but also by stressed syllables not in the leading position in the word, as in 'endure' in line 4 of the extract given below. I find this obligation no more limiting than the obligation, in composing in Romance metres, either to submit English speech rhythms to iambic rule, or to find rhyme in a language which is poorer in rhyming possibilities than such Romance-based languages as French. Yet all such formal characteristics possess, besides their limitations, their own beauties.

The head-rhyme requirement has led me as a translator into inexactitude at times, and I have already mentioned one example. That epithet *spetos* (see p. 179) actually means 'cruel', and so the poet is anthropomorphizing the Green Knight's axe. Seeking an 'h' to head-rhyme with 'helmet-smasher', I came up with 'hideous', which is not far off in effect, though of different meaning from 'cruel'. Were I to revise the translation, I should now prefer 'hateful'.

Unlike Romance metres, of which there are a number, medieval alliterative verse is a single metre, and therefore it seems appropriate to conclude with only a single example of the translation of a passage in the narrative mode, one of three modes, the other two being descriptive and homiletic, in which practitioners of fourteenth-century alliterative verse excelled. Here, set out in alternate lines with the original, are lines 397–417 of my translation of *Cleanness*, in which the final rising of the Biblical Flood is described:

> By now the flood was flowing at their feet and still rising,
> *Bi that the flod to her fete flowed and waxed,*
>
> And all saw for certain they must sink in the end.
> *Then uche a segge sey wel that synk hym byhoved;*
>
> Friends clasped in fellowship, ready to fall together,
> *Frendes fellen in fere and fathmed togeder,*
>
> To endure their doleful destiny and die united.
> *To dryy her delful deystyné and dyen alle samen;*
>
> The lover and his lady looked their last farewell,
> *Luf lokes to luf, and his leve takes,*
>
> Ending everything for all time, for ever parting.
> *For to ende alle at ones and for ever twynne.*

When the forty days were finished, no fleshly thing moved.
By forty dayes wern faren, on folde no flesch styryed

For the flood had devoured all with its furious waves,
That the flood nade al freten with feghtande wawes;

Having climbed fifteen cubits above every cliff there was,
For hit clam uche a clyffe cubites fyftene,

Above the highest hill that hung over the world.
Over the hyghest hylle that hurkled on erthe.

There mouldering in the mud in mighty calamity
Thenne mourkne in the mudde most ful nede

Lay all who had heaved breath; effort was vain,
Alle that spyrakle inspranc – no sprawlyng awayled –

Save for the hero under hatches and his odd company,
Save the hathel under hach and his here straunge,

Noah who often named the name of the Lord,
Noe that ofte nevened the name of oure Lorde,

One of eight in the ark, as the high God desired,
Hym aghtsum in that ark, as athel God lyked,

That vessel in which the various survivors stayed dry.
Ther alle ledes in lome lenged druye.

The ark was thrown high on the heaving currents,
The arc hoven was on hyghe with hurlande gotes,

Rolled close to the clouds over countries unknown.
Kest to kythes uncouthe the clowdes ful nere;

It weltered on the wild waters, went where it would,
It waltered on the wylde flod, went as hit lyste,

Drove above the depths, in danger as it seemed . . .
Drof upon the depe dam – in danger it semed . . .[8]

APPROPRIATING PETRONIUS

J. P. Sullivan

❦ The seductiveness of Petronius' *Satyricon* to the translator is perhaps the variety of the challenges the novel offers. Not only does the author use prose and verse in his Menippean narrative, which demand different strategies to confront the original, but the work itself presents a number of critical and literary problems that require at least tentative solutions, if one is to take seriously Ezra Pound's exhortation to any translator: *Make it new*. (These of course are additional to the scholarly problem of reconstructing the plot from the surviving longer and shorter fragments. The *Satyricon* was a lengthy work, and it would seem that part of the extant narrative belongs to Books XIV and XV. Its original length is explained by the fact that many of the episodes – the *Cena Trimalchionis* and the Widow of Ephesus, for instance – are self-contained digressions: that is the point of them.)

Another reason for Petronius' attraction for translators in the twentieth century may lie in the strange, perhaps overly seductive, air of modernity he wears. Although the reasons for the choice of form and principles governing the work are very different, the *Satyricon* is the one classical work which most closely resembles that most popular twentieth-century art form, the novel, particularly in its more recent manifestations in the work of Saul Bellow, John Fowles, and John Barth, who manage to combine realism with a highly self-conscious, or rather self-reflective, literary structure. The Greek romances, even Apuleius, have too much of an unreal, fairy-tale atmosphere to invite such a comparison, and so Petronius remains the narrative classic that strikes the reader as modern in a way these do not. The unmistakable feeling of modernity in the fragmentary story is produced by a number of factors. Firstly, the *Satyricon* is a highly literary text, embodying a critical rather than a reverential attitude to the Greek and Roman classics, such as Homer, Virgil, Horace and Ovid, on whom nevertheless it depends for its artistic effects. Secondly, the tone of the work is one of ironic detachment; there is a sophisticated separation between the author himself and his narrative vehicle, the 'anti-hero' Encolpius. Petronius here anticipates what we think of as a very modern technique, in poetry as well as prose: the use of the persona, a narrator who is in varying degrees distinguishable from the actual writer (a tempting target anyway for deconstructionists).

Finally, the strong vein of realism, even the acutely and humorously observed sexuality of the novel, involving pederasty, impotence, and aggressively phallic females, seem pre-eminently modern. Indeed it is precisely the modern works analogous to the *Satyricon*, such as Joyce's *Ulysses*, that won the literary liberties that rescued Petronius from his earlier Victorian status as a surreptitious classic. Before this century the only serious translation was one entitled *The Satyr of Petronius Arbiter, A Roman Knight. With its Fragments, recov'red at Belgrade. Made English by Mr. Burnaby of the Middle-Temple, and another hand.* This was published in 1694. The flat and literal Bohn translation of Walter K. Kelly (1854), like the later literal Loeb version of Michael Heseltine (1913), left the franker parts of the *Satyricon* in the original Latin. The first complete translation in this century (1902), by 'Sebastian Melmoth', the pen name of Oscar Wilde (although the version is not his) had to appear in Paris; that of W. C. Firebaugh (New York, 1922) was produced in an expensive and limited edition to avoid any problems with the law. And it was the same with *The Complete Works of Gaius Petronius* by Jack Lindsay in 1927. J. M. Mitchell's inappropriately rollicking version in the Broadway series of translations (1922) had to revert to the practice of leaving some sections in Latin to avoid offending its popular audience. In 1953 however Paul Dinnage's lively English version had to make no concessions to propriety, and William Arrowsmith's even livelier American rendering (1959) actually tries to heighten Petronius' controlled prose in dealing with sexual matters.

This feeling of modernity, however, can prove *too* seductive for the translator, making him feel that Petronius is, as it were, 'just one of us', only writing in a different milieu. Consequently the real qualities and originality of the *Satyricon* may go unappreciated, and certain sections of the work then seem vaguely unsatisfying, because they do not measure up to our preconceived notions of Petronius' realism and modernity. The tone may therefore seem uneven and the novel-reader may find himself uncomfortable with the mixture of prose and verse, or with the excessive use of coincidence, or he may find the author's tearing of the veil of verisimilitude by an aside to the reader (*Satyricon*, 132.15) too arbitrary or too precious, since it is not done consistently as in *Tristram Shandy*, *Tom Jones*, or even *The French Lieutenant's Woman*, to take a modern instance.

To dispel such doubts and reproduce the subtler qualities of Petronius' deliberately varied style and highly digressive narrative, the translator should have an understanding of the literary and historical background of the *Satyricon* and a coherent critical view not only of the work in general, but also of each specific episode, which may incorporate aims that transcend the mere progress of the basic narrative. This would allow for, even demand, a variety of stylistic techniques to deal with the differing aims and tones of the various sections. The episode of the Dinner with Trimalchio, for instance, is based on different literary premises and has different purposes from Eumolpus' critique of contemporary historical epic and his exemplary poem on the Civil War (*Satyricon* 118 ff.), and the realistic atmosphere of the action set in the *Graeca urbs*, probably Puteoli, is very different from the more dream-like, even nightmarish, atmosphere of the events at Croton (*Satyricon* 124.2 ff.).

The most important thing for the translator to apprehend is that we are not dealing with a fast-paced, low-life, occasionally sexy adventure story. That is merely the narrative thread on which to hang so many other literary and social concerns.

As for prototypes and models underlying the loose story of travel and adventure in the *Satyricon*, such narratives were well established in Egyptian writings, and the longer Greek romantic novel was flourishing by the late first century AD in the work of Chariton, although most of our surviving examples of the genre date from succeeding centuries. These later romances should not mislead us into believing that all Greek novels were of this type, since an early fragment of a Greek prose narrative curiously reminiscent in tone and incident of the *Satyricon* itself has been published quite recently. In any case the true ancestor of these 'novels' was Homer's *Odyssey*, our earliest *Reiseroman*, and it is therefore not surprising that Petronius parodies the Homeric theme of Poseidon's wrath against Odysseus with the Wrath of Priapus (*gravis ira Priapi*) against Encolpius, the anti-hero of the *Satyricon*. This protagonist is young, well-educated, cowardly and immoral; his sexual ambivalence is a factor around which much of the story revolves. The starting point has been plausibly set in Massilia in Gaul and the conclusion somewhere in Egypt. A blasphemous offence against the ithyphallic but comic god sets the story in motion: this offence, robbing the god's temple or even impersonating the deity in some religious ceremony, results in a plague (a glance at Homer's *Iliad* perhaps) and Encolpius' ignominious exile, the beginning of his louche and desperate adventures with a variety of colourful low-life companions and rivals, Giton, Ascyltos, and Eumolpus. His wanderings take him to southern Italy, to Baiae, Puteoli, and Croton, where he runs foul of various enemies; these are often aggressive, indeed riggish, women such as Quartilla, Tryphaena and Circe. Allusions to Isis perhaps prepare us for a lost ending in Egypt and so it may anticipate the other great Roman novel, Apuleius' *Metamorphoses* or *The Golden Ass*, written over half a century later.

With this basic structure, a parody of epic, the Wrath of an Offended Deity, it is not surprising that much of the humour consists of treating low-life personages and their shady doings with all the careful style and literary allusiveness that were customary for more elevated themes. This comedy of contrast between style and content is nowhere better seen than in the case of Eumolpus, whose lofty moral views are at complete odds with his immoral behaviour.

Many of the episodes involve the narrator personally, generally as victim, but Encolpius can also play the part of the detached observer, providing for us a satiric portrait of the great vulgarian Trimalchio, for example, one of the self-made freedmen so common in first-century Rome. Oddly enough, the comic creation involved in this Dickensian character, for all the sarcastic comments of Encolpius, leaves the reader in the end with a sympathetic impression of Trimalchio. It is the novelist rather than the satirist in Petronius that finally gets the upper hand. We are given Trimalchio in the round, first by Encolpius' description of his physical appearance and environment, then, more dramatically, by Trimalchio's own speeches and general behaviour, culminating in his quarrel with his wife and his long, boastful description of his rise to fortune. The sources Petronius drew upon for this elaborate portrait are many and varied. Plato's *Symposium* and Horace's *Cena Nasidieni* (*Satires*, 2.8) supplied the literary framework and some of the incidents; a keen observation of the contemporary *milieu* supplied most of the matter; and for the portrait of the host Petronius drew on Seneca's philosophical writings. Yet this parodic motive in no way interferes with the characterization. Trimalchio is self-subsistent and the *Cena* again illustrates the Petronian method of blending a realistic subject-matter with a highly literary treatment: the humour of the episode is the same as the humour of the whole work.

A more complex problem for the translator is presented by the lecherous old poet Eumolpus, whose two rhetorical invectives against the moral decay of the age and the arts (*Satyricon* 83.8ff.) contrast comically with his amusing *conte* of his seduction of the boy of Pergamum. At the end of this episode in the picture gallery, Eumolpus recites, apparently impromptu, sixty-five iambic senarii on the fall of Troy. The poem is a free reworking of part of Book II of the *Aeneid*, and its aim is a parody of Senecan tragedy. The problems it presents for the translator are those presented by Eumolpus' long poem (or short epic) on the civil war in Rome – the so-called *Carmen de Bello Civili*, the first piece of Petronius ever to be translated into English. (A version by Sir Richard Fanshawe prefaced his 1655 translation of the *Lusiads* of Camoens.)

These two long verse insertions dispel the misleading impression a mere summary of the plot of the *Satyricon* might give. The picaresque romance is only the occasion for many digressions on literary, philosophical, and social themes, prose and verse parodies, and even self-conscious reflections on the character of the work itself.

For the translator to do justice to these dimensions of the work, he must see it against its historical background. For all its picaresque plot, the *Satyricon* is a highly sophisticated work, which, despite the doubts of some scholars later than Joseph Scaliger, was written for the amusement of Nero's court circle, itself a highly artistic group which included Seneca, Lucan, Silius Italicus, Nerva, and others. Its author was almost certainly the unconventional T. Petronius described by Tacitus as Nero's *arbiter elegantiae* (*Annals* 16.18).

Tacitus' description of Petronius' downfall in AD 66 indicates that there were powerful personal rivalries at work around Nero, and the *Satyricon* proves that, in these power struggles at court, literary competition played a large part. The *Satyricon* contains several scarcely veiled attacks on contemporary Neronian writings in the form of amusing parody and *ad hoc* literary criticism. The critique put in the mouth of Eumolpus (*Satyricon* 118) is clearly directed at Lucan: Eumolpus criticizes the rhetorical taste for unassimilated *sententiae* in poetry and strongly opposes the abandonment of the traditional divine machinery of epic used by Virgil and now replaced by more Stoic modes of the supernatural in the *Pharsalia*. The poem that follows, with its constant allusion to and re-treatment of Lucanian material, is a sort of Virgilization of Lucan's theme, as well as a revisionist version of the history of the war in favour of Caesar as against the Republican side.

Furthermore much of the moralizing put into the mouths of Eumolpus and the equally disreputable Encolpius is comic parody of the subjects, sentiments, and phrasing of Seneca's philosophical works, particularly of that near-contemporary work, written towards the end of Seneca's life, between AD 63 and 65, the *Epistulae Morales ad Lucilium*. The echoes and reminiscences of Seneca found in Petronius must be taken as parody because the contexts in which they occur are uniformly humorous or ironic. For example, in the elaborate and, at least initially, satiric portrait of Trimalchio, he is given an absurd and drunken speech on the common humanity of free men and slaves (*Satyricon* 71.1). This strongly resembles the Stoic doctrine on the subject expounded by Seneca in *Epistulae Morales* 47. Trimalchio is not obviously kind to his slaves elsewhere in the *Cena*, and Encolpius criticizes the confusion caused by Trimalchio's tasteless invitation of his slaves to the table. This therefore constitutes an aesthetic, and Epicurean, criticism of the social consequences of such Stoic themes.

The *Satyricon* therefore, like Seneca's own *Apocolocyntosis*, is a much more topical and, in a way, more *opportunistic* work than was sometimes realized by those who wish to see in it a Neronian equivalent of T. S. Eliot's *Waste Land*. And the nature of the audience may also explain what is perhaps the most striking feature of the *Satyricon*, the combination of low characters, vulgar milieux, and sometimes bizarre sexual incidents, with a terse, artistic narrative Latin, constant literary allusions and parodies, and occasional ornate passages of a more elevated style. The basic humour implicit in this is reinforced by Petronius' literary sophistication. The Homeric parody in the Wrath of Priapus against Encolpius is echoed by a pastiche of Virgil introduced to describe, of all things, Encolpius' limp sexual organ (*Satyricon* 132.11). The artistry is a reflection of the high degree of literary culture during the Neronian period, but the choice of subject-matter, even for humorous treatment, has to be explained by a certain *nostalgie de la boue*, which not infrequently accompanies material and intellectual refinement. The same *nostalgie de la boue* sent Nero the *artifex* wandering in disguise through the lower quarters of Rome like an imperial Dorian Gray (Suetonius, *Nero*, 26).

Obviously a number of factors interacted in suggesting to Petronius the subjects, the treatment and the form of the work. Petronius' critical decision to choose for his vehicle a form of *satura*, which represented the earthy, more Italian strain in Roman literature and provided Quintilian with one of his more justified literary judgements (*satura quidem tota nostra est*), did not mean that there had to be a stern moral purpose underlying his creative work: satire was an art form like any other, not versified sermonizing.

Petronius is not a satirist in any high moral sense: he is an artist developing the potentialities of certain traditional satiric themes. For instance, that impressive comic creation, Trimalchio, generates sympathy and amusement, not disgust – and Petronius has achieved this by undercutting the moral and aesthetic criticisms of Encolpius, who comes off as a rather timorous, impressionable and gauche commentator on the action. The choice of form, however, would suggest certain themes and subjects, and others, such as legacy-hunting, would be suggested by his predecessors in satire.

With these antecedents, Petronius could defend his work on the grounds that such writing represented reality, as opposed to unreal rhetorical exercises, philosophical moralizing, or the mythological poems that Martial and Juvenal despised. Moreover, in contrast to Stoic writers such as Lucan and Seneca, Petronius was an Epicurean and his work is clearly based on Epicurean principles. Unlike Stoic literary theory, Epicurean theory, as we know it from Philodemus and others, did not take literature to be the servant of morality; literature's purpose was pleasure. Petronius' well-known defence of his work (*Satyricon* 132.15) has therefore to be taken seriously: it disposes of attempts to see him as a moralist rather than an artist, and also reveals most clearly the basic intention of the work.

The defence is put in the mouth of Encolpius, the narrator, just after he has been chiding his sexual equipment for having failed him with Circe: the humour of the episode in no way undermines its validity. The defence amounts to this: although some censorious critics will frown on my work since it is not narrowly instructive and moral, yet it is a reaction against our present high-flown style of writing and against old-fashioned puritanism; it has its own literary intentions; its pure Latinity aims to charm you, not instruct you; my subject is human behaviour and the narrative is realistic and humorous, in fact, *honest*; everyone knows the important place sex has in ordinary life, so who can object to harmless and natural sexual enjoyment? Epicurus' doctrines on the importance of sexual pleasure are sufficient philosophical defence.

The poem of course does not embrace all the aspects of the *Satyricon*; the literary allusiveness, for instance, and the topical parody are not mentioned, but it does stress what we know from other sources such as Macrobius (*In Somnium Scipionis*, 1.2.8), that there were large areas of sexual matter in the work, and the basic plot, a comic and sexual *Reiseroman*, is properly represented by its original title, *Satiricon libri*, namely *Books of Satyric Matters*. The poem also brings out that Petronius was an Atticist in style, Epicurean in his philosophy and literary theory, and a realist strongly opposed to the writers of moral tracts and far-fetched declamations.

From this critical view, certain conclusions for the translator naturally follow. The narrative style of the work, which belongs to the *genus tenue*, is an educated, plain, rhythmical Latin; it should therefore be represented by a spare but elegant English with unforced speech rhythms. Similarly, Petronius' careful avoidance, in accordance with Attic principles, of the large Latin vocabulary of obscenity, even when he is dealing with quite bizarre sexual incidents, is lost in certain translations that conceive the work merely as pornography.

But the basic tone modulates at times into ironic or high-flown parody of contemporary writing: for instance, in Encolpius' fake moralizing on the uncertainty of life over Lichas' corpse (*Satyricon* 115.9ff), and perhaps also in the opening chapters, where Encolpius, in a suitably ornate style, delivers himself of an elaborate criticism of contemporary declamation. Here the language of the translation must be suitably shrill and forced, and the translator should use the rhetorical and exclamatory style that he would find appropriate for a translation of Seneca's philosophical works. Too restrained an English might lose the mocking and parodic tone of the original. One may even have to resort to *equivalences* rather than close translation, if the complex surface of the work is not to be reduced to monotony and flatness. The translator must leave the impression of parodying *something*.

The question of parody immediately brings up two difficult problems that face the translator: the *Troiae Halosis* and the *Bellum Civile*, two long poems of 65 and 295 lines respectively, which describe the capture of Troy and the causes and opening events of the Civil War, the first bearing an obvious relation to Seneca's tragedies, and the second to Lucan's *Pharsalia*. A straightforward modern translation of these would misrepresent Petronius' intentions by offering dull, undistinguished poetic versions; the reader is then likely to take them as two unsuccessful poems seriously intended by Petronius. He may take them, at best, as deliberately mediocre, as a way of concretely presenting to us the poverty of Eumolpus' talent. Eumolpus, however, is not the target here, but rather Seneca and his nephew Lucan.

Now clearly there is no well-known and accepted twentieth-century translation of Senecan drama that could be utilized to represent adequately what Petronius is doing. Certainly some sort of artificial language is necessary. If a contemporary solution is desired, one might suggest a parody or imitation of the plays of T. S. Eliot.

My own solution, which was to imitate Anglo-Saxon alliterative poetry somewhat in the manner of Ezra Pound's translation of 'The Seafarer', may not satisfy all readers, but Pound had to be evoked early, because his work presented an acceptable solution to the larger problem of Petronius' imitation and critique of Lucan's *Pharsalia* in the *Bellum Civile*. No modern verse translation of Lucan can play the host to this parasite: there is none, and if there were, this would be far too unreal. A straight translation would be insufferably tedious – the *Bellum Civile* is in itself a dull and, linguistically, not very poetic treatment of Lucan's subject. For Petronius' audience the interest would lie predominantly in catching the interwoven echoes and reminiscences of Lucan and Virgil. Now the one obvious modern poet whose style and technique would be instantly recognizable is Ezra Pound, particularly the Pound of *The Cantos*, the nearest thing the twentieth century has to an epic poem. If the *Bellum Civile* were translated into a pastiche of the *Cantos*, then its function as a literary exercise, with a definite relationship to an original, would be immediately seen, at least by the reader conversant with modern poetry. And fortunately some passages in Petronius' poem which relate to usury, a trite Roman topic, bear striking resemblances to *Canto* XLV ('With usura hath no man a house of good stone ')

The other verse insertions in the work present little difficulty. None of them are particularly ambitious, although they are sometimes amusing and function in their context very adequately as *vers d'occasion fictive*. They present no more problems than would face any translator of a work which involves poetry and elaborate verbal wit. The wide diversity of metres employed in the shorter poems has to be reproduced somehow in English. Naturally any attempt to imitate the actual metres themselves has to be eschewed: the genius of English versification is quite different from that of Latin (as translators who use six-foot stress lines to reproduce the Latin hexameter so frequently forget). The translator has in each case to find an appropriate metre or stanza form – and sometimes *vers libre* may offer the only solution, provided it is not always used, for that would substitute uniformity for Petronian variety and versatility. Reproducing the puns and the many (and frequently risqué) *doubles entendres* requires work, but provided a responsible freedom is exercised, all should yield to time and thought.

One important problem has been left to the last: the colloquial language of the *Cena Trimalchionis*. The problem in these sections is the delicate matter of translating first-century Latin conversation into an acceptable English form. Fortunately one can find contemporary parallels in various modern novels. It may well be that the *populus minutus* talks in the same way all the world over and all through the centuries: about money, about morality, about the degeneracy of the present compared to the past. But there are differences in the idiom (and in the particulars harped upon) that should not be smothered. With the *Cena*, if we use a modern dialect too tied to its particular place and time, the reader might feel that Roman freedmen simply did not talk like this.

My own solution was to adopt a language based upon English vulgar language which would give the impression of a dialect, but not the dialect of any particular modern period or place in England. (An American translator's solution would be roughly similar, *mutatis mutandis*.)

As ever, *traduttore traditore*: to represent the alienness, the elegance, and the economy of Petronius' artistic pastiche of plebeian dialogue means sacrificing the native immediacy, the natural impact, that it would have had even on the sophisticated ears of the Neronian circle. Yet the members of that circle would be as interested in the artistry of the imitation as in its truth to life. Accordingly, to transpose the language freely into convincing modern idiom and strenuously local colloquialisms may result in a subtle injustice to Petronius' refined art, for he is *not* trying to write in the style of the Pompeian *graffiti*. The translator has to decide where the proper compromise is to be made. Freedom and fidelity are mistresses whose claims conflict, yet neither of them can be discarded.

Although this problem, the language of the conversation in the *Cena*, is the hardest that faces the translator of Petronius, it is similar to those that confront the translator of any Latin work in what one may call the 'Italian' tradition, the tradition that uses an artistic version of down-to-earth, ordinary idiom. It is this tradition, perhaps even more than the loftier genres such as epic, that makes one reflect that the classics have to be retranslated almost every generation. And their translatability in each age will be the measure of their vitality and relevance or their moribundity and unimportance.

TRANSLATING GREEK TRAGEDY

Philip Vellacott

❦ Betty Radice, like the founder of the Penguin Classics whom she so worthily followed, believed in translation as a necessary and honourable province in the world of literature. She was herself a gifted translator; and in the help she gave, as General Editor, to other translators, her combination of spontaneous friendship and firm guidance was invaluable. I welcome the opportunity to take part in this tribute to her memorable personality, and to her achievement in a wide-ranging contribution to English literary life.

Translation is an activity that covers a broad spectrum. A friend who recently returned from a holiday spent driving across France told me that the curt warning offered to English motorists, 'No road markings', becomes in French, 'Absence de significations horizontales'. This stirred my curiosity to turn from the ridiculous to the sublime and speculate about what could happen, on the stage of a French theatre, to some of Shakespeare's monosyllabic hammerings. Yet Shakespeare has long been a constant in the French theatre repertoire; which suggests that in a poetic drama the poetic and the dramatic elements are not separable, that each offers a flavour of the other; so that when in a translation the poetry vanishes – as often it must – action for a while supplies the loss. The next question is: what happens in a language even remoter from English, such as Russian? Tolstoy's gentlemanly soldiers in *War and Peace* are familar with Shakespeare as a normal part of their theatre diet; so are the modern musicians and artists who move and talk vividly in Shostakovich's memoirs, *Testimony*. Clearly, it is possible for great drama to speak to audiences and readers with a popular and passionate voice that surmounts language barriers, dwarfs cultural obstacles, and forgets the gulf of centuries.

This was the thought that moved me when, a year or two before the Second World War, I made my first translation of a Greek play, Euripides' *Andromache*, for a class of students. I found plenty of incidental interest in the various linguistic and textual puzzles that presented themselves in that play; but I recall also the satisfaction of knowing that here, written on paper in comprehensible English, was something that could perhaps function as a complete and organic work of art, with power to hold an audience, and reflecting, even if dimly, the unlimited potential created by the poet when he conceived and executed his dramatic design. In fact, an excellent – and prize-winning – amateur production of this version was staged, soon after the war, by Hugh Willatt, who later took charge of the theatre section of the Arts Council.

Within the rapid quarter-century that followed the war the Penguin Classics, under the guidance of E. V. Rieu and Betty Radice, published all the surviving works of the three Greek tragedians, and a number of the comedies of Aristophanes, and of Menander, in English translations. Hundreds, probably thousands, of productions of these plays were staged by amateur groups all over the country; and I know from personal experience what delight this activity gave to both actors and audiences. Yet during that period Greek drama almost completely failed to win for itself an assured and enjoyed status on the English professional stage; it showed no sign of achieving anything to approach the status of Shakespeare in European theatre. It seems unlikely that the English translations of Greek tragedy then available were so much worse than the French, Russian, or German translations of Shakespeare as to account for this. There were occasional productions. I recall a *Medea*, and an *Electra* (of Sophocles); but both were ill at ease, unintegrated, and in spite of some good individual performances made no lasting impression. Even Olivier and Thorndike, in Sophocles' *King Oedipus*, could not make Sophocles for the English theatre-goer what *Hamlet* and *Lear* apparently are to the Russian. Aeschylus was hardly ever attempted professionally before the recent *Oresteia* at the National Theatre; while intense pieces such as *Philoctetes* or *Ion* or *Orestes* were virtually not even heard of except in amateur groups. This situation is the more curious when we consider the highly professional nature of the ancient Greek theatre – so clearly depicted by Mary Renault in *The Mask of Apollo*.

Why such a situation persists, as it does to this day, is hard to understand; but I do know that there is, in this field, only one activity more pleasurably compulsive than directing a cast of keen amateurs in a Greek tragedy, and that is writing the translation. If British audiences are ever to become aware of the rich treasures of Greek theatre, translators will have a large share in accomplishing it. There is no shortage of competent actors. Directors are less reliable: when confronted with a Greek play they tend to become nervous, either carried away by over-confident ambition, or beguiled by diffidence into seeking for novelty. Translations vary widely in the demands they make on the literary education of their audience; some translators expect far too much, others far too little. Yet every translator is also a member of the poet's audience, and has a right to enjoy the Greek original just as he himself finds it. The Athenian tragedians themselves knew that, at least for their own lifetime, the proof of the pudding must be in the eating. They wrote for their friends and fellow-poets, for Pericles, for Thucydides, and for Socrates; and at the same time for the citizen-soldier, the tradesman, the corrupt juryman, the athlete, the artist; for Strepsiades and Pheidippides and for the coarse and stupid nobody.

The art of translation is – can only be – a makeshift business; yet it can claim a place among the interpretative arts, and, when it handles great literature, is only to be practised by a writer with an artist's devotion to his own language. In all great writing there is an intimate blending of form and content, not only with each other but with the author's awareness of the world he lives in. The translator of ancient literature can account fairly well for content. Some features of the form he can represent by one device or another, so long as in every doubtful choice he allows priority to meaning; other features he knows he may have to abandon. The way he conceives the author's awareness of his world will vary not only with the nature of the translator's scholarship but also with his moral attitude to his own world. This is true in general for scholars who write on tragic drama, whether they are translators or not, since moral issues are more specifically the concern of tragedy than of other kinds of writing. A translation made with sincerity must therefore remain a highly personal product; which may be the reason why a translator often finds the work of other translators uncongenial.

Such considerations are naturally disturbing for the reader. He wants to know whether what he is reading can be relied upon as a 'true' version of the original work; and a translator should try not to feel impatient at so over-simple a question. Drama is imaginative writing; and the imaginative elements of Greek drama are several. There is the myth, on which each story is based. There is the character which the dramatist gives to each traditional figure. There is the moral argument which is brought to life in the story and the characters. There is the pattern of imagery distilled from myth, characters, and moral argument, and blending all into a single poetic statement of tragic experience. When the original material is as complex as a play of Aeschylus, Sophocles, Euripides, what chance has the translator, whose work – in Platonic terms – is an imitation of an imitation of an imitation, to achieve or approach truth?

The first answer to this question is simply that drama, unlike other forms of writing, carries within itself something more than words. Its traffic is not only with our minds but with our eyes; its material is not only the voice but a group of mutually opposed voices, a pattern of bodies, costumes, objects, with music and scene, and with the mind of a director at work in his own interpretative art of composing all into a living organism. If you translate a love-song of Sappho into English, what you have to offer will be something between a tantalizing explanation on the one hand and a new English poem on the other – something fairly remote from the original experience. If you translate Homer, you can offer the story, the characters, the heroic glow of antiquity – and that is a grand offering; but the *Iliad* was made to be sung and heard, and what the first listeners to Homer heard – that we shall never hear. In translating Thucydides or Plato the proportion of what is lost is less destructive but still serious. And in translating Greek tragedy the loss, so far as the language itself is concerned, is at least as serious as in lyric or epic or history. But in tragic drama there is more than language. There is Clytemnestra facing Agamemnon, Creon facing Antigone, Oedipus facing Teiresias, Medea facing Jason, Pentheus facing Dionysus. There is the door that will close on Cassandra, the door that will open to reveal dead Phaedra, or drunken Heracles, or blinded Oedipus; there is the music that mourns for Prometheus, for Astyanax, for Neoptolemus. The fact that these visible and audible images, and still more these combating persons in victory and defeat, can find life even through a poor translation makes the attempt to provide a good translation all the more inviting.

A translator needs to be a person with fairly clear views on the use of English; someone who, confronted with a line of lyric or dialogue, knows at once whether he would wish to be credited with that line or not. Translation from a remote language is a good apprenticeship for a young writer seeking a style; because when you are faced with an idea presented to you in the elusive precision of another world, you are forced to forget style in the search for meaning;

whereas, if you are trying to create both your meaning and your phrase together, you will not only adapt style to suit meaning, but from time to time you will bend meaning to capture an alluring phrase, so that the two impregnate each other, like an alternating current. But this condition of the translator's work – that his meaning is first given to him complete and precise – this condition, which is a help to the beginner, may well be a recurrent headache for the experienced translator, for this reason: in so far as a writer writes a consistent style, he does so because the character of his thoughts is consistent, because his reason and his imagination flow in channels natural to him; but when he is translating, this instinctive process of production is interrupted, the flow of meaning comes in from an alien source, sometimes combatively demanding submission; and the writer may well find himself, in dealing with a stubborn passage, teased right out of his spontaneity, and settling for some word or phrase which months later stares at him out of the typescript, or worse still, the print, like 'a thwart disfeatur'd torment' challenging him to deny parenthood.

We all know that, in creative writing, '*Le style c'est l'homme.*' How true is that in the translation of a play? Naturally one says that the style of a translation ought to reflect not the translator but the original author; and in translations of contemporary writers I know this can happen. In translations from ancient Greek the degree of metamorphosis necessarily becomes so great as to allow much wider scope to both the strength and the weakness of that individual perception which the translator provides. No two people carry in their memory the same image of *Hamlet* or *As You Like It*. When we read a tragedy in Greek the field open to our imagination is wide; in translating it, each writer's knowledge of Greek must have its personal emphases; and in reaching a balance between accuracy of sense and the nature of the English tongue, individual instinct, prejudice, ability, will be decisive. People sometimes say, 'When translating you must never look at anyone else's version, or you inhibit your own free flow.' I have not found this. In translating some thirty plays, I once wrote with another translation open before me. It was by a good scholar and a good writer, and it was a helpful commentary on the text; but in 1,400 lines there were only two short phrases where I wanted to use the same expressions. Thus a translation of a Greek play is a very personal work, which, while it is fresh, one regards with tender appreciation; when it is old, one recognizes in it those flaws in one's own self which are all too familiar, and which would probably reappear, like the devil peeping under the angel's wing, in whatever new version one might labour to make. However, what chiefly gives translation its reward is the twofold experience of close contact with the mind of the author, and the free range of the English language for one's own adventuring.

The gulf to be bridged between modern English and ancient Greek is widc and dcep. It is a bridge that can be crossed in both directions. But such are the pressures of education today that few classical scholars are allowed time to taste the pleasures of learning to write decent prose and verse in Latin and Greek. On the subject of translation from ancient poetry to modern English, some of the best remarks I know are made by Gilbert Highet in the introductory chapter to his *Poets in a Landscape*. His translations from Latin poetry beautifully illustrate the principles he expounds; and I even feel that they reproach me for not attempting to follow them in my versions of Greek tragedy. But once again my plea is the difference of drama from all other kinds of poetry: it has to be not only spoken, but acted: not only felt, but suffered by both actor and audience who together create another world. Many important elements of the original action are lost to us; what remains is what we call the 'argument' – and a modern production must make the most of this. Therefore I feel it is right for us to forget the fact that in the ancient productions many of the audience probably missed the point of the argument (we may remember how eighteenth-century audiences accepted Nahum Tate's version of *King Lear*) and were absorbed in the more incidental elements of the performance; and our priority should be to concentrate on clarity of statement, so that the one central element we still possess can operate in full intensity.

For example, the pounding rhythms of the Furies' 'binding song' in Aeschylus' *Eumenides* could doubtless be closely reproduced in English words; but the natural English medium for such passionate emphasis is the use of rhythms native to our tongue, short rhymes, and firm rhyme-pattern. (It is often forgotten how powerfully rhyme can hold an audience.) However, I am reluctant to defend my own versions by citing examples; I am content to regard my work as one kind of translation among others equally valid and useful. Perhaps the most important truth I have learnt from translating is this: that meaning is always something prior to speech, yet at the same time dependent for its life on the words which it invents and uses as its tools, and which by their limitations inevitably modify meaning itself, bring it down to earth, set it to the music of mortality.

Thus it is that in attempting to 'translate' (the word is itself presumptuous) the powerful meanings that operate in the Greek tragedies, a dedicated writer can enjoy, among other privileges, that close contact with the author's mind which I have mentioned. A translator can accept gratefully the fruits of erudite textual and linguistic groundwork carried out by generations of scholars, without feeling obliged to receive as infallible their pronouncements on those moral and emotional issues that provide the fabric of the dramas. He will remember – what the formal scholar sometimes forgets – that such issues are in fact what obsessed the tragedian's mind as he wrote. The complex linguistic and intellectual structures which are the material of academic study were to the poet a part of himself, operating with scarcely conscious effort as the tools of his expression. How honestly did Aeschylus' Orestes judge his own action in avenging his father? How heroic, or patriotic, was Eteocles? How far did Oedipus elude the knowledge which, if accepted, would have barred him from the throne of Thebes? Can we assess the integrity of Phaedra, Ajax, Ion? Can we allow any to Demophon or Pentheus? Such questions were the stars by which the dramatists navigated the intricacies of their plots and their characters, piloting the more sensitive among their audience through the dark seas of tragedy. It is certain that each poet knew the answers to his own questions, and that these answers were seldom the same as the conventional answers that satisfied the fifth-century audience, who went home after seeing *Medea* or *Hippolytus* and – as is clear from Aristophanes' *Frogs* – told their wives they had seen a play about a murderess or a whore.

The two years during which most of my leisure was absorbed by Aeschylus' *Oresteian Trilogy* was a happy time, but tinged with an inarticulate unease. I had read *Eumenides* at seventeen in school, under that delightful enthusiast C. G. Botting. I recall being aware at the time that we were following him contentedly in pious acceptance of absurdities – but we were not to regard them as absurdities; rather they were exotic features in the morality of an ancient world, a world utterly different from ours, full of wonders which we were destined to explore. So we were not worried by the incongruity of Orestes posing as a hero, by an Apollo lacking both dignity and honesty, by Athena's trampling underfoot of every serious and tragic issue agonized over in *Agamemnon* and *Choephori*. The splendour and fascination of Aeschylus' Greek induced in us then an attitude of blind faith which was underpinned by every influence operating in our years of university Classics that followed. When, much later, I wrote my translation of the *Oresteia*, the uneasiness was still there, and the acceptance yet more reluctant. It was not until I had made translations of all Euripides' plays, and written a book about them, that I at last felt ready to undertake the task I could no longer avoid: to search for the real meaning of the *Oresteia*. Whether I found it will (I hope) remain open to dispute; but the exhilarating shock of incredulous discovery was an experience I am glad not to have missed.

I will give only one example of what I think a translation should not do. It is from Euripides' *Orestes*. Early in this marvellous but neglected play there is a short scene between Electra and Helen. Helen speaks only thirty-six lines; but, though she does not appear on the stage again, she is spoken of repeatedly in every scene, until at last a slave comes in and tells how Orestes murdered her. In the epilogue she appears above the stage, as a mute figure, with Apollo. It is obviously important to know what sort of character Helen is. Her one scene shows little more than that she is afraid to be seen in the streets of Argos, where people are ready to stone her on sight. For the rest, her words are modest and gentle; but Electra hates her, and as soon as she has gone speaks about her to the audience in bitter condemnation. A widely read translation of *Orestes*, which for the most part I think very good, in this one scene undertakes to interpret. Whereas Euripides has, I would say, left the character somewhat veiled, uncommitted, this version so phrases every line of Helen's part that she appears unmistakably as a shallow, malevolent, insincere, and selfish person. This is today the usually accepted view of the scene, and of Helen's role, as it was in the ancient world. Yet in the play itself every character who hates Helen is morally corrupt, and the only three pleasant characters all love her. Euripides spent much of his life combating accepted views. The Greek lines in themselves do not justify the assumption that Euripides meant to present Helen in this derogatory light; and the translation ought, I believe, to be as veiled, as uncommitted, as the original. Here the translator, following most scholars, has taken Electra's view of Helen to be the poet's view. This is an error, especially in Euripides. When one person in a play voices an opinion about another, it is always possible that the dramatist may in those lines be telling us something about the speaker rather than about the subject. The point of using irony in a play is to speak with one voice to those who can hear irony, and with another to those who can't. The translator's function is, where he finds ambivalence, to preserve it.

Finally, I would recommend the reader of Greek plays in translation to read always with Thucydides' *History* at his elbow. It provides a unique first-hand account of the world of fifth-century Greece. That world, rich as it is in splendours and miseries, inspiration and disastrous waste, shows its family likeness to Greek myth. Thucydides too wrote with the tragedian's ironic view both of events and of individuals. The most admirable translation of a Greek tragedy can mislead, if the reader has no notion what happened between the battle of Marathon and the final defeat of Athens eighty-five years later. An uninspired translation can bring enlightenment and pleasure, if read with imagination guided by some basic instruction. Still more, if acted with intelligence and feeling, and with a not too sophisticated commitment to the values of our modern theatre, even an unambitious version can convey something of the power and profundity of its original. There is no reason to abandon the hope that Greek drama, both tragedy and comedy, may yet win a permanent, popular, and revered place in the English theatre.

TRANSLATOR'S CHARITY

Benedicta Ward

> For I have translated in the charity, which makes things better,
> and so I trust that I shall be translated myself at the last.
>
> Christopher Smart, *Jubilate Agno*

❦ It is often supposed that the mention of 'charity' in connection with academic or literary work automatically leads to a lessening of truth and accuracy. In theory, of course, the reverse should be the case; God who is truth is also and equally love. There is, in the end, no question of priorities:

> There we shall be still and see; we shall see and we shall love; we shall love and we shall praise. Behold what shall be in the end without end! [1]

The art of the Christian translator rests in both 'seeing' with the clear eye of truth and 'loving' at the same time, in the light of the 'end without end'. There is a long tradition of 'charitable' translation, in the sense of Christopher Smart's 'in the charity', which enhances rather than lessens accuracy and truth. This is not to suggest that Christian translators have any kind of monopoly of charity about their work; clearly, an honourable translator does his work because he loves both the text and its transmission, and the basis of that love is a concern for accuracy and truth. For the translator of Christian texts, the obligation to seek truth through accuracy is underlined and not contradicted by the equal obligation to charity. It is in fact more astringent because most Christian literature, above all the Bible, is not translated for antiquarian or aesthetic purposes but for practical utility in the work of prayer. The translation therefore must be transparent for the orginal inspiration to shine through clearly, but also made available for the reader to use as a way to God for himself, without the distraction of thinking about the text as a translation. It is not meant to be a literature for casual curiosity. The author of *The Cloud of Unknowing*, for instance, insists in his prologue that

> whoever you may be who possess this book, . . . you should, quite freely and of set purpose, neither read, write nor mention it to anyone,

nor allow it to be read, written or mentioned by anyone unless that person is in your judgement really and wholly determined to follow Christ perfectly.[2]

Presumably that same stricture would apply to the same author's translation of the *Mystica Theologia* as *Dionise Hid Divinite*. Christian literature is designed for the purpose of aiding conversion of the heart towards God, and the demands of truth and love in conveying it from one language to another are part of the process. It is, of course, easy to corrupt such a pragmatic approach and make it a political one, and at once examples leap to mind of tendentious translations of Christian literature, where the translator is determined to support his own ideas about right thinking through his text, but this is always at the expense of truth. It is the balance of love and truth that 'makes things better', not either one without the other. This ideal is not an easy matter to write about; nevertheless it is an ideal, and one related to a concern of all Christian scholars, the pursuit of learning and the desire for God.

Christians were concerned with translation from the start. The Old Testament was used by the early Church not in Hebrew but in the Greek translation known as the Septuagint, simply because Christians in the Greek-speaking world did not generally read Hebrew, and as Christianity spread among Latin-speaking converts, translations into Latin of both Old and New Testaments were not so much desirable as essential. Even so fine a scholar as St Augustine seemed reluctant to read Greek where Latin was available. He was certainly aware that the young Christians of north Africa would be more accustomed to using translations into Latin of the New Testament than reading the text in Greek. The best way, of course, and this is always so, was for them not to need translations, and when St Augustine provided directions about reading in *On Chrisian Doctrine*, he says at once that some knowledge of Hebrew and Greek at least should support the use of the second-best way of using translations:

> The sovereign remedy [against being misled] is a knowledge of languages, and Latin-speaking men, whom we have here undertaken to instruct, need two others for a knowledge of the Divine Scriptures, Hebrew and Greek, so that they may turn back to earlier exemplars if the infinite variety of Latin translations gives rise to any doubts.[3]

Like any modern university teacher, St Augustine had to set his sights low; he knew, as we all do, that very few would actually know enough Greek and Hebrew to read the Scriptures regularly in the original languages. But he was alert to the dangers of translations and required his students at least to be able to check. Accurate knowledge of what the authors actually wrote is his first requirement for the Christian scholar. Some words, he says, are in fact untranslatable and he cites 'amen', 'alleluia', 'racha', and 'hosanna'[4] as instances of this. But it is not for this that he recommends a working knowledge of two languages; it is for checking words and phrases when confronted with a wide variety of divergent translations, since, 'in the early times of the faith anyone who found a Greek codex and thought that he had some facility in both languages attempted to translate it'. Clearly the pitfalls for translators as regards accuracy were no different in the fourth century. A poor knowledge of either language could wreck translation: 'many translators are deceived by ambiguity in the original language which they do not understand so that they transfer the meaning to something completely alien to the writer's intention'. In a long passage St Augustine takes a practical stance about what is possible for the average student who cannot check faulty translations for himself. To these, he recommends the use of 'those who translate word for word, not because they suffice but because by means of them we may test the truth or falsity of those who have sought to translate meanings as well as words'. Literal, word-for-word translation is not sufficient to convey the content of the text, but it is helpful in determining meaning.

Grammar, then, for St Augustine, mattered; the meaning of the original writer must be understood as accurately as possible; it should then be conveyed to the reader as clearly as possible in his own language; and a translation should be regarded as a way into the text, not a substitute for it. But St Augustine surrounds this basic, fundamental demand for accuracy with another kind of hard work for the scholar: the first section of *On Christian Doctrine* is about a preliminary requirement: the love of God, charity: 'It is to be understood that the plenitude and the end of the Law and of all sacred Scriptures is the love of a Being which is to be enjoyed'.[5] And after his instructions on the necessity for careful attention to the text, St Augustine asserts again the primacy of charity in its interpretation:

> Thus when the tyranny of cupidity has been overthrown, charity reigns with its most just laws of love for God for the sake of God, and of one's self and of one's neighbour for the sake of God. Therefore in the considera-

tion of figurative expressions a rule such as this will serve, that what is read should be subject to diligent scrutiny until an interpretation contributing to the reign of charity shall be produced.[6]

Love and truth cannot be in opposition; what is true will also be charitable, and what is charitable will also be true.

St Augustine does not mean by 'charity' a woolly kind of niceness that will distort the text. He has already defined charity as 'the motion of the soul towards the enjoyment of God for his own sake and enjoyment of one's self and of one's neighbour for the sake of God'.[7] If a translation does not promote this desire for and enjoyment of God, then it cannot be the true meaning of the text. For St Augustine, charity is the context as well as the content of a translation. Translation must be accurate, and part of that accuracy is to discover charity towards the writer and towards the readers, and towards God within the text. It must also be then a truth transmitted in words appropriate to the truth. Here St Augustine was dealing with a matter which is not quite the same in translations into English, though the principle is applicable. Latin versions of the Scriptures in the fourth century were for reading aloud, and the pointing and stress of the language could help or hinder its intelligibility. Thus, while St Augustine takes a brisk line with those who worry about pronouncing '*ignoscere* . . . with a long or a short syllable', when their concern should be with 'asking God to forgive . . . sins',[8] he is equally sure that correct and even elegant language should be used in the reading aloud of a text; the speaker must 'teach, delight and persuade',[9] if he does not take care to make the form of his discourse attractive, he will simply not be heard at all. Nor is this idea of 'enjoyment' a mere trick of pedagogy; for those who love the true God in all things, St Augustine speaks in the language of desire and enjoyment from his own heart:

I have learned to love you late, Beauty at once so ancient and so new! I have learned to love you late . . . I tasted you and now I hunger and thirst for you. You touched me, and I am inflamed with love of your peace.[10]

Enjoyment of language for its own sake is not a concern of St Augustine. Beneath the work of the translator there is always the fact of utility and service rather than aesthetics. The transmission of the true meaning of a text through another language is not primarily for the enjoyment of the translator, who is after all well able to read the original. To undertake translation is in itself a part of charity. It is primarily when there is widespread ignorance of the original language that those who do understand it must undertake translation. It is a service, a way of offering treasure to others. This primary motive of charity towards those less well equipped for reading has been a constant motive in translation from other languages into English, just as it was for St Augustine from Greek and Hebrew into Latin. The difference is that translators into English have rarely supposed that their translations would lead readers towards the original languages; in fact, rather the contrary. Translations, it is true, have often been treated in England as cribs, and therefore to be outlawed and confiscated presumably because of a hidden certainty in the minds of preceptors that children will not go to the trouble of learning a language if they can get the meaning out of a text in any other way. Nevertheless, it is not as cribs but as new texts that translations have been most popular with the English, and this began very early indeed in our history. Two Englishmen in the early middle ages in particular exercised this charity towards others by providing translations of ancient texts, and both followed the ideals and precepts of St Augustine in doing so. The first of these was Bede (*c.* 673–735).

Bede himself wrote primarily in Latin, the literary language of the newly formed Church among the Anglo-Saxons. He was however concerned that the Gospel should be understood by those who knew no Latin, in fact, the vast majority of the new converts. In the *Ecclesiastical History of the English People*, he notes with approval that King Oswald of Northumbria acted as translator for the Irish monk, Bishop Aidan, when the latter preached to the English:

> While the bishop, who was not yet fluent in the English language, preached the Gospel, it was most delightful to see the king himself interpreting the word of God to his ealdormen and thanes; for he himself had obtained perfect command of the Irish tongue during his long exile.[11]

For Bede, translation was necessary for the ignorant, and it should therefore be the duty of the translator to work carefully in order not to mislead those who were made completely vulnerable by their ignorance. He says that he himself corrected and clarified 'a book on *The life and sufferings of Saint Anastasius*, which had been badly translated from the Greek, and worse amended by some unskilful person'.[12] And the monk Cuthbert described how Bede continued to work at translations into English on his death-bed:

He translated into our language, for the profit of the church of God, from the beginning of St John's Gospel to the place where it is said, 'but what are they among so many?' and some extracts from the works of Bishop Isidore, for he said, 'I would not that my children should read a lie and labour therein without fruit when I am gone.'[13]

In a letter to Bishop Egbert, Bede had insisted that the teaching and prayers of the Church should be made available to 'those who are acquainted with no language but their own'.[14] He had himself taught the Lord's Prayer and the Creed in English to both laymen and priests. Significantly, his purpose was neither academic nor artistic but practical:

For thus is it brought to pass that every band of the faithful may learn how to be faithful, by what steadfastness they ought to fortify and arm themselves against the assaults of the unclean spirits; and that every choir of suppliants to God may understand what especially should be sought from the Divine clemency.[15]

As for St Augustine, translation for Bede was part of the greater 'charity' of a whole life turned towards Christ.

The task of translation was taken up two hundred years after Bede by another Englishman, in the same spirit of service for the use of those otherwise cut off from the Latin past. King Alfred the Great, occupied, as he says, in a great many other tasks, still found time for translation. In his preface to his first translation, that of St Gregory the Great's treatise for the use of bishops, *On Pastoral Care*, Alfred says that he translated

sometimes word for word, sometimes sense for sense . . . I translated it into English as best I understood it and as I could most meaningfully render it; I intend to send a copy to each bishopric in my kingdom.[16]

It was meant to be a useful book, to help bishops care for the Christians in their churches, not an academic exercise for the literate. Alfred allowed himself more liberty with the text than either St Augustine or Bede. Like Queen Elizabeth after him, he also translated the *Consolation of Philosophy* of Boethius into English, and gave a freer rendering than in his work on St Gregory, rearranging the order, re-casting it as a dialogue between the inquirer's mind and the personification of Wisdom, and giving personal reflections on God and the world in place of some of the more autobiographical sections. His translation of the *Soliloquies* of St Augustine were still more free, but in his translation of the first fifty psalms into English, a text above all meant for prayer, he returned to a literal yet readable rendering of the text. These royal translations, the work of a busy man, were not for ornament but for use. They were for those who could 'derive very little benefit from [Latin] books because they could understand nothing of them since they were not written in their own language'.

Both Bede and Alfred, like St Augustine, translated in order to transmit to others poorer than themselves the riches of the past, and each had also the intention of increasing charity for others as well as for themselves by so doing. The whole man, mind and body, was to be brought into the service of Christ, and the living word of the Scriptures was to reach everyone for their response. By translation, other Latin writers who had commented on the text of Scripture or given advice about the conduct of Christian life were also to be opened to the ignorant present. For those undertaking this task three things were needed: first, a thorough knowledge of the original text; then the humility which stands back and allows what was written by someone else to be transmitted; and thirdly a command of the new language so that readers could appropriate the text and use it for the extension of the kingdom of God which is the reign of love.

The late middle ages and pre-eminently the Reformation saw the flowering of English translation, most of all in 'Bibles fair and old', and in particular that monument to the translator's art, the King James version of the Bible. But in the nineteenth century, English churchmen seriously undertook this task of charitable translation again, and for very much the same reasons as their predecessors. The Oxford Movement was primarily concerned with the revival of religion in England, where its members saw an alarming growth of secularity, which they called 'liberalism', in all parts of the Church. Against such 'liberalism' Pusey, Newman and Keble decided to set the zeal and purity of faith in the early Church. Themselves excellent classical scholars, and members of the senior common room at Oriel, their acquaintance with the ancient Latin and Greek fathers was fluent and easy. They naturally read the Scriptures in Hebrew and Greek, and Pusey at least was well acquainted with many other languages too. Yet they were aware, and it surprised and pained them, that there were many other members of the Church of England, even among the clergy, who could read only English. There must, therefore, be translations as well as editions of texts. The series which occupied their energies they called 'The Library of the Fathers', a phrase first coined by Bede. It was a project of translation undertaken for a purpose as missionary-orientated as that of St

Augustine, Bede or Alfred. Like them, they bowed down their proud and scholarly necks before the yoke of translation for the ignorant, like them they insisted on the highest standards of accuracy, and like them also they had in mind no mere antiquarian effort, but a living contact with the tradition of the Church. Unlike their predecessors, however, their work was undertaken in a new scholarly atmosphere, for both texts and translations. The critical editions of ancient texts had been undertaken already, and the editions of the Maurists[17] provided far more texts and alternative readings of the Church Fathers than were available to any one person in the whole of the ancient or medieval world. Moreover, the work of translation was already being discussed as an art, most notably in Matthew Arnold's essay *On Translating Homer*. The Tractarians were well aware of the critical gaze their colleagues turned upon their enterprise, which gave to their translations the edge of debate as well as the content of devotion. Newman at once disagreed with Arnold's plea for 'translation from poesie into poesie', and urged, in his *Reply*, verbal exactness above all. The translation of the Fathers of the Church, Tractarians and classicists all agreed, should be above all accurate; but a division arose between Pusey and Newman about the amount of freedom to be allowed translators in turning Latin or Greek into readable English. Pusey was in favour of exact literal translations, which preserved the Latin sentence structure as far as possible; Newman, for all his opposition to Arnold, feared the unreadability which was already a characteristic even of Pusey's original writings in English, and therefore cautiously suggested a certain measure of idiomatic English. In a letter to Pusey, Newman wrote:

> I do not like diffusive translations. Unliteralness is no more diffuse than the contrary; I only meant not word for word. *Placet mihi* may be Englished 'it pleases me' or 'I please'. Here, what is least literal, whether better or not, is shorter. All I meant was idiomatic translation.[18]

Pusey replied that while he agreed with Newman on 'the principles of translation, I think that one might even sacrifice idiom, if one may call it so, to retain the effect of the original'.[19] His own translations were in a rigid style, as indeed were those of John Keble. But for the direction of those who undertook translations for the series he eventually wrote to Keble:

> My instruction to translators is a clear, nervous, condensed unparaphrastic style, and thus as free and as like the original, and idiomatic as may be.[20]

In his Preface to his translation of St Augustine's *Confessions*, Pusey set out his theory of translation more fully:

> The object of all translation must be to present the ideas of the author as clearly as may be, with as little sacrifice as may be of what is peculiar to him; the greatest clearness with the greatest faithfulness.[21]

Any paraphrase he suspected as changing the meaning of the original, interpreting it for the reader, so that it became no longer a translation but a commentary on the text.

Pusey and Keble preferred literal translations and at the expense of their English style. Newman, however, and his younger contemporary John Mason Neale, sat more lightly to the precise order of the ancient languages. Newman, a superb stylist in English, and Neale, a storyteller and novelist, as well as a translator of liturgical texts for use in church, regarded translations of ancient texts as vehicles for right doctrine, but even more as means by which men would learn to pray. Neale wrote novels and short stories based on events and persons of the past to stimulate devotion, as well as translating with a free genius which at times extended to downright invention; while Newman, whose translation of St Athanasius was as pedantic as Keble's version of St Ireneus, also produced edifying novels in an attempt to make the past available in English prose. They both went a step further in translation than either Pusey or Keble in making one text in particular available for private meditation. This was the *Preces Privates* of Bishop Lancelot Andrewes, a seventeenth-century divine, who himself prayed as easily in Greek and Latin as in English. In Newman's translation and in the further selection which Neale later translated, Andrewes's compilation from the ancient languages flowered into original compositions in English. The original copy of Andrewes's book, now lost, was stained and tattered and 'watered with his penitential tears',[22] evidence that the prayers were used constantly and with deep emotion. Andrewes arranged the material as a series of devotions for each day of the week, drawing mainly on the Scriptures and the liturgy, in Hebrew, Greek and Latin, but set out as personal prayers of adoration, thanksgiving, confession and intercession. Newman translated the main part in No. 28 of *Tracts for the Times* (1840) and Neale added the rest in an equally fine version. Neither Newman nor Neale needed a translation to use Andrewes's book of prayers. Their undertaking was entirely for the use of others poorer than themselves; and it is noteworthy that the pedantry of the Newman of the *Reply* to Arnold is here replaced by something that could well be seen as 'poesie into poesie'. It is a rare thing for a translation to become a new and excellent work in its own right, but that is what these two achieved. In this work, the charity of the past became the charity of the present in its most direct and personal form; it is the finest example I know of the combination of truth with love in the process of translation into English.

The main virtue of a translation of any ancient text is that it should be a translation and render the original meaning clearly. But the art of the translator is rather more than an attempt at transliteration, as a comparison between the translations of Pusey and Newman shows. The past is to be placed in the hands of the present, and it is here that the translator of Christian texts about or containing prayer has a particularly delicate job. Penguin Classics have presented this kind of material in, for instance, translations of English mystics, the *Prayers and Meditations of St Anselm of Canterbury*, Helen Waddell's *Mediaeval Latin Lyrics*, and, in some sense, in Betty Radice's own translation of *The Letters of Abelard and Heloise*. The aim of such translations is to be transparent, but also readable and usable. The transparency comes first, but where 'charity' is applied this does not cloud but clarifies the sense; as Charles Williams put it, 'accuracy is fruitfulness . . . it is the first law of the spiritual life'.[23] In the quotation given at the beginning from Christopher Smart, as fine a classicist as any, the comma after 'better' is not an accident; the second clause is not related to the word 'charity' but to the whole preceding phrase. Smart does not claim, nor does any true translator, that he has used charity in his work in order to make what he translates more acceptable to the reader; he claims that he has translated in the charity which is Christ, and it is this fact that 'makes things better'. So, like St Augustine, Bede, Alfred, or the Tractarians, Christopher Smart can conclude with the longing of the Christian translator for his own salvation also: 'and so I trust that I shall be translated myself at the last'.

NOTES ON TRANSLATING CATULLUS

Peter Whigham

They who have listened, patiently and supinely, to the catarrhal songsters of goose-grazed commons, will be loth and ill-fitted to mount up with Catullus to the highest steeps in the forests of Ida, and will shudder at the music of the Corybantes in the temple of the Great Mother of the Gods.

Walter Savage Landor, *The Poems of Catullus* (1842)

As first on the list, a reminder that all such lists are (or should be) largely ignored in the act of composition. Codes may be useful when revising, or when teaching, but the reasons that lead a writer to settle for this rather than that solution, as he reaches for a phrase or a rhyme, are seldom fully apprehended even by the writer himself. The way the light falls on the paper, a sound in the street outside . . .

Peter Whigham, Addendum to
Do's and Don'ts of Translation (1982)

❦ Were it not for the blandishments of a publisher's contract, who but the foolhardiest would undertake a verse rendering of any poet's *complete* works? All nod now and then; why render their snores? It is true that having what I can only describe as 'stumbled' into translating the *Collis o Heliconii* (that is, having found some sort of dance movement for two or three of the stanzas, I found myself unable to quit, unable, literally, to get the dance movement out of my head until I had worked my way through the whole poem) – having stumbled into translating one of the longest and most difficult ('difficult', because least Roman) of the *Carmina*, the question arose, 'Why not some of the other long poems?' At that time, 1950, these had suffered undue neglect and, in the case of the *Peleus and Thetis*, misunderstanding. Father Thomas Symons, OSB, cousin of Arthur Symons – admirable translator of Catullus, whose volumes in Father Thomas's cell were a constant stimulus to me: *he* has done *this*; what if *I* were to do *that*? – put the question directly, and it was following his suggestion that I set myself to translate *C*.62 to 68. From there, it was only a step, foolhardy or not, to attacking the whole *Carmina*. There is, after all, very little waste matter in what we have left of Catullus. To scruple over the lesser poems would be to act a little after the fashion of the princess with the pea under her mattress. Indeed, the lesser poems represent a special challenge. A translator is as tested by the failures as by the successes of his originals. Perhaps more so, since some element of successful work is amost bound to carry over; not so with relatively marred or failed work. In any event, Penguin's contract effectively ironed out any wrinkles of conscience which I may be supposed to have had.

The above is of more than historical interest, since it was because of the piecemeal manner in which I came to the *Carmina* that consistency emerged low among my aims. There is both virtue and vice in this, though which outbalances which I find it hard to say. Each poem was picked up arbitrarily, as mood impelled, and examined with an eye solely to its own challenge, and not, or very little, to how it is related to the other poems in the *Carmina*. It was the specifics, isolated in the poem under consideration, which, to the extent that one's technique permitted, had to be possessed and made a part of one's own verbal experience. Since the whole undertaking assumes in retrospect the aspect of disconnected jumps from poem to poem, it would seem natural that these notes should follow suit, rather in the manner of Landor's essay. Thus, item by item, as memory allows

Catullus' epigrams are not to be thought of as confined to the poems written in elegiacs, *C*.69 to 116; many of the shorter poems from *C*.1 to 60, though written in a variety of metres, also come under this head. They are, however, epigrams with a difference – not at all like Martial's, in spite of Martial's wish to be esteemed 'second only to Catullus'. It is the difference between the inclusive and the open-ended. With Catullus, an allusive quality attaches itself hauntingly to the incised phrase. The same thing is to be found in our day in some of the short poems of Ezra Pound, poems such as 'The Gypsy'. 'Lyric epigrams' may sound like a contradiction in terms, but that is what such poems are.

C.1.* Epigrammatic point is provided by the exchange between the last two words of the first line and the last two words of the last: *novum libellum . . . perenne saeclo*. Any translator should try for this.

* References are to *The Poems of Catullus*, translated with an introduction by Peter Whigham (Penguin Books, 1966).

If formal equivalence is looked for, the two enjambments, *cartis/doctis* and *libelli/qualecumque*, should be noted, balancing each other as they do. As for the pathos implicit in the contrast between Nepos' volumes, so well equipped, and Catullus' *nugae*, so little equipped, for immortality, this is evoked, in the Latin, in the mild mockery of *doctis* and *laboriosis*. Irony is required, and one of the simplest ways of achieving ironic effects when translating from Latin is to use the same, or closely derived, word. Thus 'doctoral' for *doctis*. Transposition of *cartis* into 'volumes' or 'tomes' will give 'weighty' for *laboriosis*: *cartis, / Doctis, Jupiter, et laboriosis*, – the line on which the poem turns, and to be preserved as such, even if Jupiter has to be sacrificed, invocations to the gods not now having the effect they once had.

*C.*2 & 3. A young lady, a pet bird, and a 'tripping' metre. How to avoid sentimentality? First, eschew the tripping metre. Eschew anything readily evocative of young ladies and pet birds. Applied sentiment to be held at a discount, there being enough sentiment and to spare in the situation as it is. Required: straightforward statement, reliance on juxtaposition of images and emphasis on definitive rather than decorative rhythms – decoration tending to the sentimental. Unless he use a set metre, the translator should consider building his rhythms in one sustained movement, so that each poem is felt as moving towards the condition of a single sentence. Several of the poems offer themselves to this approach: *C.*5, 7, 11, and the dedicatory epistle, *C.*65, the aim being to use syntax as a means of mirroring the lyric impulse of the original.

There will always be a choice for the translator, whether he is to include the traditional last three lines in the body of his poem, or whether he is to keep them separate, perhaps tacking them on as a tailpiece. Since we can know the poem only as we have received it, I have never been able to see how the putative 'original', the pristine version, fresh from Catullus' pen, or stylus, can be of more than abstract, archaeological interest. *C.*5 and 7, the two kissing poems, come to us after Ben Jonson (and Ferrabosco with him) have done their best with them. We are translating not merely the words Catullus may be presumed to have written, but what those words have subsequently come to imply, the nuances they have gathered about them. Even if we were able to scrape the patina of the years away, we should not wish to. Poems, we know, have lives of their own, beyond anything their author could have dreamed for them.

Am I, for example, to disregard the bow Callimachus' poem takes to an eighteenth-century audience in Pope's *Rape*, when I come to translate *C*.66? I think not. Let, then, the traditional inclusion of the last three lines of *C*.2 stand.

C.4. The boat, as reported by Catullus, tells its story, as the lock of hair in *C*.66 tells its. In both, the conceit is magnificently preserved, the last lines coming full circle in confirmation of the opening. The translator must contrive an equal emphasis. The metre, pure iambic, although it has its use, seems inessential to the poetry. Metres and rhythms need not in themselves strain the translator's attention: what should, to the utmost, is the part they play in the poem; for this, the translator must find metrical and rhythmical analogues in the language in which he is writing. *C*.4 is an imagist poem and Catullus' unusual choice of metre prevents the succession of images from getting in each other's way. This can be achieved in English by splitting up the lines. Rhythmically, the important thing to capture is the strong, sonorous, at times onomatopoeic effect. Lines where sound values seem particularly important are 8, 9, 12 and 24. There is humour in some of this, especially in the jawbreaking lines 8 and 9: *Rhodumque nobilem horridamque Thraciam/Propontida trucemve Ponticum sinum*. A possible aim, if metre is abandoned: juxtaposed images, clean in the half-line, held together by longer lines that imitate some of Catullus' more striking sound effects.

C.5 & 7. Even 'rare' Ben Jonson falls short when confronted with the extraordinary resonance of *nox est perpetua et una dormienda*, although his treatment of the two poems, with Ferrabosco's setting, is by far the best we have. The chime of *lux* . . . *nox* is fortunately to hand in English, and Jonson uses it, which is no reason for us not to. The line is an example of a device we have already found in *C*.1 and that occurs again and again in Catullus, that of the hinge line. He will strike out a line as focus to the whole poem, which can be seen as moving towards it, cresting on it, and then receding. The structure fits perfectly with Catullus' love of endings in diminuendo, the unexpected zeroing in on a significant detail, the use of the image as coda. When coming to a poem of Catullus, the translator must look for the hinge line, since, if such exists, that will be the nexus around which he must order his poem. His next task should be to plot the relation between syntax and metre. Only thus can he assess the import of the metre. In *C*.78, for instance, the sentence structure sprawls all over the metre. Here, in the two kissing poems, the hendecasyllables seem of the essence of the poetry. The translator therefore seeks his analogue, always remembering that it is not the metre itself, but its function that has to be conveyed. In Catullus' hendecasyllables I have read lightness, kinesis, the impact of the single line without loss of kinetic effect – but above all lightness. The metre works best in short poems. Its danger is that the single line will predominate and the onward movement become a series of disjunct little steps – unfortunate, even if they be dance steps. In the four-syllable, mostly two-stressed line that I have used for hendecasyllables, the challenge has been the other way round – not to let the kinetic element obscure the single line. To this end, the hyphen at the end of a line can be very useful. In *C.*5, *Rumoresque senum severiorum* can become 'the sour-faced strict-/ures of the wise'; while in *C.*10, in my version, there occurs, 'a/not unlady-/like young lady,/of obvious "charms" '.

*C.*6. The attentive translator will not miss the repetition of *inlepidae* (line 2), applied to Flavius' new mistress, in *lepido* (last line), applied to Catullus' poem. The swarm of Latinate polysyllables which I bring to bear ('unattractive', 'unacceptable', 'accompaniment', 'discretion', 'attenuated', 'preoccupation') allows for the heavy-handed irony – the note of masculine camaraderie – which I have chosen for my approach. It was an ill choice. I find that, when, in these boulevard pieces, I have wished to emphasize the ironic note and have therefore felt the need for Latinate diction, I have been inclined to overlook the uses of Catullus' metric. The delicacy and point of his hendecasyllables have too often been lost in favour of heavier effects.

*C.*8. One of the three by Catullus that Macaulay was unable to read (he tells us) without being moved to tears. (The other two were *C.*45 and 76.) The poem is full of repeated words and even has one repeated line. These can be seen as registering the twistings and turnings of Catullus' thoughts. In such instances, when some trick of rhetoric is very much to the fore, it is permissible to use it where it is not used in the original, but where the translator feels it might have been used had local needs dictated. As for *miser*, the rhetoric of such words will always be a problem. Latitude must be allowed for the fashion of the day, whether it be to underplay or overplay. The main thing, in this poem, is to strike the hinge line, which is the repeated line, *Fulsere vere candidi tibi soles*, at which point the nostalgic mood abruptly changes to one of indifference too exaggerated to be convincing. 'Methinks the poet doth protest too much,' we murmur. Essential here that the translator allow the stabs of jealousy to fall in quickening recurrences as the poem ends, the emotional impact of the poem lying in the paced relation between its two parts.

C.11. The litany of foreign names should be rendered with relish, *ore rotonda*. The whole known world is called to witness his opinion of Lesbia. Besides which, all poets like lists of names, and the translator may be sure he is close to his poet when he is rendering, rhyming if need be, one of these lists of his. (After all, what are poems but proper names for things? Rather complicated ones to be sure, but names for the emotions, none the less.) Ironic enumeration breaks on *non bona dicta*, the hinge line, and is succeeded by hyperbole, *identidem omnium/Ilia rumpens*, which itself gives place to litotes in *tactus aratrost*. It was a grave error, when I came to the end, to try to sustain the hyperbole. The entire effect of the poem is destroyed and one of Catullus' loveliest diminuendo endings literally 'slashed', since it is, misguidedly, by the word 'slashed' that I have sought to translate *tactus aratrost*, 'touched by the plough'. Apart from this, in *Qui illius culpa cecidit*, 'that you, tart, wantonly crushed', 'wantonly' for *culpa* renders 'tart' otiose. As one of the only two poems Catullus wrote in sapphics, it would be as well to render it in the regular metre and not in some reminiscence thereof. The pathos of the poem, as so often in Catullus, rests in the relation of part to part: irony, hyperbole, litotes. Here is the translator's test.

C.17. Where the insertion of a word or phrase will save a footnote, I believe such an insertion to be justified. The river Gua, provided in my poem, does not exist in Catullus'. There is, however, a river Gua at Cologna Veneta, near Verona, where a *ponte di Catullo* preserves the tradition of the poem. The mercurial tone is Catullus at his most Catullan: satirical, lyrical and imagistic by turns. As for the ending, C.11, 15, 25, 38, all bear the same imprint. He signs off in a phrase, or with an image in miniature, as complete and summary as an oriental seal. I know of no other poet so consistently successful and original in the concluding stamp he puts on a poem. A husband's sexual indifference, as a mule's shoe cast in the slough: *Ferream ut soleam tenaci in voragine mula*, 'as the pack-mule casts/its iron-soled slipper/in the obstinate mud'. A study of Catullus' endings would be a good place for a translator to start.

*C.*21. The translator should look to Landor's paraphrase: one of his best.

*C.*23. The test is a simple one: to keep a poker-face. I remember once seeing Malvolio played straight. It was a performance by Harold Lang at the Theatre Royal, Brighton. The result was very funny indeed, and not without pathos. Lang understood that all the humour was there already, that there was no need to underline it. (As with sentiment in *C.*2 and 3.) Underline it and you will enervate it. Every phrase must be played straight. The poem will then emerge for what it is: one of the funniest of the *Carmina*.

*C.*25. How irrationally *deserving* we feel when a line comes out with no more trouble than it takes to transcribe it! *Vel pene languido senis situque araneoso* . . . and one writes, 'or the cobwebby penis of an elderly gentleman'. We all, in hallucinatory moments, dream of possessing a magic xerox machine, in which one has only to insert the most intractable of loved poems, and – test of one's love – they will emerge word for word, cadence for cadence, as they went in, but now possessed in one's own language. The point is, that such moments are necessary if we are to approach our Sisyphan task in the first place. When not hallucinating, we are aware that there are three modes of translation: metaphrase, paraphrase, imitation. The line just quoted is metaphrase. We are delighted when this happens and know in our hearts that it has nothing really to do with our merits or demerits as translators, but is like a 'birdie' in golf. The use of paraphrase and transposition is of particular help when 'placing' the original in our tradition. Imitation, or 'persona' as we now call it, dares to walk on equal footing with the translated. All three modes are equally reputable, equally available, to be used as the translator pleases. He should feel free to move from one to another within the confines of the same poem, certainly within the confines of the same *oeuvre*.

*C.*26. 'Draught', 'overdraft'. All accidents of language, all fortuitous plays on words, should be treated as grist to the mill. This is one of the three poems Pound translated, the other two being *C.*43 and 85.

*C.*31. I have used 'brilliant' to describe the brilliant effects Catullus achieves in his closing lines – brilliant in the pianistic sense, although the word does not itself occur in the Latin. Epithets of aesthetic description, such as this, because they are an explicit confession of failure, should be used with caution.

C.34. Required: absolute transparency of phrase united to what the Romans called *gravitas*. A simplicity that is serious without being solemn. Add the dance.

C.35. I should have the translator first try his hand at this and *C*.17 before being permitted to proceed further. Can he match the shifting moods and attitudes of this most volatile of poets? First, Catullus addresses the papyrus on which the poem is written that he is sending to his friend inviting him to join him at Sirmione; second, he addresses the friend, Caecilius; then, Caecilius' mistress, and, between these, inserts acknowledgements of the power of the Mother Goddess, Cybele, the subject of a long poem on which Caecilius is engaged, and who, by means of Caecilius' devotion, is revealed as the cause of the situation in which all three now find themselves. All this in the compass of eighteen hendecasyllabic lines. If the translator can so interweave these themes that each contributes to the force of the other, he is right for Catullus.

C.45. The translator should be a mimic of all the possible modes of verse, not in the language from which he is translating, but in his own. Should he feel the need of 'placing' his original, he must be able to draw on seventeenth-century lyric, or eighteenth-century couplet, at will. What a limitation were a translator to permit himself to draw only on contemporary fashions of verse technique! At times the violation of some general principle of writing English may seem called for. The opening of *C*.45 is a case in point: *Acmen Septimius suos amores/Tenens in gremio* . . . Our lack of case endings makes it undesirable to place a subject and an object side by side. On the other hand, the reason for doing so here seems of more importance than the general rule. The poetic point is, 'girl/boy', 'beloved/lover': thus, 'Phyllis Corydon clutched to him/ her head at rest beneath his chin'.

C.46. *Furor*, 'fūror': an opportunity of using the identical word in one's translation, though with altogether changed nuances. *Iam caeli furor aequinoctialis*, 'now the *furor* of March skies'. *C*.58 provides another example in the line, *Glubit magnanimos Remi nepotes*, 'magnanimous' yielding an added bitterness.

*C.*51. A direct translation from Sappho. I should not now, were the line to be printed in italics, hesitate to supply the missing Adonic (a dactyl followed by a trochee) at the end of the second stanza. It is instructive to note that Catullus does not blush to insert a phrase of his own (line 2) not in the Sappho. The last four lines present the translator with the same problem as the last three lines of *C.*2. (The unity of *C.*55 and of 68 is similarly disputable.) To translate Catullus' sapphics as though they were written from beginning to end in the Adonic close strikes me, today, as nothing less than an absurdity. Fortunately, when I came to Sappho's original, I was more circumspect. But it was uphill work. Eleven Greek syllables, I knew, were not the equivalent of eleven English syllables. The weights of languages differ; but what this implied, I failed to grasp. Undaunted, I was two weeks constructing a metrical carbon. Perched at a window a hundred stairs up, face to face with the wall of the Duomo in Perugia, I sweated at fitting the Greek syllables to English words. The doves swooping between me and the holes they had made in the Duomo walls kept me at it. The result bore none but a dictionary resemblance to the Greek. An image here and there survived. None of the music. Deep dissatisfaction. A recognition that one was neither Swinburne, master of sapphics, nor Pound, no bad hand at them. Further dissatisfaction. Recourse to reading. Campion's essay on the English sapphic. One knows the essay as though it were one's own. 'Rose-cheeked Laura.' Illumination. Laura has been intimate from many years, but one had never thought to *use* her. A hendecasyllabic line of five or six words will be a lot lighter and take less time to say than a hendecasyllabic line of eleven words. A line of Sappho will contain more syllables though fewer words than the same line in English. Cut eleven syllables to eight, five to four. The weights of languages differ. Another two weeks at the window facing the Duomo. The doves again. Dissatisfaction lightens as poem results. Not good, not even 'good enough', but a failure in a different cause. From now on, the dictum (self-evident) holds: Don't count the number of syllables in the line, but the time it takes to say them. Time, not number, is the key to equivalence.

*C.*55. There are two lines that, above the rest, should be preserved intact, although to do so will strain the best talent. *Num te lacteolae tenent puellae?* and *Verbosa gaudet Venus loquella*. The second should have a proverbial ring.

C.57. There are times when the original language may be used. Sometimes for an exclamation, or an invocation, such as here; sometimes when a term is so technical that there is no exact equivalent: the philosophical term, *virtù*, in Dante; or even when some shade of foreignness is required, not otherwise obtainable, as *quid pro quo*, in a version I made of Martial, Book v.84, where I could equally have used 'tit for tat'.

C.58. The pauses and the repetitions must be retained. The poem is shaped by them and much of its tone of yearning is derived from them. The famous, or infamous, last line, to which I have already referred in my note on *C*.46, caused me trouble when I came to translate it. George Santayana, writing from the Convent of the Blue Nuns in Rome, had quoted the line as illustrating the degradation of the city at the hands of the allies. Was he justified in applying '*glubit*' so precisely in that context? I wrote to Ezra Pound asking his opinion. Pound replied by return. 'Can't,' he wrote, 'recall vicinage at San Stefano whence Santayana could have observed very exactly, but reckon old Jarge must've been leanin' over the fence 'nd using a pair of opry glarsses.' Since when, I have been unable to read Catullus' words without the image of Santayana thus incongruously engaged rising between me and them.

C.61. An imagist poem with a dance rhythm that is overtly sexual, the climax coming, after many approaches and as many delays, in the sixth stanza from the end.

C.62. The hexameter has resolutely refused anglicization. A partial solution would be to do what I did in *C*.11 with sapphics and 'remind' the reader of hexameters by making free play with dactyls and spondees, the spondees coming, where possible, at the ends of lines. This is what I have done, frequently splitting the hexameter into half lines, liberating the images within the line. Unfortunately, loose rhythms and exact rhythms point in opposite directions aesthetically. To write in regular metre is one thing; to write in an approximation of one is quite another. In the former, grace appeals by reason of her constrictions: assumed to her they become her, and she them; in the latter, the appeal is of the uncorseted.

C.63. Galliambics. Since there is no other example of them, there is no tradition on which to draw in our approach to the poem –

except, of course, what can be deduced of Cybele's rites. The drum-beat slaps – two or three at the end of each line – should be reproduced in any version, however free rhythmically. The diction is frequently bizarre owing to the exigencies of the metre. Similar oddities should by no means be shunned in English, even without a difficult metre to excuse them. The overall impression is one of extreme urgency. The last three lines are addressed directly to Cybele. In them, Catullus recognizes himself in the figure of Attis. He begs Cybele not to let what happened to Attis happen to him. Whatever the means, the translator should be sure that the waking world, which these lines represent, is held separate from the visionary world of the ninety lines preceding them.

*C.*64. It was Donald Carne-Ross who, in a kindly review, first observed that I had tried to make a Poundian Canto out of the poem. He was quite right, and I still think that this was a reasonable approach. Metric is subordinate to overall structure. The poem is cinematic in concept. This can be brought out by using radically different rhythms for the different sections, the technique required being that of the cutting-room floor. Landor came to the poem twice in his *Conversations*, treating it in verse as well as prose.

*C.*65. Encourage the tendency to one sentence. Note the pivotal lines 13 and 14, marking the very Catullan switch: 'You think I am writing about *this*, but in truth I am writing about *that*.' Note also the breadth of the successive clauses in the first half of the poem, and the focus at the end, narrowing to the exquisitely specific miniature of the last phrase. As with the hexameters of *C.*62, I should advise that the translator disentangle the parts of the elegiac couplet from each other and string them imagistically down the page.

*C.*66. Among the translator's first thoughts should be: 'Are there any acknowledgements to be made, debts to be discharged?' When the past was considered alive in the present, this was a natural approach. With the invention of historical perspective, at the beginning of the nineteenth century, all the ages intervening between the translator and his original were thrust from sight and the poem denied the independent life it had acquired. The interlocking of past and present, with the poet-translator as mediator between them, is first laid before us in the episode of Odysseus and the blind minstrel at the court of King Alcinous. We should stick with Homer and make sure that we do not separate the poems by which we are confronted from the traditions whence they have reached us.

Transposition on a large scale, where spritual affinities are discerned, is to be approved of: Johnson's London, for Juvenal's Rome; on a small scale, however, it is often sounder policy to recognize the differences. Rome was a slave state. Slaves were sexually available. Homosexuality was considered neither a vice nor a disease. Infibulation was practised, *etc.*, *etc.* Smoothing out awkward differences is not the way to understanding and so to that 'in-feeling' which Vernon Lee used to regard as basic to the contemplation of any work of art. For these reasons, I now regret the use of 'Debrett' in the fourth couplet.

In lines 75 and 76, the lock of hair regrets its 'translation to the brilliant skies'. In my version it reasserts its dissatisfaction, adding, 'my heavenly lustres shine (to me) less clear/ than those that hung from Berenice's ear'. There is no sanction in the Latin for this couplet. At this late date I find myself unwilling to cut and unable to justify. A verse translation is a poetic commentary (among other things). Where does one draw the line in one's 'commentary'?

C.68. My main discovery here was the use to which the metrical divisions of the elegiac couplet could be put in sustaining English rhythms in a long meditative poem. Since C.68 is meditative and not, like C.64, narrative, there is no need to change rhythms and metres to meet the needs of the different sections. There is no variation in pace, nor need there be. As elsewhere, I have used dactyls and spondees to an extent not common in English. 'Oblivion's veil', at the point where some say the poem ends and so-called 68(a) takes over, represents a token of homage to Walter Savage Landor, as though to say, 'He is the man whom I should like to have rendered these lines; let me do it for him, as he might have done it.'

The remaining poems comprise Catullus' epigrams pure and simple. They have nothing of the lyric quality of what I have described as the 'lyric epigrams'. They are all in what was then the traditional metre of the epigram: elegiacs. Over the years, I have become increasingly dissatisfied with the excessively loose manner in which I have handled these. Their revolutionary quality lies in the personal use to which Catullus put the form. I now feel that for this part of the *Carmina* I should have done better to use syllabics, as I have recently done with Martial, allowing the turbulence of Catullus' subject to beat against their formality.

C.70. Lovelace helped here. No translator should miss his versions.

C.76. The only approach to blank verse I have used in rendering Catullus, or, I believe, any classical poet. The self-pitying note, as in some of Shakespeare's soliloquies, may have led me to this. In any event, the result is rhetorical, and the rhetoric is of a received sort. The poem stands out from the other poems at the end of the *Carmina*: the model for the subsequent Latin love elegy.

C.85. One of the Catullan test poems. As with *C*.58, the pauses are everything. *C*.93, in its minor mode, is another such test poem. Landor, I find, fails in the first, but he comes out well in the second: *Nil nimium studeo, Caesar, tibi velle placere,/Nec scire utrum sis albus an ater homo*. 'I care not, Caesar, what you are,/Nor know if ye be brown or fair.'

C.86. I confess to being unduly under Arthur Symons's influence, though he would never have written anything as loose as this. He manages, however, to capture something of the boulevard aspect of Catullus, which is not surprising given his milieu. His versions, from this point of view, deserve attention. In his day, the Popean couplet was popular for much classical translation. Its advantage is not only that it is as exact as the Latin elegiac, but that it divides, if there are antitheses within the lines, as the elegiac does, into four parts, with the added balance of the two whole lines against each other. Occasionally, with Martial, though never with Catullus, I have used a ten-syllable line against an eight-syllable one.

C.95. Landor helped here. He was always best in the (apparently) occasional poem such as this.

C.96. Distinctly a poem that should go into the strictest of formal arrangements.

C.99. As with the detail of the opening names of *C*.45, 'Phyllis Corydon', so here with the first and last words, which are 'to steal' – the subject of the poem, a stolen kiss, being what comes between them. Of such details are poems made.

*C.*101. The final phrase, customary in funerary inscriptions, must be preserved. Retain – even add to – the repetitions. Pile on the spondees.

And so to *C.*116, the last in the order we have – not, almost certainly, Catullus'. We find him signing off with a flourish: the poet as toreador, the object of the epigrams the unfortunate Gellius, whom we have met before, though read simply nowadays as standing for all unfortunate adversaries of the poet.

There is an observation in the introduction to my Catullus which I should like to take this opportunity of revising. I wrote, in 1965, that I had tried to rewrite the poems as I imagined Catullus would have written them had he been alive and writing in English. I no longer hold this a tenable aim, since it is clear that were Catullus writing now there are quite simply a host of things he would not, could not, say, and that the sum of these things would alter very considerably his poetic nature. The circumstances of a poet's age largely decide the sort of poet he is to be. This, it may be objected, leaves the device of 'transposition' as our only guide. Not necessarily. A radical re-ordering of our relation to the past, a refusal to acknowledge an abysm between it and us, would be a surer one. Before what I have referred to as 'the invention of historical perspective', which occurred around 1800, people *possessed* the classics, which, as a result, were never translated to better effect. Many of Landor's versions are scattered through his essay on Catullus, which is concerned almost entirely with the minutest of textual matters. They were written for people who had Catullus by heart. Today's versions are written for those who will not only never have him by heart, but who will never know enough Latin to read him even with a crib. Landor's textual concerns are rigorous in their demands *ad literam*. His literary approach is that of one taking a walk with an old friend and happy that we should eavesdrop on the occasion. His versions are what I have called 'poetic commentaries'. Sadly, it seems that the time for that sort of thing may have passed for good. There are those who demand, with all the fervour of the bereft, that the classics be resurrected – recovered as in their heyday. There are those who believe the classics are still with us – that all they need is a little artificial respiration. What the first want is impossible. What the second believe is untrue. One's own versions inhabit uncomfortable middle territory.

The letter to Ezra Pound, called forth by Santayana's quotation from *C.*58, brought me, in 1961, to live with the poet's family in their castle in the Italian Tyrol. There I translated the remainder of my Catullus. As luck would have it, Santayana's companion of many years, Daniel Cory, was living there. His advice and encouragement helped me to complete the work. Now, in Daniel Cory's old apartment, at the table at which, some years after I had left the castle, he died, I find myself, a quarter of a century later, typing out these notes on that work. The mention I have made of placing a work in its tradition seems to be exemplified here, circumstances contributing to the very essence of the thing made. It remains only to trust that these notes may have a value beyond the obvious one of setting the record straight: that is, that they may be of interest – even help – to the next translator of Catullus, who is even now waiting, with a fresh bundle of poetic predilections, round the next corner.

TRANSLATING 'THE SOUND OF WATER': DIFFERENT VERSIONS OF A *HOKKU* BY BASHŌ

Nobuyuki Yuasa

❦ Even in translating such a short piece as a *hokku*, a translator from Japanese to English has to face numerous problems. In what follows, I should like to discuss some of the problems I had to face in translating a *hokku* by Bashō, and by comparing my translation with others, explain how I arrived at my own solutions. Readers are kindly requested to take my writing not as a defence but as a confession. I frankly admit that some of my solutions are far from being happy ones, but it would perhaps be useful to explain the thinking that lies behind them.

The *hokku* in question reads: *Furuike ya, kawazu tobikomu, mizu no oto*. It is probably the best known of Bashō's *hokku*, and is contained in the anthology called *Haru no Hi* (*Spring Days*). My translation is:

Breaking the silence
Of an ancient pond,
A frog jumped into water –
A deep resonance.

Mr Tadashi Kondō collected fifty other translations of this *hokku* in his MA thesis. Here are some examples:

Old pond! the noise of the jumping frog.
Masaoka Shiki

Old pond – frogs jumping in sound of water.
Lafcadio Hearn

An old pond –
A frog jumps in –
A splash of water.

Nitobe Inazō

Old garden lake!
The frog thy depth doth seek,
And sleeping echoes wake.

Saitō Hidesaburō

The old pond, yes!
A frog jumping in.
The water's noise!

G. S. Fraser

The ancient pond
A frog leaps in
The sound of the water.

Donald Keene

Old pond –
and a frog-jump-in
water-sound.

Harold G. Henderson

An old silent pond . . .
A frog jumps into the pond,
splash! Silence again.

Harry Behn

An old pond –
The sound
Of a diving frog.

Kenneth Rexroth

The old pond,
A frog jumps in –
Plop!

Reginald H. Blyth

The quiet pond
A frog leaps in,
The sound of the water.

Edward G. Seidensticker

A glance through this list makes us wonder if all these translations are really based on a single original, so varied are the impressions we get from them. However, what seems to be an utter confusion is to a considerable degree due to the gaps in the original text, as I hope to demonstrate later. But there is some outside help which might be useful for a translator. In the case of this *hokku*, we have the following testimony by Kagami Shikō:

One spring, our master shut himself up in his cottage in the north of

Bukō. The rain was falling quietly, and the low cooing of a dove was heard. In the soft wind, cherry blossoms were scattering, petal by petal. Probably it was late March, full of sad feeling about its going. Frogs dropped into the water, and the sound was heard not frequently but with long intervals. A profound emotion mounted in our master's heart, and he finally produced the seven–five syllables: *kawazu tobikomu mizu no oto*. Shinshi was with our master and suggested the five syllables: *yamabuki ya* to crown our master's composition. However, our master made a simpler choice and decided on *furuike ya*. The yellow roses are beautiful and gay, but the old pond is honest and true to the feeling. I find a great deal of profundity in the thought of our master who preferred the sombre honesty of the old pond to the gay beauty of the yellow roses.

This passage tells us a great deal about the occasion of the poem, and no doubt it is a help for a translator, but it is too dangerous for him to rely solely on this testimony for a number of reasons. First, in spite of the realism of his description, Shikō seems to admit that he was not present when the poem was composed. Second, the landscape he describes is so typical that it makes one suspect idealization, if not fiction. Third, Shikō was criticized by Etsujin, another disciple of Bashō, when he said in another essay that the frog poem marked the beginning of his master's mature style. Taking all these things into consideration, a translator must decide for himself how much of this testimony is to be trusted. I myself took a middle course, and while disregarding such things as a dove's cooing and cherry blossoms as being unnecessary, accepted that the place of composition was Bashō's cottage with an old pond in the garden, the time being late spring, and that the general aim of the poet was to communicate the sense of profound mystery rather than a mere description of the sound of water caused by a jumping frog. With this basic premise (which can be either right or wrong; no one can be sure about this point), let us proceed to the question of gaps in the original text.

The first word in the text is *furuike*, which is a compound noun consisting of the adjective *furushi* meaning 'old' and the noun *ike* meaning 'pond'. If a translator could satisfy himself with this simple explanation and end the whole matter by saying 'an old pond', his job would be easy. Somehow, however, I found this English equivalent to *furuike* unsatisfactory, and I wondered why. First, I sensed that the English equivalent was too weak, far too abstract and general, to convey the landscape suggested by the original word. It is true that the original word itself is not so precise in its representational quality; it is in fact far from 'the direct treatment of the thing'. Nevertheless, I thought it was the responsibility of a translator to say more than 'an old pond' to give a little more sense of the presence of the poet by the pond. Second, I noticed that *furuike* was not the same thing as *furuki ike*. The latter is perfectly conversational, even prosaic, but the former is unlikely to be used in ordinary conversation: being a compound, it has a bookish Chinese flavour, is even somewhat archaic. To give a greater sense of presence by the pond, I decided to add the word 'silence'. Unlike Shikō's dove's cooing and cherry blossoms, this word would not carry the reader's attention away from the pond, and yet it suggests by implication the presence of a listening ear. And to convey the archaic flavour of the original word, I decided to use the word 'ancient'. I am not perfectly happy with this solution, for the word has some unpleasant connotations. Still, it is better than 'old' and makes a better preparation for what follows. Thus, 'the silence of an ancient pond' was established.

The second word in the original text, *ya,* presents a great deal of difficulty, partly because there is no equivalent word in English and partly because it performs a function rather difficult to define. In its ordinary usage, it expresses a sense of wonder and excitement, and the closest English equivalent would be an exclamation mark. But in *hokku*, it performs the function of *kireji*, which literally means 'a cutting word'. When a *kireji* is placed at the end of a poem, it gives the poem a dignified ending, concluding the poem with a heightened sense of closure. When a *kireji* is used in the middle of a poem it cuts the stream of thought for a brief moment, thereby indicating that the poem consists of two thoughts half independent of each other. The subtlety of *kireji* is such that Bashō is reported to have said, 'The use of *kireji* alone does not always ensure cutting, and in some poems, cutting is achieved without using a *kireji*.' When I looked at the *hokku* under discussion with these words of Bashō in mind, I noticed one curious thing. In spite of the use of the *kireji* at the end of the first five syllables, it seemed to me the real cutting occurred between the middle seven syllables and the last five syllables, although grammatically these syllables were inseparably linked together. This consideration induced me to place a dash at the end of the third line in my translation, and I am rather pleased with the result because this way I could foreground 'the sound of water' which is obviously the most important thing in the poem. I chose a dash, rather than an exclamation mark, because in this particular case I needed a quiet pause. A comma would not yield a pause long enough, and a full stop would break the unity of the poem. The *kireji* cuts the stream of thought only for a brief moment, and the poem as a whole should stand as one stream, or in the words of Bashō, 'like gold beaten into thinness'. I also added the word 'breaking' at the beginning of the poem in order to smooth the flow of the poem until it reached the pause indicated by the dash. I am not very happy with the addition of this word, because there is hardly anything that corresponds to it in the original poem, but without it, the poem would break into three separate sections, losing the unity of the whole.

The third word in the original text, *kawazu*, presents two problems: one is grammatical and the other biological. Owing to the peculiarity of Japanese nouns, we do not know whether *kawazu* is singular or plural. Shikō suggests that it is plural, but also adds that the sound was heard not frequently but with long intervals between each sound. I went further than this, and opted for the singular, for I thought that psychologically the poem described a singular action complete in itself, and that to think of its recurrence was totally unnecessary. I think I am supported by many critics in my option, but most notably by Masaoka Shiki who says that the poem describes 'a single action in a single moment'. I shall later discuss Shiki's opinion in greater detail, but here I wish to use it as evidence to show that I am not alone in opting for the singular. The ambiguity of the number can pose a serious problem for a translator, as in the case of the famous cicada poem, but fortunately in this case the superiority of the singular to the plural is more or less self-evident. The biological problem is more difficult to handle. There is no clue within the poem itself as to what species of frog the poet is talking about. The word *kawazu* is a poetic term, and has been used in various anthologies of *waka* since the times of the *Manyōshū*. Its more colloquial synonym *kaeru* also existed, but it has not been used in poetry. In the *Manyōshū*, the word *kawazu* was used most frequently to refer to the singing frog commonly known today as *kajika* that lives on the pebbled banks of a rapid stream, and rarely used to refer to an ordinary frog that lives and croaks in marshy places. In the *Kokinshū*, the word was used to refer exclusively to the first kind, and its status as a poetic word was so elevated that it often came to represent the image of the poet himself, like the word 'swan' in English. In the *Shinkokinshū*, however, the word *kawazu* was used again to designate the second kind of frog as well. Since our poet was sitting by an ancient pond, not beside a fast-flowing stream, I surmised that he was referring to the second kind, but could not determine what particular species he was talking about – whether he was talking about the fairly big frog known as a bullfrog, or about the relatively small one known as an earth-frog. Therefore, I decided to use the generic term 'frog' in my translation, though the choice is far from being satisfactory, because the word does not have the poetic quality of the original. Why did our poet use the poetic *kawazu* rather than the colloquial *kaeru*? I think the answer to this question can be found in his principle of *zokugo o tadasu*, which literally means 'rectifying vulgar terms'. *Haikai* poems as opposed to classical *waka* are characterized by the bold use of vulgar terms, but Bashō wanted to rectify them by using them as the vehicle of a noble message. In this particular poem, the image of the ordinary frog is humble enough, but the poet used the poetic term *kawazu* to indicate that the frog was more than an ordinary frog – that it was a vehicle of profound mystery. Short of any English word that might achieve this effect, I had to postpone the solution of this problem till the final line in my translation.

The fourth word in the original text, *tobikomu*, is a verb meaning 'to jump into'. Semantically the word presents no problem, but there is some ambiguity about its tense. If you take it to be the present tense, the action of the frog becomes simultaneous with the sound of water, while if you take it to be the present perfect tense, you allow some lapse of time, though little more than a fraction of a moment, between the action of the frog and the sound of water. There is a version of this poem in which Bashō says *tondaru*, which emphatically stresses the present perfect tense. It is generally agreed, however, that this is an earlier version, less successful than the standard version. I think Bashō revised the earlier version for two reasons. First, *tondaru* with its colloquialism smacks of the vulgar diction of the *Danrin* school against which Bashō revolted, and second, it carries with it the implication that the action of the frog was completed when it jumped into the water, making the sound of water a kind of additional thought, rather than an integral part of the poem. In other words, the strong emphasis on the perfect tense cuts the poem between the middle seven syllables and the last five syllables, thereby destroying the unity of the poem. And yet, even in the revised version, a trace of the earlier version remains. Hence the ambiguity of the tense, and the psychological pause in spite of the grammatical continuity between the middle seven syllables and the last five syllables. I think the superiority of *tobikomu* to *tondaru* is in the double function it performs: it both links and cuts. The grammar implies continuity, but the rhythm slows down gradually, indicating a pause.

I felt a strong need to indicate this effect of the pause in my translation, and so I rather boldly departed from the original text, and adopted the past tense for the verb 'jump' in my translation. Moreover, instead of closing my line with a preposition, I said 'jumped into water', for I thought this was a more conclusive way of closing a line, more conducive to the emphatic cutting I needed in my translation. But, of course, the line must glide into the next line. That is why I added a dash. Thus I sought to achieve something like the double effect of cutting and linking. Although I admit that there is much room for criticism in my use of the past tense here, I am rather pleased with the result myself, for it indicates more clearly than the present tense that there was a pause, a lapse of a fraction of time, between the action of the frog and the sound of water that followed. I think the existence of this pause is of the utmost importance from a psychological or aesthetic point of view.

We come then to the last five syllables. In my opinion, this is the most important part of the poem, and it is a real test for a translator's ability. The original text says *mizu no oto*. *Mizu* is a noun meaning water. *No* is a particle indicating possession. Its equivalent in English is the preposition 'of'. *Oto* is a noun meaning sound. Thus, on the surface level, there is no problem at all. 'The sound of water' seems to be a perfectly adequate translation. In fact, there is some charm in the simplicity of this expression. Nevertheless, it was my belief that the complexity of the feeling roused by the original text could not be conveyed by the simple expression 'the sound of water'. I have already pointed out that Masaoka Shiki thought that the poem described 'a single action in a single moment'. He goes on to say that the poem has no 'spatial extension' nor 'temporal continuity'. I find it difficult to accept this view. I think Shiki was misled by his own theory of *shasei* (sketching). In his attempt to emphasize the importance of realistic description, Shiki often refused to go beyond description. He even preferred Buson to Bashō because of the greater 'objectivity' of the former. Bashō is also an objective poet in the sense that he describes an image (rather, a sound in this particular poem) without commenting on it. But Bashō is far from being an objectivist. He is reported to have said that if a poet said all that he wanted to say in his poem, it would lose its beauty (*Iioosete nanika aru*). This means that he stressed the importance of what is commonly known as *yoin* (lingering echoes) or *yojō* (lingering emotions). Bashō invites us to listen to the sound of water, but he does not want us to stop there. He wants us to listen to the echoes that ultimately end in deep silence again. This reflection led me to say more than 'the sound of water' in my translation. The words I chose after much deliberation were 'a deep resonance'. I thought these words were close enough to the sound of water and yet a clear indication of the importance of the lingering emotions that followed. I believe that through these words I have succeeded in showing that the poem indeed does have spatial extension and temporal continuity. Without an expression of this kind, the world of the poem shrinks. In short, my choice was based on the conviction that the greatness of the poet was in his ability to show a phase of eternity in an action of a moment.

Before closing this short essay, I should like to comment on the list of the translations I placed at the beginning. Masaoka Shiki's translation is almost a verbatim translation of the original text. He is determined to say neither more nor less than what the original text says, and yet it reads amazingly well. I think this is mainly due to the fact that he put the middle seven syllables and the last five syllables together to form a natural sequence of English words. The only thing I find difficult to accept is the word 'noise', on account of its unpleasant connotations. Lafcadio Hearn's translation is unique in the use of the plural 'frogs'. And yet 'sound of water' does not suggest repetition. I do not know how to account for this contradiction. He also insisted on retaining the order of the original text and placed 'frogs jumping in' before 'sound of water'. This compelled him to use two dashes, which makes the poem too fragmentary. Nitobe Inazō's translation is similar to Lafcadio Hearn's in the order of words, but he uses the singular 'frog' and 'a splash of water'. I think the use of the onomatopoeic 'splash' is rather unfortunate because it only represents the surface sound. Saitō Hidesaburō's translation is an attempt to go beyond the surface. The use of the words 'depth' and 'echoes' shows that the translator had a policy similar to mine. However, my objection to this translation is twofold. First, the adoption of strict iambic metre in the second and third lines makes the poem rather monotonous, and second, the use of such expressions as 'garden lake' and 'sleeping echoes' together with the archaic 'thy' makes the poem sound too much like a piece of Pre-Raphaelite writing. As a result, this translation is more like an imitation of an English poem than a translation. G. S. Fraser's translation is unique in its attempt to recreate the effect of *kireji* by using the emphatic 'yes!' at the end of the first line. I find it difficult, however, to account for so much excitement. Moreover, the use of the full stop at the end of the second line breaks the poem into three separate lines. Fraser gains in strength and excitement, but loses the quiet meditative quality of the original poem. Donald Keene's translation is characterized by his neglect of traditional punctuation. Until he comes to the full stop at the end of the third line, he uses neither commas nor dashes. I find it doubtful, however, whether this really puts the three lines together. Moreover, the neglect of traditional punctuation is a trademark of modernist poetry. As a result, Keene's translation reads too much like a piece of a certain kind of modern poetry. I think the same can be said about Harold G. Henderson's translation. He ignores not only traditional punctuation but also traditional grammar. I do not know if anyone can account for the grammar of the second and third lines. I am convinced that this kind of bold departure from traditional grammar is alien to the spirit of the original poem. Harry Behn's translation seems to have been well thought out. I think the addition of 'silence again' at the end of the third line brings out the basic structure of the original poem: silence-action-silence. The only criticism I have about this translation is that there are too many cuts within the short space of the poem. Kenneth Rexroth's translation is unique in the use of the word 'diving'. The word with its suggestion of downward movement gives weight and sobriety to the poem. I think 'the sound of a diving frog' is an obvious improvement on Shiki's 'the noise of the jumping frog'. What I do not understand in Rexroth's translation is why he broke 'the sound of a diving frog' into two lines. I think, poetically, this should stand as a unit. Reginald H. Blyth's translation differs from the rest in the use of the onomatopoeic 'plop'. I think there is hardly any doubt that 'plop' with its downward movement is superior to 'splash'. But whether the use of an onomatopoeia is desirable or not is another matter. I believe that in general sound symbolism is superior to onomatopoeia; that is to say, the suggestion of the sound of water is better than its overt expression. Edward G. Seidensticker's translation is somewhat similar to Donald Keene's in phrasing and punctuation, but he uses 'quiet' for 'ancient' and a comma at the end of the second line to show where the cutting occurs. I can see why he rejected 'ancient', but 'quiet' has its own problems. It sounds not only too soft but also trite. Also, the unpunctuated first line leaves me in doubt as to whether I should take it as independent, or as continuous with the second line.

I think I have said enough (perhaps more than enough) about the translations of other people. Of course, I had no intention of glorifying my own translation at the expense of the others. I simply wanted to show that no translation could be completely satisfactory. That is why a new translation has to be produced now and then. However, one thing probably emerges as a result of the comparison. Most of the translations I have discussed belong to what Dryden called 'metaphrase', while mine leans towards what he called 'paraphrase'. 'Metaphrase' is translation faithful to the words; in its extreme form it is verbatim translation. 'Paraphrase' is translation faithful to the experience evoked by the words; in its extreme form it becomes free rendering. Dryden says, 'It is best to steer a middle course between literal translation and paraphrase. The aim is to make the ancient author speak as he would have done if he had lived in the present age.' Bashō also recommends the following words of a famous priest: 'Do not slavishly follow the footsteps of the ancients. Seek rather what they sought after.'

THE SAYINGS OF THE SEVEN SAGES OF GREECE

Betty Radice

❦ In the summer of 1976 Dr Giovanni Mardersteig of the Officina Bodoni in Verona brought out one of his exquisite hand-printed books in an English edition limited to 160 numbered copies: *The Sayings of the Seven Sages of Greece*. The Greek lettering for the names of the Sages was copied from the decree in honour of Oeniades of 408/7 BC (No. 6796 in the Epigraphic Museum in Athens), and the aphorisms themselves were printed in the beautiful Greek capitals originally cut by Francesco Griffo of Bologna about 1494 for the press of Aldus Manutius in Venice. It proved to be the last of the magnificently printed books which came from the hand press in over fifty years. Giovanni Mardersteig died at the end of 1977, shortly before his eighty-fifth birthday; until his final illness he had retained all his mental vigour and zest for new projects. Sir Roger Mynors once spoke of him to me as 'the Aldus of our times' and 'the last of the great scholar printers', and the writer of the obituary in *The Times* mourned the loss to the world of 'an author-scholar-printer without compare'. He was certainly one of the most remarkable men I have ever known.

It had been my privilege for some years to provide English translations for his books, mainly from Italian and classical or renaissance Latin, copies of which are treasured possessions. I gladly agreed to work on a Greek text of the Sayings of the Seven Sages and to supply an English version. Neither of us at our first discussion quite realized what this would involve. Dr Mardersteig was an excellent classical scholar, trained in the German universities of his youth, but his main interest was the Greek lettering. He was to visit Crete to examine the Gortyn inscription and Athens to copy the Oeniades dedication, and his preface had some new and percipient observations on the formation and development of Greek capitals. I knew very little of these wise men except some of their names and the much-quoted Delphic maxims, and was soon to find that the Greeks in general shared my ignorance.

In Plato's *Protagoras* Socrates argues that the Spartan gift for laconic and pointed comment showed that their intellectual ability was well-trained, and that certain people in the past had realized

> that to frame such utterances is a mark of the highest culture. Of these were Thales of Miletus, Pittacus of Mitylene, Bias of Priene, our own Solon, Cleobulus of Lindus and Myson of Chen, and the seventh of their company, we are told, was a Spartan, Chilon. All these were emulators, admirers and disciples of Spartan culture, and their wisdom may be recognized as belonging to the same category, consisting of pithy and memorable dicta uttered by each. Moreover they met together and dedicated the first-fruits of their wisdom to Apollo in his temple at Delphi, inscribing those words which are on everyone's lips: 'Know thyself' and 'Nothing too much.' I mention these facts to make the point that, among the ancients, this Laconic brevity was the characteristic expresson of philosophy. In particular this saying of Pittacus, 'Hard is it to be noble', got into circulation privately and earned the approval of the wise.[1]

This is the earliest account we have. Myson was later replaced by the better-known Periander, tyrant of Corinth. In all the variations of the list (as many as seventeen claimants are quoted in Diogenes Laertius 1.42) Thales remains constant and was often treated as the foremost Sage. Thales is said by Herodotus (1.74) to have predicted the eclipse of the sun now dated to 585 BC, and Diogenes Laertius (1.22) adds that he was the first to be given the title of *sophos*, in the archonship of Damasias (582/1), 'when the epithet was applied to all the Seven, as Demetrius of Phalerum says in his list of archons'.[2] But why *seven* Sages? As sometimes today, seven seems to have been regarded as a number of special significance.[3] There were seven wonders of the world, seven heroes marched against Thebes, and we are told there are seven deadly sins.

In *Charmides* 164d Plato refers again to the three maxims to be seen on the temple at Delphi, putting forward the view that the first was earlier than the other two. He is of course referring to the Alcmaeonid temple of his own day, completed in 510, whereas if the Seven belong to the early sixth century, theirs was an earlier temple, which burned down in 548. It seems unlikely that the maxims were more than popular proverbs; certainly the first two, *γνῶθι σαυτόν* and *μηδὲν ἄγαν*, especially the first, continued to be frequently quoted.[4] 'Know yourself' and 'Nothing too much' could be read as homely good advice. The third maxim, *ἐγγύα, πάρα δ' ἄτα,* 'Give a pledge (or Go bail) and ruin faces you', was too specialized and archaic in sentiment to remain popular: perhaps the legal machinery of the classical age made it out of date.

The maxims were open to various kinds of re-interpretation by philosophers. Plato, in the *Charmides* passage, suggested 'Know yourself' really meant 'be temperate', while the Aristotelian polymath Clearchus of Cyprus (fl. *c.* 340–*c.* 250 BC) thought it was the oracular response given by the Pythia to Chilon of Sparta.[5] Diogenes Laertius (9.71), writing about Pyrrhon (*c.* 360–*c.* 270) and the Sceptics, says: 'Some say that Homer was the founder of this school, for he more than anyone is always giving different answers at different times to the same questions, and is never definite or dogmatic about the answer. The maxims of the Seven Wise Men they also call sceptical; for example, "Nothing too much" and "Give a pledge and ruin faces you." ' But in general the Sages were thought of as being contemporary with and known to each other, all connected with the worship of Apollo, giver of wisdom to men. The three popular proverbs at Delphi were assigned to them, and eventually four more 'Delphic maxims' were listed, to give them one apiece.

The connection of the Seven with Apollo and with each other is brought out in the story of the golden tripod which they dedicated to the god at Delphi. There were many versions of this, embroidered with what sound like folk-tales of the Ionian seaboard. In one the tripod was found by fishermen and sent by the people of Miletus to Delphi for the oracle to pronounce on its owner. They were told it should belong to the wisest of men, and gave it to Thales. He modestly passed it on and it went the round of the Sages until either he or Solon sent it back to Delphi. In other versions it was a golden bowl bequeathed by Bathycles the Arcadian, or a golden cup presented by Croesus, or the tripod was made by Hephaestus as a wedding present for Pelops, stolen by Paris along with Helen and thrown by her into the Coan sea lest it should be a cause of strife. Whatever it was, it passed through the hands of the Sages and ended up at Delphi.[6]

The ascription of sayings to sages was the result of the Greek desire to find historical origins for practices or knowledge useful in everyday life. No doubt the historical truth about them is impossible to discover: the tradition is hugely complicated by speculation and invention, especially in Hellenistic times. Diogenes Laertius, of whom little is known but who can probably be dated to the first half of the third century AD, has been much quoted, for the account in his compendium of the lives and opinions of the philosophers is the earliest attempt we have at establishing the names of the accepted Seven and putting together the aphorisms ascribed to them. His descriptions are discursive and confused by his loose mixture of historical anecdotes, snatches of verse and quoted sayings, as well as by lengthy extracts from apocryphal letters improbably supposed to have been exchanged by the Sages; but here at least are plenty of examples of practical wisdom.

We know rather more about Joannes Stobaeus, who lived probably in the early fifth century AD and was the author of an anthology of excerpts from prose-writers and poets for the instruction of his son Septimius. He simply lists (III 1,172) up to twenty Sayings for each Sage, without discussion, and gives Demetrius of Phalerum as his source. The list is printed in full under the heading *Die Sieben Weisen* by H. Diels in Volume I, section 10, pp. 61–6, of *Die Fragmente der Vorsokratiker.*[7] It is fuller than a list in comparable form from Diogenes Laertius would be; the two coincide to a limited extent, but not always in the same wording and ascription.

This seemed the most practicable text for the Officina Bodoni's purpose, but the translation of moral aphorisms pithily worded and lacking in context was not at all easy. I should sometimes have been hard put to guess what the sayings were getting at but for timely and generous help from Professor Hugh Tredennick, who is not, of course, responsible for errors of mine. And when set out, the sum of wisdom, inspired as it is by a sort of basic common sense, is not always particularly edifying. Diogenes Laertius (I.40) quotes Dicaearchus[8] as saying that the Seven 'were neither sages nor philosophers, *συνετοὺς δέ τινας καὶ νομοθετικούς*', which one might perhaps translate as 'but sensible men with a flair for legislation'; and indeed that seems fair comment. But there is variety and charm, and the interest of echoes of older literatures and cultures. 'Most men are bad' (Bias 1) recalls *Odyssey* 2.277. 'Nothing too much' appears first in Theognis 335. 'Call only the dead happy' (Chilon 7) is a common sentiment which is the central feature of Solon's discussion with Croesus in Herodotus 1.31ff. 'Give a pledge and ruin faces you' is close to Proverbs xi.15: 'Give a pledge for a stranger and know no peace; refuse to stand surety and be safe' (NEB translation). There is indeed a fair amount of emphasis on self-preservation, keeping up appearances and the prudence of loving friends and hating enemies. Where the tendency is towards the more civilized virtues and the merits of education and self-discipline, it sounds less like pre-Socratic morality than a Hellenistic attitude, the kind of warnings and precepts, often in quotable form, which are scattered through the plays of Menander. And to me at least, injunctions against gesticulation and pushing to the front (Chilon 17 and 18) are an irresistible reminder of Aristotle's *μεγαλοψύχος*, the magnanimous man who must not lose dignity by running with his arms waving (*EN* 1123b31). There is also a good deal to suggest the peasant outlook of Hesiod, the earthy Russian proverbs beloved of Nikita Krushchev or the spoken thoughts of Chairman Mao, well-worn platitudes and little more. The practical wisdom of the people rises to no great heights, even when it gains prestige from being attached to a famous name. Certainly Solon, Thales and the rest did not need to be credited with popular proverbs to be outstanding figures in history and in legend, but it is the Sayings believed to be theirs which have brought them the honour of featuring in a wise man's last great work.

(1978)

(i)

Cleobulus of Lindos, son of Evagoras, said:

1. *μέτρον ἄριστον.*
   Due measure is best.
2. *πατέρα δεῖ αἰδεῖσθαι.*
   A man should respect his father.
3. *εὖ τὸ σῶμα ἔχειν καὶ τὴν ψυχήν.*
   Be healthy in body and soul.
4. *φιλήκοον εἶναι καὶ μὴ πολύλαλον.*
   Be a good listener, not a great talker.
5. *πολυμαθῆ ἢ ἀμαθῆ.*
   Better much learning than none.
6. *γλῶσσαν εὔφημον κεκτῆσθαι.*
   Cultivate a reverent tongue.
7. *ἀρετῆς οἰκεῖον, κακίας ἀλλότριον.*
   Be a friend to goodness, a stranger to evil.
8. *ἀδικίαν μισεῖν, εὐσέβειαν φυλάσσειν.*
   Hate injustice, cherish piety.
9. *πολίταις τὰ βέλτιστα συμβουλεύειν.*
   Give your fellow-citizens the best counsel.

10. *ἡδονῆς κρατεῖν.*
    Control pleasure.
11. *βίᾳ μηδὲν πράττειν.*
    Do nothing by violence.
12. *τέκνα παιδεύειν.*
    Educate your children.
13. *τύχῃ εὔχεσθαι.*
    Make your prayers to Fortune.
14. *ἔχθρας διαλύειν.*
    Put an end to enmities.
15. *τὸν τοῦ δήμου ἐχθρὸν πολέμιον νομίζειν.*
    Regard an enemy of the people as a foreign foe.
16. *γυναικὶ μὴ μάχεσθαι μηδὲ ἄγαν φρονεῖν ἀλλοτρίων παρόντων· τὸ μὲν γὰρ ἄνοιαν, τὸ δὲ μανίαν δύναται παρέχειν.*
    Do not quarrel with your wife nor make too much of her before strangers; for the one can suggest folly, the other madness.
17. *οἰκέτας παρ' οἶνον μὴ κολάζειν· εἰ δὲ μή, δόξεις παροινεῖν.*
    Never rebuke your servants over wine, or you will appear the worse for drink.
18. *γαμεῖν ἐκ τῶν ὁμοίων· ἐὰν γὰρ ἐκ τῶν κρειττόνων, δεσπότας, οὐ συγγενεῖς κτήσῃ.*
    Marry within your own rank; for if you marry into a higher one you will gain not relatives but masters.
19. *μὴ ἐπιγελᾶν τῷ σκώπτοντι· ἀπεχθὴς γὰρ ἔσῃ τοῖς σκωπτομένοις.*
    Do not laugh when a man mocks at others, for that will make his victims dislike you.
20. *εὐποροῦντα μὴ ὑπερήφανον εἶναι, ἀποροῦντα μὴ ταπεινοῦσθαι.*
    Do not be overbearing in prosperity nor abject in penury.

(ii)

Solon of Athens, son of Execestides, said:

1. *μηδὲν ἄγαν.*
   Nothing too much.
2. *κριτὴς μὴ κάθησο· εἰ δὲ μή, τῷ ληφθέντι ἐχθρὸς ἔσῃ.*
   Do not sit in judgement, or the one convicted will hate you.
3. *ἡδονὴν φεῦγε, ἥτις λύπην τίκτει.*
   Shun pleasure if it breeds sorrow.

4. *φύλασσε τρόπου καλοκαγαθίαν ὅρκου πιστοτέραν.*
   Preserve nobility of character, which is more to be trusted than an oath.
5. *σφραγίζου τοὺς μὲν λόγους σιγῇ, τὴν δὲ σιγὴν καιρῷ.*
   Seal up your words with silence, and your silence at the right moment.
6. *μὴ ψεύδου, ἀλλ' ἀλήθευε.*
   Do not lie, but speak the truth.
7. *τὰ σπουδαῖα μελέτα.*
   Pursue worthy aims.
8. *τῶν γονέων μὴ λέγε δικαιότερα.*
   Do not speak more righteously than your parents.
9. *φίλους μὴ ταχὺ κτῶ, οὓς δ' ἂν κτήσῃ, μὴ ταχὺ ἀποδοκίμαζε.*
   Do not make friends in haste nor hasten to reject those you have made.
10. *ἄρχεσθαι μαθὼν ἄρχειν ἐπιστήσῃ.*
    You will understand how to command by learning to obey.
11. *εὔθυναν ἑτέρους ἀξιῶν διδόναι καὶ αὐτὸς ὕπεχε.*
    If you require others to render accounts you must submit your own.
12. *συμβούλευε μὴ τὰ ἥδιστα, ἀλλὰ τὰ βέλτιστα τοῖς πολίταις.*
    Give your fellow-citizens the best counsel, not the most pleasant.
13. *μὴ θρασύνου.*
    Do not be over-confident.
14. *μὴ κακοῖς ὁμίλει.*
    Avoid bad company.
15. *χρῶ τοῖς θεοῖς.*
    Ask the gods for guidance.
16. *φίλους εὐσέβει.*
    Respect friends.
17. *ὃ ἂν ⟨μὴ⟩ ἴδῃς, μὴ λέγε.*
    Do not speak of what you have not seen.
18. *εἰδὼς σίγα.*
    When you know, keep silence.
19. *τοῖς σεαυτοῦ πρᾶος ἴσθι.*
    Be patient with your own people.
20. *τὰ ἀφανῆ τοῖς φανεροῖς τεκμαίρου.*
    Judge uncertainty in the light of what is certain.

(iii)

Chilon of Sparta, son of Damagetes, said:

1. γνῶθι σαυτόν.
   Know yourself.
2. πίνων μὴ πολλὰ λάλει· ἁμαρτήσει γάρ.
   Do not chatter much when drinking, or you will fail of your purposes.
3. μὴ ἀπείλει τοῖς ἐλευθέροις· οὐ γὰρ δίκαιον.
   Do not threaten free men, for it is not right.
4. μὴ κακολόγει τοὺς πλησίον· εἰ δὲ μή, ἀκούσῃ, ἐφ' οἷς λυπηθήσῃ.
   Do not speak ill of your neighbours, or you will be called names which will annoy you.
5. ἐπὶ τὰ δεῖπνα τῶν φίλων βραδέως πορεύου, ἐπὶ δὲ τὰς ἀτυχίας ταχέως.
   Go slowly to your friends' banquets, but quickly to their misfortune.
6. γάμους εὐτελεῖς ποιοῦ.
   Arrange your wedding thriftily.
7. τὸν τετελευηκότα μακάριζε.
   Call only the dead happy.
8. πρεσβύτερον σέβου.
   Respect your elders.
9. τὸν τὰ ἀλλότρια περιεργαζόμενον μίσει.
   Hate a meddler in another's affairs.
10. ζημίαν αἱροῦ μᾶλλον ἢ κέρδος αἰσχρόν· τὸ μὲν γὰρ ἅπαξ λυπήσει, τὸ δὲ ἀεί.
    Prefer a loss to a dishonest gain; the one will distress you once, the other for all time.
11. τῷ δυστυχοῦντι μὴ ἐπιγέλα.
    Do not laugh at another's misfortune.
12. τραχὺς ὢν ἥσυχον σεαυτὸν πάρεχε, ὅπως σε αἰσχύνωνται μᾶλλον ἢ φοβῶνται.
    If you are a rough person act gently, so as to win respect rather than fear.
13. τῆς ἰδίας οἰκίας προστάτει.
    Be master in your own house.
14. ἡ γλῶσσά σου μὴ προτρεχέτω τοῦ νοῦ.
    Do not let your tongue outrun your thought.
15. θυμοῦ κράτει.
    Control your feelings.

16. μὴ ἐπιθύμει ἀδύνατα.
    Do not set your heart on impossibilities.
17. ἐν ὁδῷ μὴ σπεῦδε προάγειν.
    On the road, do not press to take the lead.
18. μηδὲ τὴν χεῖρα κινεῖν· μανικὸν γάρ.
    Do not gesticulate, for it looks mad.
19. νόμοις πείθου.
    Obey the laws.
20. ἀδικούμενος διαλλάσσου, ὑβριζόμενος τιμωροῦ.
    Seek reconciliation if wronged but vengeance if treated outrageously.

(iv)

Thales of Miletus, son of Examyes, said:

1. ἐγγύα, πάρα δ' ἄτα.
   Give a pledge and ruin faces you.
2. φίλων παρόντων καὶ ἀπόντων μέμνησο.
   Remember friends both present and absent.
3. μὴ τὴν ὄψιν καλλωπίζου, ἀλλ' ἐν τοῖς ἐπιτηδεύμασιν ἴσθι καλός.
   Do not beautify your face but be beautiful in your behaviour.
4. μὴ πλούτει κακως.
   Do not get rich dishonestly.
5. μή σε διαβαλλέτω λόγος πρὸς τοὺς πίστεως κεκοινωνηκότας.
   Do not let talk prejudice you against those who have won a place in your confidence.
6. κολακεύειν γονεῖς μὴ ὄκνει.
   Do not hesitate to flatter your parents.
7. μὴ πατρὸς δέχου τὸ φαῦλον.
   Do not take after the bad side of your father.
8. οἵους ἂν ἐράνους ἐνέγκῃς τοῖς γονεῦσι, τοιούτους αὐτὸς ἐν τῷ γήρᾳ παρὰ τῶν τέκνων προσδέχου.
   You should expect in old age from your children the same provision as you made for your own parents.
9. χαλεπὸν τὸ ἑαυτὸν γνῶναι.
   It is difficult to know oneself.
10. ἥδιστον οὗ ἐπιθυμεῖς τυχεῖν.
    The sweetest thing of all is to gain the heart's desire.

11. ἀνιαρὸν ἀργία.
    Lack of occupation is grievous.
12. βλαβερὸν ἀκρασία.
    Lack of self-control is hurtful.
13. βαρὺ ἀπαιδευσία.
    Lack of education is burdensome.
14. δίδασκε καὶ μάνθανε τὸ ἄμεινον.
    Teach and learn the better course.
15. ἀργὸς μὴ ἴσθι, μηδ' ἂν πλουτῇς.
    Do not be idle even if you are rich.
16. κακὰ ἐν οἴκῳ κρύπτε.
    Keep quiet about what is wrong in the home.
17. φθονοῦ μᾶλλον ἢ οἰκτίρου.
    Better be envied than pitied.
18. μέτρῳ χρῶ.
    Use due measure.
19. μὴ πᾶσι πίστευε.
    Do not trust everyone.
20. ἄρχων κόσμει σεαυτόν.
    When in power, control yourself.

(v)

Pittacus of Lesbos, son of Hyrras, said:

1. καιρὸν γνῶθι.
   Know the right moment.
2. ὃ μέλλεις ποιεῖν, μὴ λέγε· ἀποτυχὼν γὰρ καταγελασθήσῃ.
   Do not say what you intend to do, for if you fail you will be laughed at.
3. τοῖς ἐπιτηδείοις χρῶ.
   Cultivate the right friends.
4. ὅσα νεμεσᾷς τῷ πλησίον, αὐτὸς μὴ ποίει.
   Do not do yourself what you resent in your neighbour.
5. ἀπραγοῦντα μὴ ὀνείδιζε· ἐπὶ γὰρ τούτοις νέμεσις θεῶν κάθηται.
   Do not reproach one who shuns public life, for the wrath of the gods judges such cases.
6. παρακαταθήκας ἀπόδος.
   Restore what is entrusted to you.

7. ἀνέχου ὑπὸ τῶν πλησίον μικρὰ ἐλαττούμενος.
   Put up with it if your neighbours get the better of you in small ways.
8. τὸν φίλον κακῶς μὴ λέγε μηδ' εὖ τὸν ἐχθρόν· ἀσυλλόγιστον γὰρ τὸ τοιοῦτον.
   Speak no ill of a friend nor good of an enemy, for such conduct is irrational.
9. δεινὸν συνιδεῖν τὸ μέλλον, ἀσφαλὲς τὸ γενόμενον.
   It is dangerous to envisage the future, safe to survey the past.
10. πιστὸν γῆ, ἄπιστον θάλασσα.
    Land is a loyal, sea a faithless thing.
11. ἄπληστον κέρδος.
    Love of gain is insatiable.
12. κτῆσαι ἴδια.
    Acquire what is yours to have.
13. θεράπευε εὐσέβειαν, παιδείαν, σωφροσύνην, φρόνησιν, ἀλήθειαν, πίστιν, ἐμπειρίαν, ἐπιδεξιότητα, ἑταιρείαν, ἐπιμέλειαν, οἰκονομίαν, τέχνην.
    Cultivate piety, education, self-control, prudence, truthfulness, good faith, experience, dexterity, companionship, diligence, household-management, and skill.

(vi)

Bias of Priene, son of Teutamides, said:

1. οἱ πλεῖστοι ἄνθρωποι κακοί.
   Most people are bad.
2. εἰς κάτοπτρον, ἔφη, ἐμβλέψαντα δεῖ, εἰ μὲν καλὸς φαίνῃ, καλὰ ποιεῖν· εἰ δὲ αἰσχρός, τὸ τῆς φύσεως ἐλλιπὲς διορθοῦσθαι τῇ καλοκαγαθίᾳ.
   Look in a mirror, and if you appear beautiful, your conduct should be the same; but if you look ugly, you must correct your physical deficiency by doing what is both beautiful and good.
3. βραδέως ἐγχείρει· οὗ δ' ἂν ἄρξῃ, διαβεβαιοῦ.
   Be slow to undertake anything, but once you have started, carry it through.
4. μίσει τὸ ταχὺ λαλεῖν, μὴ ἁμάρτῃς· μετάνοια γὰρ ἀκολουθεῖ.
   Shun hasty talk lest you make a mistake, for regret will follow.

5. μήτ' εὐήθης ἴσθι μήτε κακοήθης.
Be neither guileless nor suspicious.
6. ἀφροσύνην μὴ προσδέχου.
Do not open the door to folly.
7. φρόνησιν ἀγάπα.
Love prudence.
8. περὶ θεῶν λέγε, ὡς εἰσίν.
About gods, say that they exist.
9. νόει τὸ πραττόμενον.
Think what you are doing.
10. ἄκουε πολλά.
Listen constantly.
11. λάλει καίρια.
Speak only in season.
12. πένης ὢν πλουσίοις μὴ ἐπιτίμα, ἢν μὴ μέγα ὠφελῇς.
Do not blame the rich if you are poor, unless you are doing them great service.
13. ἀνάξιον ἄνδρα μὴ ἐπαίνει διὰ πλοῦτον.
Do not praise a worthless man because of his wealth.
14. πείσας λαβέ, μὴ βιασάμενος.
Gain your end by persuasion, not by force.
15. ὅ τι ἂν ἀγαθὸν πράσσῃς, θεούς, μὴ σεαυτὸν αἰτιῶ.
Attribute any good deed you do to the gods, not to yourself.
16. κτῆσαι ἐν μὲν νεότητι εὐπραξίαν, ἐν δὲ τῷ γήρᾳ σοφίαν.
Cultivate success in youth, wisdom in old age.
17. ἕξεις ἔργῳ μνήμην, καιρῷ εὐλάβειαν, τρόπῳ γενναιότητα, πόνῳ ἐγκράτειαν, φόβῳ εὐσέβειαν, πλούτῳ φιλίαν, λόγῳ πειθώ, σιγῇ κόσμον, γνώμῃ δικαιοσύνην, τόλμῃ ἀνδρείαν, πράξει δυναστείαν, δόξῃ ἡγεμονίαν.
You will gain memory by work, caution by right timing, nobility by character, self-control by hardship, piety by reverence, friendship by riches, persuasiveness by speech, dignity by silence, justice by discernment, courage by daring, power by action, and leadership by good repute.

(vii)

Periander of Corinth, son of Cypselus, said:

1. μελέτα τὸ πᾶν.
Practice is everything.

2. *καλὸν ἡσυχία.*
   It is a fine thing to be quiet.
3. *ἐπισφαλὲς προπέτεια.*
   Impetuosity is dangerous.
4. *κέρδος αἰσχρόν.*
   Love of gain is disgraceful.
5. *φύσεως κατηγορία.*
   ⟨and⟩ a reproach to a man's nature.*
6. *δημοκρατία κρεῖττον τυραννίδος.*
   Democracy is better than tyranny.
7. *αἱ μὲν ἡδοναὶ θνηταί, αἱ δ' ἀρεταὶ ἀθάνατοι.*
   Pleasures are mortal, virtues immortal.
8. *εὐτυχῶν μὲν μέτριος ἴσθι, ἀτυχῶν δὲ φρόνιμος.*
   Be moderate in prosperity, prudent in adversity.
9. *φειδόμενον κρεῖττον ἀποθανεῖν ἢ ζῶντα ἐνδεῖσθαι.*
   Better die thrifty than be in want while alive.
10. *σεαυτὸν ἄξιον παρασκεύαζε τῶν γονέων.*
    Make yourself worthy of your forebears.
11. *ζῶν μὲν ἐπαινοῦ, ἀποθανὼν δὲ μακαρίζου.*
    Be praised in life and counted happy when dead.
12. *φίλοις εὐτυχοῦσι καὶ ἀτυχοῦσιν ὁ αὐτὸς ἴσθι.*
    Be the same to your friends, whether their luck is good or bad.
13. *ὃ ἂν ἑκὼν ὁμολογήσῃς, ⟨διατήρει⟩· πονηρὸν ⟨γὰρ τὸ⟩ παραβῆναι.*
    Keep any agreement made willingly, for it is wicked to break it.
14. *λόγων ἀπορρήτων ἐκφορὰν μὴ ποιοῦ.*
    Do not publish secrets.
15. *λοιδοροῦ ὡς ταχὺ φίλος ἐσόμενος.*
    Rebuke a man as if you are going soon to be his friend.
16. *τοῖς μὲν νόμοις παλαιοῖς χρῶ, τοῖς δὲ ὄψοις προσφάτοις.*
    Keep to old laws but fresh fish.
17. *μὴ μόνον τοὺς ἁμαρτάνοντας κόλαζε, ἀλλὰ καὶ τοὺς μέλλοντας κώλυε.*
    Do not only correct wrongdoers, but also prevent those about to do wrong.
18. *δυστυχῶν κρύπτε, ἵνα μὴ τοὺς ἐχθροὺς εὐφράνῃς.*
    Conceal your misfortune, lest you delight your enemies.

* The text is defective; possibly what should be one saying has been divided into two.

ENVOI

FOLLY SPEAKS

❦ . . . Now let me say something about publishers and printers, a race of men devised by almighty Zeus for the frustration of scholars. The manuscript to which a learned man has devoted a good part of his life, as he pores over dictionaries and searches through reference books, they keep for months and sometimes years, and then return it smudged with thumb prints and scribbled with cabbalistic signs, ems and Lower Case and Superior Numbers (the only sort of superiority they can claim), and what is worse, marked with changes in his well-chosen words and carefully planned numbering, to the confusion of the whole. With it comes a demand for the printed words to be sent back within a month, and so the scholar may be on his travels abroad or languishing in hospital, his wife may be in labour or his children home on holiday, but Proofs must be read and returned. And if he questions what they've changed in their ignorance, he is passed from editor to copy-editor and thence to typographer, but no one's to blame for an error unless it be one who left their company a month ago. They have two all-powerful authorities they can quote, the Computer which rules necessity itself and is the fount and source of all delays, and the House Rules to which they attach more importance than to the Sibylline Books. Such people would re-number the Ten Commandments if it pleased them, or reword the Beatitudes in the interests of a 'clean page'. One lot whom I won't name lest nemesis descends on me can drive one distracted with their vagaries and follies until at last *parturient montes, nascetur ridiculus mus*, the mountains will be in labour and a little mouse be born in the shape of a paper-covered book under the emblem of some bird from the snowy wastes of the antipodes, not even the owl of Minerva.

NOTES AND REFERENCES

MICHAEL GRANT

Translating Latin Prose (pp. 81–91)

1. P. Selver, *The Art of Translating Poetry* (1966), p. 10, quoting from Thorley's volume *Fleurs-de-Lys* (1920).
2. *Delos*, II, 1968, pp. 46ff.
3. *On Translation* (Cambridge, Mass./London, 1959), p. 272.
4. *e.g.* (to quote E. A. Nida), 'Truly, truly I say unto you' would not be very effective in the Hiligaynon language of the Philippines, in which repetition has a weakening effect.
5. Cited by P. Selver, op. cit., from *Le Vrai Ami du traducteur anglais-français et français-anglais* (1930). Cf. examples in T. H. Savory, *The Art of Translation* (London, 1957), pp. 14ff.
6. *Delos*, I, 1968, p. 213.
7. *Delos*, II, 1968, p. 39.
8. M. Proust, *Remembrance of Things Past* (Penguin Books, 1983), p. xi.
9. M. Grant, *Latin Literature* (Penguin Books, 1978), p. 7.
10. 'Epilogue to the Satires', Dialogue I, ll. 73–4.
11. *The Letters of the Younger Pliny* (Penguin Books, 1963), p. 30.
12. *Arion*, vii, 3, 1968, p. 477.
13. I have given examples in *Ariel* (University of Calgary), 2,2,1971, pp. 7ff., to whose editors, and especially Professor A. W. Jeffares, I owe acknowledgements for a substantial portion of the present essay.
14. *Arion*, loc. cit., p. 397.
15. Preface to *Ovid's Epistles Translated by Several Hands* (1680).
16. Tacitus, *The Annals of Imperial Rome* (Penguin Books, 1956), p. 24.
17. For some detailed comments on this edition see *Ariel*, loc. cit., pp. 24ff.
18. Apuleius, *The Golden Ass* (Penguin Books, 1950), p. 10.
19. Tacitus, op. cit., p. 24 (revised ed., 1977), p. 26.
20. Pliny, *Letters and Panegyricus* (London/Cambridge, Mass., 1969), II, pp. 317ff.
21. Pliny, *Panegyricus*, xvii, 1f.
22. Livy, *War with Hannibal* (Penguin Books, 1965).
23. *Arion*, vii, 3, 1968, p. 477.
24. P. MacKendrick and H. M. Howe, *Classics in Translation* (1952).

25. *Delos*, I, 1968, pp. 173, 212f. John Florio's English version of Montaigne appeared in 1603.
26. ibid., p. 173.
27. ibid., pp. 62ff.
28. For these opinions, see *Delos*, II, 1968, pp. 47, 30, 35, 34. Proust's knowledge of English was very imperfect when he elegantly translated John Ruskin, but his mother provided him with a word-for-word version of *The Bible of Amiens*: G. D. Painter, *Marcel Proust* (Penguin Books, 1983), pp. 258f.

PETER GREEN

Metre, Fidelity, Sex: the Problems Confronting a Translator of Ovid's Love Poetry (pp. 92–111)

1. In *Ovids Ars Amatoria und Remedia Amoris: Untersuchungen zum Aufbau* (Stuttgart, 1970), ed. E. Zinn, p. 109.
2. *Am.* 1.1.3–4, 2.17.21–2, 3.1.9–10, 65–6: *RA* 373–4.
3. *Am.* 1.1.27.
4. In his essay *On Translating Homer* (London, 1861): cf. T. H. Savory, *The Art of Translation* (2nd ed., London, 1968), pp. 44–5: Paul Selver, *The Art of Translating Poetry* (London, 1966), pp. 69ff.
5. Selver, ibid., Savory, pp. 49–89.
6. F. W. Newman, preface to *The Iliad of Homer: faithfully translated into unrhymed English metre* (1st ed., London, 1856), cited by Savory, op. cit., p. 65.
7. Preface on translation prefixed to the *Second Miscellany* (1685), reprinted in *The Works of John Dryden*, ed. G. Saintsbury (Edinburgh, 1885), vol. XII, pp. 281–2.
8. The perpetrator of this curiosity was none other than the late Sir Maurice Bowra: see *The Oxford Book of Greek Verse in Translation* (Oxford, 1938), no. 166, p. 217. Clearly, a discipline which – at least as formerly taught in England – did not hesitate to make students turn Pope into Latin elegiacs or Shakespearian speeches into Greek tragic iambics could not be expected to frown on a converse process.
9. See George Saintsbury, *A History of English Prosody* (London, 1906), vol. i, pp. 318–21, vol. ii, pp. 167–95, and especially vol. iii, chapter 3, 'The later English hexameter', pp. 394–436; and T. S. Omond, *English Metrists in the Eighteenth and Nineteenth Centuries* (London, 1907), 108–13, 124–5, 134–6, 157–61, 219–20, and Appendix A, pp. 243–55; cf. Selver, op. cit., pp. 65–87.
10. op. cit., p. 109.
11. Cited by Selver, op. cit., p. 67.

12. *The Works of Tennyson*, ed. Hallam, Lord Tennyson (London, 1913), p. 243.
13. H. B. Cotterill, *Homer's Odyssey* (London, 1911), p. 85. This is by no means the only attempt to render Homer in English accentual or pseudo-quantitative hexameters: see, for example, George Ernle's *The Wrath of Achilleus* (London, 1922). Ernle's is the most thoroughgoing attempt, not excluding Bridges's, to produce rational quantitative metrics in English, and his analytical preface (pp. 5–17) is still worth reading, not least for his description of Meredith's experiments with quantity in *Love in the Valley*. But in the end he is still forced, by his own logic, to produce such grotesque pieces of scansion (in what obstinately remains a stress-language) as 'bālefŭllÿ | brōūght sŭffĕr | īngs', or 'ānd thĕ găl | lānt Ăchĭl | lēūs': and an unwary reader, not knowing what the translator was up to, might well, following his own accentual instincts, take 'Now ever as the battle grew deadlier and the Achaeans' as highly resolved blank verse.
14. In the 'Epilogue on Translation' to his new prose version of the *Odyssey* (Oxford, 1980), p. 308, cf. p. 303.
15. Beram Saklatvala, *Ovid on Love* (London, 1966); L. R. Lind, *Ovid: Tristia* (Athens, Georgia, 1975).
16. *Ovid's Amores*, English translation by Guy Lee (London, 1968).
17. op. cit., pp. 199–200.
18. op. cit., vol. III, pp. 417, 414.
19. Virg. *Aen.* 10.649.
20. Homer *Od.* 3.30–34; Virg. *Aen.* 4.232–7. The English versions are by Lattimore and Day Lewis respectively.
21. Reprinted, with considerable revisions, in my *Essays in Antiquity* (London, 1960), pp. 109–35, under the title 'Venus Clerke Ovyde'.
22. Gilbert Highet, *Poets in a Landscape* (London, 1957): see pp. 12–14 for a brief and characteristically lucid statement on his position as a translator. The specimen quoted here can be found on p. 183.
23. J. W. Mackail, *The Odyssey* (2nd ed., Oxford, 1932), p. 268 (*Od.* 13.93ff.). In his preface Mackail wrote that he had chosen the metre before ever reading Fitzgerald, and says of his translation: 'Its aim throughout must be to suggest . . . the combination of leisureness [*sic*] and rapidity, of swift motion with the stateliness in which, as Aristotle observes, the Homeric hexameter is unequalled.' The idea of inappropriate associations seems not to have occurred to him.
24. For Ovid's somewhat self-conscious reference to his own *nequitia* see *Am.* 2.1.2, cf. 3.11.37, *Tr.* 2.280.
25. *Am.* 1.5.25.
26. *AA* 3.769–808.
27. *AA* 3.209–35.

28. John Osborne, *Look Back in Anger* (London, 1957), p. 24.
29. cf. *AA* 1.277–82, 360, 459ff., 755–72; 2.372–86; 3.101–32, and E. W. Leach, 'Georgic Imagery in the *Ars Amatoria*', *TAPhA* 95 (1964), pp. 142–54.
30. I am grateful to Professor George Doig for letting me see his unpublished research on this fascinating topic.
31. e.g., G. Némethy, *P. Ovidii Nasonis Remedia Amoris* (Budapest, 1921), p. 68; F. W. Lenz, *Heilmittel gegen die Liebe* (Berlin, 1960), p. 93; A. A. R. Henderson, *P. Ovidii Nasonis Remedia Amoris* (Edinburgh, 1979), p. 135.
32. For Achilles' oath see *Il.* 1.233–44; Agamemnon swears by Zeus, Earth, the Sun and the Furies (*Il.* 19.260ff.).
33. *Carm. Priap.* xxv, ed. F. Buecheler (5th ed., Berlin, 1922), p. 154.
34. *Am.* 2.1.21–8, 3.6 *passim*, 3.9.27–30; *AA* 2.91–106; *RA* 251–2.
35. *Juvenal: The Sixteen Satires* (Penguin Books, 2nd ed., 1974), pp. 60–61.
36. Paul Brandt, *P. Ovidi Nasonis de Arte Amatoria Libri Tres* (Leipzig, 1902), p. 10 suggests, in common with most commentators, that the reference is zodiacal, and means when the sun is in Leo, i.e., during July, the association with Hercules being through his killing of the Nemean Lion (Apollod. 2.5.1, cf. Hes. *Th.* 326ff., Theocr. 25.162ff., etc.). But what is required by the context, as advice, would seem to be a *time of day* rather than a month of the year. When the sun *terga leonis adit* suggests noon, or soon after; siesta time. 'Hercules' lion' will then have been part of a well-known statue-group (as familiar, probably, to Ovid's readers as Landseer's lions in Trafalgar Square would be to a modern Londoner). This may have stood outside the temple of Hercules Custos near the Circus Flaminius, or perhaps in Pompey's colonnade, the centre of which was laid out as a garden, and contained various works of art (Prop. 2.32.11–12, Plin. *HN* 35.59, 114, 126, 132).

An earlier version of this essay appeared in the pages of *Echos du monde classique/Classical News and Views*, 25.3 (1981), pp. 79–96, and I am grateful to the editors for permission to reproduce here material first published in that article. All translations from Ovid, unless otherwise attributed, are from my Penguin Classics volume, *Ovid: The Erotic Poems* (1982).

WENDY DONIGER O'FLAHERTY

On Translating Sanskrit Myths (pp. 121–8)

1. 'Queen Alice', Chapter 9 of *Through the Looking Glass* by Lewis Carroll.
2. See Daniel H. H. Ingalls's remarks on the difference between Sanskrit and English in this regard, in his introduction to his *Anthology of Sanskrit Court Poetry* (Cambridge, Mass., 1965), especially pp. 5–10.
3. See Martin Gardner, *The Annotated Alice* (1960).
4. 'A New Approach to Sanskrit Translation, applied to Kalidasa's Kumarasambhava Canto VIII', in *MAHFIL: A Quarterly of South Asian Literature* (Michigan State University), 7, 3–4 (Fall–Winter 1971), pp. 129–42.
5. John Brough, *Poems from the Sanskrit* (Penguin Books, 1968), introduction, p. 31.
6. Daniel H. H. Ingalls, op. cit., introduction, pp. 3–4.
7. Wendy Doniger O'Flaherty, *The Rig Veda: An Anthology* (Penguin Books, 1981), pp. 15–16.
8. ibid., p. 11.
9. Claude Lévi-Strauss, *Structural Anthropology* (New York, 1963), p. 210; cited by Wendy Doniger O'Flaherty in *Hindu Myths: A Sourcebook* (Penguin Books, 1975), p. 21.
10. Rudyard Kipling, 'Proofs of Holy Writ', published in *The Strand Magazine*, April 1934. It was David Grene – himself a very great translator indeed – who brought this story to me.

BARBARA REYNOLDS

The Pleasure Craft (pp. 129–42)

1. Translation by Dorothy L. Sayers (Penguin Books, 1955).
2. From an address entitled 'What Dante means to me', delivered at the Italian Institute in London in 1953.
3. ibid.
4. Translation by Barbara Reynolds (Penguin Books, 1962).
5. *Inferno*, VII, 13–18, translation by Dorothy L. Sayers (Penguin Books, 1949).
6. loc. cit., ll. 22–7.
7. Translation by Barbara Reynolds (Penguin Books, 1962).
8. Canto XXXII, 13.
9. Introduction, p. xvi (London, 1974).
10. Canto X, 96.
11. Monterey, California, 1976.

NOTES

N. K. SANDARS

Translating the Translators: Peculiar Problems in Translating Very Early Texts (pp. 143–51)

1. Thorkild Jacobsen, *Treasures of Darkness* (Yale/London, 1976), p. 191.
2. N. K. Sandars, *Prehistoric Art in Europe* (Penguin Books, Pelican History of Art, 2nd edition, 1985), p. 139.
3. Translation by J. F. Goodridge (Penguin Books, revised edtion 1966), pp. 220, 224, 226.
4. Milton, 'Ode on the Morning of Christ's Nativity', verse 14.
5. Book v, pp. 130–31, in the translation by Helen M. Mustard and Charles E. Passage (New York, 1961).
6. *The Mabinogion*, Everyman translation by Gwyn Jones and Thomas Jones (London, 1949), p. 39.
7. Robert Lowell, *Imitations* (London, 1962), p. xi.
8. 'Still Growing', No. 96 of 'English Traditional Verse' from the MSS of Cecil J. Sharp, in James Reeves, *The Idiom of the People* (London, 1958), p. 200.

TREVOR J. SAUNDERS

The Penguinification of Plato (pp. 152–62)

1. *Poetry Review*, June/July 1949.
2. George Borrow, *The Bible in Spain*, chapter 25, 'Translation is at best an echo.'
3. See *Classical Quarterly*, xxiii (1973), pp. 232–44, especially p. 237.
4. Aristotle, *De Anima* (Cambridge, 1907), vii.
5. See my *Bulletin of the Institute of Classical Studies*, Supplement 28 (1972), note 119.
6. *The Dialogues of Plato*, i (3rd ed., Oxford, 1892), p. xxii.
7. ibid., pp. xvi–xvii.

This essay is an extensively adapted version of a documentary entitled 'On translating Plato', broadcast by the Australian Broadcasting Corporation in August 1973. It was originally published by the Oxford University Press in *Greece and Rome*, 22 (1975), 19–28. The author is grateful to the Corporation and the Press for permission to reprint it, with minor alterations and additions.

BRIAN STONE

False Friends and Strange Metres (pp. 175–86)

1. George Steiner, *After Babel* (Oxford, 1975), p. 170.
2. Davis and others, *A Chaucer Glossary* (Oxford, 1979).
3. See D. W. Robertson, jr, *Essays in Medieval Culture* (Princeton, 1980), pp. 51–2, 72.
4. George Steiner, op. cit., p. 65.
5. *Sir Gawain and the Green Knight*, ll. 209–10.
6. Gerard Manley Hopkins, *Selected Prose*, ed. Gerald Roberts (Oxford, 1980), p. 66.
7. P. M. Kean, *Chaucer and the Making of English Poetry* (London, 1972), vol. I, pp. 179–80.
8. Translation: Brian Stone, *The Owl and the Nightingale, Cleanness, St Erkenwald* (Penguin Books, 1971), pp. 94–5, with an emendation in line 411. Text: ed. A. C. Cawley and J. J. Anderson, in *Pearl, Cleanness, Patience, Sir Gawain and the Green Knight* (London, 1983).

BENEDICTA WARD

Translator's Charity (pp. 206–15)

1. St Augustine, *City of God*, translated by Henry Bettenson (Penguin Books, 1984), p. 1091.
2. *The Cloud of Unknowing*, translated by Clifton Wolters (Penguin Books, 1978), p. 51.
3. St Augustine, *On Christian Doctrine*, translated by D. W. Robertson (Oxford, 1958), Book II, XI, p. 43.
4. ibid., p. 43.
5. ibid., p. 30.
6. ibid., p. 93.
7. ibid., p. 88.
8. ibid., p. 46.
9. ibid., p. 142.
10. St Augustine, *Confessions*, translated by R. S. Pine-Coffin (Penguin Books, 1961), pp. 231–2.
11. Bede, *A History of the English Church and People*, translated by Leo Sherley-Price (Penguin Books, rev. ed. 1968), III, 3, p. 145.
12. ibid., V, 24, p. 337.
13. Letter of Cuthbert, quoted by C. E. Whiting, 'The Life of the Venerable Bede', in *Bede: Life, Times and Writings*, ed. A. H. Thompson (Oxford, 1935), p. 34.

14. Letter to Egbert, in *English Historical Documents*, vol. 1, ed. D. Whitelock (Oxford, 1979), p. 801.
15. ibid.
16. From *Alfred the Great*: Asser's *Life of King Alfred* and other contemporary sources, translated by Simon Keynes and Michael Lapidge (Penguin Books, 1983), p. 126.
17. The work of the Benedictine monks of the Congregation of St Maurus in editing texts is discussed by David Knowles in *Great Historical Enterprises* (London, 1963), pp. 35–62.
18. H. P. Liddon, *The Life of Edward Bouverie Pusey* (London, 1894), vol. 1, p. 422.
19. ibid.
20. ibid., p. 423.
21. *Confessions of St Augustine, Revised from a former translation by Rev. E. B. Pusey D.D.* (Oxford, 1838), preface, pp. xxxi, xxxii.
22. *The Private Prayers of Lancelot Andrewes*, ed. H. Martin (London, 1957), introduction, p. 9.
23. Charles Williams, *The Figure of Beatrice* (London, 1943), p. 133. I am grateful to Dr Barbara Reynolds for drawing my attention to this remark.

BETTY RADICE

The Sayings of the Seven Sages of Greece (pp. 241–53)

1. *Protagoras* 343 a–b, translated by W. K. C. Guthrie (Penguin Books, 1956). The saying quoted is also ascribed to Pittacus by Diogenes Laertius (1, 76–7), who quotes a reference to it in the poet Simonides (d. 468).
2. Demetrius of Phalerum, b. 350 BC, Athenian philosopher and statesman, was evidently a prolific writer; see *Oxford Classical Dictionary*.
3. See W. D. Ross, *Aristotle's Metaphysics* (Oxford, 1924), II, pp. 496–7.
4. e.g. Xenophon *Mem.* 4.2.24; Plato, *Phaedrus* 229e; Isocrates *Or.* 12.230; Pausanias, 10.24.1; Pliny *H.N.* 7.119; Juvenal 11.27. For a fuller list see H. W. Parke and D. E. W. Wormell, *The Delphic Oracle* (Oxford, 1956), vol. 1, p. 392, note 24.
5. Discussed in Parke and Wormell, vol. 2, p. 171, no. 423.
6. The tales are told by Plutarch in his Life of Solon (4) and by Diogenes Laertius (1.27ff.).
7. 6th edition, 3 vols., edited by W. Kranz (Berlin, 1952).
8. Dicaearchus, a pupil of Aristotle, fl. 326–296 BC, wrote extensively on politics, history, philosophy and geography; see *Oxford Classical Dictionary*.

BIBLIOGRAPHY

TRANSLATIONS AND OTHER PUBLICATIONS BY BETTY RADICE

The Letters of the Younger Pliny (Penguin Books, 1963; with select bibliography, 1969), translated with an introduction

Terence, *The Comedies* (Penguin Books, revised edition, 1976, amalgamating *The Brothers and Other Plays*, 1965, and *Phormio and Other Plays*, 1967), translated with an introduction

Livy, *The War with Hannibal, Books XXI–XXX of The History of Rome from its Foundation* (Penguin Books, 1965; with index, 1972), translated by Aubrey de Sélincourt, completed with an introduction by B. R.

Erasmus, *Praise of Folly and Letter to Martin Dorp 1515* (Penguin Books, 1971), translated by B. R., with an introduction and notes by A. H. T. Levi

The Letters of Abelard and Heloise (Penguin Books, 1974), translated with an introduction

Livy, *Rome and Italy, Books VI–X of The History of Rome from its Foundation* (Penguin Books, 1982), translated and annotated by B. R. with an introduction by R. M. Ogilvie

Who's Who in the Ancient World, A Handbook to the Survivors of the Greek and Roman Classics (Anthony Blond/Stein & Day, 1971; Penguin Books, revised edition, 1973), selected with an introduction

Edward Gibbon, *Memoirs of My Life* (Penguin Books, 1984), edited with an introduction

Horace, *The Complete Odes and Epodes, with the Centennial Hymn* (Penguin Books, 1983), translated with notes by W. G. Shepherd with an introduction by B. R.

Propertius, *The Poems* (Penguin Books, 1985), translated with notes by W. G. Shepherd with an introduction by B. R.

Erasmus, *Praise of Folly* (Folio Society, 1974), translated with an introduction and notes

Abelard and Heloise, *The Story of His Misfortunes and The Personal Letters* (Folio Society, 1977), translated with an introduction and notes

Pliny, *A Self Portrait in Letters* (Folio Society, 1978), translated with an introduction

BIBLIOGRAPHY

Edward Gibbon, *The History of the Decline and Fall of the Roman Empire* (Folio Society, Volume 1, 'The Turn of the Tide', 1983; Volume 2, 'Constantine and the Christian Empire', 1984; Volume 3, 'The Revival and Collapse of Paganism', 1985; Volume 4, 'The End of the Western Empire,' 1986), edited with an introduction

Pliny, *Letters and Panegyricus*, with an English translation by B. R. (Loeb Classical Library, London/Harvard, 1969, 2 volumes)

Erasmus, Panegyric for Archduke Philip of Austria/*Panegyricus ad Philippum Austriae ducem*; Praise of Folly/*Moriae encomium*; A Complaint of Peace/*Querela pacis*; translated with introductions and notes by B. R. in *The Collected Works of Erasmus*, Volumes 27 and 28, Literary and Educational Writings 5–6, edited by A. H. T. Levi (Toronto University Press, 1986)

Petri Bembi de Aetna Liber/Pietro Bembo on Etna, original Latin text with an English translation by B. R. (Editiones Officinae Bodoni, Verona, September 1969)

A Comedy of Terence called Andria, Richard Bernard's prose translation of 1598, edited and revised by B. R. with a note on the translation (Editiones Officinae Bodoni, Verona, November 1971)

The Alphabet of Francesco Torniello da Novara, with an English translation of the treatise and of Giovanni Mardersteig's introduction by B. R. (Editiones Officinae Bodoni, Verona, January 1971)

The Fables of Aesop, Caxton's English translation, with six fables missing from Caxton's text translated from Latin by B. R. (Editiones Officinae Bodoni, Verona, February 1973)

Bernardino Barduzzi, *A Letter in Praise of Verona*, original Latin text of 1489 with an English translation by B. R. (Editiones Officinae Bodoni, Verona, December 1974)

The Sayings of the Seven Sages of Greece, original Greek text, edited with an English translation by B. R. (Editiones Officinae Bodoni, Verona, April 1976)

Francesco Petrarca, *Lettera a Giovanni Anchisea* [*Lo incarica di procurargli libri*], English version 'To Giovanni of Incisa' [Commissioning him to search for books] by B. R. (Stamperia Valdonega di Verona, 1967; a gift from Carlo Alberto Chiesa to his bibliophile friends)

'The Letters of Pliny', in *Empire and Aftermath*, Silver Latin II, edited by T. A. Dorey (London, 1975)

'The French Scholar-Lover: Heloise', in *Medieval Women Writers*, edited by Katharina M. Wilson (University of Georgia Press, Athens, 1984)

'Como and the Villa Pliniana', in *Rivista*, The Journal of the British Italian Society, No. 171, November/December 1962

'Bembo's Etna', in *Rivista*, No. 247, July/August 1975

'A Letter in Praise of Verona – 1489', in *Rivista:* Part I in No. 256, January/February 1977, Part II in No. 257, March/April 1977
'Edward Gibbon's Journey from Lausanne to Rome', in *Rivista*: Part I in No. 294, July/August 1983, Part II in No. 295, September/October 1983

Note Betty Radice's translations of Terence and Abelard and Heloise are scheduled to appear in the Loeb Classical Library and the Oxford Medieval Texts respectively. For further information on the Officina Bodoni see Giovanni Mardersteig, *The Officina Bodoni, An Account of the Work of a Hand Press 1923–1977*, edited and translated by Hans Schmoller (Edizioni Valdonega, Verona, 1980).

PENGUIN CLASSICS EDITED BY BETTY RADICE

The following is a complete list of Penguin Classics translated from ancient or oriental languages and published between 1964 and 1985. It includes revised versions of books originally edited by E. V. Rieu. It is roughly chronological, but grouped according to language. Books published since her death that Betty Radice commissioned and guided – such as Walter Hamilton and Andrew Wallace-Hadrill's *Ammianus Marcellinus*, 1986 – should also perhaps belong to the list.

From Greek

Aristophanes, *The Frogs and Other Plays*, translated with an introduction by David Barrett, 1964
Marcus Aurelius, *Meditations*, translated with an introduction by Maxwell Staniforth, 1964
Aristotle, Horace, Longinus, *Classical Literary Criticism*, translated with an introduction by T. S. Dorsch, 1965
Eusebius, *The History of the Church from Christ to Constantine*, translated with an introduction by G. A. Williamson, 1965
Plato, *Timaeus and Critias*, translated with an introduction by Desmond Lee, 1965 (*Timaeus*), 1971 (with *Critias* and an appendix on Atlantis), 1977 (revised edition)
Plutarch, *Makers of Rome*, translated with an introduction by Ian Scott-Kilvert, 1965
Procopius, *The Secret History*, translated with an introduction by G. A. Williamson, 1966
Michael Psellus, *Fourteen Byzantine Rulers*, translated with an introduction by E. R. A. Sewter, 1966
Theophrastus, *The Characters*, Menander, *Plays and Fragments*, translated with an introduction by Philip Vellacott, 1967, 1973 (second edition)

BIBLIOGRAPHY

Early Christian Writings (The Apostolic Fathers), translated by Maxwell Staniforth, 1968

Longus, *Daphnis and Chloe*, translated with an introduction by Paul Turner, 1956, 1968 (unexpurgated)

The Alexiad of Anna Comnena, translated with an introduction by E. R. A. Sewter, 1969

The Odes of Pindar, translated with an introduction by C. M. Bowra, 1969

Plato, *The Last Days of Socrates*, translated with an introduction by Hugh Tredennick, 1954, 1959 (new edition with additions), 1969 (revised edition)

Greek Political Oratory, selected and translated with an introduction by A. N. W. Saunders, 1970

Philostratus, *Life of Apollonius*, translated by C. P. Jones, edited and abridged with an introduction by G. W. Bowersock, 1970

Plato, *The Laws*, translated with an introduction by Trevor J. Saunders, 1970, 1975 (minor revisions)

Xenophon, *Memoirs of Socrates and The Symposium*, translated with an introduction by Hugh Tredennick, 1970

Apollonius of Rhodes, *The Voyage of Argo* (The Argonautica), translated with an introduction by E. V. Rieu, 1959, 1971 (second edition)

Arrian, *The Campaigns of Alexander*, translated by Aubrey de Sélincourt, 1958, as *The Life of Alexander the Great*; revised with new introduction and notes by J. R. Hamilton, 1971

Pausanias, *Guide to Greece*, translated with an introduction by Peter Levi, 2 volumes, 1971, 1979 (revised edition)

Plato, *Gorgias*, translated with an introduction by Walter Hamilton, 1960, 1971 (revised edition)

Plutarch, *Moral Essays*, translated with an introduction by Rex Warner, notes by D. A. Russell, 1971

Euripides, *Orestes and Other Plays*, translated with an introduction by Philip Vellacott, 1972

Herodotus, *The Histories*, translated by Aubrey de Sélincourt, 1954, 1965 (with index), revised with new introduction and notes by A. R. Burn, 1972

Plutarch, *Fall of the Roman Republic*, translated by Rex Warner, 1958, revised with new introduction by Robin Seager, 1972

Thucydides, *The Peloponnesian War*, translated by Rex Warner, 1954, revised with new introduction and appendices by M. I. Finley, 1972

Xenophon, *The Persian Expedition*, translated by Rex Warner, 1949, new introduction by George Cawkwell, 1972

Aristophanes, *Lysistrata and Other Plays*, translated with an introduction by Alan H. Sommerstein, 1973

Euripides, *The Bacchae and Other Plays*, translated by Philip Vellacott, 1954, 1973 (revised with new introduction)

BIBLIOGRAPHY

Hesiod, *Theogony/Works and Days*, Theogonis, *Elegies*, translated with an introduction by Dorothea Wender, 1973

Plato, *Phaedrus & Letters VII and VIII*, translated with an introduction by Walter Hamilton, 1973

Plutarch, *The Age of Alexander*, translated with notes by Ian Scott-Kilvert, with an introduction by G. T. Griffith, 1973

Euripides, *Three Plays* (Alcestis, Hippolytus, Iphigenia in Tauris), translated with an introduction by Philip Vellacott, 1953, 1974 (revised edition with new introduction)

Greek Pastoral Poetry, translated with an introduction and notes by Anthony Holden, 1974

Plato, *The Republic*, translated with an introduction by Desmond Lee, 1955, 1974 (revised edition)

Demosthenes and Aeschines, translated by A. N. W. Saunders, with an introduction by T. T. B. Ryder, 1975

Aristotle, *Ethics*, translated by J. H. K. Thomson, 1955, revised with notes and appendices by Hugh Tredennick, introduction and bibliography by Jonathan Barnes, 1976

Greek Literature – An Anthology: Translations from Greek Prose and Poetry, chosen by Michael Grant, 1976 (first published as a Pelican, *Greek Literature in Translation*, 1973)

Aristophanes, *The Birds and Other Plays*, translated by David Barrett and Alan H. Sommerstein, 1978

Polybius, *The Rise of the Roman Empire*, translated by Ian Scott-Kilvert, selected with an introduction by F. W. Walbank, 1979

Xenophon, *A History of My Times*, translated by Rex Warner, 1966, new introduction and notes by George Cawkwell, 1979

Aristotle, *The Politics*, translated by T. A. Sinclair, 1962, revised and re-presented by Trevor J. Saunders, 1981

The Greek Anthology and Other Ancient Epigrams: A Selection in Modern Verse Translations, edited with an introduction by Peter Jay, 1973 (Allen Lane), 1981 (revised edition)

Josephus, *The Jewish War*, translated by G. A. Williamson, 1959, 1970 (revised edition), revised with new introduction, notes and appendices by E. Mary Smallwood, 1981

Plato, *Philebus*, translated with an introduction by Robin A. H. Waterfield, 1982

Hippocratic Writings, edited with an introduction by G. E. R. Lloyd, translated by J. Chadwick & W. N. Mann, I. M. Lonie, and E. T. Withington, 1950 (Blackwell), 1978 (Pelican Classics), 1983

Aristotle, *The Athenian Constitution*, translated with an introduction and notes by P. J. Rhodes, 1984

Sophocles, *The Three Theban Plays*, translated by Robert Fagles, introduction and notes by Bernard Knox, 1982 (Allen Lane), 1984

BIBLIOGRAPHY

From Latin

Plautus, *The Rope and Other Plays*, translated with an introduction by E. F. Watling, 1964

Cicero, *Selected Works*, translated with an introduction by Michael Grant, 1960, 1965 and 1971 (revised editions)

Petronius, *The Satyricon*, Seneca, *The Apocolocyntosis*, translated with an introduction by J. P. Sullivan, 1965

Plautus, *The Pot of Gold and Other Plays*, translated by E. F. Watling, 1965

The Poems of Catullus, translated with an introduction by Peter Whigham, 1966

The Poems of Propertius, translated with an introduction by A. E. Watts, 1961 (Centaur Press), 1966 (revised edition)

Seneca, *Four Tragedies and Octavia*, translated with an introduction by E. F. Watling, 1966

Caesar, *The Civil War*, translated with an introduction by Jane F. Mitchell, 1967

Horace, *Odes*, translated with an introduction by James Michie, 1964 (R. Hart-Davis), 1967

Juvenal, *The Sixteen Satires*, translated with an introduction by Peter Green, 1967, 1974 (revised edition)

Cicero, *Selected Political Speeches*, translated with an introduction by Michael Grant, 1969, 1973 (revised edition)

Seneca, *Letters from a Stoic*, selected and translated with an introduction by Robin Campbell, 1969

Tacitus, *The Agricola and the Germania*, translated with an introduction by H. Mattingly, 1948, translation revised by S. A. Handford, 1970

Cicero, *On the Good Life*, translated with an introduction by Michael Grant, 1971

The Last Poets of Imperial Rome, translated with an introduction by Harold Isbell, 1971

Livy, *The Early History of Rome*, translated by Aubrey de Sélincourt, 1960, new introduction by R. M. Ogilvie, 1971

Tacitus, *The Annals of Imperial Rome*, translated with an introduction by Michael Grant, 1956; 1971, 1973, 1975, 1977 (revised editions)

Cicero, *The Nature of the Gods*, translated by Horace C. P. McGregor, with an introduction by J. M. Ross, 1972

Tacitus, *The Histories*, translated with an introduction by Kenneth Wellesley, 1964, 1972 (with bibliography), 1975 (revised edition)

Tibullus, *The Poems*, translated with an introduction by Philip Dunlop, 1972

Horace, *Satires and Epistles*, Persius, *Satires*, translated with an introduction by Niall Rudd, 1973 (*Satires* only), 1979 (with Horace's *Epistles*)

Cicero, *Murder Trials*, translated with an introduction by Michael Grant, 1975

Lives of the Later Caesars, translated with an introduction by Anthony Birley, 1976

Livy, *Rome and the Mediterranean*, translated by Henry Bettenson, introduction by A. H. McDonald, 1976

Cicero, *Letters to Atticus*, translated with an introduction by D. R. Shackleton Bailey, 1965–8 (Cambridge University Press), 1978

Cicero, *Letters to his Friends*, translated with an introduction by D. R. Shackleton Bailey, 2 volumes, 1978

Martial, *The Epigrams*, selected and translated by James Michie, introduction by Peter Howell, 1973 (R. Hart-Davis), 1978

Justinian, *The Digest of Roman Law*, translated with an introduction by C. F. Kolbert, 1979

Suetonius, *The Twelve Caesars*, translated by Robert Graves, 1957, revised with a new introduction by Michael Grant, 1979

Caesar, *The Conquest of Gaul*, translated by S. A. Handford, 1951, revised with a new introduction by Jane F. Gardner, 1982

Ovid, *The Erotic Poems*, translated with an introduction by Peter Green, 1982

Virgil, *The Georgics*, translated with an introduction by L. P. Wilkinson, 1982

Quintus Curtius Rufus, *The History of Alexander*, translated by John Yardley, introduction and notes by Waldemar Heckel, 1984

Virgil, *The Eclogues*, translated with an introduction by Guy Lee, 1980 (Liverpool Latin Texts), 1984

From post-classical Latin

Thomas More, *Utopia*, translated with an introduction by Paul Turner, 1965

The Age of Bede, translated by J. F. Webb, 1965, edited with an introduction by D. H. Farmer (and with the Lives of the Abbots of Wearmouth and Jarrow added), 1983

Geoffrey of Monmouth, *The History of the Kings of Britain*, translated with an introduction by Lewis Thorpe, 1966

Bede, *A History of the English Church and People*, translated with an introduction by Leo Sherley-Price, 1955, revised by R. E. Latham, 1968

Boethius, *The Consolation of Philosophy*, translated with an introduction by V. E. Watts, 1969

Einhard and Notker the Stammerer, *Two Lives of Charlemagne*, translated with an introduction by Lewis Thorpe, 1969

Richard Rolle, *The Fire of Love*, translated with an introduction by Clifton Wolters, 1972

BIBLIOGRAPHY

Gerald of Wales, *The Journey through Wales and The Description of Wales*, translated with an introduction by Lewis Thorpe, 1978

St Augustine, *City of God*, translated by Henry Bettenson, with an introduction by John O'Meara, 1984 (first published in the Pelican Classics with an introduction by David Knowles, 1972)

From Old English

The Earliest English Poems, translated with an introduction by Michael Alexander, 1966, 1977 (second edition)

Beowulf, translated with an introduction by Michael Alexander, 1973

The Exeter Book of Riddles, translated with an introduction by Kevin Crossley-Holland, 1978 (Folio Society), 1979

Alfred the Great, Asser's *Life of King Alfred* and other contemporary sources, translated with an introduction and notes by Simon Keynes and Michael Lapidge, 1983

From Middle English

Sir Gawain and the Green Knight, translated with an introduction by Brian Stone, 1959, 1964 (revised edition), 1974 (second edition)

Medieval English Verse, translated with an introduction by Brian Stone, 1964

Julian of Norwich, *Revelations of Divine Love*, translated with an introduction by Clifton Wolters, 1966

William Langland, *Piers the Ploughman*, translated by J. F. Goodridge, 1959, 1966 (revised edition)

Geoffrey Chaucer, *Troilus and Criseyde*, translated with an introduction by Nevill Coghill, 1971

The Owl and the Nightingale, Cleanness, St Erkenwald, translated with an introduction by Brian Stone, 1971

Geoffrey Chaucer, *The Canterbury Tales*, translated with an introduction by Nevill Coghill, 1951; 1958, 1960, 1975, 1977 (revised editions)

The Cloud of Unknowing and Other Works, translated with an introduction by Clifton Wolters, 1978 (first published without the Other Works in 1961)

Geoffrey Chaucer, *Love Visions*, translated with an introduction and notes by Brian Stone, 1983

The Travels of Sir John Mandeville, translated with an introduction by C. W. R. D. Moseley, 1983

BIBLIOGRAPHY

From Celtic languages

A Celtic Miscellany, translations from the Celtic literatures by Kenneth Hurlstone Jackson, 1951 (Routledge & Kegan Paul), 1971

The Mabinogion, translated with an introduction by Jeffrey Gantz, 1976

Early Irish Myths and Sagas, translated with an introduction and notes by Jeffrey Gantz, 1981

From Icelandic

The Vinland Sagas, translated with an introduction by Magnus Magnusson and Hermann Pálsson, 1965

King Harald's Saga, translated with an introduction by Magnus Magnusson and Hermann Pálsson, 1966

Laxdaela Saga, translated with an introduction by Magnus Magnusson and Hermann Pálsson, 1969

Hrafnkel's Saga and Other Icelandic Stories, translated with an introduction by Hermann Pálsson, 1971

Egil's Saga, translated with an introduction by Hermann Pálsson and Paul Edwards, 1976

Orkneyinga Saga, The History of the Earls of Orkney, translated with an introduction by Hermann Pálsson and Paul Edwards, 1978 (Hogarth Press), 1981

From Middle Eastern languages

The Epic of Gilgamesh, translated with an introduction by N. K. Sandars, 1960; 1964, 1972 (revised editions)

The Koran, translated by N. J. Dawood, 1956, 1966, 1968, 1974 (revised editions)

Poems of Heaven and Hell from Ancient Mesopotamia, translated with an introduction by N. K. Sandars, 1971

The Jewish Poets of Spain, translated with an introduction and notes by David Goldstein, 1965 (Routledge & Kegan Paul), 1971 (revised and expanded edition)

Tales from the Thousand and One Nights, translated with an introduction by N. J. Dawood, 1973 (revised and combined edition; originally published in two parts, 'The Thousand and One Nights', 1954, 1955, and 'Aladdin and Other Tales', 1957)

The Book of Dede Korkut, translated with an introduction and notes by Geoffrey Lewis, 1974

Birds through a Ceiling of Alabaster, Three Abbasid Poets, translated by Abdullah Al-Udhari and George Wightman, 1975

The Psalms, translated by Peter Levi, introduction by Nicholas de Lange, 1976

BIBLIOGRAPHY

The Ruba'iyat of Omar Khayyam, translated by Peter Avery and John Heath-Stubbs, 1979 (Allen Lane), 1981

Farid ud-Din Attar, *The Conference of the Birds*, translated with an introduction by Afkham Darbandi and Dick Davis, 1984

From Indian languages

Poems from the Sanskrit, translated with an introduction by John Brough, 1968

The Upanishads, translated with an introduction by Juan Mascaró, 1965

The Dhammapada, The Path of Perfection, translated with an introduction by Juan Mascaró, 1973

Speaking of Śiva, translated with an introduction by A. K. Ramanujan, 1973

Hindu Myths, A Sourcebook, translated with an introduction by Wendy Doniger O'Flaherty, 1975

The Rig Veda, An Anthology, selected, translated and annotated by Wendy Doniger O'Flaherty, 1981

Three Sanskrit Plays, translated with an introduction by Michael Coulson, 1981

From Chinese

Lao Tzu, *Tao te Ching*, translated with an introduction by D. C. Lau, 1963

Poems of the Late T'ang, translated with an introduction by A. C. Graham, 1965

Anthology of Chinese Literature, compiled and edited by Cyril Birch, associate editor Donald Keene, 1965 (New York), 1967

The Golden Casket, Chinese novellas of two millennia, translated by Christopher Levenson from Wolfgang Bauer and Herbert Franke's German version, introduction by Herbert Franke, 1959 (Munich), 1964 (USA), 1965 (Allen & Unwin), 1967

Mencius, translated with an introduction by D. C. Lau, 1970

Six Yüan Plays, translated with an introduction by Liu Jung-en, 1972

Cao Xueqin, *The Story of the Stone*, translated with an introduction by David Hawkes, Volume 1, 'The Golden Days', 1973; Volume 2, 'The Crab-Flower Club', 1977; Volume 3, 'The Warning Voice', 1980; Volume 4, 'The Debt of Tears', translated by John Minford, 1982

Li Po and Tu Fu, selected and translated with an introduction and notes by Arthur Cooper, calligraphy by Shui Chien-t'ung, 1973

Wang Wei, *Poems*, translated with an introduction by G. W. Robinson, 1973

Confucius, *The Analects*, translated with an introduction by D. C. Lau, 1979

BIBLIOGRAPHY

Shen Fu, *Six Records of a Floating Life*, translated with an introduction and notes by Leonard Pratt and Chiang Su-Hui, 1983

From Japanese

Anthology of Japanese Literature to the Nineteenth Century, introduced and compiled by Donald Keene, 1955 (Grove Press), 1956 (Allen & Unwin), 1968 (revised edition)

Bashō, *The Narrow Road to the Deep North and Other Travel Sketches*, translated with an introduction by Nobuyuki Yuasa, 1966

As I Crossed a Bridge of Dreams, translated with an introduction by Ivan Morris, 1971

The Pillow Book of Sei Shōnagon, translated and edited by Ivan Morris, 1967 (Columbia University Press/Oxford University Press), 1971

Murasaki Shikibu, *The Tale of Genji*, translated with an introduction by Edward G. Seidensticker, 1976 (Secker & Warburg), 1981

NOTES ON CONTRIBUTORS

MICHAEL ALEXANDER

Michael Alexander's verse translations, *The Earliest English Poems* and *Beowulf*, are Penguin Classics. Other publications include *Twelve Poems*, *Old English Riddles from the Exeter Book*, *The Poetic Achievement of Ezra Pound*, a history of Old English literature and books on Chaucer. He has written and broadcast on modern poetry. A lecturer at the University of Stirling for seventeen years, he is now Berry Professor of English Literature at St Andrews, where he lives with his three children. His wife, Eileen, died in 1986.

ARTHUR COOPER

Arthur Cooper served in the Foreign Office from 1938 to 1968, and then returned to a special interest in Chinese poetry and script. He published *Li Po and Tu Fu* (Penguin Books) in 1973 and a monograph on *The Creation of the Chinese Script* (China Society) in 1978 (reprinted 1985). He has contributed to the forthcoming *Oxford Companion to the Mind*, and is now completing for OUP *'Heart and Mind': Ancient Language-Making as Recorded in the Chinese Script*; showing how similar were the beginnings of all human language, often by comparing English etymologies with ancient Chinese characters.

JEFFREY GANTZ

Jeffrey Gantz was born in Washington, DC, in 1945. He was educated at Amherst College (BA, English literature) and Harvard University (PhD, Celtic languages and literatures); currently he is associate arts editor at the *Boston Phoenix* (a weekly newspaper), where he also writes occasionally about art, classical music, film, theatre, books and Italian politics. His poems and reviews have appeared in *Poetry*, *Medium Aevum*, *Dickens Studies Newsletter*, *Boston Review*, *Michigan Quarterly Review* and elsewhere.

DAVID GOLDSTEIN

David Goldstein was born in London in 1933. He read English at Oxford, and then specialized in Hebrew and Jewish studies at University

College, London. He was ordained as a Liberal Rabbi, and served congregations in south London and St John's Wood. He is now Curator of Hebrew Books and Manuscripts at the British Library. His volume of translations *Hebrew Poems from Spain* received the Jewish Chronicle Book Award in 1966, and was reprinted in Penguin Classics in 1971 under the title *Jewish Poets of Spain*. Other works include *The Religion of the Jews* (Open University), 1978; *Jewish Folklore and Legend* (Hamlyn), 1980; and *The Ashkenazi Haggadah* (Thames & Hudson), 1985. He is co-editor of the Littman Library of Jewish Civilization (OUP), and is currently seeing through the press a three-volume translation, *The Wisdom of the Zohar*.

MICHAEL GRANT

Michael Grant, CBE, has been successively Fellow of Trinity College, Cambridge, Professor of Humanity at Edinburgh University, first Vice-Chancellor of Khartoum University, and President and Vice-Chancellor of The Queen's University, Belfast. He has been President of the Royal Numismatic Society, the Virgil Society and the Classical Association, and is the holder of honorary degrees and prizes in Britain, Ireland, America, Sudan and Italy. His recent books are *History of Rome* (1978), *The Etruscans* (1980), *From Alexander to Cleopatra* (1982), *History of Ancient Israel* (1984) and *The Roman Emperors* (1985). He has translated Cicero's *Selected Works*, *Selected Political Speeches*, *Murder Trials* and *On the Good Life*, and Tacitus' *Annals* for the Penguin Classics, and has edited two Penguin anthologies, *Latin Literature* and *Greek Literature*.

PETER GREEN

Peter Green was born in London in 1924, and educated at Charterhouse and Trinity College, Cambridge. He obtained a PhD with a dissertation on Graeco-Roman magic, but temporarily abandoned a career in classics to work as a freelance writer, translator, and literary journalist. In 1963 he emigrated to Greece, where he returned to professional teaching as a lecturer in Greek history and literature. In 1971 he became Visiting Professor in Classics at the University of Texas at Austin; he now holds a permanent position there as the Dougherty Centennial Professor of Classical Studies. His books on antiquity include a history of the Persian Wars, a biography of Alexander the Great, and a forthcoming major study of the Hellenistic Age. He has translated numerous works from French, Italian, Latin, and Greek (both ancient and modern), including Juvenal's *Satires* and Ovid's *Erotic Poems* for the Penguin Classics.

NOTES ON CONTRIBUTORS

WALTER HAMILTON

Walter Hamilton was born in 1908 and was a Scholar and Prize Fellow of Trinity College, Cambridge, where he wrote a dissertation on Plutarch's philosophical myths. He went on to become assistant lecturer at Manchester University (1931–2), a master at Eton College (1933–46), fellow of Trinity College, Cambridge, and University Lecturer in Classics (1947–50), Head Master of Westminster School (1950–57), Head Master of Rugby School (1957–66), and Master of Magdalene College, Cambridge (1967 78), of which he is now an honorary fellow. He has published articles and reviews in the *Classical Quarterly* and *Classical Review*, and has translated Plato's *Symposium* (1951), *Gorgias* (1960), *Phaedrus & Letters VII and VIII* (1973), and *The Later Roman Empire* of Ammianus Marcellinus (with A. F. Wallace-Hadrill, 1986) for the Penguin Classics.

WENDY DONIGER O'FLAHERTY

Wendy Doniger O'Flaherty was born in New York in 1940 and trained as a dancer under George Balanchine and Martha Graham before beginning the study of Sanskrit at Radcliffe College in 1958. She holds doctoral degrees in Indian literature from Harvard and Oxford Universities, and is now Mircea Eliade Professor of the History of Religions and Indian Studies in the Divinity School at the University of Chicago. Her publications include *Asceticism and Eroticism in the Mythology of Siva* (1973), *The Origins of Evil in Hindu Mythology* (1976), *Women, Androgynes and Other Mythical Beasts* (1980), and *Dreams, Illusion and Other Realities* (1984), as well as numerous articles on Indian history, literature, and mythology. She has translated *Hindu Myths* (1975) and *The Rig Veda* (1981) for the Penguin Classics.

BETTY RADICE

Betty Radice read classics at Oxford, then married and, in the intervals of bringing up a family, tutored in classics, philosophy and English. She became joint editor of the Penguin Classics in 1964. She translated Pliny's *Letters*, Terence's *Comedies*, Erasmus's *Praise of Folly*, *The Letters of Abelard and Heloise* and Livy's *Rome and Italy*, and also wrote introductions to Horace and Propertius, all for the Penguin Classics. She edited Gibbon's *Memoirs of My Life* for the Penguin English Library, her own translation of Pliny for the Loeb Classical Library, and translated from Latin, Greek and Italian for the Officina Bodoni of Verona. She collaborated as a translator in the Collected Works of Erasmus, and was the author of the reference book *Who's Who in the Ancient World*. She was an honorary fellow of St Hilda's College, Oxford, and a vice-president of the Classical Association.

WILLIAM RADICE

William Radice was born in 1951 and went to Westminster School. He read English at Magdalen College, Oxford, winning the Newdigate Prize for poetry in 1970. He went on to do a diploma in Bengali at the School of Oriental and African Studies, London. After working as a psychiatric nurse and a schoolmaster, he returned to Oxford in 1979, researching on the Bengali epic poet Michael Madhusūdan Datta for the degree of D Phil (1987), and teaching Bengali in the Faculty of Oriental Studies. He has published three books of poems, *Eight Sections* (1974), *Strivings* (1980) and *Louring Skies* (1985), and two translations from Bengali, *The Stupid Tiger and Other Tales* (1981) and *Rabindranath Tagore: Selected Poems* (Penguin Books, 1985). He was given a Bengali literary award, the *Ānanda Puraskār*, in 1986.

BARBARA REYNOLDS

Barbara Reynolds was for forty-one years a lecturer in Italian language and literature at the universities of London, Cambridge and Nottingham. Since retirement she has lectured widely in the United States. She is the General Editor of *The Cambridge Italian Dictionary*. When Dorothy L. Sayers died in 1957, E. V. Rieu invited her to finish the translation of Dante's *Paradiso* and to provide the introduction and commentary. Later she translated, also for Penguin Classics, Dante's *Vita Nuova* and Ariosto's *Orlando Furioso*. For the latter she received the Monselice International Award for Translation.

N. K. SANDARS

After the war N. K. Sandars studied archaeology at the London Institute of Archaeology and in Oxford at St Hugh's College. She took part in excavations in England, Scotland and Greece, and carried out archaeological research, travelling in Europe, the Aegean and the Near and Middle East, including Iran and Soviet Georgia and Armenia. She published a study of *Bronze Age Cultures in France* (CUP), followed by *Prehistoric Art in Europe* (Penguin Books, Pelican History of Art), and *The Sea Peoples: Warriors of the Ancient Mediterranean*. She has made English translations of *The Epic of Gilgamesh* and *Poems of Heaven and Hell from Ancient Mesopotamia*, both in Penguin Classics, along with contributions to periodicals on prehistoric art and religion and on David Jones. Recently she visited China and is working on the Silk Road.

NOTES ON CONTRIBUTORS

TREVOR J. SAUNDERS

Trevor J. Saunders was born in Wiltshire in 1934, and was educated at Chippenham Grammar School, University College London, and Emmanuel College, Cambridge. He has taught at the universities of London and Hull, and is now Professor of Greek at the University of Newcastle upon Tyne. He has been Visiting Member of the Institute for Advanced Study, Princeton, and Visiting Fellow at the Humanities Research Centre, Canberra. His main interest is in Greek philosophy, especially political, social and legal theory, on which he has published numerous works, including a translation of Plato's *Laws* in Penguin Classics and an extensive revision and re-presentation of T. A. Sinclair's Penguin version of Aristotle's *Politics*. Most recently he has been contributing editor of Plato, *Early Socratic Dialogues*, in the same series.

W. G. SHEPHERD

W. G. Shepherd was born in Kent in 1935. He was educated at Brentwood School and at Jesus College, Cambridge, where he took the English tripos. His National Service was spent in the Royal Artillery: he was commissioned. He lives now in north London with his wife and two sons, and is a contracts executive in an electronic capital goods company. Three collections of his poems have been published (in 1970, 1980 and 1983) by Anvil Press, and his *Horace, The Complete Odes and Epodes* and *Propertius, The Poems* (both with introductions by Betty Radice) are in the Penguin Classics.

BRIAN STONE

Brian Stone has recently retired from the Open University, where, as Reader in Literature, he wrote, broadcast and taught on poetry and drama, and was active in the planning of arts teaching throughout the university system. Of his four books of verse translation for the Penguin Classics, *Sir Gawain and the Green Knight* is the best known: his fifth, which is nearly completed, will be of the stanzaic *Le Morte Arthur* and the alliterative *Morte Arthure*.

During the war he was awarded the Military Cross, and wrote an account of his experiences, *Prisoner from Alamein*, for which Desmond MacCarthy wrote a foreword. In 1951 Brian Stone was joint runner-up in the English Festival of Spoken Poetry. He is a freelance lecturer and reader of poetry.

NOTES ON CONTRIBUTORS

J. P. SULLIVAN

J. P. Sullivan was born in 1930 in Liverpool, and read Classics at Cambridge. He has taught at Oxford and the universities of Texas at Austin and New York State at Buffalo. He is at present Professor of Classics at the University of California, Santa Barbara. He has edited the classical journals *Arion* and *Arethusa*, as well as various books on Ezra Pound, women in antiquity, and Latin elegy and satire. Besides translating Petronius' *Satyricon* and Seneca's *Apocolocyntosis* for the Penguin Classics, he is the author of *Propertius: A Critical Introduction*; *Ezra Pound and Sextus Propertius: A Study in Creative Translation*; *The Satyricon of Petronius: A Literary Study*; and *Literature and Politics in the Age of Nero*. He is currently working on *Martial: The Unexpected Classic*.

PHILIP VELLACOTT

Philip Vellacott taught classics for many years at Dulwich College, where he was also in charge of drama, and produced Shakespeare plays and some others. In his spare time he wrote translations of Euripides and Aeschylus. He was the founder, and for some time the chief director, of the Attic Players, a group which produced annually Greek plays in translation in small London theatres. In the past twenty years his classical work has been chiefly in the United States, where he has lectured on Greek tragedy in many university departments. He is also the author of a book on Euripides, *Ironic Drama* (1975), and a book on Aeschylus, *The Logic of Tragedy* (1984), and has recently completed a book on Sophocles.

BENEDICTA WARD

Sister Benedicta is a member of the Community of the Sisters of the Love of God. She holds a doctorate from Oxford University for a thesis now published under the title *Miracles and the Medieval Mind* (Scolar Press, 1980). Her other published works include *The Prayers and Meditations of St Anselm* (Penguin Books, 1973), *Sayings of the Desert Fathers* (Mowbray, 1979), *Lives of the Desert Fathers* (Mowbray, 1982), *Wisdom of the Desert Fathers* (SLG Press, 1979). She teaches for the Centre for Medieval and Renaissance Studies, Oxford, as well as for the university.

PETER WHIGHAM

Peter Whigham was born in Oxford in 1925. He is married to Margaret Kiers and lives in San Francisco, where he lectures in Comparative

Literature at the University of California, Berkeley. His publications include *The Poems of Catullus* (Penguin Books, 1966), *The Blue Winged Bee* (Poetry Book Society Choice, 1969), *The Poems of Meleager* (with Peter Jay, 1975), *Things Common, Properly: Selected Poems* (1984), *Letter To Juvenal* (1985) – these last four volumes published by Anvil Press Poetry, London. He is co-editor (with J. P. Sullivan) of *Martial, Englished by Divers Hands*, for the University of California Press. He is at present engaged on a verse translation of Dante's *Inferno*.

MARGARET WYNN

Margaret Wynn was Betty Radice's contemporary at Oxford. They met again during the last year of the war with firstborns in hand on the steps of a nursery school and found they were neighbours. She is the author of two pioneering books, *Fatherless Families* (1964) and *Family Policy* (1970). With her husband she has visited European countries and North America to study the prevention of handicaps in children. They published *Prevention of Handicap of Perinatal Origin* in 1976, *Prevention of Handicap and the Health of Women*, 1979, and *Prevention of Handicap of Early Pregnancy Origin*, 1981.

NOBUYUKI YUASA

Nobuyuki Yuasa was born in Tokyo in 1932. He took a BA in English at Hiroshima University in 1954, and an MA at Berkeley in 1956. He returned to Hiroshima, becoming lecturer in English in 1961 and Professor of English in 1982. From 1970 to 1971 he was Visiting Professor of Japanese at Stanford University. He has published *The Year of My Life, A Translation of Issa's Oraga Haru* (University of California Press, 1960), and translations of Bashō's *The Narrow Road to the Deep North and Other Travel Sketches* (Penguin Books, 1966) and Ryōkan's *The Zen Poems* (Princeton University Press, 1981). He has also written papers in English on Spenser, Sidney, Shakespeare and the 'Rainbow Portrait' of Queen Elizabeth.

JOHN GAY

John Gay is a professional photographer and has published several books, amongst others, one on Victorian railway stations, with John Betjeman, one on Highgate Cemetery, and one on cast iron. He and Betty Radice were friends and neighbours, and his relaxed portrait of her was taken on one of those occasions when she dropped in for a chat, on her walk with her dog.

NOTES ON CONTRIBUTORS

SHUI CHIEN-T'UNG

Shui Chien-t'ung, painter, scholar and calligrapher, was born in the far west of China. He has studied Chinese epigraphs inscribed on ninth-century BC bronzes, and has translated Homer into Chinese. The ancient Buddhist cave paintings of Chinese Turkestan were a primary influence on his own paintings.